Warrior's
Song

*Also by Catherine Coulter
in Large Print:*

Calypso Magic
The Countess
The Courtship
The Deception
Earth Song
Fire Song
The Heir
The Hellion Bride
Midsummer Magic
Moonspun Magic
The Offer
Riptide
Secret Song

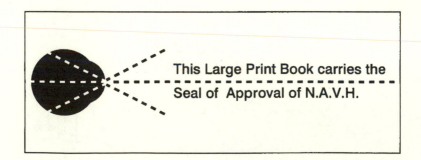

This Large Print Book carries the
Seal of Approval of N.A.V.H.

CATHERINE COULTER

Warrior's Song

Medieval Song Quartet #4

Thorndike Press • Waterville, Maine

Copyright © Catherine Coulter, 1983

Medieval Song Quartet #4

All rights reserved.

Published in 2001 by arrangement with Signet, a division of Penguin Putnam Inc.

Thorndike Large Print Basic Series.

The tree indicium is a trademark of Thorndike Press.

The text of this Large Print edition is unabridged.
Other aspects of the book may vary from the original edition.

Set in 16 pt. Plantin.

Printed in the United States on permanent paper.

Library of Congress Cataloging-in-Publication Data

Coulter, Catherine.
    Warrior's song / Catherine Coulter.
        p. cm. — (Medieval song quartet ; 4)
    ISBN 0-7862-2354-5 (lg. print : hc : alk. paper)
    1. Great Britain — History — 13th century — Fiction.
2. Crusades — Eighth, 1270 — Fiction.   3. Large type
books. I. Title.
PS3553.O843 C48 2000
 813′.54—dc21   99-055836

To Henrik, the second time around

Chapter 1

Croyland Castle, near the northern Welsh border
May 1272

She saw him across the vast expanse of barren land scored with jagged rocks, scrubby pine trees and thick, low-lying fog.

He was astride a black destrier, at least thirty men behind him, fanned out across the horizon. His armor shone bright silver under the sun. His surcoat was black velvet, and even from their distance, Chandra could see its richness. A scarf of black silk trailed from his helmet in the breeze. He sat perfectly still, waiting.

Perhaps she would have thought him magnificent if he and his men weren't strung in a long, solid line between her and Croyland. There were only six men with her, two of them carrying the boar between them, tied to a pole — a boar she herself had brought down.

She turned only slightly on Wicket's back and said low to the gnarled old man at her side, who had taught her how to throw a knife to split the core out of an apple, "Ellis, that man — do you know who he is? He looks like some sort of statue sitting there so quietly. Why does he not come to us? Why this show of force?"

"Aye, mistress, I know who he is." Ellis sounded grim, more grim than he had just an hour ago when Ponce, one of her father's squires, hadn't managed to kill the charging boar with a clean throw of his spear, and the boar had nearly taken both of them down before Chandra's knife was planted deep into its small brain. Ellis said now, pointing, "See the three silver wolves on his black banner? It's Lord Graelam de Moreton. Why is he here? I don't know. He is a long way from his home — Cornwall."

She shook her head. Perhaps she'd heard her father mention his name, but she didn't remember.

"I wonder why he doesn't come forward to greet us."

"I don't know, but I don't like this, mistress. I don't like it at all. He has too many men with him not to mean some mischief."

It all fell into place. Chandra said, her voice colder than the frozen water in the cistern that morning, "By all that's holy, I understand now. Father was tricked. That scrawny little man we caught lurking about Croyland, who finally admitted to my father that Cadwallon's bandits were near — it wasn't true, none of it. It was a ruse to draw my father and many of our men away from Croyland. But why? This Graelam must know that he could not hold Croyland for long. My father's vassals would be gathered within the week. He would be killed and all his men with him."

"Mayhap his presence here isn't what we think. He is a mighty lord from Cornwall, as I told you. He holds lands aplenty, and great wealth. He is friends with the king's son, Prince Edward, so there is might behind him. He is dangerous and powerful. I do not like this. Listen to me. You remain here while I speak to him. We can't let him see that you are a woman."

The man suddenly spoke, his voice hard and deep across the expanse. "Lady Chandra." For the first time Graelam de Moreton's black stallion sidled gracefully forward, his strength held in check by the man upon his back. Another man in armor rode at this side.

"He already knows I am a woman, Ellis, and exactly who I am. It is I who must see what he wants. No, Ellis, stay back. Do not argue with me. My father left me in charge.

Look at all his men, all armed and ready. There are too many of them. We would have no chance against them. I want no needless deaths on my hands. It would be a slaughter and you know it."

Ellis knew she was right, but he didn't want to put her at risk. She knew that, but she was in charge when her father was away from Croyland. Her father trusted her above anyone to protect his castle, her young brother, John, Lord Richard's only heir, and her mother, Lady Dorothy, that purse-mouthed lady who'd disliked her own daughter for as long as Chandra could remember. Her endless cruelties and meanness had ended only when Chandra had turned eleven years old and was large enough and skilled enough to stand up for herself.

Chandra said now, "It will be all right, Ellis. I will see what he wants." She gave him a small salute and dug her heels into Wicket's lean sides, sending him galloping forward over the barren, rock-strewn ground. She drew Wicket to a halt some twenty feet from the man with the three silver wolves on his banner.

His voice again, deep, dark as the velvet surcoat he wore, a voice that made her want to dive for cover behind the boulders just beside her. She was frightened, more frightened than she'd been when Lady Dorothy locked her in the dungeon when she was nine years old. Chandra couldn't remember what she had done to deserve a day and a half in a cell filled with filth and rats and only a sliver of light.

He called out, "Lady Chandra, daughter of Richard de Avenell." Not a question, not a bit of uncertainty, she thought. He knew exactly who she was. But how could he have known? She was dressed in leather breeches, a leather cap on her head, covering her hair, a sword and a knife strapped on the belt at her waist. Her boots came to her knees, the leather cross garters splattered with the boar's blood. Her black wool coat fluttered a bit in the slight breeze. She called out, "And you are Graelam de Moreton, I am told by my man. I ask you what you wish here at Croyland. Why have you spread your men across our path?"

He paused for just the slightest moment before saying calmly, "I have come for what is mine, Chandra."

"There is nothing here that is yours, my lord. Come, enough of this."

"I agree. It is enough." He rode closer, the other man in armor close behind him. The long line of his men stood silently, not

11

moving, the fog swirling about their horses' legs, making them look otherworldly.

"Tell me what you want and there will be no battle between us." At that moment, she heard her mother yelling at her, a small child, helpless, but filled with bravado, *"Brave words, you godless little slut, brave words!"* And what she'd just said to this man, they were also just brave words. She knew she was as helpless now as she had been when Lady Dorothy had screamed those words at her so many years before. She flinched, then calmed. Brave words indeed, but she would back them up this time. She had to. But what she'd said to Ellis was true. Graelam de Moreton and his men could cut her down in a second, her six men with her.

The man behind Graelam de Moreton yelled out, "What absurdity from a girl dressed as a man with but six ragtag men behind her, don't you think, my lord?"

Graelam turned to the man beside him and spoke in a low voice. She couldn't hear what he said, but the man just shrugged and drew his warhorse back a few more paces.

"My man meant no insult," Graelam said. "It's true that if I didn't know you, I would believe myself facing a boy. But I do know you. I know everything about you. I know of your bravery, your training as a knight, your strength of character, your endless pride. However, you are not a boy, despite your prowess with weapons, despite the trust your father places in you to see to the safety of his castle. Now, pull off that ridiculous cap. I would at least see you as a woman."

He knew too much, but how? And he believed her all those things? She was brave? Proud? They were just words, she thought, just words to gain her compliance; they meant nothing. Calm, she had to be calm, to be reasoned, as her father had taught her. She threw back her head and said, "No, Graelam de Moreton. Now, I will ask you once more. Why are you here?"

Slowly, he removed his helmet and handed it to the man behind him. She saw that he was dark, his hair thick, black, slicked to his head with sweat. His face was swarthy, his eyes black as a starless night. Even from the twenty-foot distance that separated them, she could see the blackness of his damned eyes. He looked like the devil, particularly garbed in all that black. Then, suddenly, he smiled, his teeth white and strong, and she felt a bolt of fear that nearly knocked her off Wicket's back. The devil, she thought. That was indeed who he was. Her hands shook on Wicket's reins. No, no, she couldn't show him that he frightened her. She couldn't let her men see her fear either, she couldn't, or all would be lost.

"I am here for you, Chandra."

For her? By all the saints' sins, what the devil did he mean? "Damn you, that makes no sense. You wish to carry me away for ransom? Are you mad? My father would hunt you down and carve your guts out of your belly."

He laughed, a full, deep, rich laugh. "No, that is not it at all. Have a bit of conceit, madam. I have come to take you back to Wolffeton with me. You will be my wife, the mistress of my holdings, the mother of my sons. There will be no killing, no looting, if you will but agree."

She turned as cold and still as a rock, sitting tall astride Wicket, her back straight, and the fear licking at her very heart, making it pound hard and harder still as the seconds passed. Well, she had demanded to know and he had told her.

She didn't know how she managed it, but she laughed, threw back her head and laughed even more. "Your wife? This is madness. It is impossible. I have perhaps heard my father mention your name once or twice, my lord. You are a stranger. I do not know you, nor do you know me."

"You are wrong. I have told you. I know

everything I need to know about you. Before the day is done, you will be my wife."

"No," she said, calm, her voice low, but carrying far enough for him to hear her. She raised her chin, and her voice was filled to overflowing with contempt and disgust. "What is this, my lord? Are there no ladies in Cornwall for you to attempt to steal? Tell me, are you so ugly, so brutal, so dishonorable, that you must needs come to the North to find yourself a mate?"

Again he laughed. "You sharpen your wits on my head, do you? You want taming, Chandra."

"What I want is my knife to cut your bastard's throat."

She heard Ellis's angry voice behind her, and the other men, talking in furious voices now. She heard the two men who carried the boar between them drop it to the ground. She knew all of them had their swords drawn, their knives held in their other hands.

She was a fool to have baited him. She would be dead six times over before she would manage to stick her knife in his neck. Oh, God would he kill all of them now, all of them except her? But the fact was that she would die as well because she would fight until he had no choice but to run a sword through her.

Why had she said those things to him? She was a fool and she would die a fool, die when she was only eighteen years old, so much life ahead of her, but she would be dead and buried. Her beautiful, brave father would be alone, for surely her mother would be no comfort to him. Her mother would be happy to see her gone. And John, his heir, too young, too self-important to give comfort to him.

Chandra looked at the long line of his men that still hadn't moved. There was no going around them, only through them. Six men couldn't possibly do it. All those men would be on her and her men in but a moment with a signal from him. She waited, her tongue dead in her mouth, to see what he would do.

What he did was throw back his head and laugh. When he had laughed his fill, he said, "I look forward not only to the taming of you, my lady, but to showing you that you have no chance at all against me. It will afford me great amusement. Come now, it is over. Do not let the violence begin. I have no wish to draw blood, nor do I wish you to be hurt."

But it was Ellis who would be hurt, not she. Oh, God, she heard his furious shout, watched him stab the heels of his boots in his horse's side, raise his sword high. He yelled at Graelam even as he rode with dead reckoning straight at him, "You bastard son of a witch! You want our lady? Not likely! I'll carve your miserable heart from your chest."

She didn't think, just acted. She yelled for him to stop, but of course he didn't slow. She yelled at the five men behind her, "None of you move. If you do, I'll gullet you. I swear it. First I'm going to gullet Ellis."

She kicked Wicket's sides and sent him straight at Ellis. She came up beside him in but an instant, for Wicket was fast, and she was determined. She slapped her fist as hard as she could against his arm. "Listen to me! My father would flay me alive if you were hurt. You damned hero, stop it!" It slowed him, but just for a moment.

She heard Graelam shout, "Keep him back, Chandra. I don't want to kill an old man." His destrier was dancing forward, eager for combat.

Ellis yelled foul curses. He was out of control. She realized then that there was simply no choice. She threw herself at him and knocked him clean off his horse, sending them both crashing to the rocky ground.

For a long time, she simply couldn't breathe. She heard Ellis groaning beneath her, heard a roar of laughter. She thought she was dying, but then breath slammed into her lungs and she sucked it in as hard as she could. Finally, she realized she was alive, that she'd only knocked the wind out of herself.

She saw de Moreton riding slowly toward them. She rolled away from Ellis, grasped his sword and knife, and threw them away from him. "Don't you move, damn you," she yelled at him, and rose slowly to her feet, her hand on her own sword. She pushed back her cloak and slowly pulled the sword out of its scabbard. She stood there, facing him, her legs slightly apart, waiting.

He was nearly on her, his horse black as night, blowing. Graelam dismounted and walked toward her. He was big, she realized, taller than her father, thicker, much younger. He looked intently at her, saying nothing, just kept walking to her.

She held her sword in one hand, ready, ready, moving it slightly back and forth so he couldn't be certain of her point of attack. She couldn't just let him take her — she wouldn't. That was something she couldn't bear.

She took several steps back, keeping herself between him and Ellis, who was still now, lying on his back. She heard him moaning, but doubted he was conscious. He still hadn't moved. She said, "I won't be your wife. I won't be any man's wife, ever. Do you hear me? I will never wed. I am my father's daughter, and I belong here with him. Leave now and I won't fight you."

"You truly wish to fight me?" he said the words slowly, no disbelief in his dark voice, but rather a sort of pleased joy.

"I would like to stick my sword through your belly. Ah, but you are wearing armor so that leaves me your throat. A good target."

He drew his own sword and held it easily in his right hand, his left hand empty. He had tossed his shield to the ground beside his destrier. It was obvious he didn't believe her to be any sort of threat. Indeed, how could she be? She was half his size. Very well, he had to be slow; his size and the weight of his armor would make it so.

"It is between us, Graelam de Moreton. You have no choice but to fight me. Tell your men to stay back. If I beat you, you will tell them to leave here."

He cocked his head to one side, and still there was that amazed look on his face that mirrored both pleasure and anticipation. He didn't look away from her as he shouted

back toward her own men, "All of you remain where you are."

She said again, "Tell them that they will
leave if I beat you."

"Oh, no, I will not tell them that. It would
make them fall off their horses with
laughter. You can't beat me, Chandra. Give
it up." He had the gall to hold out his hand
to her.

It was too much. She gave an animal
growl deep in her throat and lunged forward
toward his left side. Her sword struck his.
She nearly dropped like a stone. There had
been no give, no weakening at all. It was as if
she had slammed her sword against a rock.
She remembered her father's words, spoken
over and over during the years, "Keep your
damned head, girl. Don't panic, ever, for if
you do, you're dead. If you're alive, then
there's hope, but you must keep your head.
If you fail with your first attempt to bring
your man down, then keep seeking until you
find his weakness. Every man has a weakness."

"You have no weaknesses," she'd said to
him, but she knew that every other man did.
Lord Richard had grinned at her and cuffed
her shoulder just as he would a boy's.

And so she stepped quickly aside and
hammered her sword against Graelam's,

high, near his hand. He leaped back, releasing. She'd made him retreat. Just a step, but it was a beginning. Then she heard his laugh. He was laughing at her.

He thought she was amazing, a girl who aped a man's ways, a girl who dared to raise a sword at him, and her anger nearly sent her straight at him. No, she had to be calm or it would be all over. She slipped her right hand into her cloak and slowly pulled her knife from its sheath at her belt. She looked steadily at her own sword, distracting him, readying herself. Ellis was yelling behind her, quite conscious now. She could see him from the corner of her eye struggling to get his sword, clutching at his right leg.

Graelam engaged her this time. He slammed his sword against hers, slicing downward, dragging her sword with his. He didn't pause, just hammered again and again, giving her no respite. She knew he would crush her soon; his strength and his skill were simply too great. She fell back, slowly, slowly, her eyes on his face, hoping to see his strategy mirrored in his eyes. Soon now. Soon she would make her move. His blows were rhythmic, unending, and it seemed to her that each new blow was harder than the last. She wondered if he ever tired. Soon now. She danced to the side.

When he turned slightly to come after her, she knew it was the moment she'd waited for. She leapt toward him, her knife out and raised. She struck her knife with all her strength at his naked throat.

Chapter 2

She saw her knife driving forward, straight and strong toward his unprotected neck, felt her own power behind that driving blow, limitless, focused, and then, suddenly, he had twisted about, and his hand in its leather gauntlet had somehow closed around her wrist and he was only inches from her face.

"A trick your father taught you, I assume," he said, and she saw that he wasn't breathing hard at all. She was nothing to him, nothing at all. The pain of knowing that was nearly as great as the pain in her wrist.

He squeezed slowly until she felt she would die from the pain. "Stop this. I have no wish to break your wrist. Drop the damned knife." And in the next moment, her knife dropped from her numb fingers. She tried to bring up her sword, but he grabbed her and pulled her back against his chest. Both of their swords clattered to the rocky ground. He held one arm around her, and with his other hand, he pulled off her cap.

He was silent for a moment; then he said, very close to her ear, "You smell like sweat and fury and boar's blood, but now it is over. I have won."

So very easy for him, she thought, wanting to grab her wrist and rub it, the pain was so great, but she didn't. She saw Ellis lying there, just staring at them, and there was defeat on his face.

She had lost. She wanted to curse him, but she said nothing.

Graelam called out to her men, "It is over, as I just told your mistress. There will be no looting, no killing, if you will drop your weapons and come with us into the castle."

She heard her men speaking in low, angry voices.

Then they were riding slowly forward, toward that long line of Graelam's men. The man who had ridden behind Graelam sat tall on his horse's back, calling out calmly, "My name is Abaric. Attend me. No one will be hurt. Just keep riding." He looked toward Graelam. "You will bring her, my lord?"

"Aye," Graelam said, "I will bring her." She heard the possession in his voice, his triumph and pleasure, and she wanted to slink away in shame. She had failed.

"Have her men collect the old man, but don't let him near a weapon. He would gullet me if he could."

She felt his arm hard beneath her breasts and said, "My men will never lower the drawbridge, never."

He said nothing.

"You will see."

He merely shook his head. His man handed him his helmet and he put it back on. He was faceless again, and that was more terrifying because he was no longer just a man.

It seemed that such a short time had passed when Graelam, Chandra seated in front of him on his powerful destrier, one arm holding her against him, rode forward to take position in front of his men. He came to a stop twenty feet from the castle walls. He yelled up to the battlements, where all her father's remaining soldiers stood poised, his voice reaching every part of Croyland castle, "I have Lady Chandra. You will lower the drawbridge or I will cut her throat."

She felt a knife edge against the naked flesh of her neck.

"He won't," she yelled. "He doesn't want me dead. Don't lower the drawbridge!"

The knife nicked her flesh and she felt a

sharp sting, felt her blood, hot and heavy, seep out.

She heard their voices from atop the ramparts, but there was no hesitation at all.

"It is a fine holding," Graelam said as they rode into the inner courtyard. There were horses and cows and chickens, at least a half-dozen dogs and a good dozen children, most of them quiet now, staring at the enemy who had just come into their world. Even the Croyland rooster, King Henry, he was called, had backed up, comb high, and was staring at them. Chandra watched as his men rounded up all the Croyland soldiers, watched the man Abaric lead them toward the dungeons.

Once in the huge Great Hall, Graelam looked at the black-beamed ceiling high above his head, the fresh-scented reeds that covered the floor, the well-scrubbed tables, the rich tapestries that hung on the walls to keep the sea's dampness from seeping into the castle. There were few servants in evidence, however, and not more than a half-dozen men, their heads down, and Graelam said as he nodded, "This will do. You and I will be wed here, this evening, by your priest, Father Tolbert."

"I will never wed you," Chandra said. "There is no way you can force me."

He looked at her a moment, then nodded again, as if he'd known she would say that. He said, "Tell me, where is Lady Dorothy and Lord Richard's heir, John?"

"You will not find them," Chandra said.

"You think not?" Graelam said. She was held loosely now by two of his men. "I will find them and then we will see how long your stubbornness lasts."

She knew he wouldn't find her young brother and her mother, and he saw that knowledge in her eyes. She lowered her head, a bitter smile on her mouth. They were in the small hidden room beneath the granary that lay just above the dungeons. It was a standing order from Lord Richard. Trouble of any kind, and they were to remain hidden there until he came for them. They were safe. But at what cost? She didn't yet know.

But she did know that Graelam de Moreton would gain no leverage. Whatever the cost, she would bear it.

"Find them, Abaric," he said to his man. "Also, bring me the priest."

Never had a keep been taken so easily, so very effortlessly, she thought as she watched Lord Graelam sit in her father's chair at the head of one of the long tables, one of the serving girls, her hands shaking, giving him bread and cheese and a goblet of the fine Croyland ale. She stood silently between his men.

"I will not marry you, my lord. All this is for naught. You will not find my brother to use to gain my compliance. You will leave soon, and I will see the back of you."

"You thought never to wed?"

"No."

"That is very strange."

"Not at all. My father needs me."

"Your father has his heir — a boy, who will someday be a man, something you will never achieve, Chandra, no matter how much skill you have with weaponry. You are meant to be a wife and the mother of warrior sons."

"No," she said again.

He said, looking at her now, "There is much you do not know, Chandra, much your father has not told you. Speak to the dwarf, Crecy. He will tell you that I have sought an honorable marriage alliance with Lord Richard for two years. I was at first refused, your father's reason being that you were too young for a husband, which I accepted even though you were sixteen and surely old enough. Since that time he has sent Crecy to me with empty promises to keep me at bay. I grew tired of waiting, tired of all the lies, and now I have come to take what is mine. Your father will not come after you, Chandra, for I will wed you this evening in the Great Hall of Croyland, by your priest, with all honor that is due you. And this night, you will share your bed-chamber with me and your virgin's bed will become our marriage bed."

Of all he had said, she heard only that her father had kept him away from her. She felt warmth in her heart. He wanted her to re-main here with him. She smiled as she said, "From what you say, it is obvious that my fa-ther didn't want an alliance with you. It is as I told you. He wants me here at his side. He would never sell me to another man."

He drank deeply from his goblet, his eyes never leaving her face. He said slowly, "You speak of your father as if he were your lover."

Graelam saw the shock on her face, her sudden pallor. "Does that notion distress you? It should. You are a woman, meant to serve a husband honorably and bear his children. You are not meant to remain with your father, despite any feelings you may have for him and he for you. Now, enough."

When he had drunk his fill of the Croyland ale, he led her through the great hall, eerily silent now, for the servants had hidden themselves. She heard his men, some of them yelling, some giving orders, one of them even singing. Crecy, the dwarf, stood in the open door.

"Well, Crecy," Graelam said. "I have come for what is mine."

The dwarf bowed low. "It would appear so, my lord. It is a pity that you would not wait. Lord Richard will not be pleased."

"He should not have played me false. Now he will lose his precious daughter anyway. Tell her that I have dealt honorably with her damned father."

Crecy said, "What he says is true, mistress."

"It matters not. I will not wed him, Crecy. My father was right not to want an alliance with him. He has shown what he is — a thief who must needs steal what he wants."

Graelam didn't say anything to that, just continued to Crecy, "Tell me where the boy and Lady Dorothy are hidden."

She yelled at him, "Even if you find them, I will not wed you."

He turned to smile at her then. "Of course you will. If you do not, then I will take both you and the boy back to Cornwall with me. Do you think that your father would want you returned more than his son, his only heir? Surely he must prize his son more than you."

The pain sliced deep. It always did because she knew he was right. "You will not find him, so it won't matter," she said.

"I cannot tell you, my lord," Crecy said, and he drew himself up to his full four and a half feet. "I cannot, or Lord Richard will kill me. If you kill me for not telling you, why then, I have only lost perhaps three days of life."

Graelam dismissed him, then said to Chandra, "I wish to see the rest of the keep." He said to the two men with him, "Keep an eye out."

"There are no soldiers hidden about to come out and slit your throat. More's the pity."

"Come."

But where he wanted to go was her bedchamber. They went up the winding stone staircase. He knew where she slept, she realized, watching him stride toward the door at the landing of the second level. He opened the door and walked in, motioning his two men to bring her. The shutters were drawn over the narrow windows. The room was dim and chill.

Mary stood in the center of the room, a pale hand pressed against her breast. Chandra heard one of the men draw in his breath behind her.

"One of your servants, Chandra?"

"No, she is one of my ladies. Mary is the daughter of Sir Stephen of Yarmouth, a vassal to my father. She has lived with me since we were children. She is too young to understand what is going on here. Have your men leave her be."

"How old are you, Mary?" Graelam said to her.

"I am seventeen, my lord."

He smiled at Chandra. "Not a child at all." He walked to Mary. He took her chin in the palm of his hand and forced her face up. "Tell me where the boy is hidden, Mary."

She stared up at the man, dark as a moonless night, his voice deep and calm as the waters in the Edze River she had fished in just the previous day. She shook her head. She wasn't a fool. She understood exactly what he would do if she did not tell him. He would kill her. But she wasn't a coward and she said, "I cannot tell you, my lord."

Graelam said over his shoulder, "Hold Lady Chandra."

Her arms were grabbed and pulled behind her.

"You really must tell me, Mary," Graelam said.

She was terrified; he knew that, as did Chandra, but Mary just looked at him, mute, and shook her head.

"You are a lovely maid," he said, and Mary realized then that he wouldn't kill her. No, he would rape her.

His men were looking at Mary. Chandra could taste their lust; it weighed down the very air. They were focused on what their lord was doing and so it took but an instant for Chandra to free herself. She lunged at Graelam, trying to grab his knife from its sheath. He whirled about as she yelled at him, "Damn you, leave her alone!" He grabbed her, again slamming her back against his chest to take away her leverage, his arms wrapped around her. He had great respect for her fists and her knee. He said against her cheek, "You fight me like a mad-woman. What is this? Is this why you do not wish a husband? This girl is your lover?"

She twisted her head to look up at him, and he saw the utter bewilderment in her eyes. "You will not touch her, Graelam. She is my friend."

"Then tell me, where is your brother hidden?"

Chandra said nothing.

Graelam turned to Mary. "Where is the boy?"

Mary shook her head. She knew this man was the enemy. She had no idea how he had managed to take Croyland. He wanted Croyland's heir. John had to be kept safe, kept hidden until all threat was gone. His safety was paramount — at least it was paramount in her world.

Graelam said to his men, "Take Lady Chandra and hold her this time."

He lightly shoved her toward his men. Chandra kicked out at him, but her foot struck his armored leg. It was hard not to cry out because it felt as if she'd broken her toes. Then the men jerked her backward, twisting her arms, and she breathed hard through her mouth to control the sudden pain.

"God's blood, you fools, don't hurt her! Just hold her." When Graelam was satisfied, he turned slowly back to Mary. "Take off your gown. Your first man will be Graelam de Moreton. Perhaps it is also a good thing for your lady to see what her future husband is about."

Mary knew, oh yes, she knew what he would do. She whispered, "No, please do not, my lord."

"Then tell me where the boy is."

"You know I cannot."

"Your gown, Mary. Take it off or I will have to rip it from you."

Chandra yelled at him, cursed him, called

him a coward, but he said nothing, merely watched Mary slowly remove her gown.

"Mary, no, don't!"

"I must," Mary said, her voice firm now, set. "The heir to Croyland must be protected. Do not, Chandra, plead for me." Then she smiled at her friend, just a bit. "It really doesn't suit you."

She began to unfasten the soft leather belt at her waist.

"Graelam, no, you must not, no!"

He heard the fear in her voice, the impotent rage, but he paid her no more attention.

Chandra heard the men's breathing catch as Mary slipped off her gown and her linen shift. She stood perfectly still, her eyes on the floor at her feet. Her body was white, newly matured. She was a pretty girl, soft, untouched.

Graelam stood back from her, deliberately studied the young body, waiting for Chandra to speak. But she didn't. He saw that her eyes were tightly closed. He had been certain that she would break.

He didn't really wish to do this, but now he had backed himself into a corner. Perhaps yet the maid would tell him. He sighed even as he began to remove his armor. It took him some time without the assistance of his squire. When he leaned over to unfasten his cross garters, he saw that Chandra was now looking at him, all of him. He raised a black brow in silent question.

She swallowed, but said nothing.

He stood straight, naked now. She closed her eyes against the sight of him. He moved toward where Mary stood, her head still down.

"No, damn you, no!" Chandra struggled against the men, struggled until her eyes were dark with pain.

"You have but to swallow your pride and tell me where your brother is hidden," he said over his shoulder. "I have no wish for this. Nor does your poor friend here. Give over, Chandra, and tell me. Tell me and I won't touch her."

Chandra shook her head, beyond words. She looked at him now, his body, hard and powerful, so dark he was, the hair black on his head and on his chest, and at his groin, and his sex, thrusting out, ready, just as she had seen her father's sex, full and hard, and she'd hated it, hated the sounds he'd made, hated the sounds the woman had made. Not just one woman — there had been so many over the years, one of them even her own serving maid, only fourteen years old, who had told her later, a stupid smile on her face, just how grand her father was, how very deep he went inside her.

"No," she whispered, "no, I cannot. You know that I cannot. Leave her be. If you wish to rape someone, then rape me, not Mary."

"No," he said.

He wasn't golden like her father. No, he was the devil, black as night, black as a heathen's darkest sins. He was terrifying, overwhelming, and he would hurt Mary.

Graelam motioned for Mary to lie on her back on Chandra's bed. "I will try not to tear you," he said quietly, as he opened her thighs, pulling her toward him. "Just don't fight me, and it will be over soon. It is your first time, so there will be a bit of pain." He spat on his fingers and Chandra saw his hand going between Mary's legs, and Mary whimpered.

Chandra closed her eyes. She couldn't bear it.

His hands were still between Mary's legs even as he turned to look at her one last time. "Chandra, you will learn that you will obey me, in all things. Where is your brother?"

She opened her mouth, but Mary lurched up and yelled, "No, Chandra! Keep your mouth shut!"

Graelam went into her. It was over soon, just one anguished cry from Mary, making her arch with pain. Graelam said even as he was moving deep inside her, "It was your maidenhead. There won't be any more pain."

The pain wasn't as awful now, but Mary hated the feel of him inside her, too big, too big, and she knew she was crying, but she just couldn't stop. Mary wondered if he'd torn her somehow. He had said he would try not to tear her. But if he had, then she would die. She closed her eyes and waited, willing herself to bear the pain, to bear him. She'd held firm. She had saved John. She'd saved Chandra. She hadn't fallen to cowardice. It must be worth it, it must. Yes, it was a small sacrifice.

Graelam pulled out of her and stood there a moment, breathing hard with his release. There was blood on her legs and on him as well, her virgin's blood. But she hadn't broken.

Neither had her friend. He turned slowly to face Chandra. She wasn't yelling at him now. Truth be told, he had expected her to be cursing him to the beams of her bedchamber. But no, she was on her knees, her head bowed, and he watched her vomit. His men had released her, jerking back, staring down at her, not knowing what to do. She remained kneeling on the floor, her body heaving until there was nothing more in her belly. Graelam walked to the small table and poured some water from a carafe into a goblet. He came down on his haunches in front of her. "Wash out your mouth."

She took the goblet and did as he bade. She spat the water out into the rushes. Then she drank deep. She was shaking, couldn't seem to stop it. She felt a vast emptiness, and it alarmed her because she didn't understand it. But it was deep, so deep inside her, it seemed an integral part of her. What he had done, so passionless it was, so matter-of-fact, with no purpose but to dominate, to gain his way. And the humiliation for Mary, forced to accept him, and she'd let it happen. Because of her, now Mary was no longer a maid. She was used.

"Chandra."

She raised her face at the sound of his quiet voice. Gone was the deadening blankness. He was naked, standing right in front of her and she saw Mary's blood on him. She moved faster than he could have imagined, grabbing for his sword that lay beside his clothes and his armor, and the hilt was in her hands before he managed to wrench it from her. She hooked his leg in a wrestler's grip and drove her fist hard into his naked groin.

Graelam's legs buckled. He heard his men, but yelled for them to stay back. He lurched to the side, managed to grab her thick braid, and jerked her backward to land on top of him. He couldn't believe the pain, knew it would get worse, and it did, and he closed his eyes against it even as he held her so tightly against him that he could feel her ribs pressed into his chest.

In that instant, he realized that if he were as intelligent as he'd always been told he was, he would drag himself and his men from Croyland and send his blessings to God that he had survived. He was a fool to force this woman to wed him. He had no doubt that she would try to bring him low. He wondered then if he would ever tame her, ever make her accept him. He imagined fighting her in bed, wondered if he would have to tie her down, and knew then that he would indeed have to.

Why had she vomited? Merely watching him take her friend had sent this proud, arrogant girl to her knees, retching in the flower-scented rushes? His pain slowly receded, almost too slowly for a man to bear, and finally he said, "I will have to think about your payment for that."

"What will you do? Kill me? Well, then, you savage, do it now."

Chapter 3

He didn't kill her, of course. What he did was make his men hold her again while he slowly dressed himself. He left off his armor, saying, "I will go to Lord Richard's bedchamber. I will make use of his clothing." And then he'd smiled, for the pain was gone from his groin and he knew he would live again. Once again, he was filled with optimism and determination. He had worked too hard to get her. He would have her, no matter the cost. He had absolutely no doubt that she would kill him if she had the chance. It didn't worry him. It fascinated him.

"As for you, Chandra, you will either agree to wed me, whether or not I find your brother, or I will simply take you back with me and you will live as my mistress until you agree to marry me. I know you —"

He never finished, for just then the bedchamber door burst open and Abaric yelled even before he saw Graelam, "We have them!"

Lady Dorothy and John came stumbling

into the bedchamber, a half dozen of Graelam's men behind them.

"We have them," Abaric said again, and rubbed his hands together.

Chandra stared at her mother, then at John. She couldn't believe it, just couldn't, yet here they both were, standing right in front of her, no torn clothing, no signs of any struggle. She said slowly, feeling her heart beat with slow, deadening strokes, so loud they were, "How is this? You were well hidden. How did they find you, Lady Dorothy?"

Why, Graelam wondered, did she call her mother Lady Dorothy?

She was a gaunt woman, as tall as her daughter, but the life seemed sucked out of her. Her hair, once a rich black, was streaked with coarse gray strands, her mouth seamed so tightly, it was only a thin, pale line. She looked, he thought, as unforgiving as his own witch of a mother. She looked as though she'd never had an ounce of joy in her life and that she would do her best to see that no one around her had any joy either.

Lady Dorothy shook off the hands of the men behind her. She looked first at Graelam, then at Mary, who was standing beside Chandra's bed, her face pale, looking blank and stupid. Lady Dorothy sniffed the air. The room smelled of sex. But how could that be? Both Mary and Chandra were fully clothed, as were the men.

Lady Dorothy turned to Chandra and her face hardened. Filthy she was, boar's blood all over her, her hair matted to her head with sweat. Lady Dorothy said, her chin up, "You look disgusting."

Graelam stared at her, not believing what had come out of her mouth, but Chandra said only, "I know. It doesn't matter. Who found you?"

Lady Dorothy shrugged and said, quivering at that smell she still believed was sex, "No one. I did not like it in that small dark room. I never have. I've told your father many times that it is too rude a place for me ever to remain for more than a few minutes. There were rats, the sound of men's boots clattering overhead, yells and cursing. John fretted. I did not wish him to be frightened. I did not wish to dirty my gown."

"Because you did not like the room, because you did not want John to whine, because you did not wish to soil your gown, you broke Father's rule? You actually came out by yourselves, of your own free will? You simply chose to disregard my father's orders?"

"Your father isn't here," Lady Dorothy

said. "Even though you like to pretend that you are the one who is important here, you are not. It is my responsibility to see to the castle. Just look at you, a dirty hag, here in your bedchamber with this man, nearly alone with him. Why is there the smell of vomit?"

"I was ill," Chandra said. "It doesn't matter."

"No, it doesn't. I hope you weren't ill in front of our guest. Why ever did you bring him to your bedchamber? You should be seeing to his comfort. By all the saints, Chandra, you aren't good for anything, must less protecting your father's precious holdings. John, come here."

The boy, small and slight, moved to stand beside his mother. He was, Graelam saw, looking over at his sister, and there was a smirk on his small face. He looked very pleased with himself. Graelam wanted to pick him up and throw him out one of the narrow windows. What was going on here?

"I didn't like that room, just as Mother told you," John said, and he put his hands on his hips, daring his sister to say something. "Who is this man? Is he really a guest and not one of father's enemies?"

Chandra said, still not wanting to believe what they'd done, "You really came out of

44

hiding because you decided you wanted to?"

"I am the mistress here, not you," Lady Dorothy said. "I will do as I please. Now, answer your brother. Who is this man?"

Mary made a very small sound in her throat and slowly fell to the floor.

"What is wrong with her?" Lady Dorothy asked to no one in particular.

"She seems to have fainted," Graelam said. He walked to Mary, picked her up and gently put her on Chandra's bed, the bed he would share with Chandra this very night. When he straightened, he said, "I am Lord Graelam de Moreton of Wolffeton in Cornwall, my lady. I am here to wed your daughter."

Lady Dorothy just looked at him.

John said, "Chandra doesn't want to marry, ever. Everyone knows that. She won't marry you, will she?"

Lady Dorothy said slowly, tightening her fingers on the boy's shoulder, making him wince, "Welcome, my lord. I am pleased to give my precious daughter over to you, a great lord, who will see that she becomes what she is meant to become, if it isn't, of course, too late."

Chandra felt such pain that she wanted to fold in upon herself, but she couldn't. She heard John say, "It's about time she was gone from Croyland. It's mine, Mother, just as you're always telling me, not hers. I'm the important one here, not her. I don't want her here."

"That's right, my love. Soon you will rule Croyland, as you were always meant to, with no more interference from your sister. Now, Chandra, I will see that the servants prepare a lovely wedding feast. I will see to Lord Graelam's comfort since you have not bothered. Now, bathe the filth off yourself. My lord, I am pleased that you have come."

Lady Dorothy actually gave him her hand. He bowed low over it, then watched her walk out of the bedchamber, the boy swaggering beside her. He turned to Chandra, his forehead furrowed in thought, his voice calm. "It is just as well that you will soon be gone from here. I should not have liked to have her for my mother, although my own was just as vicious. Ah, Mary is coming around. I will speak to Father Tolbert now. Then I will go to your father's bedchamber. Prepare yourself, Chandra."

He paused at the doorway, saying over his shoulder, "I hope you will now agree to wed me. I should hate to be forced to take that boy back with us to Cornwall, although several good thrashings just might improve him, something it appears your father hasn't done."

"My lord, you'll not believe this, but Croyland has been taken."

Lambert, tall, skinny as a tent pole, nearly fell off his horse, scrambling not to lose his balance as he ran to Jerval. "I didn't believe it myself at first, but one of the villagers told me to keep clear of the castle because Lord Graelam de Moreton and thirty of his men hold it now."

"This is madness," Jerval de Vernon said slowly, trying to understand. "How is this possible?" He was tired. He and his twenty men had ridden for three days to get to Croyland, and now, Lord Richard had somehow been overcome?

"Lord Richard isn't there," Lambert said, still panting from his wild ride back to their campsite in a protected inlet by the water. The waves made a gentle, rolling sound, constant and low, and the sun was brilliant overhead. "It was a trick, a ruse. The villager told me that Lord Richard had caught a man skulking about, and the man finally admitted that he was scouting around for Cadwallon, that Welsh bandit. He was planning a surprise attack on Lord Richard when he and his men left Croyland to hunt.

Lord Richard took his men to catch the bandit. But Cadwallon is nowhere about. It was Graelam de Moreton who sent the spy there. Another villager said that de Moreton caught Lady Chandra out hunting with some of her men. It was over then. Another villager said that he held a knife to her back and told them that he would slit her throat if they didn't lower the drawbridge. It was quickly done."

"But why would he do that?" Sir Mark asked, slapping his leather gloves against his thigh. "He must know that he could never hold Croyland. Why?"

Lambert said, "He doesn't want Croyland. He came because he wants Lady Chandra. He plans to wed her this very night, done by Croyland's own priest."

"By all the saints' buried sins," Jerval said, grinning like a madman, "this is something that will surely invigorate the blood." Then he laughed and rubbed his hands together. "The little princess got her comeuppance, did she?" He laughed again. "My father tells me that she is known for her pride — bred, he claims, into her very bones. Her valor as well, though that makes little sense. Well, I suppose that we must do something about it. It wouldn't do to have Lord Graelam wed her, not when we have ridden three days to get here ourselves so I could marry her."

"You know you don't have to wed her, Jerval," Sir Mark said. "Your father just asked you to look her over."

Jerval just smiled. His father, Lord Hugh, was eager for the alliance. Camberley was close enough to Croyland to provide mutual protection, and his father had raved on and on about her beauty after he'd seen his only son back away when he spoke of her fierce pride, her bravery. No woman, he'd said again and again, was as beautiful as Chandra of Croyland.

Jerval didn't believe that for a moment, but he had agreed to come and see her for himself. This glorious creature, according to his father, had hair golden as a sheaf of wheat ripening under the summer sun, flowing hair spun into minstrel's verses, and ah, her eyes — the color of the sky in early July when it was warm and still and so clear it made you weep. What tripe. There was no female in the known world who looked like that. Of course, his father had seen her only once when he had been visiting Croyland some four years before. He shook his head. His father really wanted the alliance. Jerval had a very bad feeling about her.

On the other hand, Graelam de Moreton had taken Croyland just to get her. Perhaps his father had somehow spread the same exaggerations to Lord Graelam, and he'd believed them.

Why had Lord Richard left so few men to guard the castle? Why had she left to go hunting? Her small, dainty falcon was bored? Didn't she have a brain? He didn't want a stupid wife. No matter, he would save her from her own folly. Then he would very likely go home without her, pleased to escape.

Jerval left his men to their talk and walked down on the beach. He watched the waves, low, gentle, fan out onto the shore, then slowly fold back. He watched the sun lower in the sky. Mark looked after him as he said to Lambert, who was scratching his ear, "Now, he goes to think and plan. What do you say, Lambert? How long will it take him to come back with a strategy?"

"Ten minutes," Lambert said. "No longer. It's not all that difficult a problem."

"Nay, I disagree. It's a knotty problem."

Exactly ten minutes later, Jerval called out as he strode back up from the beach, "Let's go. I have a plan to save the little princess." He looked very pleased with himself.

Mark dug a coin out of his tunic and tossed it to Lambert, who bit on it out of habit, and chuckled. Soon all the men were laughing.

Jerval frowned at them as he mounted his horse. "What is the jest?"

Crecy, wearing his best wine-colored robe, which really required very little precious material since he was so short, walked beside Chandra down the deep stone stairs into the great hall. He saw that Graelam stood in front of her father's huge chair, with its high carved back and its lion's-head posts, waiting for her. On his left sat Lady Dorothy, John next to Graelam's man, Abaric.

"He is an honorable man," Crecy said in his low, soothing voice, knowing there was no hope for it now. "He will not mistreat you. You will not have to protect yourself from his violence, for there will be none. He will treat you well, if you will but allow him to. He admires you. Give over, mistress." He paused a moment, alarmed by her pallor. "Cornwall is a beautiful land, harsh along its northern coast, but just a few miles to the south there are palm trees and the water is balmy. It will please you. His holding, Wolffeton, is magnificent."

"I have no wish to go to Cornwall." She shook her head. "I don't understand. Why me, Crecy? A powerful lord like Graelam de Moreton shouldn't select a wife who brings him nothing, a wife who would carve out his heart if she had the chance. He must know that I will always hate him, that I will never bow to him."

Crecy said, "That you, a girl, would have the skill and the courage to actually fight him, to kill him if you were the more skilled, the more ruthless — it fascinates him. Two years ago when you were but sixteen, a wandering minstrel came to Wolffeton. It was Henri of Agris. Do you remember him? He was a young Frenchman who worshipped you."

"Yes, I remember him. He was annoying with all his drowsy-eyed looks, but he did sing sweetly."

Crecy thought that Henri was a credulous puppy, beyond annoying, what with all his sighs of adoration, making him miss his footing and trip into piles of muck as he followed the mistress around, but no matter. "After he left Croyland, he went to Cornwall. He sang of you in vivid verse to Lord Graelam, painting you as the virgin warrior of great beauty who rode and hunted like a man. He painted you as a woman more desirable than any lady in the king's court, a woman without a woman's wiles, a woman who held honor dear."

"I look like no warrior now," she said, bitterness hard and flat in her throat.

"No," Crecy said, his voice at its very driest, "you do not." She was dressed in a pale yellow silk gown that made her look soft and white, and very much a lady. Her father had brought the fabric with him from London for her birthday, just three months before, and had it sewn for her to his own directions. This was only the second time she had worn the gown. Its arms were long and tapered at her wrists; a woven yellow belt hung loose at her hips. Her hair fell halfway down her back, nearly dry from its washing. There was no more stench of boar's blood; even the bits of blood and dirt from beneath her fingernails were gone.

Crecy cleared his throat, ran a short, thick finger over his sparse beard, and said, "When Henri was there two years ago, Graelam's wife, a whining lady from the French court, had just died birthing a stillborn child. Graelam had wed her to please his father and to fill his father's coffers. But then his father died, followed by both his wife and the babe, and he was his own man and the lord of Wolffeton. He now wants a wife like none other in all of England. He wants you."

Chandra said, "The man is an idiot to believe anything that a minstrel would put to verse."

"He just told me a while ago, whilst he was dressing, that if he could find Henri, he would give him a handful of gold. Your beauty came as a surprise to him, for, like you, he said that only a fool would believe a minstrel's weeping verses."

Chandra saw Mary, seated on the other side of Graelam's man, Abaric, who was leaning very close to John, set there, undoubtedly, to guard him and see that he kept to his place. Mary's head was down, but Chandra could tell from where she stood that Mary was very pale. Graelam had raped Mary, even though he said there'd be no violence, no brutality. He'd just done it as if it was nothing at all, and it was over and nothing had changed. Mary's silence had bought naught. But for Mary, Chandra knew, nothing would ever be the same again.

Chandra realized that no one must ever know what had happened, particularly Mary's father, Sir Stephen, a hard man who looked at his young daughter with the sole thought of selling her to the richest man he could find. If he ever found out that she was no longer a virgin, he would kill her, for she would have no more value to him.

Very little in life, Chandra thought, was fair, particularly when it came to women, particularly when it was the men making the decisions, which they always did.

She saw a dagger hanging loose in a man's belt. She could get it, she knew she could, and she could kill Graelam. She would die, but it would be over.

Slowly, she sidled nearer and nearer to the man and that dagger of his. He was laughing, talking, drinking her father's ale, paying no attention. She was close now, her hand stretching out now to ease the dagger out of his belt.

Chapter 4

"Ah, mistress," Crecy whispered against her ear, "do not, I beg you. Graelam is looking at you. He will see you take it. It's possible that he would kill John as a punishment." Crecy knew this wasn't true, but it stopped her cold. He watched her draw in a deep breath, gain control again.

"I want to kill him, Crecy. Then it would be over."

"Graelam is a very hard man to kill. Leave go, mistress."

There was really no choice. She sighed as she saw her mother staring at her from across the Great Hall. The pleasure in her faded brown eyes was stark and clear. So pleased she was to be rid of her daughter. But it didn't hurt, not the way it had when she was small. Ah, yes, and Lady Dorothy was now smiling, a triumphant smile. Why had her mother so disliked her only daughter? Chandra nearly laughed aloud. Not just dislike, that was too tame a word. All those years of abuse, done in the privacy of Lady Dorothy's bedchamber, and she had never complained to her father about it, knowing, even as a child, that if she ever said anything, Lady Dorothy would somehow manage to kill her. A mother killing her own daughter — but she'd felt it, known it would happen. At age eleven, Chandra had been large enough to protect herself, and she had. She would never forget when her mother backhanded her for some misdeed, and she had known at that instant that she wouldn't be beaten anymore. She'd growled like a young animal, deep in her throat, and leapt on her mother, her hands going around her neck. She'd nearly choked her to death before her old maid, Alice, had pulled her off.

Since that time, Lady Dorothy hadn't ever raised her hand or fist to her again.

If she were forced to leave Croyland, she would not miss her mother. She saw that John was also looking toward her, and like her mother, he too was smiling, but there wasn't real meanness there. She realized that he was afraid — the fear was stark and livid in his eyes. She was thankful that he wasn't entirely blind, that he realized that his home was now in the hands of an enemy. As for his pleasure at this wedding of hers, he simply followed his mother's example. Of course he knew bone-deep jealousy at his father's treatment of him, resented her because his father gave her all his attention and affection. But she wanted to tell him that he was just a little boy and soon he would go to another great lord's keep and learn to be a knight. And once that happened, he would be very important to their father, very important indeed.

Crecy gave her over to Lord Graelam, who bowed slightly to her, never taking his eyes from her face. "Your beauty pleases me."

She said clearly, looking past him at the magnificent tapestry on the stone wall, at the golden unicorn who sat beside a beautiful maiden, the two of them woven so beautifully into the thick wool, "Aye, I am now clean, well garbed and useless."

He looked from her thick, burnished hair, still damp, to her light blue eyes, to the fine bones in her face, to her breasts, to her feet in the soft leather slippers. He had indeed believed the minstrel Henri must have exaggerated, but he hadn't. By all the saints, he hadn't. "Yes," he said easily, "the skirt to your gown is very narrow. It would be hard for even you to fight me wearing that. Sit down, Chandra. It is our wedding feast. Your mother did well."

"Yes, I did," Lady Dorothy said, raising her voice. "I would do anything for my dearest daughter, as you see, my lord."

The servants, terrified of getting clouted if they didn't move quickly, served Lord Graelam's men first, then the few Croyland men Graelam had allowed at the feast. The other thirty or so men were locked in the dungeons.

There was delicious boar's meat, laid out on huge platters. There were large bowls of leeks and sops in wine to pour over the bread laid in the trenchers. There was haddock with onions dipped in breadcrumbs and broiled until brown, served with brown ale. Chandra chewed on a bit of fresh bread, saying nothing, listening, watching. All of Graelam's men were loud, laughing, cursing, punching each other, celebrating their lord's wedding. The ale flowed freely.

No choice, Chandra thought as she drank some of the sweet wine from Aquitaine, the pride of her father's cellars, kept for only very special occasions. She kept her eyes on her plate. She wasn't hungry. When she looked at the boar steaks, she saw only her blood-smeared clothes, Mary's virgin blood on Graelam. She was aware of Graelam next to her, felt the heat from his body, saw that he was wearing one of her father's robes, a brilliant red silk that didn't come all the way to the floor as it did on her father. She hadn't realized he was the larger. He smiled on her, but offered her no pieces of meat from his trencher.

She thought about the coming night. She'd seen what he did to Mary, something so quickly over, so easily done, but the pain of it, the loss of pride and dignity, the lack of choice, it could bow a woman to her knees. She couldn't imagine a man doing that to her, overcoming her, sticking himself into her, sending pain throughout her body, reducing her to nothing. She remembered clearly the times she had seen her father take any female he happened to fancy, any female who chanced to be near when the need was on him. It never seemed to matter how old or young they were for either the women or for him. Just heaving and laughing, and the women seemed to be enjoying themselves as well. She couldn't begin to imagine such a thing.

"Your home is Wolffeton," Graelam said. "It was built by my great-grandfather, back when Eleanor of Aquitaine was Queen of England. He was smitten with her, I have heard it said. He died when her son Richard the Lionhearted came to the throne. Wolffeton is a mighty keep. I have many vassals, many men-at-arms. You will always be safe there."

She looked at him, but said nothing.

"I will try to get you with child this night," he said, and this time she attended him, her head jerking up, her eyes cold and frightened, until she gained control and her eyes became blank. "I do not believe so," she said.

"I will take time with you. There will be some pain, but for a warrior like you, it will be nothing. Perhaps you will even enjoy my taking you."

"I will enjoy nothing about you, save your death," she said.

He smiled, pleased. The thought of bending her to his will, of her submitting to him, her yielding to him, made him want to yell with the power he felt flowing through him. He would have her, at last he would have her.

Graelam wanted very much to get the ceremony over. He wanted her, had wanted her for so very long that just the thought of her made him hard. He let her be. Soon, he thought, soon.

Time passed. The air grew thick, heavy with the men's laughter and jests. Graelam appeared not to care that she didn't speak to him, that she merely sat beside him, mute. A servant came to her side, slowly pouring more of the sweet wine into her goblet. She was so locked into herself that when the man spoke low, close in her ear, she didn't hear him. He said again, more loudly this time, right in her ear as he poured her wine, "Look around you, my lady. I am Sir Mark de Gwen, here with Jerval de Vernon and twenty men. We are here to save you. When Father Tolbert comes forward for the ceremony, that is the signal. Get your brother and your mother to safety. Can you do this?"

She nodded slowly, staring into her wine goblet. And then he slipped away, back into the shadows before she could think of anything to say, which was just as well because Graelam was looking at her again. Someone was here to save her? Chandra looked around the Great Hall. This time she easily picked out all the strangers, men all, at least twenty of them as Mark had said, wearing servants' clothing, serving all the men ale and more ale. They were getting them drunk. She smiled. Now there was a chance. She saw one cowled priest walk slowly forward. He didn't move like Father Tolbert; he was much larger than the meager priest who had spewed his foul breath into her face since she'd been a child. Jerval de Vernon, she thought. She waited, muscles tense, ready to leap into action, and wished the stranger had given her a dagger, anything.

"It is time," Graelam said, and lightly stroked his fingers over the back of her hand. Her flesh was very cold. He frowned a moment, then said, "It will be all right. All you must do is bend to me, trust me. I will be your husband, your master. I will protect you and our children. Give over, Chandra. It is too late for you to fight me now."

She said nothing, merely pulled her hand away and nodded.

He didn't like that, she realized, but he said nothing. She was afraid that if she spoke, he would hear something in her voice, the anticipation, the hope.

Graelam stood and called to the priest, "We are ready, Father."

The man walked toward them, his head down, covered by a thick, dark-brown woolen hood, a scribe following behind him carrying a rolled parchment.

Then, suddenly, the man threw back his hood, pulled off the wool robe, and shouted, *"À Vernon! À Vernon!"*

All the soldiers garbed as servants grabbed for their swords and knives and jumped at Graelam's men. As for Graelam, he flung himself at Chandra before the words were out of the priest's mouth — no, the bastard wasn't a priest. He was a young giant and his sword was already freed from his cloak.

He missed her. Chandra managed to knock the chair into him as she slipped out of it. His men were slow because they were drunk. Before he knew what had happened, Chandra had jerked Abaric's knife from its sheath and stabbed it into his shoulder even as he yelled in shock, knocking him out of his chair. Chandra shouted, "John, quickly, quickly. Get under Father's chair. Hurry!"

"But, Chandra —"

"Do as I tell you! Lady Dorothy, get you to safety with him, now!"

The Great Hall was in pandemonium. Even as Graelam was methodically working his way to her, his sword drawn, he was shouting orders. Food and ale were hurled to the rushes as his soldiers tried to get themselves together. They were well trained, but they had drunk more ale than usual and they were slower, their brains sluggish, for they hadn't expected anything like this. But soon enough they had their weapons in hand and were fighting.

Suddenly, the doors to the Great Hall burst open, and Lord Richard's men who had been locked in the dungeons came running in, shouting, *"À Avenell! À Avenell!"*

Chandra saw Graelam hacking his way toward her, his face grim, his concentration complete. Unlike his men, he had drunk little. She stuffed her stolen knife into her belt, then leaned down and grabbed the sword of a fallen soldier.

Mark saw her with that sword and blanched. What the devil was she doing? Was she mad? Hysterical? He yelled, "Lady, run, get out of here, hurry."

Chandra saw that Lady Dorothy had stuffed John beneath his father's chair. She herself was pressed back against a tapestry, out of danger.

Chandra heard one of Graelam's men yelling curses, even as he raised his sword to drive it into Mark's back. Without hesitation, she rammed her sword through the man's side.

Mark whirled about and gaped at her, at the bloody sword in her hand. She'd saved his life? This was the little princess Jerval spoke of, the girl he believed was overproud, filled with her own worth? He yelled at her, "Lady, thank you, but for God's sake, get you to safety. I told you to hide yourself!"

"If I had run, you fool, you would be dead." And she laughed, pure and deep, wheeled around to drive her sword into the arm of another of Graelam's men who was hacking his way toward John.

Graelam was drawing nearer to her even though three men were on him. He was very skilled, she thought matter-of-factly, not at all surprised, and very strong. His endurance was amazing, probably as amazing as her father's endurance when he had been Graelam's age. She felt a man's hand on her shoulder and jerked about, her sword coming up. "No, lady, I am not the enemy. I'm Jerval de Vernon. Please, let me take you out of here."

"Oh, no," she said, and smiled at the young man whose face was streaked with sweat and trickling blood from a wound near his temple. Then he whirled about and motioned two of his men to join him.

Three men surrounded her now. They wouldn't let her free, hacking, hacking, keeping their backs to her, keeping her in a tight circle, guarding her with their lives.

She heard a yell of fury, saw that Graelam was at the head of a knot of his men, his sword arm moving in great arcs as he fought his way back toward the doors of the Great Hall. He'd given it up, realized he couldn't overcome all the men, and she knew he hated it, but he would escape, damn him. Abaric, holding his shoulder, his face without color, was staggering behind Graelam, and Graelam was protecting him. No, she couldn't allow him to escape. She managed to break through her circle of protectors, simply because they believed her safe now and grateful for it, and ran toward him. Her skirt ripped up the side, but it didn't matter. Suddenly Jerval de Vernon, the young man who had pretended to be Father Tolbert, was there between them and she froze for an instant. She really looked at him now, really saw him. By all the saints, she was looking at her father in his youth. This was a young man so golden, his eyes so brilliantly blue, his body large, so very hard with muscle, that he should have been her father's son. He was big, sweating, his arm never tiring.

"Let me by you!"

He gave her a quick smile. "Not as long as I am still alive."

She tried to run around him, but he blocked her. Then he leapt toward Graelam, yelling, "Come, Graelam de Moreton, fight me!"

Graelam saw Chandra behind Jerval de Vernon, and knew she wanted to take his place. For an instant, he felt deep pleasure at the sight of her, at the taste of her rage, the bloodlust in her eyes, the rip in her gown, the blood on that incredible fabric. Damnation, he knew he couldn't get to her. He looked at the man who faced him now and knew he was a man of his own strength.

"Damn you to hell and beyond," he said low, and swung his sword in a powerful arc directly down at Jerval de Vernon's bare neck. But Jerval's sword blocked his. They hacked at each other, the clash of steel on steel ringing above the cries of the wounded soldiers.

The great oak doors were flung wide. Graelam's men streamed through them and down the narrow outside stairs, Abaric with them. Graelam drew Jerval with him. He heard his men getting the horses together, gathering their weapons and their supplies. No, he didn't want it to end like this. He hated failure, tasted it, strong and hot in his mouth.

With a sudden cry of rage, he plunged his sword downward with all his strength, shearing away Jerval's shield.

They were both panting, sweat blinding them. Graelam saw Owen, his father's man, bold and coarse, weakening under the on-slaught of a younger man. Graelam swung his sword in great arcs, pushing Jerval back, but he was too late. Owen fell hard into a

68

pool of his own blood. Graelam lunged at Jerval as Owen's death yell sounded loud in his ears.

They were evenly matched until Jerval slipped on a slick of blood. He saw Graelam's sword above him as he flailed the empty air to find balance.

Suddenly, Jerval heard a soft, hissing sound. Graelam staggered back, his hand clutching at his shoulder. A dagger lay deep in his flesh. Jerval turned quickly to see that she had thrown it, that she was staring at Graelam, at the knife in his shoulder. She moved now to stand beside Jerval, her hand on his arm. "I'll kill him now. Quickly, quickly, give me your sword."

Even knowing what she'd done with the dagger, even seeing her save Mark's life, even knowing she'd saved his own life, he hesitated, unable to comprehend what she had done.

"There will be another time, Jerval de Vernon!" Graelam grunted in pain as he jerked the dagger from his shoulder. He started to fling it to the ground when he saw it was Abaric's knife, given to him by his father. He cursed, then shouted, "Your aim is that of a girl, Chandra, not a warrior. The next time, I shall teach you." He laughed then even as his men pressed him back, out

the great oak doors, into the inner courtyard.

She grabbed Jerval's sword and ran after
him. Jerval grabbed her arm and pulled her
down beside him. "No, don't go after him.
Even with your father's men, we cannot be
certain to defeat him. Let him go."

The men of Croyland and Camberley
were pressing about them, running down the
outside stairs into the bailey. They stopped
then, shouting in victory as Graelam's men,
helping their wounded friends, managed to
get onto their rearing horses and ride out
over the lowered drawbridge.

Save for the moaning of wounded soldiers
and the soft wails of women in the Great
Hall, there was silence.

Jerval looked into her face. There were
streaks of blood running down her temple,
her hair was tangled about her head, her
gown was ripped and covered with gore and
filth. She was smiling. His father hadn't lied.
Jerval had never seen a more beautiful
woman in his entire life. The little princess,
soft and adored, helpless and submissive,
that he had pictured in his mind's eyes, died
a swift death.

He said slowly, "You are Lady Chandra,
daughter of Lord Richard de Avenell?"

She helped him to his feet, then said as

she looked up at him, "I am."

"Graelam was wrong. Your aim was that of a warrior. It was your anger than blinded you." He turned to Mark. "Send some men to the walls. We must be certain that Graelam takes his leave. Bring up the drawbridge."

He turned again to look at the woman he was here to consider for a wife. If he had not seen her fight with his own eyes, he would have thought himself in the presence of a delicate young maiden, one in need of protection and rescue. Ah, but she didn't need anyone. The bloodlust was fading from her eyes, and she slowly relaxed her grip on the bloody sword, letting it hang loosely at her side.

She said, cocking her head at him, "Who are you, Jerval de Vernon? How came you to be here?"

So her father hadn't told her of his visit. He said slowly, "I am here to visit your father, an ambassador from my own, Lord Hugh de Vernon."

"You are welcome here, as either priest or warrior." And she punched her fist into his arm, threw back her head and laughed. "We won!"

Jerval looked over to see Mark staring at her, just standing there, staring.

"Yes," he said, "we won."

71

Chapter 5

"Crecy, tell me the truth," Lord Richard said as he absently pulled the ears on his huge wolfhound, Graynard, who was lolling at his booted feet, "you swear that he did not touch her?"

"I swear, my lord. He wanted her in marriage, honorably. He did tell her precisely what he wanted of her, what he wanted her to become, what he would allow her to become. But I think he did that because he took pleasure in her rage and in her spirit even though she was helpless against him. I think that when she threw the dagger into his shoulder, even that amazed and pleased him."

"Is the man an idiot?"

Crecy had to smile. "I think he is so fascinated by her that if she stabbed him through the heart he would compliment her strength before he died. But he is gone now, my lord."

"The son of a bitch," Lord Richard said as he looked across the Great Hall at his daughter in conversation with Jerval de Vernon, a young man who made him feel as though he was looking at himself twenty years before. Not yet twenty-five he was, and he had already gained a reputation as a fearless warrior, a man of honor, a man to trust at your back. *And he is nearly as comely as I was at his age,* Richard thought. For a moment, he felt jealousy sear through him at what this young man was, at what he would become, and most importantly, that he would have Chandra.

He said to Crecy, the taste of his own voice rancid with jealousy, "I knew the day would come when I had to give her to another man." He hadn't said that exactly right, he thought, though Crecy hadn't even raised an eyebrow at his words. Richard scratched Graynard's head, cleared his throat, and tried again. "She is turned eighteen now, old enough to have been wed for three years, and I know I must let her go. She is not meant to remain a virgin. I will give her to Jerval de Vernon. Look, Crecy, he hangs on her every word. He is laughing."

"I am not surprised. He also saw her fight. It did not repel him."

"No," Richard said slowly, "I would not have selected him for her had I believed that he would see her as unnatural."

"You saw him when he was only twenty years old, my lord, scarcely a man grown, newly wearing his spurs. How did you know what manner of man he would become?"

Richard said simply as he rose and shoved Graynard aside with his boot, "His is my mirror image. His father, Lord Hugh, even told me — jealousy leaping out of his mouth as he spoke — that his boy was just like me. I believed him and I did spend three days at Jervel's side, watched him fight, jest, drink." Richard paused a moment, and he frowned. "I did not watch him wench. I hope he does not —" He broke off, then added, "And, I know to my soul that Jerval de Vernon will want her until death drags him from her. Now, where is my wife? I would know why the bitch disobeyed my orders."

Crecy, the only human in this huge holding who was the recipient of Lord Richard's true feelings about everyone, said, "I believe she is with her ladies. She sews. She plots. She probably keeps John close to her skirts."

"More than likely she is hiding from me. I should beat her, Crecy."

"You might well find your food poisoned if you do, my lord, or a dagger slipped between your ribs some dark night."

"True enough," Richard said. "But there is one thing I can do. I am sending John to the Earl of Grantham within the month. It is time. I fear that she's turning him into a mewling little puke."

"It is well past time to send him away, some would say, my lord."

"I wanted to toughen him up, but I realize that he will not do much of anything that is admirable until I have him away from his mother."

"I will write immediately to Lord Grantham, my lord," Crecy said, and bowed deeply.

Lord Richard frowned toward his daughter. "Yes, see that you do, Crecy. I wonder what they're talking about."

There was a wicked glint in her eyes even as Chandra was saying with all the earnestness of a penitent facing a priest, "It is said that I am very nearly amazing with a bow and arrow. Perhaps even beyond amazing. My father taught me, and there is no one better than he is. I am giving you warning, Jerval, if you want a competition, your manhood will suffer grave sorrow. Perhaps you will even weep in your humiliation. Dare you take the risk?"

The little princess, Jerval thought, wanting to kiss that delicious smirk off her

75

mouth. Did his father truly believe that he would not want her if he knew about her warrior skills? That he would be appalled that she would insult his own skills and his manhood in one breath and make him want to laugh at her cockiness in the next? Probably so. Men saw women in one way only, and he knew he always had, but that was different now. All in the course of one single evening, his life had changed irrevocably. Perhaps he would allow himself to judge her, a woman, by some of the standards a man was judged by. That was difficult, when it came right down to it. But to listen to her bravado, to play at all her games, it amused him, pleased him to his soul, and made him want to strip off her clothes and kiss every inch of her. But he'd also seen her fight like a man, seen her with his own eyes yell her triumph, seen her splattered with blood, and yet she still looked at him as only a big playmate, when all he wanted to do after he kissed every patch of her was to lie with her on that grassy knoll just beyond Croyland's walls.

He was harder than the stone beneath his feet. If there were an enemy behind him, it wouldn't be a good thing. He shook his head at himself.

She hit her fist into his shoulder. "Attend

me, sir. Do you wish to grovel at my feet when I have made you look the veriest beginner?"

What was she talking about? Oh yes, a competition — bow and arrow. He smiled, wanting to stroke his fingers over her face, wanting to kiss her mouth, feel his tongue play between her lips. By all the saints, he was in a bad way. He saw that her head was angled to one side, that she was looking up at him, eagerness and laughter in her blue eyes. Nothing else, dammit. A playmate, he was naught but a playmate to her, but no matter. It was early days and despite her prowess, her courage, her audacity — or perhaps because of them — she was innocent in the ways of women, appallingly so. He said easily, straightening taller so that he looked down on her more, "You bray like a cocky young lad. I will send you weeping into the dirt, Chandra, when you lose to me. You are a girl and I am a warrior. You haven't a chance."

He watched her puff up — her pride, her defenses all in place, ready to bash him — when Lady Dorothy said from behind her, "I trust you are thanking this blessed young man for saving us, Chandra."

Jerval watched her stiffen as taut at a bowstring, all the fun, all the laugher, dying out of her face. There were problems here between mother and daughter, big ones. Mark had told him that Lady Dorothy had willingly given her over to Graelam, had come out of her hidey-hole, disobeying Lord Richard's express order. What kind of mother would do that?

Chandra said, her voice carefully neutral, "If he hadn't come, then I would be in Cornwall and you and John would still be safe here at Croyland. Only I would be gone."

"There is that," Lady Dorothy said, and frowned. "Still, the young man is here now and things have changed. We must all adapt."

By the saints, Jerval thought, was she going to say something about why he had really come to Croyland? No, he couldn't allow that — it was too soon. Jerval said quickly, "Ah, Lady Dorothy, this daughter of yours has thanked me for saving her until I have grown dizzy with the repetition of it. I beg you not to encourage her to thank me more. I feared she would burst into tears, she holds me in such high esteem. My head aches from all her gratitude."

Chandra poked him in the ribs, hard. She was very nearly laughing at what he'd said. He was charmed to his feet when she said, "He knows his own worth, ma'am. I do not need to add to his conceit."

"You should if it would perhaps reduce your own," Lady Dorothy said. She looked up then to see her husband striding toward her. She said quickly, "Chandra does not thank men, sir. If you think that she did, you are wrong. You are blinded by her beauty, which is of no importance at all, as anyone with a working mind knows. I crave solitude. I believe I will go to the solar now. There is that new tapestry I have designed."

Lord Richard saw his wife look back at him, then hurry away toward the tower stairs. He had believed her to be in her solar and now, likely, that was where she was going. He wondered what she had said to Chandra and Jerval. He knew he wanted to beat her. Maybe this time he would.

What would her father say to his wife? Chandra wondered, seeing Lord Richard turn to stride after Lady Dorothy. *I hope he locks her in her bedchamber for a week,* she thought, but of course he wouldn't. "I am going riding, Jerval," she said, turning back to face him. "If you wish to come with me, I will show you our beautiful countryside."

"I don't suppose you will challenge me to a race?"

If she hadn't thought of it yet, he could tell by the quick lighting of her eyes that she was thinking it now. Excitement, anticipation, both were there, and he wondered, not for the first time in the two days since he'd first seen her dressed as a bride in this Great Hall, what this damned girl had done to him.

They did race, of course, and Wicket beat out Jerval's destrier, Pith, by the length of his shadow, showing bright and stark against the black rocks that lined the hills above the beach. Oddly, she only crowed for a moment; then she frowned at him, even waved her fist under his nose. She was wearing a tunic and breeches, a belt around her waist and a knife in its sheath fastened to that belt, her boots cross-gartered to her knees. To have to untie cross garters, then to pull down breeches so he could make love to a woman — he'd never before done that, never even considered such a thing. The thought made him hard, something he was growing used to, then made him smile. Her hair was windblown, nearly pulled out of its thick braid. Her lips were chapped by the harsh winds and he said, "Have you cream for your mouth?"

"What?" She touched her fingers to her lips. "Oh, I don't know. Does it matter?"

He wanted to kiss her chapped lips, he wanted to lift her off Wicket's back and lay her on her back, over on that soft bed of green spread beneath those pine trees. He could see himself now pulling those breeches off her, could see how she would lift her hips as he did it, could see himself coming over her. Oh, God. He reached out his hand and lightly touched his fingertips to her mouth. She cocked her head to the side, staring at him. "It matters. Your lips are dry. Have your servant give you cream."

"Surely it isn't that important." She gave him a strange look, her own fingertip now rubbing against her mouth. What did he care about her mouth? Her lips were chapped, just that, nothing more.

"When you are given something perfect, something beautiful, then you should take care to keep it that way."

"You are saying that I must take special care of my mouth because it is perfect and beautiful?" There was absolute astonishment in her voice.

"Yes, see to it."

Then she remembered and said, waving a new fist, "You let me win. I saw you pull Pith back at that last turn."

"I didn't want to knock you off your horse," he said easily. "Had I continued, I would have hit you and —"

"The chances are that I would have sent

you flying into the dirt. I do not like it that you tried to play the chivalrous knight. Don't do it again."

Jerval wasn't stupid. He knew she was serious, and he knew he couldn't let it pass with simple silence, a jest, or a smile of amusement. He had to apply the spurs, but gently, slowly. Beginning now. He said, perfectly serious, "Or what will you do?"

Without hesitation, she said, "I will wrestle with you and bend your arm behind your back until you howl."

Wrestle with her? As in the way men wrestled? He simply shook his head at her as he saw himself pulling her beneath him, flattening her with his body. No, he couldn't imagine a girl wrestling like a man. In bed, surely, but in jest and in pleasure, not the way men wrestled in the practice field, sweating and grunting and trying to maim the opponent. No, surely — he couldn't help himself. He forgot about beginning to apply some limits to her, for he was equally amused and excited, and said with utter seriousness, "I will rub your nose in the mud before you manage to do that."

She laughed and laughed. He watched her kick Wicket in his lean sides, watched her horse leap forward, heard her laughter floating in the soft air back to him.

"I mean it," he called after her, but she didn't hear him. Perhaps, if she pushed him, then that was exactly what he should do.

Before the midday meal, Jerval found himself with Lord Richard, warming himself in front of the fire set in the great fireplace. "She wants to wrestle with me. It is not a jest — she means it. This is impossible."

Richard thought it was rather impossible himself. "If she wants to wrestle, you will have no choice, Jerval. You will simply have to control yourself. Naturally she will try to kill you. She is good. I taught her. When she sends pain crashing through you, your mind will forget your lust."

"She doesn't realize she is a woman."

"No, she does not. That is why you are here. It is time for her to learn."

"You set me a problem, my lord, a very large one."

"Perhaps," Lord Richard said very deliberately, "just perhaps I should have given her to Graelam."

"No, damnation, no! He would have tried to break her — or perhaps not. I don't know what was in his mind. But he did not want her to —"

"To what?"

"I don't know. It no longer matters. I

drove him from Croyland. He lost and he will never have another chance at her." He looked into the fire and stretched out his gloveless hands to warm them. Large hands, Richard thought, competent hands, strong and sure. Graynard tried to shove him aside, but Jerval held firm and the dog collapsed next to him on the brick hearth, his huge head on his paws.

"She craves freedom," Richard said then. "She always has. Even as a child, she wanted the wind tearing at her hair, all the speed her pony could give her, wanted to throw her small spear farther than my squire could throw his own. Ah, I can still remember her laughter, her absolute joy, when she won her first knife-throwing competition. She beat six young men, and I will tell you, their resentment was palpable even though they knew she practiced more than they did, knew that she wasn't like other girls, knew that she wanted victory at least as much as they did. One of them even said something to her about going back into the castle and sewing. She bloodied his nose. Just one blow with her fist, and he was yelling his head off. Of course I had taught her how to use her fists."

Actually, Jerval had no difficulty at all picturing that scene.

"I have never reined her in, never stopped her from doing something she wanted to do. She wanted a suit of armor, and so I had one made for her. The flat rings don't quite overlap, so there is more space between them and thus less weight. In a true battle, she wouldn't have the same protection a knight has. But she is content, and when she jousts, there is at least some protection. Naturally, my men would let themselves be slaughtered before they would ever take the chance of hurting her."

Jerval couldn't begin to imagine a girl wearing armor. His disbelief was so obvious that Lord Richard hurried to add, "She rarely wears the armor, just occasionally on the practice field when there is jousting practice. Some of the men even demand that she wear hers when they wear theirs to keep the games fair. She gives no quarter, you know. I taught her that compassion only comes into play when your sword is pressed against your foe's gullet.

"But attend me, Jerval. There is no mean-ness in her, no pettiness. Perhaps some jeal-ousy of another's better skills, certainly, but what is wrong with that? That just makes her work all the harder. She does not recog-nize her own beauty. Even if she did, it would not count greatly with her. It is what she has to offer, what she can gain by the skill of her own hand, her own wits — that is what she values."

"As I said, you have set me a problem."

"You will decide if the problem is too great for you to deal with."

Lord Richard had struck him hard in the face with that challenge, one, Jerval thought, that he knew he would not hesitate to take on. Dear God, what was he getting himself into?

Lord Richard left the young man, who, in truth, looked like Chandra's brother, and went to search out his wife, who had been hiding from him for two days now. He'd nearly caught her once, but she'd gone to the jakes, not her solar. He found her in her solar this time, sitting tall and proud in her high-backed chair, ready, he supposed, to face him.

He still wanted to beat her. Even after two days, his blood hadn't cooled. His hands clenched into fists at his sides. He ordered her women from the chamber. Six colorful pigeons, giggling, talking about him behind their hands, their eyes full on him. He came to stand in front of her, his fists on his hips, his legs spread. *She looks old,* he thought, *and there is no bigger bitch in all of Christendom.*

"Why did you come out of the hidden chamber?"

Lady Dorothy started to repeat her litany, for it sounded quite reasonable, but she realized he wouldn't believe her, not for an instant. She gave a shrug that she knew enraged him. "You want the truth, do you? Very well. I wanted her gone. Lord Graelam de Moreton actually wanted to take her, something I cannot begin to imagine, but it was true. He wanted to wed her. He wanted to take her away with him. I was overjoyed. I gave him my blessing."

"You are a stupid cow."

"You never said a word about Jerval de Vernon, not even a hint to me of your plans for her. Graelam was a perfectly good match for her, a powerful man, a wealthy one as well. He is much better than she deserves, truth be told. I did what I thought right. She is past old enough, eighteen now. She needs to be married. You need to gain worth from a marriage alliance. What better alliance than with Graelam de Moreton?"

"You considered none of this. You wanted to be rid of her, and you saw your chance. You wouldn't have cared if he'd raped her on the floor of the Great Hall, if he'd captured her and ridden away with her, if he'd been a Welsh bandit on a raid."

"Aye, that is true enough," she said, and she smiled at him. For a moment, he saw the remnants of beauty in her that had given him a very brief period of satisfaction so many years before. Her hair was once black as the hills of Wales just to their west, drenched in darkness. Now it was threaded with coarse gray strands, weaving in and out. There was no gray in his golden hair. There were lines of discontent fanning from her eyes, creasing her face beside her mouth. She was old, he thought again.

"Damn you, you should have known that I had made plans for her. You did know, didn't you? You simply chose to get rid of her as quickly as you could."

She had the gall to shrug again.

"You knew I would do what was best."

"Ah, best for whom, Richard? Perhaps for yourself since you have molded her into your own image, kept her with you year after year, allowing her to do what she pleases, allowing her to show me her contempt for all things that a woman must know and —"

"I know that you abused her," Lord Richard said abruptly, cutting her off, and he took a step away from her, his desire to clout her was so great. He said the words again, "You abused her."

"So," Lady Dorothy said slowly, "the perfidious little bitch went whining to you, did she? Well, it isn't true. I only struck her when she deserved it, as any good mother would do."

"She told me nothing. You, lady, are a liar. You hit her whenever you wished to. Unfortunately, I did not learn of what you had done all those years until old Emily was dying and confessed it to me just this month. I wanted to kill you."

"Why didn't you try?"

"I am not a murderer," he said, "although you tempt me greatly. Why in the name of all the martyrs' graves did you beat a child?"

"Why?" She could but stare at him. "You have the gall to ask me why? By all the saints, she is nothing to me. No, that isn't true. She is a blight, an unnatural whelp who should never have been born. She is nothing but the bastard from your slut in London, your proud lady who gave her to you so her reputation could remain unsullied and her family could arrange a great marriage for her. Aye, you made me take her, pretend she was my daughter. You thought I would love her, want her near me? That little bastard was nothing but a thorn in my side. I have hated her since the day you forced me to hold her in my arms."

So many bitter, venomous words, so much

89

malevolence. He'd known she hadn't liked Chandra — natural enough, he supposed — but this hatred, this viciousness? He said slowly, "Old Emily told me that when Chandra was eleven, she was strong enough to protect herself. She said Chandra nearly strangled you when you hit her that last time, and she saved your worthless life. It is me you should hate, Dorothy, not Chandra. She never did anything to you. She always was, and still is, innocent."

"She existed," Dorothy said, and thought of that child who stared at her, pain in her vivid eyes, bowed over from the blow in the ribs her supposed mother had dealt her. No, she wouldn't think of that small, silent child, her silent tears. "Emily would never betray me. Chandra told you. I know she did."

"I only wish that she had. She never said a word against you. I remember when she began calling you Lady Dorothy, and I did wonder about that, but if that's what she wanted, and it appeared it was what you preferred as well, then why should I question it?"

"She's naught but a bastard. And the name you gave her — Chandra. A ridiculous name — the name of that ancient priestess who ruled in the land of men. Do you think if Jerval de Vernon knew the truth about her birth, he would still be here to look her over for his wife?"

"He will never know," Richard said, and his hands clenched into fists now.

"I won't tell him — you needn't worry about that. I want her gone, the sooner the better. She will make him a miserable wife since she knows nothing of what a woman is meant to be, meant to know, meant to do. She might even stick a knife through his ribs when he tries to bed her." Lady Dorothy laughed. "Ah, then she would be hanged. I should like that."

"You damned bitch." Richard didn't strike her. He kicked her chair, then shoved it, and it fell backward, taking his wife with it. She lay there on her back, her knees bent over the side of the chair, the toes of her leather slippers sticking in the air, looking up at him. She didn't move, just looked at him with that blend of contempt and triumph.

"Damn you, I would like to kill you."

Still she didn't move, just lay there in that overturned chair. She smiled up at him now. "Do you really think she will allow him to bed her? Did you know that Chandra first saw you rutting with one of the serving wenches when she was about five years old? Naked you were, pumping into her, and the girl was laughing and moaning and telling you how grand a stallion you were. Aye, Chandra saw you. I know because I saw you as well. And I saw the expression on the child's face. Aye, and that wasn't the only time. Emily told me that she saw you taking one of the visiting ladies against a wall, with her husband swilling ale in the Great Hall, and she said Chandra vomited, emptied her belly at the sight. How many more times? She became as she is only because she despises what a woman must be, what she must do for a man. She will never accept having a man plow her belly, controlling her, rendering her helpless, as she has seen you to do to so many different women all her life."

"Shut up, you filthy-mouthed bitch! I have never forced a woman, never. If she saw anything, she would realize that it was naught but pleasure, that it was natural, that it was not a man's will overcoming the woman's. Damn you, I will kill you if you don't be quiet. I will."

"Aye, you would like to, but you can't. My father still lives. He is still powerful. You would be dead within a sennight were you to hurt me. Even if he were dead, there is my brother, who hates you more than you can imagine. He is jealous of you, of course. He wouldn't hesitate to kill you, to crush you like a bug. You know this, Richard. You aren't stupid."

No, he wasn't stupid. She'd sickened upon occasion over the years and he'd prayed she would die, but she never did, and she always smiled at him, knowing what was in his mind. She might look like a bitter old woman, with her coarse graying hair, all those deep lines in her face, but she was stronger than his destrier, curse her foul soul.

"You have also taught John to despise his sister."

"Naturally. He is your heir. He is of my body. He will be the lord at Croyland after you're dead. She has no claim to his affection. She is nothing to him."

Richard said then, because he knew at last that he could cut her deep, "I am sending John to foster with the Earl of Grantham. He is leaving within the month." He looked down at his fingernails.

"No!" She scrambled to her feet, nearly falling because her skirts tangled in the fallen chair cushions.

Richard rubbed his hands together. "Aye, the boy is my heir, and if he remains here you will make him into a mean-spirited, puling little coward, craven and spoiled."

She was shrieking at him, curses he was certain Father Tolbert had never heard from her mouth. He smiled at her as he turned on his heel and left the solar. Her women were gathered outside the door on the narrow landing, listening, he knew, and he smiled at each of them. There were six ladies of different sizes, different ages. He had bedded four of them. He wondered if Chandra had seen him with any of them. But what did that matter? He didn't want her to be innocent going to the marriage bed. He was a strong man, well built, and he gave a woman pleasure. Surely he had shown her that lovemaking between a man and a woman was something pleasurable. He didn't believe that she had vomited. His bloody wife would say anything to make him pay. Jerval de Vernon would teach her, would give her endless pleasure — no, Richard didn't want to think about that.

Chapter 6

Chandra smoothed down the figured buckle over her shoulder, as she always did; it always brought her luck. She pulled an arrow from her leather quiver, set it into its notch against the bow, and drew it back until her bunched fingers touched her cheek next to her mouth. She released slowly, so carefully, watched the arrow as it arced smoothly upward, crested, and embedded itself with a thud in the center of the target.

A shout went up from Lord Richard's men, a murmur of surprise from Jerval's.

Mark said to Jerval, his voice full of laughter, "Lord Richard's men must believe they will make their fortunes today. I will lose my own wager if you do not split Chandra's arrow. The pride of Camberley rests on your shoulders, Jerval, as well as my money and the money of your men."

Jerval smiled, flexed his arm, and stepped forward to stand beside Chandra. She was grinning like a fool; he saw it even though she kept her head down. He wished she didn't make him want to laugh with her endless show of bravado, her guileless show of pleasure in her own triumphs.

He said, "You told me that you would crush me into the dirt," he said. "I will admit that wasn't a bad shot. Perhaps it was even a very lucky shot. Not as interesting, perhaps, as seeing you dressed in a man's tunic and a man's wool breeches — that makes quite an impression on a poor man's wits. My men were shocked, naturally, even though they shouldn't have been, since I had warned them not to stare at you, knowing what was beneath those breeches. Thank the saints, now they are even getting used to you." He looked as if he would say more, and she interrupted him, wanting to clout him, wanting to laugh. "Will you keep blathering or will you shoot?"

He was stroking his chin. "Actually, I'm wondering if I should let you win."

"Let me win? You can't beat me, you fool. Soon you will be on your knees eating the dirt beneath your feet. Come, you can't put it off much longer. Swallow your conceit and make your shot."

"I am really very good, Chandra. I told you that."

She chewed this over for a minute, then said slowly, those incredible eyes of hers hard and cold, "You mean you would allow me to win the way you allowed Wicket to beat Pith?"

"I was only protecting you, trying to keep you safe — you, a small weak girl who is so lovely the sun glints in her hair."

She snorted.

"Very well. The distance is far too short for me, but if it pleases you, if it makes you feel superior, then I will declare that you are the winner of this paltry beginner's competition."

"You bleating goat, I am no beginner."

"Then why don't we have a competition that would mean something, that would truly show which of us is the more skilled?"

She called out to Cecil, her twelve-year-old page, "Go to the target. Yes, that's right. Now, Jerval, tell him the distance you wish."

Jerval shouted, "Move it to the base of the hill."

He'd doubled the distance. She had her limits, and he knew it, damn him. Actually, she was anxious to see how well he would do. But now she had to shoot again. She felt a leap of uncertainty, perhaps even a kick of panic.

Jerval saw that she hadn't creamed her mouth and now she was chewing on her bottom lip, and he knew she was wondering what to do. Oh, she would shoot, he had no doubt about that, but she was frightened she wouldn't do well. He said, "I do not wish to see you humiliated. You did very well with your other shot, but this is no longer so easy. Would you like to choose a champion?"

She jumped to the bait like the trout he had caught in Camberley's lake just two weeks before. "I don't need a champion. I told you, I am amazing with the bow and arrow. I have the eye of an eagle." *But I don't have the strength,* she thought. She saw her father from the corner of her eye, standing beside Ellis, watching the match. She swallowed hard, waved toward him and stepped forward, stretching straight and tall with her side to the target, measuring the distance. She released her arrow and stood motionless, watching it soar upward. There was a bit of wind and it carried it further than she deserved, thank the saints.

The arrow missed the center, but who cared? It slammed itself into the dark blue outer rim of the target. "I hit it," she said, so surprised, she said again, "I hit it. Did you see that? I really hit it!" She hadn't meant to say it out loud, but it was too late now. Never would she willingly have given him even a hint that it had been a lucky shot, very lucky and helped forward by a friendly wind.

However, she still wished her father's men didn't sound as astonished as Jerval's. Had they expected her to miss it altogether? Well, truth be told, she had herself expected to miss, have her arrow fall from the sky into the dirt, well short of the straw target.

Jerval heard Crecy say to Lord Richard, "By all the saints' crooked toes, it was a great distance, too great a distance, but she hit it."

Ellis said, "Few of the men could do better."

That was a fact, Jerval thought. He was so pleased with her that he wanted to grab her and swing her into the air. And then he simply couldn't help himself. He did lift her high in his arms and swing her until she was shouting with laughter. Then, very slowly, he let her down again.

No playmate would do that, and she knew it. She stood very quietly.

John, who was on his haunches chewing on a blade of grass near his father, raised his head and said, "I will do it easily someday, Father. Avery has said that I have your eye."

"So does your sister," Lord Richard said.

"Aye, but I will also be as strong as you someday. I will be a man. She won't."

If Chandra heard her brother, she gave no

sign. She was jesting with her father's men now, laughing, looking at Jerval, waiting, wondering what he would do.

Jerval met Mark's eyes, and winked. He drew an arrow from his quiver and set it against the bow. He took his time, aware now that Chandra was utterly silent, tapping her foot just behind him.

He would not ruin her pleasure — he couldn't. His arrow shot straight toward the target, its speed so great, it was a blur. It slammed into the packed straw with a loud thud.

A smile played about Lord Richard's mouth as Ponce ran to the target and dropped to his knees in front of it. When he rose, he cupped his hand to his mouth and shouted, "Sir Jerval's arrow split Lady Chandra's. Thus a part of hers is closest to the center."

"By all the saints' tight-lipped smiles, I can't believe he did that," Richard said. "He is perhaps even a better diplomat than Crecy. His obvious skill blasts her in the face and yet she still wins."

Jerval smiled down at her, seeing the recognition in her eyes that he was the better, but it didn't matter, and he hoped that she realized that. A competition with no one to lose. He said, "I pronounce you the winner, Chandra. Must I drop to my knees and stick my mouth in the dirt? Or perhaps lick your dirty boots?"

He had defeated her, not beaten her cleanly, quickly, utterly. He'd let her keep her triumph.

"What say you?"

She said, so low that only he could hear her, "You showed me you are the more skilled, but you did it so charmingly, so nicely, I want to kill you because I don't think I have your generosity. I also want to swing you up in my arms and yell with laughter. I think you are the most clever man I have ever met, other than my father, of course. That is what I say."

"All that?"

"Yes, all that."

"I am — very pleased to hear those words from you. I should like for you to swing me about."

He stuck out his arms. She laughed, drew a deep breath, wrapped her arms around his waist and tried to lift him off his feet. She managed to pull him to his toes, but no more. And so she simply squeezed her arms as tightly as she could around his waist and hugged him. Jerval closed his eyes with the feel of her. His men were laughing. Any moment now there would be jests, probably very crude ones. He couldn't allow that. It would ruin everything.

He quickly backed away from her. She was smiling, and there was a softness in her eyes that scorched him to his booted feet.

"I knew Sir Jerval would win," John said, his child's voice overloud. "She is only a female. She is weak."

Lord Richard looked for a moment at his son's upturned face. He had his mother's pointed chin and his mother's querulous voice. John was indeed spoiled, but not for much longer. Grantham was a man of moods, many of them black, but most important, he was strong and mean and fair. He would accept no petulance from John.

Lord Richard said to Crecy as he strode back toward the keep, "Jerval controls her well. Did you see her throw her arms around him? I have made the right decision."

"He also pleases her, something I have never seen before. But still, my lord, she doesn't see him as a suitor. She seems him as —" Crecy couldn't find the right word and so Richard said, "Jerval told me she regards him as her playmate. But he wasn't completely the playmate today. Progress, Crecy, progress."

"Aye," Crecy said. "Perhaps you are right, my lord. But still, I am worried."

"If Jerval wants to wed her, then he will

make her understand all of it. Don't fret. He isn't a fool. I just hope he can keep from — no, never mind that."

"Ellis said that if any man could woo her and tame her, it was Jerval."

"My girl doesn't want taming. Now, Ellis is limping badly. I don't believe he will ever again ride into battle."

"Ah, Ellis is gnarly as an old oak tree. He will improve, my lord. He will improve."

Richard was thinking that he would have Crecy write immediately to the king, asking his permission for the alliance between Croyland and Camberley. It would be ready for the messenger to take to London as soon as Jerval made his decision.

The following afternoon, Jerval rode silently beside Chandra away from the tiltyard toward the sea. Her face was streaked with sweat; her thick braid, plaited tightly about her head, was dulled with dirt.

In the tiltyard, her lance held firmly against her side, urging her beast of a destrier at full gallop, she had showed nearly his own skill when he had been her age. He had no particular wish to turn their every encounter into a competition, but it was she who wanted it, forced it on him, and in the most natural way imaginable. If only she'd been a man . . . but she wasn't. *I am still her good friend,* he thought, *her companion, and she looks up to me, admires me, never becomes angry when I best her, never pouts or sulks, merely laughs and smacks me on the arm. What in the name of God am I to do?*

He wanted to talk to her, simply spend time sitting beside her, looking at her, may-hap even holding her hand, but really, just talking, learning what was in her mind, in her heart, not these continuous challenges and competitions, pitting them against each other. Like two brash young men bent upon impressing each other, he thought. Damnation.

He thought of his cousin, Julianna, how all she wanted to do was sit with him and talk and talk. It had made him restless, all those soft words of hers, made him desperate to do something, stride about, run with his father's dogs, anything. But with Julianna, it was always just those sloe-eyed looks of hers and so much talk that he sometimes wanted to stuff one of his mother's beautifully sewn bathing cloths into her lovely mouth. Julianna had learned to tease and flirt by practicing on him. He'd believed her an angel, perhaps a bit tedious, but that wasn't important, and then he'd seen her turn red in the face and shriek like a fishmonger at a hapless serving maid, and strike the girl. Jerval had simply walked up to her, carried her away, still shrieking, under his arm, and dropped her at his mother's feet. He'd never looked at her quite the same again.

He knew Julianna wanted him. He also knew that even if he'd wanted her, his father would never allow it. Marriage wasn't about anything other than property. He smiled, a big pleased smile. Mayhap not always.

"Chandra, pull up."

She reined Wicket in, the huge destrier nickering as he drew close to Pith.

"Am I as filthy as you are, Chandra?"

She looked at his powerful arms, still damp with sweat. His tunic was open, and the light hair on his chest was matted with dirt.

"Probably more because you are so large. There is more area for the filth to cover."

He didn't care if she was black with dirt. He still wanted to caress every inch of her, feel her with his fingers while he closed his eyes.

"You know that Father is holding a banquet tonight in your honor. Two of his vassals, Sir Andrew and Sir Malcolm, will attend." But thankfully not Sir Stephen, Mary's father. Mary believed she should confess to her father, but Chandra knew that would be a horrible mistake. She needed more time to persuade Mary not to tell anyone what had happened, particularly not her selfish and inflexible father. As if what had happened were Mary's fault. Chandra sighed. Were men so rigid, so set in their thinking that they would not be able to see that it wasn't Mary's fault that she was no longer a virgin?

"I trust you will be honoring me more than any other? You will perhaps honor me so very much that you will feed me from your own knife?"

"Yes," she said, grinning at him, "I have plans for my knife."

She laughed as she dug her heels into Wicket's sides. She was gone from him again.

After another ten minutes, Chandra drew in Wicket's reins and carefully guided his descent to the rocky stretch of beach below, cut off from the harbor at Croyland by a thick finger of land. Jerval followed her, looking at the softly lapping waves collapsing gently on the coarse black sand.

It was a bright day, the sun full overhead, no rain clouds in sight. When they reached flat ground, Chandra dismounted, pulled off Wicket's bridle, and shooed him away.

Jerval did the same, and when he turned to face her, he saw that she was eyeing him, a look he didn't begin to understand.

"About the formal banquet this evening," she said, not looking at him. "You and I have jested about it, but truly I have not really thanked you properly for saving me."

"I have never jested about it," he said.

"That is because when you remember, you feel fear again that I could have had my throat sliced open."

"If I could have sat on you to keep you safe, I would have."

Immediately, her mouth was open to defend her own skill, her cunning, her strength. He raised a hand and lightly touched a finger to her lips, still chapped. "Attend me, Chandra. You must allow a man to do what he was born to do, and that is to protect you. If you take that from him, then what good is he?"

She said slowly, looking out over the sea, "I hadn't thought of it like that. But there are so many ladies who still need protecting. They litter England. What matter does it make if only one of them doesn't need your protection? If I don't?"

He said patiently, touching his fingertips now to her arm, watching her slowly turn back to him, "A man is what he is. You could be larger than I, more vicious than King John before his barons finally defeated him, more stout of heart than King Richard, but it simply wouldn't matter. I must protect you or die trying. If I don't, then I am not worth much of anything."

"You speak like the ideal of knighthood, Jerval. I know that men can perhaps protect women, but they seem to forget all about it when one is available to be raped. Where is all your vaunted protection then?"

"Rape? What are you talking about? Graelam didn't touch you, did he?"

"No, he didn't." She'd almost said too much. Even now he was looking at her, and he was puzzled, wondering why she'd said that. Quickly, she thought, quickly, she had to distract him. "But you cannot deny that men will take what they can and it doesn't matter if it is a male or a female at their mercy. If you are different — well, I don't really know that, do I?"

She'd finally done it, just shoved him right over the edge. Anger flamed deep and hot. "Damn you, Chandra, you believe that I would harm someone weaker than I? You don't know me well enough, you said. Then why would I take my time to save your white hide? And, having saved your hide, why then didn't I simply throw you on the ground and ravish you?"

"I would have killed you and you knew it."

He wanted to clout her. Instead, he grabbed her, hurled her over his shoulder and walked to the water.

Since he wasn't stupid, he had an excellent grip on the back of her legs. She reared up, yelling curses at him, hitting him, but she couldn't hurt him overly, not if she couldn't kick him. He kept walking. The water lapped over his boots. They would be ruined. Well, no matter. He kept plowing forward into deeper and deeper water.

"What are you doing? Are you mad, you idiot? Put me down!"

He said nothing, just kept pushing his way through the water until finally it was at his waist and then he stopped. "You are arrogant. Beyond that, you are ignorant. You think only of yourself and your own value. If you have any wits at all, you have buried them under layers of your own wonderful opinion of yourself."

She fought him, nearly broke some of his body parts, but he managed to hurl her another six feet forward into deeper water.

She slammed into the water — and sank like a stone.

He strode back to the beach, then turned to see her swimming gracefully, powerfully, back to shore.

Well, damn. He'd hoped she would have a bit of trouble, perhaps need him to rescue her, but no luck. She was wearing trousers, not a gown.

When she pulled herself out of the water, she walked up to him and drew back her fist, her intent to break his jaw.

He laughed with the joy of it. He grabbed her arm, pulled her off balance toward him, then flipped her over his shoulder. She landed on her back in the sand some feet beyond him.

Instead of rage, or curses, she lay there a moment, getting her breath back, and then she grinned up at him. "That was very well done," she said. "I can wrestle and do all sorts of vicious holds, but not that throw. Could you show me how to do that?"

He said after he managed to recover, "You defy any logic that I have ever known." He gave her a hand up, then spent the next hour showing her how to gain enough leverage, to use his own momentum against him to send him over her shoulder.

She learned very quickly.

Chapter 7

When he was sitting in a large steel-banded bathing tub late that afternoon, Jerval realized that she had never thanked him for saving both her and Croyland. They'd immediately gone after each other's throats. Well, he'd simply tried to explain a man's honor to her, but he hadn't succeeded. Ah, well, doubtless Lord Richard would have her say all that was proper to him this evening. He wondered if she would do it well, if she would be gracious and mean it. He sighed and slid down until the water covered his head. Life, he thought as the water enfolded him in its calm silence, had strange byways. He wondered what he would be thinking now if she *had* turned out to be a little princess, with soft hands and softer words.

When his head cleared the water, it was to see her standing by the tub, staring down at him. She was still dirty, her hair in tangles about her face. He wanted to kiss her until she was wild for him.

"Did you come to scrub my back?"

"No."

"Do you want me to scrub yours? It would take a very long time."

"No. I realized that I hadn't thanked you."

Now this was something, he thought, and kept quiet. He was hard, but the water covered him, thank God.

She smiled down at him and lightly touched her hand to his wet shoulder. "Allow me to thank you on my own. Later — well, that will be formal and not between us."

"All there is between us now is this tub of dirty water."

She just shook her head at him.

"Have you rehearsed something for me?"

"Be quiet. Listen to me now. This is important. It comes from the deepest part of me, so to me, it is vastly important. If you had not come to Croyland when you did, if you hadn't managed to come up with such an excellent plan, if you hadn't been strong and brave, your men as well, then I would have been wedded to Graelam."

She actually shuddered as she spoke the words. He had the sudden thought that perhaps she would give an equally distasteful shudder if she'd been forced to marry him.

From the deepest part of her? He was brave and strong? "You're welcome," he said finally. "I am glad that I was close by, very glad that one of my men found out what had happened. If I had come too late, well then, so much would have been lost. I might not even ever have met you."

"Yes," she said, and smiled at him, a lovely white-toothed smiled, filled with relief. "Actually, you wouldn't have met me at all because Graelam would have murdered me by now — that, or I would have managed to slip a knife between his ribs."

Or perhaps Graelam would have taught her to bend to him, to admire him, to . . . "I would offer you my bathwater, but it is nearly as black as you are."

He watched her pick up her long braid and give it a yank. "Always dirty," she said. "Father won't let me cut it. It would be so much easier. Look at you. You simply stick your head in a bucket of water, rub in a bit of soap, and it's all done."

"You have beautiful hair. I wouldn't let you cut it off either."

"How would you like to have to sit still whilst someone had to brush your hair for an hour to get it dry?"

"I shouldn't like it at all, and that's the truth. However, when I look at you — your face, your hair, all of you — it gives me, a simple man, great pleasure. It would please me if you would continue to sit quietly for that hour to dry your hair."

"Now, what does all that mean?"

He laughed. "Nonsense, all of it is nonsense. Your hair pleases me, that's all. Now, would you like to dry me?"

She cupped her hand in his bathwater and spurted him in the face.

The Great Hall was bright with the light from countless mutton-fat rush torches, the air thick with laughter and conversation. Sir Andrew, Sir Malcolm, and their men lounged about the long tables, waiting for the servants to serve up the thick slabs of roasted beef and casks of wine.

Jerval sat to Lord Richard's left, impatient that Chandra had not yet come into the hall. He knew that he was being studied, his worth to Croyland weighed and discussed. Lady Dorothy sat at the far end of the dais. There was no expression at all on her face but the ravages of time, of perhaps a bitterness felt so long that it was etched into the shadows in her eyes. He didn't know. But whatever had made her what she was at this moment, sat deep and heavy on her face. Why did she so dislike her daughter? He raised his goblet, and a serving wench hastened to fill it.

"You threw my daughter in the water, then threw her yet again over your shoulder. I saw that move only once before, done by an Italian boy."

How did the man know that? Did he have spies everywhere?

"I watched the two of you," Lord Richard said. "I assume she pushed you over your limit and tossing her into the water was her punishment?"

"Not punishment enough."

"That throw — she learned it well, very quickly, didn't she?"

"Yes. I was surprised that she didn't know how to do it. I learned it from a Scots raider many years ago."

"Ah. Well, she knows now since you taught her." He paused a moment, his long fingers curling about his goblet. He didn't look at Jerval as he said, "She still looks at you as an oversized friend."

"Yes."

"But she trusts you now. She has never given her trust or her friendship lightly."

Lord Richard looked up then and paid him no more attention. Jerval frowned at his host, wondering, until he followed his line of vision to see that Chandra had come into the Great Hall. A father shouldn't look at his daughter that way, he thought, then wondered at himself. Lord Richard was proud of her. And why not? She was the most beautiful creature he himself had ever seen. Why wouldn't her own father think so as well? But something about it wasn't quite right. Something was just a bit wrong with everything here at Croyland.

There was no woman to compare to her. Her hair was shining, it was so clean, and it hung nearly to her waist, kept off her forehead with a narrow golden band. She was gowned in a pale pink gown that barely showed her slippers. She wore a filigree belt around her waist. To see her now, gowned as she was, made it difficult to believe that so short a time before, she'd been a filthy urchin. Actually, it was closer to amazing.

"There is no woman to compare with her, save, perhaps, her mother." The instant those words were out of Lord Richard's mouth, he looked furious. Why?

"I see no resemblance at all between her and her mother," Jerval said. "But perhaps when Lady Dorothy was younger —"

"Aye, perhaps."

She walked directly to Jerval, gave him a full curtsy, deep and graceful, and let Ponce seat her beside him.

"It took nearly *two* hours to dry my hair," she said, the first words out of her mouth.

"Did you think of my pleasure whilst you did it?"

"No, I was thinking about Wicket's hock. It is a bit swelled. Later I would like you to look at it, tell me what you think."

"I will be pleased to," he said. He heard Lord Richard choke over his wine at her words.

"Tell me about your years with the Earl of Chester," she said, chewing on a warm piece of bread. "My father tells me he is a madman on the battlefield."

"Yes, I have seen him fight." He had also seen his bloodlust turn to sexual lust after a battle if there was an available woman. Willing or not, it didn't matter to him. Chandra was right, at least about Chester. A battle brought out the worst and the best in a man. He cleared his throat and said, "But he didn't stint on praise when it was deserved. If he had seen you throw me that last time, he would have told you it was well done."

"I have also heard that Chester has four daughters and eight sons."

She looked so soft, so lovely, that it was difficult to concentrate on her words. Here she was finally doing what he wanted, just simply speaking to him, but what he wanted to do was very carefully take her out of that lovely gown and touch every single inch of her. He wanted to bury his face in all that magnificent hair of hers. Suffocate himself perhaps.

"Is that not so?"

"What? Oh, yes, there were four girls. Do you know that all his children still live? It is amazing. All but one have been wedded." He paused just a moment, then smiled at some faraway memory. "Eileen was the youngest," he said, his voice soft, "and she followed me about like a small chicken." No, that didn't sound particularly flattering to him.

"Was she was infatuated with you?"

"Oh, yes. Chester had already arranged her marriage to the Earl of Maninthorpe when she was born, but the fellow married someone else. The first wife died some months ago, so Eileen goes to him this year, I believe. She's an old woman now — near your age, I believe."

"Not old enough then," Chandra said. She gave him a hard look that he didn't quite understand until she said, her voice low, "Did you break her heart?"

He saw the banked jealousy in her eyes and wanted to shout with it. He said, toying with a piece of bread, "Perhaps."

She ate a piece of beef off the tip of her knife and chewed it viciously.

"Did she beg her father to let her marry you instead of this other man?"

"Very likely."

Actually, he had no idea. He was aware of Chandra's every movement from the corner of his eye. He saw also that Lord Richard was holding himself perfectly silent as well, listening.

"Men should not do that," she said finally. "She was an innocent. You should not have made her love you."

"Ah. Is that what you think I did? Chandra, I was her father's squire. You know what that means. I was on the practice fields until I was so sore and battered, I could scarce walk. Then I had to serve Chester, remove his armor, polish it, bring him wine in the middle of the night. I even had to rub his damned feet once when his wife refused to."

She blinked, then laughed, a full laugh that had everyone slowly turning to look at her, and still she laughed, holding her sides now, and soon everyone was laughing.

He leaned over and slapped her back just at the instant she began to choke.

Finally, her tears of laughter dried, she

said, "You did not then lead her on, tell her that her eyebrows moved you profoundly, sent you to the priest to confess your man's lust?"

"Not all that often."

"Men are rotten. You included."

"And women are always angelic and virtuous? You are a woman. So think carefully before you reply to that."

She didn't reply at all, just presented him her knife, a slice of very tender beef speared on the tip.

"Just so," he said and ate the meat.

The evening was far advanced when Richard motioned to Cecil to bring Chandra her lyre. "Whilst I was sitting there having my hair dried, I practiced," she said. "For you."

She moved to sit on a small, round stool, the huge fireplace at her back. She set the wooden instrument lightly on her lap and gently touched the strings, testing their pitch. She tried several chords, and their haunting echoes filled the hall.

Jerval sat back, the rich sweet wine lulling his senses, his eyes on her hair falling over her shoulder as she leaned over the instrument.

Chandra lightly flicked the high strings again, then turned to face the company.

"This is an old Breton legend," she said, her voice clear. "Behold the faithfulness of the lady as she laments her dead lover." She began to sing, her voice sweet and dark as a moonless night.

Hath any loved you well down there,
Summer or winter through?
Down there have you found any fair
Laid in the grave with you.

He was pleased. He found himself sitting forward. The firelight cast a halo about her.

Is death's long kiss a richer kiss
Than mine was wont to be
Or have you gone to some far bliss
And quite forgotten me?

He wanted her more than he'd ever wanted anything in his life, even more than he'd wanted to win his spurs, and that had burned very deeply inside him.

Hold me no longer for a word
I used to say or sing;
Ah, long ago you must have heard
So many a sweeter thing.
For rich earth must have reached your heart
And turned the faith to flowers;

And warm wind stolen, part by part,
Your soul through faithless hours.

Jerval watched her eyes clear, watched the small smile on her mouth. She rose, bowed slightly at the waist, and handed the lyre again to Cecil. Jerval remained still in his chair, not heeding the loud clapping and cheering from the company.

His eyes met Lord Richard's.

"She was taught by our minstrel, Elbert. She sings more sweetly than he did, poor fellow. Ah, were you surprised, then, that she sang a song of love?"

"Yes," Jerval said. "But, withal, she is a woman."

"Aye, she is."

Chandra was beside him then, and she said without guile, perhaps even a bit shyly, bringing him firmly back from the dream she herself had created, "Did you like my song?"

"Perhaps," he said. "A bit more practice, while your hair is being dried, and in ten years or so you will be acceptable outside your own hall."

She laughed, punched his arm, and sat down beside him. "I like the words, the way they sound to the ear, the way they feel deep inside me."

"Yes, I did too," he said, and he knew now why Chandra had played. Her father had insisted that she do so. Her father had wanted him to see the passion in her.

When all of the rush lights had been extinguished, only a spread of candles left to light the way, Jerval said good night to Chandra, lightly touching his fingertips to her cheek, nothing more. He remained in the Great Hall with Lord Richard. He said without preamble, "I believe our two houses must be joined."

Richard nodded. It was difficult to smile at the beautiful young man standing before him, but he finally managed it.

Chapter 8

Sir Mark nearly walked into Mary, grabbed her arms to keep her upright, then bade her a good morning. She stumbled back several steps from him, her face paling, her white hand fisting against her chest. Then she simply turned and slithered back into the chamber she'd just left.

"Good morning," Chandra called out to him, wondering why he was just standing there, staring at the closed door, his fingers stroking his chin.

"Good morning," Mark said, adding, surprise in his voice, "She is such a timid girl. I said nothing to alarm her, but she was alarmed nonetheless."

"Who is a timid girl?"

"Mary."

"She has a right to be," Chandra said.

Mark fell into step beside her. "Why? What happened?"

She paused a moment, anger at Graelam nearly bursting the words out. Oh, God, she had to keep her mouth shut. No one could ever know. She said, "You're right. She is shy, very shy. I know she meant no offense."

Mark didn't believe that for an instant, but he was too kind to pry.

She pulled away then because she saw Jerval in the inner bailey, speaking with her father. They were probably speaking of the Welsh bandits, their last round of bloody raids, the number of men they'd managed to kill, the cattle they'd stolen — just like the Scottish raiders, she thought, who plagued Camberley to the north.

Yes, they were speaking of strategy. They were speaking of how best to attack the bandits, whether or not it would be worth their while to take prisoners for ransom.

Jerval said, "I will teach her what it means to be a woman."

Richard said, "Since I have taught her the ways of men, I suppose it is right that her husband teach her the ways of a woman."

Although the words came out smoothly enough, it was an effort for Richard to actually say them. Jerval teach her to be a woman? This damned man who was far too young, far too inexperienced to know anything about how to treat a woman? Ah, but that was the point. He was young, strong, bursting with life and health. The thought of him with Chandra, knowing her in ways

Richard never could, rubbed and grated, even tore at him, deep down, but he knew there was no other way. She was his daughter, of his flesh, and there was no changing that.

He remembered clearly the day some five years ago when Chandra had run to him, her face white, sobbing low behind her fist. It had taken him a while to finally get her to admit to him that she was bleeding. She believed she was dying. She hadn't done anything. Please, Father, she hadn't. She swore it on Father Tolbert's Bible. And now she was bleeding to death and it wasn't fair. She had always come to him, never to Dorothy, and now, he understood why Chandra hadn't gone to her. He remembered he had tried, carefully, and with some tact, since he loved her and didn't want to frighten her, to explain what the bleeding meant.

She hadn't liked what he'd told her. Actually, he couldn't say that he would particularly like it for himself either. And when her breasts began to grow, she had bound herself tightly, ashamed of them because the boys didn't have them, and hunched her shoulders forward to hide them. It was Egbert, the minstrel, who had achieved the impossible. He had convinced Chandra when she was fifteen finally to wear gowns.

Her hunched shoulders suddenly straightened, and to Richard's profound relief, she seemed to come to enjoy dressing up for their guests and having her incredible hair brushed to her waist until it gleamed in the candlelight. Now she made the transition from boy to lady gracefully.

He knew that he had kept her with him overlong, knew he had, by his own hand, formed her brilliantly. He sighed. He had to admit that he had misformed her as well. She still did not understand compromise, but she was young. Learning to compromise would come. Married to Jerval, she would have to learn to bend. And if she didn't? No, he wouldn't consider that. Compromise was nothing compared to the qualities she held in the deepest part of her. Thank God that Jerval de Vernon appeared to both understand and accept her the way she was. Even though he was too young to know much of anything.

Richard said now, "Avery tells me that a ship from France has just put in to the harbor. Why don't you join me and see the wares the captain has to offer? Perhaps you will find something your bride will like."

Chandra was sitting cross-legged on a grassy patch above the promontory looking out over the sea, chewing on a blade of grass. It was early afternoon. The sun, finally, was bright overhead, and warmed the earth on which she sat. She felt the sun warm her all the way to her bones and was content. It was the sort of day that didn't demand that she do much of anything. She turned her head at Wicket's whinny and saw Jerval atop Pith, riding at a gallop toward her up the rocky slope. She felt a rush of pleasure to see him. He and her father had left so quickly, she hadn't even had a chance to bid him a good morning.

But now he was here. She'd realized almost at once that with her, he wasn't coarse in the manner of her father's men. He never boasted on the exercise field, except of course with her, and that was merely good-natured jesting. He would yell in a man's face when he failed at a task through inattention, but he was fair. Aye, he was always fair, both in his praise to his men and in his punishments.

There was much joke-telling and laughter among the men when he was about. She smiled toward him, admiring the fall of his simple white woolen tunic and the strength of his hands on his destrier's reins. His golden hair, thick and curling at his neck made her think again, a lurch of pain passing through her, that he should have been her father's son. Fate hadn't dealt kindly with Lord Richard. Jerval wasn't her brother — nothing could change that — but he was a man she admired, a man she very much liked. It wasn't his fault that he looked like Lord Richard.

Jerval dismounted and walked to her, tall, strong, the sun shining down on his gleaming hair. When he saw her looking up at him, he smiled.

By all the saints, he thought, staring at her, she was a glorious creature. Soon she would belong to him, every thought in her head, every white inch of her body, every word out of her mouth. *His.* She would belong to him, to no other man ever. He looked away from her because he wanted to leap on her, and he knew, knew all the way to the soles of his feet, that it was too soon, that with all her skills, all her talents, she was appallingly ignorant in the ways of men and women. It didn't make particular sense, but it was nonetheless true. He said, "Mark told me you rode up here."

Chandra patted the grassy ground next to her, and to her surprise, for just an instant, he hesitated before he dropped to sit beside her.

She remembered that Mark had seen

Mary's fear and wondered at it. She must speak to Mary, warn her, urge her not to flinch away whenever a man came near her. "I was just thinking about you," she said. "How much longer will you stay at Croyland?"

When would he face it? Jerval wondered. When would he tell her what he wanted of her? Soon, he knew, when he felt the time was right. He said easily enough, "My father set no limit. Why? Do you wish me to leave?"

"Sometimes."

"I don't like the sound of that."

"No, it's not what you're thinking." She shrugged, as if it weren't all that important, but he knew that it was.

"Tell me," he said. "Tell me what I'm not thinking."

"I really don't want to, but you will keep at me, won't you?"

"Aye."

"All right. It's just that you are a man, but you are also much more than that. I find you amazing. You can do everything and you do it well. You are fair. You always know what to say, what to do. Even if one of your men doesn't perform at something all that well, you do not stint with your praise on what he did do right, or on your encouragement —

and you manage to remain honest. Well, usually."

He couldn't believe she thought that highly of him. He was amazing? Fair? He always knew what to say, to do? Surely she must love him to see him through such blind eyes. She shrugged again, but he was content to wait. She said, "I do things well, but never will I be like you. I do try to treat people well, but I'll tell you — if there is a single way to offend, I will find it, very quickly. You do not."

He was staring at her, couldn't help himself. He was still stunned at her words, words spoken passionately. "Do you truly see me like that?" His heart was now beating slow and hard.

"Aye. You are so like my father."

Well, damn. Finally, he said, "I'm glad you see me in such a good way."

She shrugged. "You are you. There is no other way to see you. You are good. It's true, sometimes I wish I could be you."

"Believe me, I am very glad you are not a man, that you are nothing like me. You are, to be honest here, perfect just as you are right this very moment."

"You say that only because I have praised you, but nonetheless, I will accept that I am perfect, at least right now."

He wanted to bite her lower lip, then lick it. By all the saints' sweaty palms, it was nearly too much. "I brought you something from the captain's ship."

He handed her a small cloth-wrapped package.

Slowly she pulled the soft protecting wool apart, her fingers trembling just a bit. "I love presents," she said when she saw him grinning at her. "I have always thought that to be by yourself in a small room, surrounded by piles of presents — nothing could be better than that."

"How about also having the person with you who gave you all the presents so he could see your face as you opened them?"

"Oh yes, that would be quite fine. But such things don't ever happen. If I can have only part of my fantasy, then I will take the presents."

"I would as well. I hope you like it. I saw you in my mind's eye when the captain held it out for me to look at."

It was a gold necklace, three intertwined gold chains, beautifully formed, weaving in and out of each other. There were three black pearls set deep in the gold, dark, mysterious, incredibly beautiful. It felt wonderful to spill the gold over her hands, feeling the warmth of the pearls against her flesh.

Still she didn't say anything.

"Do you like it?"

She looked at him then. "It is beautiful. I have nothing like it. I have never seen anything so lovely as this." And to his astonished pleasure, she leaned into him and threw her arms around him, squeezing his neck until he wondered if he'd choke.

She kissed his cheek, her breath warm and sweet, and he could taste her excitement and her pleasure. If he hadn't already been sitting, it would have dropped him to his knees. Then she was laughing and pulled her braid off her neck. "Put it on me, please. Oh, it is so lovely. Thank you, Jerval."

And he fastened the lovely necklace around her neck, then let her turn to face him. She was waiting to hear what he would say, and for a moment, he simply couldn't find the right words, couldn't find any words really. He just wanted to kiss her mouth — no longer chapped, he saw — kiss every bit of her and know all the way to his soul that she was his. He cleared his throat. "I chose well. With a gown, you will look like a mysterious princess, hiding her thoughts, keeping secrets close. Though to be honest, I think you would look beautiful wearing nothing at all. Show me again how much you like it. Kiss me, Chandra."

She was still laughing, so pleased with him, with the necklace, with the feel of it around her neck, the weight against her chest, that she kissed him once, twice, even yet again, this time very close to his mouth.

Then she jumped to her feet. "Oh, my, I must show my father. He will believe you more thoughtful than Father Tolbert, who always takes great care to praise father's generosity and care of all his lands and people in his sermons."

Generous? Care of all his people? Lord Richard? Now that was a thought. Jerval had seen one of the maids slipping out of Lord Richard's bedchamber early that morning when he had risen to relieve himself. She had looked tousled, and when she saw him, she'd grinned widely before lowering her eyes and hastily smoothing her gown. In matters of sexual appetite, he thought, Lord Richard was very generous indeed, very caring, endlessly so. To be fair, though, Lord Richard was a fine liege lord, his lands well tended, his people well protected.

"No, I have changed my mind. I will show the necklace later to my father. Now I will reward your kindness. It is so warm, I will take you swimming. Come, Jerval. There's a small lake in the middle of the forest. You will like it."

He felt a leap of pleasure, but it was swiftly gone. "Wait! Swim? As in get wet? But what will you wear to swim?"

"A shift, of course. Why?"

A linen piece of cloth that might come to the middle of her thighs, a piece of cloth that would, once wet, leave nothing left unseen. Oh, God. That damned rock lying beside his right hand wasn't as hard as he was now. "And what about me?"

"I have seen naked men, Jerval," she said patiently, "from the time I was five years old and finally realized there was a difference. You can strip to your skin if you wish."

He knew of course that he couldn't — he simply couldn't. He would scare her witless. He wouldn't be able to control himself — he just knew it. It would be too painful. He said, shaking his head, "No, I don't wish to swim today. I wish to sit right here, with the nice wind off the sea blowing around us, and speak of the future."

"Very well, if that is what you wish. What future?" She sat down again, still fingering her necklace, caressing the smooth pearls, and he wished her fingers were on him, stroking him.

Now was the time. No reason to put it off. She'd kissed him. She believed him honest and kind. She believed him as fine as her father. Damn. No matter. Forget her father. Surely there was no finer opportunity than right now. He picked up her hand. Calluses, he saw, lightly touching his fingertips over her palm. Dirty nails, but not all that bad. Slowly, he raised his eyes to her face.

He felt the words rumble deep inside him, so many words, spilling over each other. He said finally, "I want you to come back to Camberley with me."

She merely smiled at him. "Now that I know you as my friend, why naturally I should like to visit Camberley. Perhaps we could go Scots-hunting."

She was as obtuse as one of the black Welsh boulders strewn across the landscape, though he might be insulting the boulders.

"I don't want you simply to visit," he said patiently. "I want much more."

At last, he thought, she was coming to understand what he was talking about. Her head was cocked to one side and she was looking him straight in the eye.

Spit it out. Just spit it out the way your father spits bones into the rushes. "I want you to be my wife, Chandra. I want you to come to Camberley with me, to live with me, to love me, to have my children, to smile at me until I am finally forced to leave you, hopefully so far

136

into the future that neither of us can grasp it."

Naturally she hadn't heard or understood his wit, perhaps just that bit of it right there at the end. It was wit, he knew it was, and he was nearly smiling at himself. But no, she was still looking straight at him, but now her mouth was hanging open, her eyes suddenly unseeing, all of her frozen, and he knew, quite simply, that she didn't want to believe this, that she wanted nothing to change between them.

She wanted him as her playmate. By all the saints' toenails, it was enough to make a man curl up on the ground and groan with frustration.

"Chandra?"

Very slowly, she pulled away from him and stood. She was still fingering the necklace. "No," she said finally, and turned away.

Instant rage turned his blood hot, made him see red. "Just no? That is all you can say to me? Just a niggardly no?"

"That's right. No." She had the gall to walk away from him, her stride long, looking like a damned boy.

"Chandra, wait! By all the saints' prayers, you did not understand me. I want you for my wife. I am asking you to wed me."

"I understand you well enough, Jerval." She stopped and turned back to him, her hands splayed in front of her to keep him away from her. "What I don't understand is why you would do this to me. I believed that you liked me, that perhaps you even believed me somewhat skilled, that you enjoyed being with me. But this? What is in your mind? Are you perhaps ill?" Her eyes lit up with that, and she nodded as she added, "Yes, that is why that rash of nonsense came leaping out of your mouth. You are ill and perhaps even fevered, and that is why you didn't want to swim with me. You know you are sick and you could perhaps die if you got wet."

He just stared at her, absolutely amazed. Could she actually be serious? "I swear to you I am not ill or fevered. I am in my right mind. It is time for us to be more to each other than simple friends. Marry me. Be my wife. Belong to me."

She said nothing at all to that; she just ran to Wicket, climbed onto his broad back, and was off and away. He rose slowly, staring after her, his hands on his hips.

His first marriage proposal hadn't gone especially well. Then he realized that he'd forgotten to say anything of love to her. Would it have mattered? Did she even have a single idea what love was between a man and a woman?

Chapter 9

Richard was speaking with Crecy when Chandra burst into the Great Hall and ran to where he was standing beside the huge fireplace. She was panting and she was pale, very pale, almost as pale as that time when she was thirteen and had been felled by that strange sweating fever that had attacked the village. He'd never left her side.

Then he knew, of course. He waited.

Chandra said, "Crecy, forgive me, but I must speak to my father now. It cannot wait."

Maybe he was wrong. Perhaps her mother had been tearing at her again, telling her how unnatural she was. No, it wasn't that. Anything Dorothy said now, Chandra merely flicked away without a thought. He said, "We will finish this later, Crecy." He waited a moment, until Crecy was out of hearing, then nodded to her.

"Father, he has changed. He must leave. There is nothing more for him here."

Her face was no longer pale; it was flushed

red now. She looked as if she'd run from the Croyland harbor back to the keep. Her hair was flying about her head, and she was still panting hard.

"Who has changed?" But he knew, knew that Jerval had spoken to her of being his wife, and this was the result. No surprise, really, but he had prayed, prayed until he'd been out of words. He sat down heavily in his big chair and tapped his fingertips on the beautifully carved wooden arms.

"Jerval, of course." She came down onto her knees beside his chair and grabbed his sleeve. "We were having such a very nice discussion of things. Look at the necklace he bought me. Everything was as it should be, as I would want it to be, and then he did that. He wants to wed me." She actually shuddered. "He said he wanted me to belong to him. Can you imagine such a thing?"

Richard gently pulled away her fingers, praying for some kind of inspiration. He knew it was coming. Why hadn't he practiced what he would say to her? He had to say something, and so he did. It wasn't much, but it was a start. "I thought you liked Jerval de Vernon."

"Of course I like him. He does everything so well and he teaches me and laughs at me, but I don't care. The men like him. He has

140

humor in him that makes everyone smile. He is strong and he is kind. He is very good."

"You have painted the image of an estimable man."

"Well, aye, I suppose that I have. But listen to me, Father. I didn't wish to hear what he had to say to me. Don't you understand? He wants me to live with him, to bear his children. He wants me to leave you and go away to this place Camberley. Father, you know that I cannot leave you, that nothing like that was ever to happen to me. That is why you didn't let Graelam have me. You wanted to keep me here, with you. I belong here. That is what you must tell Jerval. Then you can tell him he can either change back to what he was before an hour ago, or he must leave. There is no middle ground here."

Spit it out, nothing else to do, and so Richard said, "Jerval de Vernon is here because I asked him to come."

She cocked her head to the side, exactly as he did it, and said slowly, "Why would you do that?"

"Listen to me, daughter. You are a beautiful woman, the pride of my body. I have held you overlong with me, and that's the truth of the matter. If Graelam had taken you, it would have been my own fault. I should have let Jerval wed you at least a year ago."

She sat back, wrapping her arms around her bent knees. She was aware of voices in the Great Hall — there were always noise and voices and animals running about, fighting, yapping. But the voices were distant; they didn't touch her. She said even more slowly now, clearly disbelieving still, "You want me to wed Jerval? You knew? That is why he is here?"

"Aye, certainly. I wanted to give you both the chance to judge if you could like each other. You do. He spoke because he was finally ready to speak, because he knew that you were ready as well. Evidently he was wrong, but no matter. What's done is done."

"No," she said, shaking her head. "No."

He reached out his hand and lightly began to stroke her dirty braid. "Chandra, Croyland cannot be your home forever. Surely you must realize that. Don't you understand? Graelam wanted you, as have others. I even turned away Earl Malthorpe, a cousin of King Henry." He could see that she wasn't impressed. He remembered that he had agonized over that, but after having met the man, he knew that his proud daughter would slit Malthorpe's throat because he, unlike Jerval de Vernon, wasn't kind or nice

142

or anything good at all. Just rich. Just related to the damn king of England.

"I met Jerval four years ago and I knew he was the man for you, no other, just him. And now everything has come together as I wished it to. You will marry him, and our two houses will be united. It is a good alliance, Chandra." Not splendid, like the one with Earl Malthorpe, but good enough.

"You cannot mean it," she said slowly, her eyes never leaving his face. "You cannot mean to send me away."

It smote him, the rawness in her voice, that look of pain in her eyes, but he had to hold firm. "I wish it. Jerval's father, Lord Hugh, also wishes it. Jerval has decided he will have you. You like him, you have admitted it. You will continue to deal well with him. He will not try to change you, Chandra. He admires you. Why should he try?"

"He is a man, Father. Whatever else he is, he will want to rut me. He will own me. He will force me to be his broodmare. It is something I won't do. It is something I cannot do."

His voice was harsher than he'd intended. "You are a woman, Chandra. You will do what you must do, and that is bear an heir for your husband."

"How can you give him control over what I am to do and how I am to act?"

He eyed her, seeing her urgency, her fear. By the saints, he hadn't realized she was so very afraid of mating. He would speak to Jerval, caution him, tell him to go easy. He said, "Listen to me. There are few choices for any of us. Do you believe I wed your mother because I loved her? I wed her because it brought me a huge dowry, brought me even more land. That is what marriage is all about, alliances between great families. There was no choice at all for me. But I have given you to a man you like, to a man who admires you and likes you. You are a very lucky woman. At least Jerval de Vernon is besotted with you, and if you aren't utterly without sense, if you don't push him to the wall, he will treat you just as you wish."

"But a woman must obey her husband — it is her vow before God. You wish me to forget who I am and become a soft, devious creature and manipulate my husband to get what I want? When I want something, Father, I want to get it for myself, not plead and act weak and helpless to make a man do what I want. Do you hear me? I won't become his chattel, I —"

He jerked her against him, cutting off her

furious words, and buried his face in her dirty hair. He felt her holding herself stiff and unyielding, and he stroked her until she eased and nuzzled her cheek against his neck. He remembered the pain he had suffered the year before when he had been gored by a rampaging boar. Chandra had been distraught with fear for him, and had nursed him herself, ministering to his every need as if he had been her beloved child. He felt the pain again, gnawing at him, but there simply was no choice. He said, "I have taught you to be strong, Chandra. You will do what you must, just as I have done. Do you not wish to have children, be mistress of a great holding, set your own mark upon the world, see your children grow into strong men who will carry your blood into the years ahead?"

He felt her shaking her head against his shoulder, and he continued, more quickly. "You cannot remain at Croyland. You weren't fated to spend your life as a woman who does not know womanhood, a woman who does not experience all that a woman is meant to be. Perhaps I should not have encouraged you to ignore what God intends. You must trust me, Chandra, trust me that I do what is best for you."

"I want nothing more than to remain at

Croyland," she whispered, raising her face from his neck. "My life is here, not far away with a stranger, a man whom I must obey, a man I do not even know."

"You know Jerval. I have given you ample time with him. You know him much better than most girls know their future husbands. I have watched you with him, watched you smile and laugh, watched you enjoy his company. Look at the beautiful necklace he bought for you."

She just shook her head against his neck.

So stubborn she was, so utterly unbending. There was so much of him in her that it was frightening.

It was time now for obedience, time to show her that he really meant his words. "It is what you will do. You will wed Jerval de Vernon. Your loyalty to me will become his. You will trust him as you now trust me, and obey him as you obey me."

"You're forcing me to leave because I was not born your son."

"No, that isn't true. I am forcing you to face what you are — a woman who must make her life as a woman should. You have a destiny to fulfill, Chandra. You will not hide from it. You will not refuse to face it."

Words lay dead in her throat. She felt hollow, empty, like a reed flute crushed underfoot when a minstrel tossed it heedlessly away.

She started to turn away from him, but he grabbed her arm and held her still. "Accept what must be done." Then, because he knew she would probably take a knife and gullet the man who wanted to marry her, he dropped his voice until it sounded mean and low and vicious — a tone he had never before used with her — and said, "Listen to me. You will behave with the greatest respect toward Jerval, Chandra. You will not scream curses on him, you will not demand that he leave, you will not insult him to make him despise you. You will endeavor to remember that before an hour ago, you held him as a good friend. You will obey me in this or I will send you to a convent and you will spend your remaining years on your knees in endless prayers."

He saw from the utterly frozen look in her eyes that she believed him. Good.

Jerval was coming out of the Great Hall, speaking to Mark. The afternoon sun was bright overhead. It was a warm day, the smell of the jakes not particularly noxious since the breeze was from the west. He saw Chandra and felt something very warm fill him. She was wearing a gown. Her hair was

147

braided, thick and golden beneath the sunlight, and he saw that it was clean. He knew she'd spoken to her father, for Lord Richard had told him that she had. Lord Richard also said that she would wed him, no more than that. What had he said to her? Was he forcing her? Jerval prayed it was not necessary. What was in her mind now? Why was she walking away from him?

Chandra cursed her woman's long, narrow-skirted gown and walked faster. She wasn't ready to see him, not yet. Not ever.

A strong hand closed over her arm, steadying her, as she stumbled on a sharp-edged cobblestone.

"Slow down," Jerval said. "You can't race me across the cobblestones in a gown."

He turned her slowly about to face him. Chandra kept her head down, staring at her toes. He was big, damn him. He was too big, blocking the sun.

"Chandra." He wanted to tell her that she looked beautiful. He wanted to pull that braid of hers apart and rub his face in her hair. He cleared his throat. "Chandra," he said again, no amusement in his voice, "we must talk, you and I."

A raindrop fell on the tip of her nose, and she dashed it away and looked heavenward. "How can it rain? The sky was

148

blue just a moment ago. Oh dear, was it a bird?"

He laughed; he couldn't help himself. She was wonderful, this woman he would marry, no matter what she thought of him right now. "No, no bird. Come along to the stables. We can find some privacy there and not get rained on."

The stable was dim and smelled of sweet hay and manure and horse. He led her to an empty stall and watched her seat herself on a hay bale.

He said, all calm and sure of himself, "You know what your father wants. You have spoken to him, have you not? Right after you left me earlier?"

"Aye." She jumped up, shook out her skirts, and looked as if she wanted to run.

He started to grab her arm, then stopped himself. He said easily, knowing he had to be calm, go slowly, "You want to leave? We have just begun. Sit down."

Slowly, he let his hand slide down her arm until his fingers laced through hers. He pulled her down beside him on a thick bale of hay and released her hand.

"Very well. What is it you wish to say?"

She was not making it particularly easy for him, he thought, studying her profile. "I wish you were wearing the necklace. It would be perfect with that gown."

"No."

"Face me when you wish to be rude."

She didn't mean to be rude, not really. She loved the necklace, loved to touch it. "All right. Here, I'm looking right at you. You gave the necklace to me as a bribe. I realized that soon enough. You thought I would do whatever you wished once that thing was around my neck, didn't you? That I could be bought with that necklace. Well, it didn't work."

"I gave you that necklace because I thought you would like it. It pleased me to give it to you, to see your pleasure. Nothing more than that."

She said nothing at all, but she didn't have to. She thought he was a liar.

Jerval sighed. Why couldn't something this important be just a bit less complicated? "You kissed me," he said.

"Yes, as I would kiss a friend. Not a man."

"I'm a man and your friend."

Damn him, it was true, and so she forced herself to say, "Mayhap so."

"I wish you weren't so afraid of me. If you could see me clearly, then you would realize that I mean you no harm. I want you to be happy. With me. As my wife."

"I am not afraid of you. Now, Graelam —

he was a man to fear, but I wasn't afraid of him either."

He laughed and she very nearly sent her fist into his nose. Her father's threat blared loud in her brain. It stayed both her fist and her tongue. She didn't want to be sent to a convent; the mere thought of it curdled her blood.

"You are so filled with bravado. You've raised defenses that would keep out the stoutest of warriors, defenses that would likely send them running for their lives, thankful to avoid you."

"Not you, more's the pity."

"No, not me. Will you wed me now that you have had time to consider it?"

"My father believes that you will make me a fine husband."

"That is the truth. However, I do need you to agree with your father."

She wanted to smash him onto the stable floor, but she knew she couldn't even try. How to make him leave her alone? To make him not want her any longer, but in such a way that she wouldn't be sent to a convent? Oh, aye, she believed her father's threat.

She said, chin up, "I don't wish to lie with you."

That was something a man never wanted to hear, he thought, wanting very much to taste her mouth right this moment. No, he would hold firm, keep to his course. Aye, once they were wed, he would have her. He said easily, "You don't have to worry about mating with me until we are wed. Mayhap then you will change your mind."

She said nothing to that, just kept looking down at her feet in their leather slippers. "My father has bedded every comely girl within Croyland's walls. The only woman he never beds is Lady Dorothy, his wife." She frowned, shaking her head. "Were I a man and her husband, I doubt I would want to get that close to her either." She shrugged, then said matter-of-factly, "I saw him several times with a girl younger than I was. I don't ever wish to do that, ever. It is humiliating. It makes me sick to think of it. But that is the way men are. I hate it, but there is nothing I can do about it."

"You believe I would bed females at Camberley, with you as my wife?"

She simply nodded.

He hadn't realized that she'd seen so much, that it had scarred her so deeply. It was a pity. Also, there was something else going on here. There was too much between father and daughter, deep unspoken feelings that he didn't want to even think about. But all that would pass. She would forget.

She would gain years and maturity. She would be his wife, away from Croyland, away from her father.

"I will not bed other women once we are married. It is a vow I make to you. I will be faithful to you."

It was clear she didn't believe him.

He sighed. "You will come to believe me. I am not an ogre. Nor am I a liar. I love you and respect you. Why would I ever want to hurt you? This is one way I am not like your father."

She said quickly, "My father isn't that way, not really. It is simply something that a man must do. He cannot help himself, but he doesn't mean it."

He wanted to snort at that, but he didn't, saying only, "No, you are wrong, Chandra. A man makes choices. He does what he wishes to do. There is nothing or no one to force him, at least in matters of the flesh. Your father does what he does because he chooses to. He is your father, but it is better that you see him for what he is. Now, why does your mother so dislike you?"

He thought she would argue with him about her father, but she said, shrugging, "I don't know."

The chances were good that she didn't know. He, however, needed to find out everything about this girl who would be his wife. He would have to speak to Lord Richard about it.

"Truly," she said, "I never wanted to marry anyone."

"You are ready. You are eighteen. Past ready."

"I don't want to belong to any man, and that's what it would mean. It is God's commandment that a wife yield to her husband."

"Aye, it is the natural way of things. But that needn't worry you, Chandra."

"It is natural only to you, not to me. I do not want to be owned."

"Listen to me. I admire you. I enjoy being with you. I enjoy competing with you, something you and I will likely do until we grow too old to raise a bow and arrow. It is more to your advantage to wed me than, say, a man who would want you only for the wealth you would bring him, a man who would crush your spirit, mayhap even beat you. I really do not see myself as your master, and quite frankly, you would make a dreadful slave."

She jumped to her feet and began pacing about the small stall. He was content to watch her.

Finally, he said, "Everything will be all

right, Chandra, I promise you. You must trust me, just as you trust your father. Believe that I will try never to hurt you or to demand things of you that you would dislike." He rose then and cupped her chin in his hand, forcing her face upward. "Do not fret, little one, and don't curse me while I'm gone."

"You're leaving?"

He grinned down at her, wanting to kiss her. He cleared his throat. He knew well when to advance, when to retreat. "I must leave to fetch my family. I will return in two weeks for our wedding. Your life will change, Chandra. I cannot deny that. I think eventually you will prefer being a wife to being a daughter. There are many pleasant benefits, you know, over being one and not the other." Before she could kick him or yell at him, or just bite him, he quickly leaned down and kissed her. She didn't move. Still, he felt confident when he released her.

"Will you wed me?"

Her father's words were clear in her mind. Slowly, she nodded.

"Say the words."

It seemed that an eternity passed before she said, her voice low and thin, "I will wed you."

"Good." He kissed her again, hard, then

said, "I must tell the men. We will leave at dawn on the morrow. Contrive, sweeting, to miss me whilst I am gone."

He left her, his step jaunty, and she saw him smile as he raised his face into the rain.

Chapter 10

Lord Richard said calmly to his daughter, "Sir Jerval and his family are nearly here. Go remove your boy's clothes. I want you to wear the saffron gown, Chandra, and do not forget Jerval's necklace. He told me himself that he believed the necklace would look well with that gown."

He saw that she would argue and held up his hand. "Do it, now. I will not tell you again. You are a lady. You will act like a lady. You are greeting your future husband and your new family. Do not shame me, daughter." He let the unspoken threat lie heavy between them. Finally, without a word, she turned on her heel and went back up the narrow stone stairs to the upper floors.

When Jerval first saw her, standing there, tall and proud and utterly silent, he realized that he had been wrong. He had believed that no woman could be as beautiful as he'd remembered her. But she was. She was wearing the necklace he'd given her. She looked pagan, like a princess awaiting her champion. He felt something move deep inside him, fill him, and he recognized it for what it was. It was love for this woman, a caring so deep, he knew it would fill him until he died.

He strode to her, drew her against him, felt the long length of her, the softness, and kissed her, everything he felt for her in that kiss. She didn't move.

She was wary of him as a man, perhaps even afraid of him. He knew that. He would go more slowly. When he stepped away, he said, "Come, Chandra, and meet my parents and my cousin, Julianna." He wondered if she could see the naked love he felt for her shining from his eyes. Evidently not. She looked, truth be told, as cold as carved marble, mayhap even miserable if one looked deeply enough into her eyes. That would change; he would make it change. He knew her, and he knew himself. She was his mate; God had fashioned her just for him.

Lord Hugh and Lady Avicia stood just inside the Great Hall speaking to Lord Richard. Lady Dorothy stood behind her husband, making no move to greet Jerval's parents. He had assumed she agreed with their marriage, but now he wasn't so sure. Not that it mattered.

Chandra bowed to Jerval's parents. Lord Hugh was thick in the middle, his belly plumping over his wide leather belt. Lady Avicia was bountiful herself, but there was beauty there, in her large dark eyes and her black hair, barely streaked with gray. She saw that Jerval resembled neither of them. Again, she thought, he could have been her father's son. It was odd, but Lady Avicia was looking about the Great Hall with something akin to disdain. Disdain about what? It made no sense. The Great Hall of Croyland was magnificent. As for Lord Hugh, he looked quite pleased.

Chandra said little, speaking to Jerval's parents only when spoken to. They were pleasant. Then she met Jerval's cousin, Julianna, a small pretty girl with very white skin, blond hair so light it looked nearly white, and soft blue eyes that grew very hard indeed when they landed on Chandra. And Chandra wondered, *Why does she dislike me? She doesn't even know me.* Then Chandra realized that it was jealousy in Julianna's fine blue eyes, digging deep and furious, that jealousy. She wanted her cousin for herself, wanted him badly.

Chandra wished she could give Jerval to her. But no, he wouldn't be happy with Julianna, he . . . She looked at her father, saw that he was smiling, saw that he was very pleased with himself and what had come about. She wasn't going to think about Jerval and Julianna together, or what that would mean to her.

It would mean nothing. Aye, the die was cast.

Before the afternoon meal, Jerval found himself next to Avery. He smiled at the grizzled warrior, who said with grave understanding, "You wonder whether God has cursed you or blessed you. Listen, it is hard for her, sir, to leave her home and all that she has known."

"Has she been a problem whilst I was gone, Avery?"

Avery chuckled, stroking his coarse, graying beard. "Nay, my lady is never a problem, though she did yell at Ponce when he chanced to recall your skill with the bow."

"A crime indeed. I hope she didn't crush him underfoot."

"Nay, he hid behind the target to escape her. She wants taming, I suppose, but one forgets that she is a girl, and not a cocky lad."

"She was never a cocky lad to me," Jerval said.

"No," Avery said slowly, eyeing the young

man, "I know that she was not."

Jerval nodded to Avery, then went to speak to his father, who was drinking some of Lord Richard's sweet mulled wine, one hand stroking Graynard's massive head, and looking quite blissful.

Just after dawn on the morning of her wedding, Chandra slipped from the keep and made her way in the chill, low-lying fog to the east tower on the outer wall. It had been a favorite haunt since childhood, a quiet, isolated spot.

A tired guard stood silent vigil some twenty feet away, leaning forward on the crenellated wall, and did not hear her approach. She had passed but one of the guests outside the keep, a man in Sir Stephen's service, on his way to the jakes. Soon, she knew, the servants would be up and about, and the guests who had had to spend the night wrapped in blankets in the Great Hall would be jostled awake by the racket. The barracks were packed and even the wall chambers overflowed with guests.

She sighed and crouched down against the damp stone wall, pulling her fur-lined cloak close about her. She ran her finger slowly over the rough stone surface, tracing the chipped crannies that had been deep in the stone before her birth. She rested her head against the stones and felt tears sting her eyes. She could not imagine leaving Croyland.

It was there that Mary found her, curled up fast asleep, her head leaning against the hard stone.

"Chandra," Mary said quietly, touching her hand to her friend's shoulder.

Chandra jerked awake. "Oh, goodness, is it already time?"

"No, it is still early. I am sorry to disturb you, Chandra, but I wished to speak to you. I could not find you, and guessed that perhaps you would be here."

"It's the only private place left." She looked closely at her friend and said, even as she jerked her fingers through her tangled hair, "I am sorry, Mary. I'm selfish, thinking only of my own plight. Come, sit beside me."

"You have said nothing to your father, have you, Chandra? About what happened? About what Graelam did?"

"Of course not."

Mary drew a deep breath. "I cannot remain at Croyland, Chandra, once you leave. Please, take me with you to Camberley. I could not bear to return to my father's keep, knowing that he would give me eventually to

162

someone in marriage, and that I would have to tell him I am no longer a maid. I could not bear the shame of it. Nor do I know what he would do. I do not know how much worth I have to him. At least with you, I would have more time."

"You truly wish to come with me? Oh, Mary, I hadn't asked you because I didn't believe you would want to come to a strange keep, with people you don't know."

"You don't know them either."

"You're right, but I have no choice. You do. Of course you will come with me. Oh, your wretched father, he wouldn't understand that it wasn't your fault. Aye, come with me. Are you sure you can deal well enough with Lady Avicia and Julianna?"

Mary merely shrugged. "Julianna is just jealous of you, that is all. She will doubtless bite her tongue once you are wed. As for Lady Avicia, she is a bit overpowering, I will admit that, but not a malicious person. She has been kind to me."

Chandra cursed suddenly, quite vile curses she'd learned when she was six years old from her father's man, Clyde. Then she said, "I just remembered that I must ask Jerval's permission, for Camberley is his home."

"Do you think he will permit it?"

"Of course he will."

"You are right. Jerval would deny you nothing." She paused a moment, looking out toward the fog-veiled harbor. "How very lucky you are."

"How can you say I'm lucky when I must leave Croyland?"

"I can hardly imagine you wanting to spend the rest of your life here, Chandra, particularly after John grows up and becomes the lord of Croyland. He would make your life a misery. He tries to do that now. Can you imagine the kind of girl he will marry?"

"I hadn't thought of that," Chandra said slowly. "She will be a termagant, that girl — she will have to be to survive John, if he continues the way he is going. He is becoming mean-spirited. All Lady Dorothy's doing, of course. It's true. I do not belong here, do I?"

"No. You belong in your own keep, where you are both mistress and wife. You belong where all loyalty is yours, not anyone else's."

"My father said that."

"It is the truth. As I said, you are very lucky. Jerval is besotted with you. He admires you. He will treat you well."

Chandra sighed. It was true, all of it.

"You do not think him a fine man? Brave? Honorable?"

"Aye."

"I am glad you see him so clearly. I would not wish to see him saddled with a wife who would make his life a misery."

Chandra swallowed. She had never thought to do that. Actually, she had never really thought about what her new life would be like at all. "I would not be that way — that is, I wouldn't want to be that way, but —"

"Do you notice how the wind has just strengthened?"

"Aye."

"And we are both bending so it won't knock us off the ramparts."

"Aye, we are both bending into the wind, and I am not stupid."

"Bending to another's wishes, not always insisting upon holding the upper hand, makes for more peace than strife."

"Aye, I know." Chandra sighed again. "It's just that sometimes it is difficult to bend when —"

"When you feel threatened?"

She shook her head. "Oh, no."

"Oh, Chandra, think of all the joy you can have with your soon-to-be new husband if you will but allow it."

"Let us go in now. I will speak to Jerval."

"Thank you."

"Nay, it is I who am grateful to have you with me even if you must always rub my nose in the dirt when I am in the wrong."

Mary laughed at that, and Chandra realized it was the first time she had heard her friend laugh in a very long time. Since Graelam had taken both her and Croyland.

Chandra made her way through the hall, where at least fifty people were eating their morning meal, amid boisterous joking. When she reached Jerval's chamber, one that he shared with Sir Mark, she paused a moment, hearing several serving maids giggling within.

Her knock was answered by Mark. If he was surprised to see her on the morning of her wedding day, he gave no hint of it. He said, smiling, "I have just got Jerval into his bath. Do you wish to see him?"

She nodded, waiting in the doorway until the two young girls, wet and laughing, slipped beside her. They both nodded to her, smiling and smug, rolling their eyes a bit, for they'd known her all her life.

"What is it, Ema?"

"He's a lovely man, Chandra, just lovely." And Ema laughed, poked Isabel in the ribs, and laughed some more.

"Mayhap too big," Isabel said, winking at Chandra, then giggled behind her hand.

"He is large," Chandra said, "but he is a warrior and one would expect that." They both laughed even harder as they passed the corner out of sight.

Chandra walked into the small chamber to see Jerval sitting in a sturdy wooden tub, water swirling about his waist. His golden hair was plastered wet about his head. His knees were sticking up. He was a beautiful creature — she would grant him that. "Don't ask me to scrub your back."

"A pity," he said. "I would prefer your soft hands to my own calluses."

"I have just as many calluses as you do."

"Mayhap, but somehow they feel different to me."

She frowned down at him, looked at the expanse of strong back. "Perhaps another time. Heed me now. This is important."

"I thought it would be since you hunted me down in my bathing tub." He was delighted to see her, and pleased that she would search him out on their wedding morning. It was simply not done, but then again, she was unique, this bride of his. "Come, what concerns you, sweeting?"

Sweeting. An endearment that sounded natural when he said it. She liked the feel of it, the warmth of it, but there wasn't time for that now.

"It's Mary. She is Sir Stephen's daughter."

"Aye, I have spoken briefly with him. He appears a hard man, with little humor and an iron fist."

She nodded. "Mary has been my friend forever. We were raised together. I would like her to come with us to Camberley. I am here to secure your permission."

He lifted his arm to soap his chest, aware that she was looking at him now, and wondering if she believed him well made. He said, "Surely such a matter should be discussed with Sir Stephen. She is young, comely, ready to wed."

"No, we cannot do that."

"Why not?"

"I suppose you should know," she said, looking at his hand holding the sponge, rubbing over his belly now. "But you must swear to me that you won't tell anyone else of this. Please, Jerval, it is very important."

"I would never betray your confidence, Chandra."

"Lord Graelam raped Mary. In front of me and two of his own men."

Jerval leapt to his feet, sending waves of water splashing onto the stone floor. "Raped her? By God, that miserable whoreson."

He realized he was naked, and quickly eased down into the tub again.

She hadn't seen him naked before. It was a revelation even though she had seen many naked men over the years. She was very grateful that he was firmly seated in the tub again.

"Yes, he raped her."

"But it was you he wanted."

"It was to bring me into line. Neither Mary nor I would tell him where my mother and John were hidden. Without them, he could not force me to wed him. It was my fault that it happened, for had I only spoken, Mary would have been spared, but I did not speak. I held myself silent while he raped her, praying that her sacrifice would be worth the cost.

"But it wasn't, of course, for Lady Dorothy came out of the hidden room with John by herself. No one may know. Mary's father, Sir Stephen, would blame her. What you felt when you met him is true. And he would come to know the truth, for Mary would have to tell him when he sought her a husband. I doubt that he would be kind to her. He might kill her, for she wouldn't be worth anything more to him. It isn't fair, Jerval. None of it is her fault."

"No, it isn't. Of course she will come with

us. Fret no more about it, sweeting. It will be our secret. Assure Mary that I will not betray this."

"Thank you. You are a man and yet you are reasonable."

"You are a woman. Are you reasonable as well?"

"I will try to be," she said, and he smiled at that. She was chewing on her lower lip, thinking hard.

"I can already hear the merrymaking," he said, then added, "I jumped up because I was so surprised at what you said. I am sorry if I shocked you."

"You did not shock me. I have seen more men unclothed than women. You are a man."

"As in just a man like all other men?"

"No, you know that you are not like all other men. You are quite perfect. You surely are not blind to what you are. I am not blind either."

"You are saying that my body pleases you?"

"I said nothing about any pleasure. I merely speak the truth, state an obvious fact, as one would remark upon a beautiful statue or a lovely fattened pig ready to be slaughtered. I really must go now, Jerval. There is much for me to do."

"Will you believe me perfect this night when we come together for the first time?" He squeezed the sponge over his chest, seemingly intent on the rivulets of water that trickled to his belly.

She stared at him. "I do not wish to think about that," she said.

"Surely it is not a thought to distress you or frighten you."

He expected her to hurl an insult in his face, to deny that anything could ever frighten her, but she said nothing for a long moment. To his surprise, she slowly nodded. "Mayhap it is," she said, and was out of the bedchamber before he could even think of anything else to say.

Chapter 11

Chandra stood quietly as Alice pulled the soft, linen chemise over her head. When she lifted the wedding gown, fringed with magnificent ermine, over Chandra's head, and smoothed it down over her hips, Mary sighed with pleasure.

"It is really quite beautiful," she said, fingering the green silk, elegant and soft to the touch. There were full sleeves that fell beyond Chandra's fingers, and a long train. Her pointed shoes were made of vermilion leather and threaded with more gold embroidery. They pinched her toes.

"Here is the girdle," Mary said. It was made of pieces of gold, each set with a good-luck stone — agate to guard against fever, sardonyx to protect against malaria. The clasp was fashioned with great sapphires.

Since the morning was bidding to be warm, Chandra carried her mantle over her arm. Like the gown, it was of silk, intricately embroidered and dyed a royal purple.

After Alice had arranged Chandra's long

hair to her satisfaction, Mary stepped forward and placed a small saffron-colored veil held by a golden circlet on her head.

"You will not shame my son," Lady Avicia said when she walked into the bedchamber, Lady Dorothy at her heels.

"She looks well enough," said Lady Dorothy, looking at a point beyond Chandra's right shoulder.

Julianna said nothing at all.

Chandra thought to herself, as she looked at the strange exquisite girl in her silver mirror, *Aye, I look well enough,* and then she closed her eyes for a moment. She wouldn't shame her father. She was marrying the man he had chosen for her. Everything would be all right. She straightened her shoulders and smiled. It was her wedding day, the only one she would ever have. That gave her abundant food for thought.

The castle chapel was too small to accommodate all the wedding guests, so Chandra, her father at her side, walked toward the orchard, where Father Tolbert waited to conduct the ceremony.

Her brother, John, walked to stand beside Lord Richard. There was a smile on that thin little mouth, and it wasn't a nice smile. It was triumphant and smug. The paltry little kidling, she thought, then realized that

173

what Mary had said was exactly right. She pictured herself here at Croyland in ten years, when John would be eighteen and a man and ready to wed. She would be nothing once her father died, and the stark reality of it was very clear to her now.

She looked at Jerval.

She didn't belong here at Croyland any longer. She belonged with him.

He was her future. She couldn't begin to imagine it.

The servants, under Lady Dorothy's direction, had raised an archway and threaded colorful flowers in the latticework. When Chandra and her father walked beneath the arch, Jerval stepped forward to join them. He wore fine brown silk leggings and a tunic of blue sendal silk that reached to his knees. His mantle, like hers, was edged with miniver. He wore a golden chaplet, set with flashing gems, on his shining wheat-colored hair.

Jerval met her gaze, looked as solemn as a priest, and winked at her. To his surprise, and to hers, she winked back.

She heard some of the men who had seen the exchange of winks guffaw.

The guests, fifty deep, formed a half circle about Father Tolbert, who looked both stern and pompous — and, to Chandra's re-

174

lief, clean. He nodded toward Lord Richard, who stepped from Chandra's side and turned to face the wedding guests.

He unrolled a wide parchment and read aloud the goods, servitors, gold, and fine garments Chandra would bring to Jerval as her dowry. Next he read King Henry's greetings to the bride and groom, and his formal permission for them to wed.

Jerval reached out and took hold of her hand. "If the king had dared refuse, why then, I would have abducted you. Unlike Lord Graelam, I would not have bungled the job."

Probably not, she thought.

She heard only bits and pieces of the long, solemn mass of the Trinity, as, she suspected, did Jerval. He kept shifting from one foot to the other. She wondered if his shoes pinched as hers did.

At last Father Tolbert drew near the couple and pronounced his special blessing. Chandra nearly swallowed her tongue at his words.

His voice rang out, loud as church bells. "Let this woman be amiable as Rachel, wise as Rebecca, faithful as Sarah. Let her be sober through truth, venerable through modesty, and wise through the teaching of heaven."

"By the blessed saints," Jerval said out of the side of his mouth, "you will be all that?"

"He should have told me to be as strong as an Amazon queen."

"I doubt he has ever heard of the Amazons since they did not have their adventures in the Bible."

The mass ended. Father Tolbert chanted the *Agnus Dei*, then stepped back. It was the first noble ceremony he had performed since coming to Croyland, and he was quite pleased with himself.

Lord Richard was thinking about other matters — the various gifts he would be expected to distribute among the guests, gifts that had cost him dearly. He heard the *Agnus Dei*, and brought his attention back to his daughter. She was behaving well, her bearing proud, her manner gracious. More important, she seemed to have accepted the inevitable. He was suddenly aware of a tensing in Lady Dorothy. For a moment, he believed the bitch would announce that Chandra wasn't the daughter of her womb, but a bastard foisted off on her. He grasped her hand and squeezed. She made a small, pained sound, nothing more.

He watched his son-in-law embrace his new wife, watched her arms slowly go around his waist.

He felt immense relief, and immense pain.

A loud cheer went up from the wedding guests, signaling the last silent moment of the day. The jongleurs Richard had hired for the wedding puffed their cheeks against their flutes and began to dance among the laughing guests. Jerval, feeling as jubilant as their guests, pulled Chandra close to him and led the procession back to the Great Hall. "You are the most beautiful bride I have ever had," he said loudly, to be heard over the raucous singing of the jongleurs and the guests.

"I am your only bride," she said, looking straight ahead, and he shouted with laughter. "I am also the only bride you will ever have, so you can lock away all your man's dreams."

He pulled her around and kissed her mouth. "Every dream that invades my brain is of you."

He kissed her again, hard, and prepared to suffer through at least another six hours of feasting before he could have her.

It was nearly seven hours before the huge wedding feast at last drew to a close. Jerval never wanted to see another bite of food again. The haunch of roasted stag, the larded boar's head with herb sauce, beef, mutton, legs of pork, roasted swan and rabbit were strewn about on the tables, now little more than meatless carcasses, or tossed to the boarhounds, who growled happily, pulling the bones through the reeds. He was ready to throw his bride over his shoulder and run as fast as he could up the stairs when the servants staggered into the hall carrying yet more food — rabbit in gravy spiced with onion and saffron, roasted teal, woodcock, and snipe, patties filled with yolk of eggs, and cheese, cinnamon and pork pies.

He cursed.

Chandra was eyeing the pork pies when Sir Andrew, nearly as drunk as his wife, shouted, "Jerval, how will you go about bedding your warrior bride?"

"Aye," came another drunken shout. "Will the bride remove her armor?"

"Will you challenge her for her maidenhead?"

"Aye, now that's a challenge I would willingly accept," Sir Stephen yelled out.

Chandra looked ready to leap from her chair and run her sword through them all. Jerval laughed at her. "Let them bray, sweeting. It means nothing. Besides, it is a guest's obligation to tease and jest and get drunk at a wedding."

"A man's rod is his wife's dearest friend," Sir Malcolm's wife, Joanna, called out, her voice slurred after a day of drinking wine.

"How would you know, my lady?" Sir Andrew yelled. "That old man you're married to wouldn't know what to do if he discovered what he had between his legs."

"On and on it goes," Jerval said, and fed her a bite of pork pie from his fingers. "I had expected this much sooner, but it doesn't matter. That's right. You've eaten very little. Open your mouth."

"Look yon, Jerval feeds her."

"That is because he cannot yet feast his mouth between those long legs of hers. Aye, he'll see to it that she is well eaten."

Jerval grinned as he listened to the ladies and men alike, and he saw himself indeed kissing her between those legs of hers, and quickly gave her another bite of pork pie.

He doubted she even knew what they meant. That pleased him. She would learn soon enough because he would teach her. Tonight. He could nearly taste her. He sucked in his breath — and choked on his wine.

Why would Jerval wish to eat whilst he was between her legs? It made no sense to her. Chandra chewed slowly, smelled the sweet scent of mulled wine on his breath and felt the warmth of his body as he pressed close to her. She'd drunk a goodly amount of wine herself. She didn't feel any fear, any distaste, at the closeness of him.

"Will Lord Richard's men or Lady Dorothy's ladies lead the bride to her wedding chamber?" Sir Andrew shouted.

"And who will do the mounting? Sir Jerval, be you the stallion or the mare?"

Jerval yelled, "You, Hubert, and you, Mark, see that I am blessed to have both a mare and a stallion. I will have the joy of mounting and being mounted."

Richard rose suddenly from his great chair and banged his knife handle onto the table for quiet. "Avery," he shouted, "bring in the three men."

Jerval looked on in surprise as three filthy men, pale from their weeks in Croyland's dungeon, were dragged into the Great Hall by Avery and Ellis and shoved to their knees before Lord Richard.

Chandra watched her father draw a parchment from the full sleeves of his robe and wave it toward the men. "Listen well," he shouted. "This parchment is for your master, Lord Graelam de Moreton, from our beloved King Henry. I release you to return to your lord. You will tell him that the prize he sought will never be his. He will live the rest of his life knowing that my daughter is another man's wife. The king herewith orders that he will pay half of all Croyland's taxes for the next full year in just retribution for his actions." Richard thrust the parchment into one of the men's hands. "Tell your lord that the king has saved his lands from my revenge. Go now."

Richard smiled down at his daughter and bowed. "My gift to you, Chandra. Now, the dancing."

Time slowed, then stilled entirely. Jerval looked at Lord Richard, saw that he was staring at the two of them, and he didn't want to know what Chandra's father was thinking.

They danced until, finally, Jerval returned Chandra to her chair, amid more drunken wit and advice that left her pale and wild-eyed, and said to Lord Richard, "It is time. I do not wish her to be embarrassed more. I will see to her if you will control all the guests, and my family."

Lord Richard looked at his daughter and slowly nodded. He was afraid that she would bolt, and Jerval saw the fear on his face. He felt it as well.

"You do not wish to follow the traditional bedding?"

Jerval shook his head. "Nay, not with her. She has drunk a goodly amount of wine, but still, I —"

"You're afraid she will run?"

"Aye."

"Go then. I will hold everyone here."

In Chandra's bedchamber, the women had been busy. There were rosebuds strewn on the rushes, incense that smelled of lilac filled the air and the nostrils, and a dozen wax candles were lit.

It was warm and a bit dizzying in the room.

She turned slowly to look at her husband, his back against the closed door, his arms crossed over his chest.

"It has come to pass," she said, standing in the middle of the room, looking blankly around her. "You are here in my bed-chamber, and it is expected that you be here. I cannot hurl you out."

"Nay, you cannot. I hope that you do not wish to, now that I am your husband."

"I am not certain. I know nothing about this, Jerval. Perhaps it is troubling."

"Troubling? Not at all, sweeting. It is pleasure I will give you, I swear. Now, I have thought of this moment, Chandra. Come here."

He doubted she would obey him, but it

didn't matter. He simply wanted to see what she would do. Her eyes were a bit glazed from the wine she'd drunk. Mayhap she had drunk enough so that she wouldn't fight him.

Fight him? Mayhap go for his throat. She was strong, this wife of his.

"Come here," he said again, and waited.

She picked up the skirts of her beautiful silk gown and slowly walked to him. "Aye, sir?"

She was looking up at him, no fear on her face. By all the saints' elbows, she was beautiful. He knew he had to go slowly, very slowly. She was a maid, and despite all her knowledge of men and their ways, despite the fact that the wine she had drunk had eased her, she was as ignorant as a stoat.

"I'm going to kiss you now. Put your arms around me."

She did; then, to his surprise, she raised her face. It was almost more than he could bear. He kissed her mouth, very lightly, no threat at all, just a beginning exploration, a savoring.

Chandra rose to her tiptoes, and Jerval, his arms now tight around her back, let his hands fall to her hips. The feel of her through the gown and her shift — he wanted to strip her wedding gown off her, have her naked and beneath him in the next moment, but he couldn't. He had to go slowly. He wanted to curse, but since he was kissing her, it wasn't possible.

And so he did go slowly, and tried to ignore the prodding and the urgency that gnawed in his gut. He was gentle, patient, and he was rewarded by a very worried look from his bride when a small sound came from deep in her throat.

"I want that gown off you," he said then, and set her away from him. He didn't want to, but he knew if he didn't, he would rip the gown off her, and then what would she think of him? He could see the effects of the wine falling off her, leaving her cold and ready to fight him to the death.

But she didn't fight him. Indeed, she stood there, saying nothing, not helping him, but not shrinking away from him either. "Lift your arms." She did, felt the smooth silk slide against her cheek, then the linen shift, not as smooth as the silk, but soft, nearly like Leah the goat's butter. She was naked then. Standing in front of him, her arms at her sides. Naked, completely and utterly naked.

"Ah." It was all he could say. Unlike his wife, he couldn't keep himself still. He grabbed her to him, lifted her and carried her to the bed, and laid her among several rose leaves thrown on the counterpane.

He was panting hard, staring down at her, sprawled on her back, her legs spread slightly, the blond hair between her legs — no, there was a touch of gold in her woman's hair — and he wanted desperately to touch her, to kiss her, to breathe in the scent of her. Instead, he began pulling off his own clothes. He saw that her hands were fists now, and said, "It will be all right, sweeting. I will take good care of you. You are not to be afraid."

"I do not know about this, Jerval."

Was that her voice, that small reedy sound that was high and female and frightened?

"You do not have to know anything. All you have to do is trust me."

"My father told me to lie still, not to fight you. He said you would know what to do — at least he hoped you would know what to do. He is worried that since you are very young, you will be uncaring, mayhap rough, a clod."

A clod? He murmured ironic thanks to Lord Richard, wishing he had the man's neck between his hands. "He is right and he is wrong. I would sooner take an ax to my own neck than hurt you. I am not a clod." He was naked now, and she was staring at him, focused on his sex, harder than the stone beneath his feet.

She said, never looking away from his sex, "I really do not wish to do this, Jerval."

He'd left her alone too long, and that brain of hers was working again, probably yelling at her that since he was a man and that was surely a bad thing, he would surely try to subjugate her and force her to do his bidding. He eased down beside her even though he wanted to part her legs and lay his full length upon her. He had to give her time, and so he kissed her and stroked those white breasts of hers until she was making those small sounds in her throat again.

It was difficult.

He stretched out beside her, knowing she felt him hard against her leg, but he merely smiled into her eyes and lightly laid his palm over her heart, pushing her breast upward as he did so. Her heart beat smoothly, slow and steady.

"Do not worry about anything. It is just the two of us now, Chandra, and we are man and wife and all of this is exactly right."

"I really didn't want to marry you, but Mary was right."

That stopped him cold. "Not want to marry me?"

"Oh, no. Croyland is my home and all I

know and love is here."

"What was Mary right about?"

"She asked if I could imagine living here at Croyland with John as the master. I could not. She said I must have my own keep, my own family, loyal only to me."

Jerval knew then that he would hold Mary dear for the rest of his life. "Aye," he said only.

"Can you imagine the sort of lady that John will marry?"

"It fair curdles my gut to think about it."

She laughed, and the sound warmed him to his toes.

He kissed her again and yet again, then a slow kiss, not forcing her mouth to open, but she finally did open her mouth to him after some prodding, and he realized she didn't know what she should do. Now she did know, and he thought he would spill his seed at the feel of her, the warmth, her taste. It was he who groaned into her mouth. She jumped, then kissed him back, more at ease now.

He continued to caress her breasts, soft as the silk of her wedding gown, and he wanted . . . He pulled away, smiled down at her, but said nothing, merely lowered his head again to nuzzle her breasts. When he closed his mouth over her, she moaned. He thought hard about a horse race he'd lost in a tourney at York and it steadied him.

She was breathing hard, and he smiled against her flesh, tugging with his lips, licking her, suckling her, and he could feel her heart now, fast, pounding hard.

He let his hand stroke over her belly, touching her thighs, lightly pushing her legs apart, coming closer and closer, but still not touching her where a woman's need was greatest, and to his delight, she jerked her hips. He was young, Lord Richard was right about that, but he wasn't a clod, as Lord Richard believed he would be, curse the man.

No, he wasn't a clod, but he wondered if he would be able to hold himself back long enough to give her pleasure before he brought her pain, as he knew he must for she was a virgin. He also knew he must give her pleasure or he just might send her scurrying away, cursing him for a man who gave a woman only pain, a man who didn't care. He would cut off his own arm before he let that happen.

He felt her fingers in his hair, tugging, and he lifted his head from her breasts and smiled up at her, a painful smile because he hurt with need.

He said, "What do you feel?"

"It is strange," she said, and blinked and looked very worried, yet interested at the same time. "I want you to touch me — my belly — as I feel very hot there, sort of hungry, I guess, and I hurt and I do not know what to do."

"I know what to do," he said, and kissed his way down to her belly. He laid his head there, feeling her muscles tighten, relax, feeling her smooth flesh. Slowly, he thought, coming down further between her legs, parting them. When he touched her with his mouth, she froze solid as the small lake at Camberley in February, then lurched up and yelled to the beamed ceiling of the bed-chamber. He both heard and felt her pants, for they were deep inside her, making her shudder and quake, and he felt the building tension in her. Yes, he thought, yes. She was straining against him when he slowly eased his finger inside her. By the saints, she was small, and he wanted to weep with the wonder of her.

She grabbed his head between her hands, her breaths raw and harsh, her back arching off the bed. He pushed her over the edge, and she wept with the force of the feelings making her body fly out of her control. She was crying with the immense joy that filled her, the wonder that one could feel such an amazing thing. Then she felt his weight, felt his fingers on her flesh, and she lifted her hips, excited, wondering what more there could possibly be.

At least she wanted more until he came hard into her, and she screamed again, this time in pain, trying to fling him off her, but he was heavy, and so deep inside her, she felt helpless, and all the grand feelings faded into oblivion, and she continued to cry, only this time it was the pain that bowed her.

Jerval stopped. He balanced himself on his elbows, looking down at her beloved face, at the tears staining her cheeks, and he said, his jaw nearly locked from the grip he had on himself, "I am sorry, sweeting. But the pain will fade quickly. Just lie quietly and I will try not to move. By all the saints, you are more than I have ever imagined in my benighted life."

She opened her eyes and stared up at him. He was deep inside her body. It was something she had never imagined. She had seen men rutting women, but she simply hadn't imagined it being done to her. The pain was receding. But still she burned deep inside. She was stretched by him, and it was still hard to believe that he had made himself part of her. She said, "Am I really more?"

"Aye," he said and dipped down to kiss

her nose, and just that one small act did him in. He looked into her eyes as he roared to the heavens.

He felt as though he'd been clouted in the head. He fell onto his back, brought her with him, holding her tightly against him, and he was breathing in the scent of her hair, and then he knew no more.

Chapter 12

He awoke slowly, his mouth smiling even before he remembered the incredible release that had felled him the night before and sent him into a deep sleep before he could make love to his bride again. Ah, but it was morning, early still, and . . .

"Chandra," he said, his voice low and hoarse with sleep and need, and turned to gather her against him. He was warm and hard and ready.

And she was gone.

It was worse than being doused by a bucket of cold water. He sat up in bed, his sex still as hard as the handle of his sword, saw her virgin's blood on the coverlet, and again, he smiled. He'd hurt her, aye, but he'd given her pleasure first, and that had to fill her mind, not the brief pain, so small it had been, truly, so insignificant, not even worth a thought or a mention. Aye, mayhap she had awakened smiling just as he had and gone into the Great Hall to fetch him some bread and cheese, even a small flagon of ale.

It was a nice dream, one he didn't believe for more than one crazed moment. He shoved the covers back and rose. He saw her blood on his sex, and frowned, but only for a moment. He had actually pleasured a virgin before he'd come into her and caused the inevitable pain. Ah, but scarce more than the veriest prick, surely, so quickly gone, nothing at all to a strong girl like his bride. He washed her blood off himself, dressed quickly and went down into the Great Hall. It was very early, and the hall was nearly empty. He imagined all the men and the guests hanging over buckets, leaning off the ramparts, ducking behind the practice field, heaving up all the wine and ale they'd drunk the day and evening before.

He wanted his wife. He wanted to haul her over his shoulder and carry her into the forest just beyond the castle, to the east, to the large cluster of thick pine and spruce trees, hidden within from the bright sunlight, soft and dark. She would stand against a tree and he would lift her and bring her legs around his waist and he would part her with his fingers and . . .

Mark came in, slapping his gauntlets against his leg. "I could not sleep and I wanted to, but it was not to be. I shared the last watch with Roul and Abel. At least my head isn't splitting open like every other guest's at the wedding feast. Why are you here so early? Where is your wife? She has not left you already, has she?"

Jerval grinned and rubbed his hands together. "Naturally not. I am here to find her. She is a happy wife, Mark. I pleased her. Aye, I pleased her well."

"By God, you are all puffed up. You are bragging and preening. I haven't seen you like this since our visit to London three years ago when —"

"Forget that," Jerval said and laughed again. He couldn't seem to help laughing. He felt very good. "Aye, perhaps it is true that I am very pleased with what I accomplished last night. Now it is morning and there are other things I wish to do."

"Like what?"

"I want to leave this morning."

Mark stared at him. "Leave? Leave Croyland? But we are to remain here for at least three more days. There is more feasting and more sport, and your parents surely need to spend more time with Lord Richard and Lady Dorothy."

"They will. We will take only three or four men with us and return to Camberley. I wish Chandra to accustom herself to her new home before my mother returns. It is a very big change for her, Mark. I would rather begin it without my mother's — ah, forceful help."

"Do not forget Julianna. She cannot seem to wipe the malignant look off her face."

Jerval frowned, but just for a moment. "I will speak to my father about it. It is time he found her a husband."

"You are doubtless right about Julianna," Mark said, "but still. Leave this morning? When did you think of this? Surely not until after you and Chandra — well, I need not be quite so clear about what I mean."

"Nay, you do not. Actually, it came to me all of a piece, a whole cloth all intricately sewed, all formed in my mind, just five minutes ago. Now, is it possible? Can you have three or four of our men ready in an hour? Are there three or four men who won't vomit on their boots or fall off their horses?"

Mark thought about the few men who were still at least conscious. "Aye," he said finally. "There are four men. Rolfe, Bayon, Ranulfe and Thoms. They are all strong and well enough to fight off bandits should they attack. They will grumble and hold their heads, but they will do. Do you want us to take some of Chandra's dowry goods?"

"Nay, let my parents bring all the wagons, and most of the men to guard all of it. We will travel light."

"Ah . . . does Mary come with us?"

Mary. Jerval recalled that he'd mentioned her coming with Chandra to Mark. He nodded. She was now under his protection. "Now," Jerval said, looking about, "where is my wife?"

"I don't know," Mary said, coming up behind him so silently that, if she'd been an assassin, she could have easily stuck a blade in his back. She was, he saw, studying his face carefully. Did she fear that he had hurt her friend? Forced her? Probably so. He said easily, never looking away from her eyes, "When I awoke, she was gone. I had thought perhaps she had come here to fetch me some bread and cheese to break my fast."

"Oh, no," Mary said. "Surely not. Only if you were Lord Richard would she think of that."

Mark said, "You are certain you did not frighten her into running away from you?"

"Aye, I am certain. She wouldn't do that," he said, and grinned.

"Ah, then she must be here, somewhere. Mary, you have not seen her?"

Mary shook her head. She looked worried, although she tried to hide it. "Is Wicket gone? Perhaps she is riding."

Not more than a blink later, Chandra

came striding into the Great Hall, dressed like a boy, her hair stuffed beneath a dark blue woolen cap, tendrils escaping to hang about her face. Her long legs covered a goodly amount of rush-strewn stone as she strode toward him. If he did not know she was his wife, if he had not possessed that white body of hers, heard her yell, felt himself explode inside her, his fingers clutching her hips, he would have seen a simple lad, all sorts of cocky and full of bravado, coming toward him.

He didn't like it. She was a woman. She was his wife now, not this scruffy boy who looked so sure of himself. He felt anger pulse through him. She should be lying naked in his arms this very minute, up in her bedchamber, in her bed, smiling up at him, kissing him, stroking her hands over his body, asking him to take her again, to give her that incredible pleasure. Again.

He didn't think, just strode to her, his pleasant dream falling beneath the rushes. He walked over those rushes and got angrier. She should be in bed, naked, feeding him chunks of bread, laughing as he chewed.

He grabbed her shoulders and shook her, saying not an inch from her face, his voice a scratchy whisper, "I awoke and you were gone. You should not have left me unless it was to fetch me something to eat and drink. But you were not here. Where have you been? Why are you dressed like this?"

She jerked away from him, her chin up, her eyes cold, just like the Chandra before she'd become his wife, just like the Chandra before he'd brought her pleasure.

She didn't look at him, just shrugged and said, "I was riding. Wicket needed exercise."

"That is a pathetic excuse and you know it. Why did you leave me?"

She looked at him now, and there was a cold look on her face, and anger in her eyes. "I told you. I wanted to ride Wicket."

Mark and Mary were standing close, all ears. Jerval said, "Wicket will get all the exercise he needs. We leave within the hour. Get yourself ready."

"Leave? Croyland?"

"Naturally we will leave Croyland. Think you we are in London?"

"That is nonsense. My father wants us to remain here at Croyland for at least three more days. There is a joust planned, and he wants to go against you. There is no reason to leave. What are you talking about? Leave to go where?"

Her father again. Would she have yelled

for him in the competition were they not to leave? "I wish to leave today for Camberley. You have an hour. See to it."

She jerked off her cap and threw it to the rush-strewn floor. "I do not wish to leave yet. You make no sense. You shout orders, but you do not give any good reasons."

"I don't have to give you any reasons at all, good or otherwise. I wish to leave, and it is my wishes that are important. Cease your woman's prattle and do my bidding."

Mary saw that Chandra was ready to leap upon her husband of less than a day, and threw herself between them. She said quickly, her hand tight on Chandra's forearm, "Listen to me, Chandra. Jerval wishes you to become accustomed to your new home before everyone else returns. He wishes to show you everything himself, with no interference, with no other duties that would distract you, that would take your time."

Chandra stepped right into her friend's face and snarled like a wild wolf, "Get out of the way, Mary."

"No. If you want me moved, you will have to throw me out of the way."

Chandra got hold of herself. She saw that Jerval's eyes were narrowed, that he didn't believe for a moment that she would attack him. She snarled in that same voice, "Then why didn't the fool tell me that?"

He nearly set Mary aside himself. "Listen to me, wife. I want us gone before my mother starts giving you instructions that will surely make you want to clout her in the head."

She was silent a moment, then said, her voice really quite nice and calm now, "Oh, I see. That is probably a good idea." Then she smiled at both Mary and her husband, turned on her heel and strode, just like an arrogant boy, to the stairs. She was whistling. She paused there for a moment and said over her shoulder, "I will not need an hour. I will help Mary, then see to all our supplies. How many days will we be traveling?"

"Three or four."

"Very well." And she was gone, taking the deep stone stairs two at a time.

Jerval stood there in the Great Hall, listening to a few moans from men curled up amid the rushes.

"That was quite a surprise," Jerval said, staring after his wife, whom he could no longer see. He said to Mary, who stood silently not two feet from him, "You will not step between us again. Do you understand me?"

"Sometimes — no, rarely — she loses her temper. I did not know what she would do."

"She would have done nothing."

"I hoped that she would not."

"She would not dare to strike me, her husband."

"Well, mayhap, but she didn't." She slowly nodded and hurried after Chandra.

"You acted like a husband, Jerval," Mark said quietly. "I do not believe it a wise way to approach your lady, particularly when she wears a sharp knife at her belt."

"Aye, that's the truth of it," Jerval said. "By all the saints' tribulations, do you think she would have thrown herself on me? Do you think she would have gone for my throat with that knife of hers?"

"You wish for honesty here? All right, I think it is possible," Mark said. "You rode her hard, Jerval. Mayhap you should stop ordering her about, explain your reasons for things, ease her more gently into this new role she must play."

Jerval waved away Mark's words. "Next time, I will let her have at me — knife and all — and we will see." He frowned. He looked baffled. "I wonder why she doesn't seem to remember her softness and pleasure of last night."

Mark wisely said nothing at all, and Jerval strode away himself.

"You'll curse yourself, Jerval, for leaving the warmth and comfort of Croyland if those storm clouds I see to the west keep building."

Jerval slewed his head about and looked thoughtfully toward the sea. "You might be right, Mark. Let us hope the winds blow the storm southward."

Mark was silent for several minutes, his gray eyes, out of habit, searching the rugged hills to the east for robbers. They rode quickly enough since there were no baggage mules loaded with Chandra's dowry goods to slow them down. There was only one mare to carry all Mary's and Chandra's clothing.

Mark heard Mary laugh and turned in his saddle to see a seabird winging close to her. He watched her hold out her hand to the gull and hoped the bird wouldn't bite her. She was still shy around him, but she didn't flinch or slither away anymore.

What had happened to make her fear men so much? Or was it just him? Surely he had never given her a reason to fear him.

"I will ride with Mary for a while," Mark said, watching the gull fly over her head, coming no closer, simply keeping pace. "I will send your wife to you. It is to be hoped that she will not go for your throat."

Jerval smiled. "At least not whilst we are riding." They were well away from Croyland. She was his wife, his responsibility, and he felt very good about that. This morning hadn't been a natural sort of morning. She had forgotten he was her husband, her lord. But she would not forget again. He would help her not to forget by taking her again and again, until he filled her belly with his child. If he had not been surrounded by his men, he would have called a halt and taken Chandra into the fields just yon, eased her onto her back, his cloak spread beneath her, of course, and then he would . . .

"I once camped with my father in those fields," Chandra said, reining in Wicket beside Pith, who snorted and veered away.

Her damned father again. He didn't need to hear that. He said, "Aye, I was thinking of those fields, but not camping for the night there."

She was riding astride, dressed like a young squire, her mail vest beneath her tunic. Since her braid fell over her shoulder, there was no chance to mistake her this time for a boy. When she had come running down the stairs into Croyland's Great Hall, thusly dressed, he had held his tongue, for she had obeyed him. They were away within the hour, and she had said nothing more to gainsay him. Mayhap he had pulled the reins too tightly. He would go more easily with her.

He reached out his hand and laid it on her wool-clad thigh. He felt her muscles tighten beneath his palm. He was instantly harder than the boulders beside the narrow road. Surely it wasn't all that healthy for a man to be hard so quickly, so often. He cursed. "I wish this day would be over."

She stared down at his large hand for a moment, but didn't try to shove him away. "Why? It is a beautiful day. Those rain clouds that so worry Mark — they won't settle over our heads. Just breathe in that sweet air. The sea is only a half mile to the west."

She was talking, just talking about this and that, and he wanted to take her down off Wicket's back and carry her that half mile to the beach. There was sand, and so he would use his cloak again and . . .

"Why are you smiling? I said naught of anything funny."

"I am a man," he said, nothing more.

She sighed, a deep, profound sigh. "I know," she said. "I know."

"Tell me true now. Why did you leave me this morning before I awakened? Why didn't you kiss me, ease me awake so that we could come together again?"

He didn't think she would answer him, but then she simply blurted out, "I don't want you to make me feel all soft and limp. I am not really sure how it felt now, because time has passed. Even so, whatever it was, I did not want to feel it again. It isn't right. It isn't the way I should feel. It isn't the way I should act. It wasn't me — truly it wasn't."

She said slowly, a frown furrowing her brow, "Like I just wanted to lie there and touch you, mayhap smooth my fingertip over your eyebrow, and laugh and keep kissing you until I fell asleep."

By all the saints' rosaries, he wanted to kiss her until they were both unconscious. He said, "There is nothing wrong with that. I am sorry that I left you so quickly. You took all my strength, Chandra. You felled me."

"You did sleep very hard. I just lay there for a very long time. I didn't understand how you could make me feel that way. I still do not understand. However, I felt like myself again this morning, all those strange feelings gone. I left because I didn't want to stay there with you."

He gave her a big smile, his heart thumping. "Because it was too dangerous?"

"Aye," she said, looking at him straight on now. "I don't wish to feel like that again, ever."

He had her. Quite simply, he knew now that he could bring her to him, make her want him, want those dazzling feelings he gave her. He gave her an even bigger smile and leaned close. "I want to kiss you between those long legs of yours again tonight."

She nearly swallowed her tongue. He saw it and laughed aloud. "I did kiss you there, Chandra, and you are so very sweet. You nearly rolled yourself off the bed — do you remember that? And you yelled so loudly that my ears drummed."

"I did not yell that loudly."

"Aye, you did. I think when I eased my finger inside you, that you lost your breath and nearly made yourself blue, your pleasure was so great."

She said nothing at all. He was pleased to see her red in the face.

"When I came into you, I hurt you because I had to rend your maidenhead. I am sorry for that, but it is done now and there will be no more hurt for you, no more blood, only pleasure. Can you begin to imagine that, Chandra? All the pleasure I will give to you?"

"What about pleasure for you?"

He nearly spilled his seed right there, sitting atop his damned destrier. "You gave me great pleasure. And it was a husband's pleasure, not a simple man's pleasure. You will give me more. I will teach you how."

She didn't want to talk about this weakness of hers that changed her utterly in those wild, frenzied moments. But the words were out of her mouth before she could stop herself. "What is the difference between a man's pleasure and a husband's?"

"For a man, the pleasure is fleeting, since there is no caring, no feeling or longing for the woman. But for a husband, Chandra — you are my wife and I want you. To have you send me beyond myself — I thank you for that."

She said, looking between Wicket's ears, and nowhere else, "Jerval, these husband's feelings you speak of, I do not know about that. Maybe what you felt, maybe what I felt last night, was just as fleeting. Maybe it will never happen again for either of us."

"It will."

She shook her head at that, chewed her bottom lip and said, "I don't like the fact that I am no longer responsible just for myself. I must speak to you now as I would to my father."

"Oh, no."

"I can see no difference. Before we wed you didn't give me orders or critize me. Now, you wish to command me. Before, you did not demand that I obey you, but now, suddenly, you do. You have changed now that you're my husband."

Had he suddenly changed? No, surely not, but he was her husband now, and that meant that perforce things were different.

She said, "You know I did not wish to wed you."

"Aye, but you are a reasonable woman. You accepted Mary's words and you have realized that with me you will have all that you could possibly wish. I am not your father, Chandra. Do not say that again."

She shrugged. He lifted his hand from her leg. "You have but to bend a bit — toward me, not away from me."

"That is what Mary said."

"Mary appears to be a font of wisdom. She is the one I could understand fearing men, not you. You don't fear me anymore, do you?"

That stiffened her back just as he'd known it would. "I never feared you. I merely didn't wish to have a man know me the way you did last night. I am not stupid. What you did to me — it is what my father does to every comely maid within Croyland's walls."

"Mayhap, but it is no concern of yours now what your father does or doesn't do. You will accustom yourself, for I will touch you until I leave this mortal world. There will be no other comely maids, just you."

"I do not know if I can do that, Jerval," she said, then kicked her heels into Wicket's back and galloped ahead of him. He heard her yell, "I don't know that you can do it either."

She rode so well, like a boy raised on horseback. Of course she had been, but she wasn't a boy. She was his wife. Perhaps he had changed, a bit.

He cursed, but he didn't give it much heat. Over time she would come to believe him, to trust him. As for her not wanting him to bring her pleasure, he discounted it. No one, having once experienced that sort of pleasure, ever wanted to have it disappear. He would get her used to it; he would have her anticipating his hands and mouth on her.

His fingers itched to touch her. He was on the point of swearing, he was so hard, when Rolfe rode up beside him to tell him about two drunken men the night before who mistook each other for females.

Chapter 13

Chandra had never before traveled this far north of Croyland. The winding lakes of Cumbria twisting between the lush forests, dotted with small islands and set against rolling mountains, were wild and beautiful. There were very few people; they'd passed only one village, and it sat at the base of a small castle.

"Look, Jerval, the mountains yon are still covered with snow."

"Aye, the Cumbrian Mountains. Many years the snows do not melt from their caps until early summer."

"I had not guessed that such beauty lay only four days from Croyland. Indeed, I never believed that any other lands could compare to ours."

"There are many beautiful places in England. Mayhap we will visit them together."

"Oh, yes," she said. "I would like that. I

have dreamed of seeing more of the world than just our small corner of it."

He merely cocked an eyebrow at her. He felt the same way.

They cleared a gentle rise, and Jerval straightened in his saddle. "There is Camberley," he said, and there was emotion in his voice, a good deal of pride, of possessiveness.

Chandra shaded her eyes with her hand. They were descending into a gentle valley, and just beyond, high atop a craggy hill, she saw the massive castle of Camberley. Its stone walls were a deep red-brown in the fading afternoon sunlight, and four majestic towers, squared, not rounded like those of Croyland, rose like mighty sentinels. Within the walls, the circular keep rose some sixty feet upward. Two hundred yards of land on three sides of Camberley was cleared to prevent any attacker from reaching the walls unseen. A small, winding lake bounded the eastern side.

"It looks impregnable," she said.

He smiled at her. "Trust you to see the strategic advances before anything else."

"It is the most important."

He only nodded. "The last siege was in the early days of Henry's reign, when my grandfather was ill and prey to the rapacious de Audley clan. The granite rock upon which the castle is built made it impossible for them to tunnel beneath the walls. Even their war machines could not destroy the walls. They tried to starve my grandfather into surrender, but even that failed, for the harvest that year had been excellent."

"I have never heard of the de Audleys," Chandra said. "Did your grandfather kill them all?"

"He did. When my grandfather regained his health, he led a surprise attack upon their main fortress and killed every one of them. With Henry's permission — or rather, I should say, with de Burgh's, the earl marshal's, permission — the de Audley lands were forfeited to the de Vernons, with of course a healthy payment to the king. The only price to be paid was a de Vernon wedding the last de Audley daughter. My grandfather bequeathed the lands to my father's younger brother, and it was he who wed Eleanor de Audley. Since that time, our only battles have been with the Scots."

"You are as close to the Scots as Croyland is to the Welsh."

"Aye, and they are more dangerous than the Welsh when roused. We cross swords sometimes three or four times a year, when their hunger drives them to raid our demesne farms." She was sitting forward in her saddle, all her attention on him. "They scream a hoary battle cry when they attack, and move like shadows. When we fight them, we shed our armor, for it makes us too slow. They are not knights and do not fight as such."

"How I look forward to crossing swords with them," she said.

He knew it had to be said now. He was her husband, responsible for her now, and so he said slowly, "You will never fight any enemy. You may practice with the men, but the Scots — you will never even consider crossing any weapon with them. Do you understand me, Chandra?"

"You have changed, and I don't like it."

She kicked Wicket in the sides and rode away. He stared after her. He heard Mark tell Mary about the village of Throckton that was just to their right, nestled amid rich farmland, before they climbed the narrow, serpentine road that led to Camberley.

He heard Mark say, "Camberley's lands extend nearly to the border, hence our continual bouts with the Scots. At one time, Jerval's father thought to extend the de Vernon lands to the east, and considered a marriage alliance with Chester. Luckily, Lord Richard arrived just in time and turned Lord Hugh's eyes toward the lands in the south."

As they approached the castle, Chandra slowed until she once again rode beside her husband. She heard welcoming shouts from the men lining the outer walls.

"They cannot wait to meet you," Jerval said. "Look at the north tower. See that huge man hanging over the wall above the drawbridge? That is Malton, our master-at-arms. The man is the size of a bull and so strong that a hug from him could break your ribs."

The wide drawbridge flattened over a ditch bulging with dirty water, and the iron portcullis ground upward.

"Look, she is dressed like a lad."

"Aye, but there is no lad beneath those trousers."

"Jerval looks besotted with her."

And on it went.

The outer courtyard was not much different from Croyland's, Chandra saw, bustling with animals and people, yells, laughter, the constant hum of conversation, and muddy from the last rainfall. But there wasn't a rooster who strutted about here the way King Henry did at Croyland.

Jerval was yelling good-natured insults at his men, keeping a tight rein on his horse to avoid hitting the children that ran in and out of his path, greeting them by name. Like Croyland, Camberley was a huge village, enclosed within stone walls six feet thick.

The inner bailey, closed in by lower walls that were, Chandra thought, thicker even than the outer walls, made her blink in surprise. All was orderly and clean. The ground was paved with cobblestones that slanted downward to allow the rain to run easily into the outer courtyard. Low-roofed sheds were clustered about the great keep, and she sniffed the air, suddenly hungry at the smell of fresh-baked bread.

Jerval dismounted and she started to jump down from Wicket's back when something stilled her. She waited for Jerval to lift her down, which he did.

She heard all the people cheering.

"That was well done of you," he said. He called out names, so many names, she knew it would take her a very long time to remember all of them. So many new people to get to know, so many children, and the animals, more running free within the walls here than at Croyland.

She heard Ranulfe tell the men who stood around Wicket, "Aye, it is milady's destrier."

"Hard to believe," said another man, "although she handled him easily enough when they rode in."

Bayon said, "Our lady is like none you've ever known, Blanc."

"Look at that glorious hair — I'll wager Julianna isn't too pleased. She had hoped for an ugly heiress."

She followed Jerval up the winding staircase, into the Great Hall, and drew to a halt, looking about. There were no rushes on the stone floor, and there was a sweet smell in the air, as if everything had been scrubbed with perfumed soap. The stone walls were covered with thick tapestries, and the wooden tables and chairs gleamed with wax. There were at least a dozen servants, all of them looking very industrious until they saw Jerval. There were excited murmurs, and he smiled and called them together to meet Chandra.

She greeted them pleasantly, trying to memorize all the curious faces, for these were the indoor servants, and she would be seeing them every day.

After Jerval had sent them all back to work, he said, "Camberley servants respond quite well without being cuffed about. You can be certain that my mother's commanding voice keeps them in line."

"It smells so clean," Chandra said, sniffing the air. "There are no dogs about."

"No, but you'll soon accustom yourself to it. They are kept outside. I will introduce Mary to Alma, my old nursemaid and something of a seer, who will make her comfortable. There is a small room next to Julianna's that she may have. Now let me show you to our bedchamber," Jerval said.

She walked beside him up the thick, winding stone stairs to the upper floor. There seemed to be a different servant with each step.

Jerval's bedchamber, she had imagined, would look like her father's — nearly bare, its walls hung with weapons and its floor covered with thick reeds. She was dead wrong. His chamber had none of these things. The room faced south, through rows of narrow windows paned with small squares of glass, and the afternoon sunlight filled the room with reflected light. The walls were hung with colorful tapestries, and between them were tapers held in twisted silver mounts. The floor was strewn with thick, brightly colored Flemish carpets. The bed was set upon a dais, not as large as her father's, but encased in beautifully embroidered covers that touched the floor. There was a high, carved wooden screen set in a corner, and behind it was a large wooden tub and wooden racks that held linen and towels. She could not imagine that the king's chambers at Windsor were more magnificently furnished.

She stood still, her hands on her hips, and announced, "This is hardly a man's room."

He merely laughed at the heap of scorn in her voice. "I trust you are wrong," he said. "This man is your husband, and he gives you pleasure every night. I believe my mother added the carpets and racks, since it will also be a lady's room."

"My bedchamber is nothing like this."

"No, but you are a lady, and naturally, you will want to thank my mother for her thoughtfulness."

Two boys interrupted them, carrying buckets of hot water. As Jerval spoke to the boys, Chandra sat in a high-backed chair and shifted her bottom on the soft, velvet-covered cushion. She realized that her hair was tangled about her face. Her clothes were none too clean. Her smell was ripe.

After the boys left, Jerval offered her the tub. She couldn't imagine at that moment taking off her clothes in front of him. It was true that he had stripped her naked, or nearly naked, every night since they had married, but there was full daylight now. She shook her head.

She did, however, watch him pull off his clothes. She did not look away when he was naked. She saw him ease slowly down into the hot water. He grunted with pleasure. He leaned back and closed his eyes.

"You will need a tub of fresh water," he said after a time. "Four days of grime have left it black. This time I won't ask you to join me."

She said, "I do not mind waiting." She tried to focus on the orchard below the windows — apple trees, pear and peach trees, covered with tight buds. It was a beautiful, lush spot.

"It is very different here."

"Aye, I know it," he said from the tub, and she looked to see his hair and face lathered. "Will you scrub my back this time?"

There was no reason not to. She scrubbed him, no particular gentleness in her strokes. Soon, he was laughing up at her, and it was only her quickness that kept him from pulling her down into the water on top of him.

It was much later before she was in her own bath, for Mary came to visit after Jerval left, and nothing but praise flowed from her mouth.

"Everything is so neat and clean," she said for the third time, as three servants holding buckets came into the chamber. "Ah, here is water for you."

She left Chandra, humming under her breath.

Chandra accepted the help of a young girl whose name was Matta. Soon she was dressed in a soft, pale blue silk gown and fastened a blue leather belt about her waist. She looked at herself one final time in the polished silver mirror, and left the bed-chamber.

There were at least fifty people seated at the trestle tables in the Great Hall, and a score of servants served the evening meal. All their faces were upon her as she entered; all of them now stared.

Jerval rose and called to her. As she walked to the huge, high-backed chair beside him on the dais, he shouted over the hall, "My lady and wife, Chandra de Vernon." She started at her new name, and felt a crushing moment of homesickness. She smiled, seeing shock on many of the men's faces, for she had arrived looking like a grubby boy.

"That silver thing beside your trencher," Jerval said, as he handed her a fat slice of warm bread, "is called a fork. You see, it has two prongs. It makes it easier to get your food to your mouth. It takes a bit of getting used to, but I think you'll appreciate it soon enough." He picked his up and speared a piece of meat with it.

"It is particularly useful with fish," he said, watching her efforts. "Here, try it on the lamprey." He wrapped his fingers about hers, guiding her hand in the proper motion.

She scooped up the eel easily, and laughed. "It is ridiculous, this thing, but perhaps it isn't entirely worthless."

"Ah, Jerval," Malton, the master-at-arms, called out. "Sir Eustace was here. He seemed peeved that he had not been told of your wedding. I let him believe it was to Chester's squint-eyed heiress. He will be in a frenzy of jealousy when he sees your lady."

"Who is Sir Eustace?" Chandra asked.

Mark said, "Sir Eustace de Leybrun was wed to Matilda for a time — Jerval's older sister — but she died in childbed. He is not a particularly amiable fellow. He still comes about."

"Mark is too sweet-tongued," Malton said. "Your husband will want to keep you well in sight whenever Sir Eustace visits Camberley. He's a leering braggart. And when he sees you, my lady, he might even forget that one small shred of honor that lies deep within him."

Mark said lightly, "Now that you are wed, Jerval, he will have to be content with his own lands."

"Aye," Malton agreed, "with the sons you and your lady will breed, he'll never know Camberley, save as a bothersome guest."

Jerval didn't want Eustace to ever see Chandra. He knew he would take one look at her and run his thick tongue over his lips as he did whenever he saw a girl that pleased him. No, what concerned Jerval, if Eustace ever came to Camberley, was that Chandra would take offense and mayhap stick her knife between his ribs. He smiled a bit at the thought. Perhaps not a bad end for the man.

Malton called out, "Perhaps the Scots will pay us a visit before Lord Hugh returns. It was a hard winter up north, and I'll wager the heathen are hungry for our cattle."

He saw that the lady was looking at him, so beautiful she was, incredibly so, but perhaps he had frightened her, regardless of seeing her mounted on that huge destrier. "There's never much danger, my lady."

"Do you ever ride after them, Malton?"

"Aye, and it's better sport than a boar hunt. The Scots are good fighters, and it keeps the men from growing bored."

"You will not fight them, Chandra," Jerval

said, stuck a good-sized bit of lamprey into her mouth when she would have disagreed, and grinned at her. "Leave go. There is much you can do, but not that. No fighting. No trying to best any of our enemies. That is my job and I do it well. And no, do not accuse me of changing since we wed. I have always felt that way."

She chewed on the eel and said nothing more.

Mary said, as she and Chandra climbed the stairs at evening's end, "Jerval was right. The old woman, Alma, has been very kind to me. He said she was something of a seer. I believe he is right. What a marvelous banquet we were served tonight, and with no warning at all of Sir Jerval's return. I am quite impressed with Lady Avicia's housekeeping."

Chandra grunted. "I pray she will continue to take care of everything."

"Sir Mark gave me a tour of all the outbuildings. The kitchens are huge, Chandra, and the fellow who oversees the cooking is marvelous. And the jakes are set along the outer wall. Only a southerly breeze will raise an odor. And there are so many children, all of them fat, obviously well fed. Camberley is a rich keep. Ah, here we are. I'll bid you good night now, for Sir Jerval is likely to be coming soon. It is a beautiful bedchamber. You will never shudder with cold here."

"Your room is all right, Mary?"

"It is a marvel, like this one."

When Jerval entered his bedchamber some time later, he drew up short at the sight of Chandra wrapped in three blankets, curled on her side atop a carpet, a thick blanket pulled to her chin, sound asleep on the floor next to his bed. Like a damned dog, he thought. He stood over her for a moment, then leaned down and gently scooped her into his arms and carried her to the bed.

Chandra felt the soft bed beneath her back, felt his hands on her bed gown. She tried only once to slap his hands away; then she simply said, "I will not enjoy this tonight. I have suffered too much enjoyment from you. I am tired of it. I wish you to leave me alone."

And she turned over onto her side away from him.

He laughed and pulled her back. In but a moment, she was naked, spread out for him to look at her, which he did for a very long time.

"I will torture you with more enjoyment," he said, then rose to strip off his own clothes. "I want you to be brave, to bear with this dreadful enjoyment, to force yourself to

cry out when you gain your woman's release."

"I don't want to."

He merely began kissing her, and he was
grateful that he didn't have to fight her and
that she didn't try to bite his mouth. When
she cried out, her back arched, panting as if
her heart would burst from her chest, he
smiled down at her and came deep inside
her. She held him tightly when he collapsed
against her.

"I am sorry to torture you so much," he
said, kissing her mouth, the tip of her nose,
her chin.

Jerval awoke the next morning to find
himself alone in his bed. He wasn't surprised. It was thus every morning when he
woke up. Nor did he believe anymore that
she had merely left their bed to fetch him
some bread and cheese. He was whistling as
he dressed quickly and strode down to the
hall, where he was told by Maginn, one of
his father's young pages, that milady had
broken her fast early and gone he knew not
where.

Jerval ate warm, crusty bread, drank a
tankard of rich ale and set out to find her. To
his surprise, Wicket remained in the stables.
So she hadn't ridden out. That was rather
intelligent of her since Malton would most

assuredly have demanded to accompany her if she wished to leave the keep.

He knew what she had done. He was, in fact, quite sure that she had walked out, probably whistling, likely through the postern gate in the north wall.

She shouldn't have done that. She was new here, and even though she was his wife, not everyone would know that yet. She could be in danger.

He took Wicket. According to Dobbe, the wizened old graybeard who attended the cows, she had indeed left through the small north gate, alone.

He galloped Wicket alongside the lake, thinking she might have gone swimming, for the sun was warm overhead, the night storm having blown itself out. He did not find her there, so he turned Wicket onto the rutted, muddy road that led to the small village of Throckton. Suddenly Wicket reared up on his hind legs and whinnied loudly. Jerval saw Chandra walking along the narrow road toward them, Lord Hugh's most vicious boarhound, Hawk, coming up fast behind her, fangs bared. Dear God, the dog was going to attack her.

He kicked his heels into Wicket's side, yelled at the top of his lungs, and rode as hard and fast as he could to save her.

Chapter 14

No, wait, Hawk wasn't attacking. He was carrying a knobby stick in his great mouth, gobs of slobber dripping off his muzzle. What was going on here? Jerval swallowed his yell, saw that she wasn't looking at him but at the huge boarhound, coming up fast, his damned tail high and wagging. The hound stopped in his tracks. His tail continued to wag. Jerval watched her lean down, cuff Hawk on his thick neck, pull the stick from his mouth, and hurl it away from her. Hawk bounded off into the thicket beside the road to fetch the stick.

Only he and his father played like that with Hawk. No one else, not even his keeper, Dakyns.

He felt like a fool. He cursed beneath his breath. She looked up at him then, and waved. She had the gall to both wave and smile, when he'd believed her to be in grave danger of being torn apart by his father's hound.

She'd cuffed that damned vicious hound, and he'd slobbered on her hands.

Chandra dropped to her knees, ignoring Jerval now, as Hawk galloped back to her, grinding the stick between his ferocious teeth. He dove toward her, nearly tipping her over backward, dropped the stick at her feet, and licked her face with that huge tongue of his. She laughed, threw her arms about his neck, and hugged him to her. Hawk pulled back suddenly, his ears flattened to his head.

"Nay," she said, hugging him again, stroking his massive head. "It is just Jerval, come to play with us." She clutched the hound to her, but he began now to bark wildly in welcome and bounded toward Jerval.

She rose slowly, eyeing her destrier and the man on his back. He was riding Wicket. Wicket had never allowed anyone on his back save her.

Jerval dismounted, gave Hawk an indifferent pat on his head, and strode to her, wanting to grab her to him, he was so relieved that she was all right, and yell in her face for even coming close to Hawk, for leaving the safety of the keep. He came to a halt two inches from her. He opened his mouth to flay her.

"What are you doing on my horse?"

His outrage filled his craw to overflowing.

"You have the gall to face me down about riding Wicket? Have you no sense? You are out here alone. You do not know what sort of man might be lurking, eager to take you. You are with Hawk, the most vicious of all my father's hounds. He could have ripped your neck apart."

"I am not alone. I am with Hawk. He likes me. There was never a problem with him. No one would come close to me with him about. It is you who are at fault here. You are riding Wicket. He is my horse, no one else's. Why are you riding him? Why did he allow you to?"

He kept a firm hold on himself. "The only reason you are not riding him is because you knew my men would never let you out of the keep walls without protection. So you made a friend of Hawk and slithered out the postern gate. At least you had the brains not to venture out by yourself."

"Aye, mayhap that is the way it appeared."

"Don't lie to me. That is exactly what you did."

"Very well. That is very handy, that gate. It is a beautiful day. I was bored. I wanted to explore. Hawk wished to have some exercise. He is all the protection I needed. I do not like you riding Wicket. I don't understand why he let you ride him."

He plowed his fingers through his hair to calm himself. He could only shake his head. "Your horse and my father's hound have no sense. But hear me, Chandra, what you did was beyond foolish. Hawk could have chewed your arm off instead of falling in love with you. I don't understand it. Why did you leave the safety of Camberley without telling me? And don't you dare whine about me lying there snoring."

"Well, you were snoring. You woke me up. I could not go back to sleep."

"Then why didn't you kiss me to wake me up?"

She looked at him as if he were mad.

He could only shake his head. "That is no excuse for leaving the safety of the keep. I still cannot believe that my men allowed you to leave by yourself. They will not allow this to happen again, Chandra."

"I am to be a prisoner now?"

"By all God's gifts to the world, are you really so witless? Or, for some devious reason I cannot understand, are you simply torturing me?"

"I am not witless or devious."

"Then what are you?"

For an instant, her eyes went perfectly blank. Then she said slowly, and he saw the deep uncertainty in her, "I don't know anymore what I am. I am not what I was, but now? Mayhap you're right and I am witless."

He cursed, then pulled her against him. She was stiff. He stroked his big hands up and down her back, willing her to ease against him. He kissed her neck, tasted her, and said, "Listen to me. You are not a prisoner. You are my wife. That is what you are now. Have no more doubts about that. Now, you will exercise your sense — do you understand me? And no, don't accuse me of changing."

She leaned away from him. "You have changed toward me, and you are nearly spitting in my face."

"No, I wasn't spitting. I was kissing you."

She said nothing at all to that.

He looked at her face, into her eyes, wondering what she was thinking now. "Well then, that is good. You understand." He released her, turned away and mounted Wicket. "Wicket is a fine animal. He took to me readily. It seems Wicket recognizes me more quickly than you do as his master."

"I don't want you to ride him again, Jerval. In fact, you should get off him right now. I will ride him back to the keep. You will stay with Hawk."

"You walked out here. You can walk

back." He laughed and gave her a wave and galloped away. She did not know it, but Jerval didn't let her out of his sight until she was safely inside the postern gate.

Life, he thought, as he brushed Wicket's broad back in the dimly lit stable, was proving to be quite a diversion. Diversions were fine, but too many of them just might send him to his knees.

When he joined her at one of the long benches in the Great Hall, he broke off a piece of warm bread, chewed it with great appreciation, and said, "Did you enjoy the storm last night?"

She ate her own bread, chewing it for a very long time. He leaned close and kissed her nose. When she would have pulled away, he said, "At least you were warm and safe because I held you very close. You see, I continue to be useful to you even after I have felled you with pleasure."

She ate more bread and chewed and chewed before saying sourly, "Mayhap there is some truth there."

He laughed.

"Chandra," Mark called out, Mary at his side, "what were you doing outside the keep walls? Jerval was very worried about you. Were you hunting?"

"She was playing with this damned

hound," Jerval said, pointing to Hawk, who was not supposed to be in the Great Hall, but when he was trotting so happily next to Chandra, Jerval hadn't had the heart to kick him out.

"By all the saints' rigorous prayers, that curdles the blood," Mark said. He started to stick his hand out toward Hawk. The hound growled at him.

"Chandra gets along well with most animals," Mary said. "It is a gift."

"Lady Avicia won't like the hound inside, Jerval," Malton said, watching Chandra hug the hound again, his slobber wetting her arms to her elbows. "By God, but he's a good beast. He is known as the scourge of all enemies of Camberley. I don't like the look of this at all."

"Don't fret, Malton. She won't tame him," Jerval said. "I will have Dakyns fetch him soon."

"More's the pity," Chandra said. "Dogs belong in the Great Hall, by the fireplace."

All the men agreed with her, but kept silent.

Lady Avicia swept into the hall, her sweet memories of Lord Richard and his wicked compliments faded from her mind during the long, bone-jolting journey back to

Camberley. She was tired, impatient for a bath, and if the truth be told, itching to discover how Camberley had fared in her absence, with Chandra at the helm. She hugged her son, searching his face for a moment, then nodded to her daughter-in-law, all the while looking about for signs of disorder. She soon found a collection of dust on her beautiful trestle table. She ran her fingers over the table surface.

"You have been at Camberley a week, Chandra," she said, holding up her dusty fingertip.

Chandra eyed her in absolute amazement and said, "Six days, actually."

"Nearly seven. It's almost afternoon."

Jerval shouted for wine and honey cakes to be brought into the hall, then turned to greet his father, leaving Chandra alone with his mother and Julianna. He had mentioned to his wife several times that she should at least give the keep servants instructions, but she had shrugged indifferently, and he had let her be. It had been Jerval who had told the servants to carry on, but they were used to his mother's sharp eyes and attention to every detail, and he knew the wenches had grown lax in their duties. He decided to let Chandra fend for herself, at least for the moment.

"You look tired," he said to his father.

"I am too old for such journeys," Lord Hugh said, heaving his bulk into his great chair, "and this damned gout hasn't given me a moment's peace."

"All the good food and wine didn't help. Did you leave Lord Richard and Lady Dorothy in good health?"

"Oh, aye. Even Richard looked ready to take his ease by the time his vassals left. Sir Andrew broke one of Richard's ribs in the tourney — the one you didn't stay for." Hugh glanced over toward Chandra, who stood stiffly beside Avicia. "None of the men blamed you at all for leaving so quickly. By God, what a beauty she is. I trust you are enjoying her as you should?"

Jerval could not keep down a very satisfied smile.

"Aye, so it should be. What does your lady think of her new home?"

Jerval shrugged. "She knows every inch of Camberley — outside the keep."

"Ah, well then, let your mother handle that."

"It is that notion that worries me." He turned as he overheard his mother ask Chandra, "Have the servants treated you as they should, child? Have they done your bidding?"

"Aye, they have, although I have not bade them to do anything in particular."

Wrong answer, Jerval thought.

"Come, Aunt," Julianna said, looking toward Jerval beneath her lashes, "surely you do not expect a *warrior* to take interest in a lady's duties?"

"Why, Julianna," Chandra said, looking toward her, "how kind of you to explain things so nicely and so very clearly."

"Your wine, my lady," Mary said in that soothing voice of hers. "Your honey cakes are delicious. I have wanted to ask the cook for his recipe."

"It is I who gave the varlet the recipe," Lady Avicia said, softening. She found herself staring at Mary. Odd that she had not noticed at Croyland that the girl had the look of Matilda, her sweet, biddable daughter, whose memory always brought a pang of sadness. "You are thin, Mary," she said. "I hope you will be happy here at Camberley."

Lord Hugh's mouth was full at the moment, else his jaw would have dropped to his chest at his lady's words.

"I am very happy, my lady. Camberley is so lovely, and there are so many windows — I feel as if I am standing in the sunlight."

"Do you also know about armor, Mary,"

Julianna said, "or do you just polish Chandra's?"

Mary's sweet smile did not waver as she said to Julianna, "Unfortunately I have not Chandra's skill — more's the pity. Also, she always sees to her own armor."

Chandra felt a moment of envy at Mary's skill in dealing with Julianna. Julianna's eyes hardened, and then she turned to Jerval and gave him a dazzling smile. So that was the way things still were. Chandra wondered idly if she would have to clout the nonsense out of Julianna's head.

"I trust the evening meal will be well prepared."

Chandra said to her mother-in-law, "I see no reason why it should not be. The servants know now that you are returned."

"We will see," Avicia said, ready to bolt for the cooking sheds.

She was on the point of leaving when suddenly she heard Dakyns shouting. She whirled about to see Hawk bounding into the hall, barking loudly, running directly at Chandra. Avicia yelled and jerked Mary behind her to protect her.

Lord Hugh thrust out his big hand to grab the hound, but Hawk eluded him. He grabbed at his sword as the beast dove at Chandra.

"Nay, Father," Jerval said, laughing as he stayed his hand.

Lord Hugh stood stunned as he watched his most vicious boarhound plant his paws upon Chandra's shoulders and lick her face with his huge tongue.

"What is that wretched beast doing in here? Get him out, at once."

"Don't worry, Mother," Jerval said, grinning at her. "He is here because he heard Chandra's voice. It is all I can do to keep him out of our bedchamber. He is forever at Chandra's heels."

Avicia drew herself to her full height. "None of those disgusting beasts is to foul the keep. Get him out of here at once or I'll have him killed."

It was a mistake, and she knew it the moment her husband took a step toward her. "I beg your pardon," Lord Hugh said, staring at his wife.

Avicia splayed her hands in a helpless gesture that had, some thirty years ago, led Hugh to the erroneous conclusion that his bride was a soft-spoken girl who needed his strong man's protection. "You promised, Hugh. The dog is fouling Chandra and making a nuisance of himself."

"Oh, no," Chandra said, "you needn't worry for me, and he is not fouling me, for

Jerval and I bathed him but yesterday."

"He nearly ripped my arm off," Jerval said. "The men were laying bets on how long it would take him to knock me on my back."

"God and the angels," Hugh said, torn between laughter and his wife's outrage. "You actually gave this vicious hound a bath? A *bath?*"

"I did not want to bathe him," Chandra said, "but Jerval thought it would make Hawk more acceptable to you, my lady. My father's hounds are always in the keep. You, my lord, were always throwing bones to Graynard during supper."

"Aye, that's true," Hugh said, rubbing his chin, remembering Graynard's nose rubbing against his legs. He forgot that he had cursed the fleas.

"Hugh?"

"The hound is clean," Hugh said. "As long as Chandra is willing to keep him that way, he may stay here in the Great Hall."

Chandra closed her arms about the hound's neck and let him throw his great weight against her, dragging her to her knees.

"As you will, my lord," Avicia said, tight-lipped. She remembered all too well the pigsty Camberley had been when she first wed Hugh, for there had been no lady in residence for several years. She looked toward her daughter-in-law, recognizing that she was beautiful, that she had character and intelligence, but knowing to her innards that the girl saw things as a man would. That wasn't good. She would have a battle on her hands.

"Hawk is almost human sometimes, my lady," Mary said. "Indeed, when Jerval yelled at him to hold still for his bath, he seemed to understand. Alma gave me some powdery leaves to rub into his coat. She said it would keep all the vermin away from him."

The girl was diplomatic, Jerval thought, staring at Mary. Unfortunately, that quality seemed foreign to his wife.

Chapter 15

Dinner that evening was set only for the family, well prepared, and served without mishap, thanks to Lady Avicia's last-minute visit to the cooking sheds. Jerval forked a piece of roast pork into his mouth, closing his eyes a moment at the taste. His mother's voice brought his head up. "There are no idle hands at Camberley, Chandra, as I'm certain you've noticed. Everyone has duties to perform, and we do not cater to slothfulness." She directed her next words to her husband. "When we arrived, I heard that slut Glenna laughing in the solar."

Lord Hugh said between bites, "The girl has her uses, Avicia." He choked on the meat. "Er, that is, she *had* her uses."

"What do you mean, my lord?" Chandra asked.

"He means nothing at all," Jerval said.

"Tell me, Chandra," Avicia said, wondering how her daughter-in-law could be such a dolt about such matters, "what were your duties at Croyland?"

241

Chandra smiled. "There were no idle hands at Croyland either. I helped Crecy with the ledger accounts. Lord Richard despises numbers, and during the past year, I saw to Croyland's purchases and sales."

"You read?"

"Aye, my lady, my father wished it. Crecy taught me."

"We ladies do not involve ourselves in that sort of thing at Camberley," Avicia said, and wondered silently why not.

"You have an honest steward then? One who can count beyond his ten fingers?"

Avicia thought of the oily Damis, whom she had distrusted ever since the day she had seen him strutting in a new fur-lined tunic in the village over a year ago. "I don't know," she said slowly.

"Actually," Jerval said, "I handle quite a bit of that now, Chandra. Damis needs a close eye on his ledgers. My mother is thinking of that new tunic of his. I took the cost of it from his wages. The fellow does well enough now."

"But what did you do at Croyland that is appropriate for a lady?" Julianna asked.

"Chandra sings and plays the lyre beautifully," Mary said, "but you already know that, Julianna."

My little champion, Chandra thought,

looking at Mary. She said to Lady Avicia, "My mother directed the servants in the weaving, cooking, and cleaning. She never wished my help. Indeed, she didn't want anything from me. I know nothing of it."

"That makes no sense," Avicia said. "It is a mother's responsibility to train her daughter."

"That was not Lady Dorothy's view of things."

"Then I will teach you," Lady Avicia said, and she actually rubbed her hands together. "Since you are my son's wife and the future mistress of Camberley, there are many responsibilities that will be yours. There is the proper planning of the meals, seeing that the servants do their jobs well, clothes to be woven and mended, the gardens to be tended and, naturally, the care of guests. Ah, so many things to be done." Lady Avicia rubbed her hands together again as she said with too much relish, "Aye, no one will have to worry about this because I will instruct you."

Chandra didn't like that very happy look on her mother-in-law's face. She wasn't at all certain that instruction from Lady Avicia would be such a good thing. Probably not even a tolerable thing. She nearly shuddered. She'd spoken aloud about Lady Dorothy because the words had simply popped out of her mouth without her permission. She wondered what Lady Avicia would do now. She thought with horror of using a spinning wheel. Wisely, she kept her mouth shut.

Like his wife, Jerval wondered what would happen now. But what bothered him was what she had said about her mother.

Chandra said at last, "However, I believe that Croyland is the most magnificent keep in all of England."

Avicia said, "Magnificent mayhap, but the meals were ill prepared save for the marriage feast, the serving maids slovenly and shiftless and the keep filthy. There were bones and refuse in the reeds. I could not even walk about in the bailey without having my skirts soiled. Well, that is not quite true, but almost."

Jerval saw that Chandra would probably draw her knife to defend all the perfection of Croyland. He said, rising quickly, "It is late. You are all very tired, as are we. Chandra and I bid you good night."

"She insulted Croyland," Chandra said as she walked beside him up the stone stairs. "She dared to insult Croyland."

"The meals were not all that tasty," he said mildly, and leaned over to kiss her. "I do like your nose."

She shoved him back. "Leave me be, damn you. You will not make me laugh. You will not make me yowl again. You will not make my brain leap from my head."

He grabbed her hand, kept walking, and began whistling. Just before they reached their bedchamber, he stopped her and held her hands together in his. "Before we wedded, I never considered our life once it would actually begin here at Camberley. All I could think about was being inside you, kissing every bit of you. I nearly expired with lust. I still do. However, life has intruded. Now, my mother is mistress here, and her standards are exacting."

"Camberley should be like Croyland — a warrior's keep, not a sweet-smelling, useless hall where more attention is given to the cleanliness of the tables than to the fortifications."

"You have eyes. You see that Camberley is very well fortified. The keep is clean. All like it that way." He paused a moment, then said, "I am sorry that your mother didn't wish to teach you. It isn't natural. It must have been difficult for you. But no longer. Now, I know what you should do: just think of the way you feel after I have given you your woman's pleasure, then speak to my mother."

She was appalled. "I cannot. She would believe that I have lost all my wits."

"Aye, and that might be a good thing."

"She would see me as weak and soft and she would kick me."

He said thoughtfully, "Now, that's quite possible. However, I will keep a sharp lookout and see that she doesn't do that."

Chandra said, her eyes clouded with sudden memories that Jerval knew weren't good, "My mother hated me. For as far back as I can remember she couldn't bear to have me near her."

"But why?"

"I don't know. She beat me until I was big enough to fight back and then she stopped. She was afraid of me then."

"Why didn't you tell your father?"

Chandra gave him a long look, then shrugged. "I don't know why I told you that. It's not important, hasn't been for many years now."

"Why didn't you tell your father?" he asked again.

"She said she would poison him if I did. I believed her." Chandra shook herself then, as if waking from a dream. "I do not wish to be with you tonight, Jerval. I am angry because you see nothing good about me. I would very likely bite you."

A mother who hated and beat her own daughter? It made his guts churn, his belly cramp. She was right, though. It was years too late, and now this. He smiled at her. "Come. I will take my chances. I believe I will try some new things on you."

He did and she didn't bite him.

Before he fell asleep, he said against her neck, "There is so much good about you that it nearly breaks my heart."

She was soft and limp, her mind easy, vague. "What is good about me?"

But he was asleep.

Rolfe had to squint against the early-morning sun to make out the figure riding toward him. It was Sir Jerval's wife, astride her destrier. A sword was strapped at her side, and a shield was tucked under her arm. Her long woman's legs were encased in chausses, with cross garters binding them to her, and she wore a tunic of dark blue wool. Rolfe met Malton's astonished look, grinned, and spat into the dirt.

Malton drew a deep breath and wheeled about. "I don't like this, Rolfe. I don't think she is here just to cheer the men on. I must see Sir Jerval." He had seen her on the archery range with Jerval and Mark during the previous week, and of course she was a familiar sight in her men's garb riding her great destrier. But that Jerval would allow her to take part in the Scots' competition, that he could not believe. She was skilled, no doubt about that, but she was still a lady, she was a female, and she could be hurt.

He found Jerval naked to the waist, sluicing himself from a bucket of water at the well.

"Aye, Malton?" Jerval shook himself, took a towel from a giggling serving girl at his side, and rubbed it over his chest and head.

"By all the ancient gods," Malton said, "it's my lady. She's mounted on that beast of hers, in the tiltyard. She is carrying her sword. We are having the competition this morning. You know it is dangerous. She is a girl, a soft, beautiful girl who surely should not be anywhere near the practice field, and —"

"Of course she will not compete. Don't fret, Malton. She is just looking over the course."

"She looks like she is doing more than just looking."

"Nay, it is nothing more than her interest. She is well trained, so of course she would want to know how everything will be done."

Malton said nothing more. However, Jerval dressed more quickly than was his wont, mounted Pith, and followed Malton to the tiltyard. Chandra had been gone when he awakened that morning, but she always was. When, he wondered, would she not leave him? When would she stay and let him love her in the morning daylight?

He had seen her briefly when they were breaking their fast down in the Great Hall; then she had disappeared. Likely she was avoiding his mother. At least she never left the keep now without an escort. He had hope for her sense.

Jerval pressed his knees to Pith's sides and galloped to the far side of the tiltyard, where Chandra sat astride Wicket, looking everything over.

"Good morning, wife," he said, reining in Pith beside Wicket. "What do you think of the course? Have you picked your favorite to win?"

"Bayon explained it all to me," she said. "As to who will win, why, since I wish to compete, I must wager on myself."

As always, she sounded so sure of herself. He said slowly, "You must know that you cannot compete in this competition, Chandra. It is not a game. Archery, wrestling, and hunting are one thing, but not this. This is deadly serious."

"I am well used to riding at straw dummies. This course does not look all that difficult."

"It is misleading. You may watch. You might consider cheering for me." He leaned over, gripped her chin and kissed her hard. He felt the immediate response in her. He grinned as he straightened, looking directly through her tunic to her wildly beating heart, she was sure of that, and then rode away.

He rode to where all the men were mounted and waiting. "Prepare the Scots. Malton, you will keep the scores and count the seconds."

Chandra looked hard at the course. She'd studied it since early that morning. It was set the length of the practice field, with straw figures bound upright to long poles, spaced haphazardly, their heads tilted at odd angles. Her fingers fairly itched to draw her sword. She leaned forward to pat Wicket's glossy neck, guessing that success depended greatly on the destrier's skill.

As Ranulfe was readying himself for the first run, Lord Hugh rode onto the tiltyard and pulled his horse to a halt beside his son. "So, Jerval, I see your wife is here. Does she wish to show the men how to run the course?"

"She is watching, that is all. Hopefully she

will cheer for me as well."

"You do not sound certain that she will."

"Nay, I am not, but I am hopeful."

"It seems that I have saddled you with a hellion," Hugh said, grinning at his son, "but by damn, she is a beauty."

"Aye, I know it well." And the son smiled at the father. "She is exactly what I would want."

"Does she accept you yet as her master?"

"Probably not."

"I envy you the taming of her. Your mother believes that you give the girl too much rein, but all in good time."

"She bends — you just don't see it much as yet."

"Actually," said Lord Hugh, "I have seen none of it."

Maginn raised his arm, then, with a loud whoop, sliced it through the air back to his side.

Ranulfe raised his sword over his head and galloped toward the nearest straw Scot, yelling, *À Vernon! À Vernon!*" The straw head went hurtling into the air. There were thirty Scots in all, and by the time Ranulfe wheeled his horse about at the end of the run, fourteen had lost their heads.

"Not bad for a Cornishman," Jerval shouted out as the men cheered.

As the sewers raced through the course to fasten the heads back to the bodies, Chandra inched Wicket toward the field. She watched the next three men take their run, heard Malton call out their scores and their times, and wondered why they had all avoided the center of the course, where most of the straw Scots were bunched together. It was a narrow passage, to be sure, but to win, it had to be tried.

She called out, "What is the prize for winning?"

"Do not dare say it, Father," Jerval said. He called back to her, "It is two pieces of gold, Chandra." He wasn't about to tell her that he usually won and his prize was one of the serving maids, usually Glenna, because she knew how to pleasure him until his teeth ached. But that was over now, Glenna forgotten.

"That is a good prize," she said.

Lord Hugh gave a deep belly laugh. "So you will not tell her."

"Oh, no."

"It would make her jealous."

"It would hurt her. And that is different."

They turned their attention back to the course. Maginn raised his arm and dropped it, but instead of Thoms galloping toward the course, it was Chandra, shouting, *"À Avenell,*

À Avenell!" as Wicket bounded forward.

Chandra felt a surge of pleasure as her sword sliced through the first straw neck, sending its head flying upward before it landed, careening wildly on the ground. It was not so difficult. Four more heads went flying, clean strikes, all of them. Then she whipped Wicket toward the center lane. She realized quickly enough that she had to hold Wicket on a straight path, and that meant she would have to lean as far as she could, her arm extended to its full length, to have a chance of reaching the straw Scot. Then, within but an instant of time, she would have to get her sword in her other hand to lean dangerously far the other way to behead the next Scot.

She would do it. She set Wicket down the center of the course. She whipped her sword up high, extended it as far as she could, and its weight nearly pulled her from the saddle. By the time she recovered, she'd missed the Scot. She whipped her arm back, having no control now, nearly slashing her thigh. She tossed her sword to her left hand. The time cost her dearly, for a straw Scot to the left was nearly upon her. She twisted about in the saddle, unwilling to pass it by, and slashed her sword at it. It sliced cleanly through the straw man's chest but embedded itself in the pole. She did not release soon enough, and in the next moment, she was flying off Wicket's back. She landed on her bottom and rolled instantly to her side. She was laughing at herself when she managed to get to her feet.

She was trying to work her sword from the pole when Jerval galloped to her side and jumped from Pith's back. "The course is much more difficult than I thought," she said over her shoulder to him, and kept working at the sword.

He grabbed her, jerking her about to face him. "Are you all right?"

"Aye, but I was a fool to take the center. I had not realized how far the reach was, and how little leverage and time I would have. I am all right, Jerval. My bottom is sore, that's all."

She wasn't hurt. He tightened his grip about her upper arms and shook her. She tried to jerk away from him, but he held her tight. He stuck his face right into hers. "You disobeyed me."

She tried to pull away again, but it was no use. He was very strong. She said, her voice reasoned and calm, "How could I not? Your order was unfair. With a bit of practice, I could take the course as well as any of the men."

"When will I ever learn?" he asked no one in particular. "When will you recognize that when I tell you something, I mean it? That when I give you an order, there is a very good reason for it? Even if I do not choose to give you a reason, it matters not. I am your husband. You are to obey me."

"Aye, you are my husband, I realize this well every night when you force me to feel things that I never wanted to feel. Why are you not proud of me? Why do you not encourage me? Praise my skills? You would have before we married."

Jerval suddenly felt the utter silence. None of his men had moved. All just stood there, watching. Why? Did they believe he would beat her? "I have no intention of giving the men any more of a show than we already have. If I have changed it is because I'm now your husband and you, you damned girl, are now my responsibility."

Before he could drag her to Wicket, the men were no longer silent. They surged toward them and gathered about her. Ranulfe thwacked her on the back. "God's bones, lady, it was not so bad for your first time."

Malton groaned, rolled his eyes, and looked toward Jerval, who was just standing there, not believing what he was seeing. Jerval had judged wrong.

Ranulfe said, "She sliced off five heads before she tried the center. No, it was not bad at all."

Chandra grinned. "Thank you. I was a fool to believe it was easy."

"Aye, if you had realized how hard it is, you would not have a bruised butt," said Bayon, and he too buffeted her shoulder. Just as though she were one of them.

Jerval saw Malton eyeing him, shook himself, threw back his head and roared, "Back to work, all of you bleating goats, or there will be a lot of sore butts from the flat of my sword."

When they were finally alone again, Jerval said, "Do not think that all the men's praise changes a thing. Come with me."

"They thought I did well. They praised me, encouraged me."

"Aye, you did well for your first and last time. Now come." She dug in her heels, but it didn't matter. He dragged her to Wicket, grabbed her about the waist, and tossed her into the saddle. "You will follow me, Chandra."

Malton shook his head as he watched Jerval and Chandra ride from the tiltyard and swing to the east toward the lake. "Jerval's lady is in for it."

"I told him she wants taming," Lord

Hugh said. "Not an easy task even though he is one of the most strong-willed men I know. He was wrong to believe the men would agree with him and condemn what she did. They were proud of her. It was amazing."

Lord, but Chandra had made Jerval look the fool today, but perhaps his men did not realize it. Well, Malton did. He hoped Jerval wouldn't beat her too badly.

Chandra followed Jerval to the small emerald lake. He dismounted and stood waiting, hands on his hips, for her to do likewise.

"The men didn't seem to think I did badly."

"I would not care if you had beheaded each and every one of those damned Scots. That is not the point."

As soon as her feet touched the ground, he grabbed her about the waist, fell to one knee, and upended her over his thigh. He brought his hand down on her buttocks as hard as he could. She already hurt, and his hand was hard, very hard. She yelled curses at him and twisted frantically to free herself.

"You could have killed yourself," he said, and slammed his hand hard again. He wished her bottom was bare, for the thick woolen chausses protected her.

"Stop it! Damn you, my father would never give me such an order. Stop beating me."

He did not stop. Every time his palm connected with her bottom, he had something to say. "I am tired of your disobedience. That is what is important here. You must do as I say. I must be able to trust you. Don't you understand that?"

"You are not responsible for me, damn you. Stop pounding me."

To her surprise, he did. He rose abruptly and rolled her off his leg onto the slightly grassy incline; she managed to stop herself before she rolled into the water. She rose to her knees. She hurt badly. She felt tears sting her eyes and swallowed.

He stood over her, his hands on his hips. "Listen to me, Chandra, and listen well. Never again will you disobey me. Your behavior is that of a spoiled child. Furthermore, you disregard my mother's every instruction. It is time for you to grow up. Dammit, woman, do you think any of the pages, squires, or men would ever disobey me? No, keep your mouth shut else I'll take you over my knee again. From now on, you will meet with my mother every morning and learn those things you are expected to know. If you hold your tongue and become skilled at household tasks, then I will allow you to continue on the practice field in the afternoons. Do you understand me?"

"Make your own beer."

"Do you understand?"

"Aye." She managed to stand up. She walked slowly, favoring her right leg, to where Wicket stood grazing on the water reeds.

She saw that Jerval was still standing some feet away from her. He had beaten her. Slowly, she mounted Wicket, inching toward Pith. She reached out suddenly and grabbed Pith's loose reins.

She yelled at him as she whipped both horses about, "I will send Hawk back to walk with you. I dare you to beat *him!*"

She dug her heels into Wicket's sides, urging him up a steep slope to the path. Suddenly, there was a loud whistle, and in the next instant, Pith reared back, jerking at the reins in her hand. She toppled backward off Wicket's smooth rump, landed on her side in the thick grass and rolled down the slope, unable to stop herself. She heard Jerval laughing his head off.

She came finally to a stop and looked up to see her husband, legs apart and arms clasped over his chest, standing over her.

"I don't like you," she said, and he only laughed harder.

"Next time, you will know that even my horse obeys me. By all the saints' fevers, you are a mess."

She struggled, trembling, to stand up. Her tunic was ripped, and the cross garters on her right leg had come loose, leaving her chausses sagging and wrinkled like an old sack.

"Why don't you take a swim?" he called to her over his shoulder. "It will make you more presentable."

He jumped onto Pith's back and rode away from her.

It galled her so that she could think of nothing to yell after him. She pulled herself painfully to her feet and leaned over to fasten her cross garters. Then she stopped. He was right. She was a mess. She took off her clothes and dived into the small lake.

He watched her from the cover of the trees as she rubbed her bottom, the flesh reddened from his palms, before she dived cleanly into the water.

Chapter 16

Chandra sniffed, caught the smell of the jakes from a stiff south wind, and slipped back into the hall. She climbed the stairs past the family's chambers, until the steps twisted and narrowed and became finally a ladder that led to the summit of the keep. She paused on its board roof, gazing upward to the round turret that rose another twelve or so feet into the air. From atop the turret fluttered the orange banner of Camberley, embroidered with a black lion standing on his hind legs, his claws bared to all who approached.

She turned to gaze over the lush, wild countryside to the east. Small squares of tilled land set upon sloping hills dotted the thick forest. Beyond them she saw a sparkling blue lake that wound about the small village of Throckton with its thatch-roofed houses. The lake was small, but still; it reminded her of the sea, and of the tingly salt air that left tendrils of sticky, damp hair falling into her face. She felt suddenly homesick, felt immense hunger for that girl she had been, and tears stung her eyes. Then she saw herself straddling her husband, saw him as part of her, no way around that, deep inside her, and she was mewling like a weak pathetic animal, beyond herself and what she knew she had to be — strong and reliant, and alone, complete unto herself. She was astride him and she was only what he made her feel. In those moments, she had lost completely what she was, and it was just too much. She had to get away from him or that girl she had been at Croyland would die. She closed her eyes over the tears.

"I'm a weak fool." She turned away to look down into the inner bailey. People milled about below, their talk, their laughter, their yells muted by the distance. But there was one below her whom her eyes sought without her even being aware of it. Jerval was wiping down Pith, his large hands graceful, fluid. She drew herself up, for she did not wish to think about her husband, much less see him.

She heard the ladder creak and saw Mary's head. "Careful," she called out. "I don't like the sound of that ladder."

"This is like the top of a mountain," Mary said, looking about her. "I had not been up here before. It is beautiful." She sat down beside Chandra. "I saw you climbing the outside stairs, but I did not tell Lady Avicia where you were, so do not worry that she is searching the keep for you."

"What has she in store for me today?"

"I don't know," Mary said. She burst into tears.

"Mary — oh, my God, Mary, what is wrong? Did that old bat say something mean to you?"

"Oh, no, Lady Avicia is never unkind to me. Only to you. Let me stop these silly tears." She held her eyes closed for a moment, then sniffed, wiped her knuckles over her cheeks and said, "I'm sorry. There was no call for that. Oh dear, I had to speak to you away from the family and all the servants."

"Whatever is wrong if it is not Lady Avicia?"

"There is no easy way to say this. I am with child, Chandra."

Chandra stared at her. "Pregnant? You are pregnant? But how do you know?"

"Do you know naught about being a woman? My monthly flux has not come, and I feel sick to my stomach and I'm nauseated. Sometimes I vomit, particularly in the mornings. It can be nothing else."

"Graelam," Chandra said.

"There could be no other."

"But I do not understand. It was but one time. You were a virgin, how —" Even as she said the words, she felt Jerval deep within her, felt his seed filling her. How many times? Oh, God, nearly every night he'd wanted her, taken her, even two times the previous night, and it no longer even occurred her to fight him. Her monthly flux — had she missed it? She never bled the same time each month, so she didn't know. She wiped her hands on the skirt of her gown.

"It would seem that I am not very lucky."

Chandra jumped to her feet and struck her fist against the turret tower. She winced, then struck it again. "Damn men — all of them are wretched bastards, disgusting worms. They take what they want with no thought of what can come from their lust. I would slay them all if I could."

"Well, you cannot, Chandra. I do not know what to do. The de Vernons will have to know soon, for my stomach will begin sticking out, and they cannot allow me to stay, not a woman who will bear a bastard." Mary covered her face with her hands.

Chandra took Mary in her arms and held her tightly against her. "No, Mary, don't cry. I will think of something — I swear it to you. You must not despair, and you must promise me to say not a word to anyone. Now, wipe your eyes, else my mother-in-law will wonder why you are crying, and blame me for it."

Mary smiled through her tears. "You are probably right."

When they reached the solar, Chandra said again, "Don't worry. Trust me, please. Now, Mary, do you know anything about mending sheets?"

Mary smiled and nodded.

Chandra knew the only one to help her was her husband. She found the hall filled with angry, shouting men when she came in for the midday meal. "Quiet, all of you!" Jerval shouted, and turned to Malton. "Prepare a dozen men to ride within the hour. The Scots are but a few hours ahead of us, and the bastards are herding cattle, so it will slow them down."

"Hell's fires," said Lord Hugh, "I cannot ride with you, not with my damned foot swelled like a ripe melon."

"What has happened?" Chandra asked, walking quickly forward.

Jerval smiled at her — he couldn't help himself — then finished giving instructions to the servants to wrap food in the saddle pouches.

265

He walked quickly to her, kissed her mouth, and said, "The Scots attacked a northern demesne farm last night. They killed three of our people, razed the farm, and made off with the cattle. We leave shortly." He said to his father, "There is always a next time. It was only a small raiding party from the man's report, nothing to challenge us."

When Jerval entered their bedchamber, he found Chandra tying the cross garters on her men's chausses, a sword strapped at her waist, and a quiver filled with arrows fastened on her shoulder.

"You have not told me how skilled the Scots are with the bow, Jerval," she said, never pausing.

"Quite skilled."

"Then we must catch them in a crossfire."

"Aye, we will probably do that, depending on where we finally catch up with them."

When she walked past him to get her shield, he grabbed her shoulders and pulled her about to face him. "I wished you were in bed when I awoke this morning. How many times have I told you that? But you were not. Once again you ran away from me, from yourself. No, I cannot think of that right now. Listen to me, Chandra. You will remain here. Since my father is not well, I am

266

placing you in charge of guarding the keep. Do not disappoint me."

"But Malton can stay back. He is your master-at-arms."

"Yes, he will also remain." He sighed. He had tried to give her purpose, but it hadn't worked. He said now, his voice still gentle, so very calm, "I would order myself to be hanged if I were to allow my wife to ride into danger. You will remain safely within the keep. This time you will not disobey me, Chandra."

"You ride into danger, and you are my husband. What, I pray, is the difference?"

"I have twice your strength and endurance. I am far more skilled than you. I am far more experienced than you. You would be no match for the Scots. Just as you are no match for me."

"I beat Thoms in the tourney just last week."

"Thoms, like every one of the men, would give up his life before allowing you to be harmed. It is more than that. I cannot afford to have any of them distracted by your presence. They as well as I would be protecting you, not fighting with all their wits."

"I saved your life, Jerval. You were not protecting me that night Graelam nearly sent his sword through your belly."

Jerval sighed. "I have not forgotten, Chandra, but it changes naught. It is my responsibility to keep you safe. You will remain here."

"It is not fair."

He could think of nothing more to say. No, there was something more. He gripped her upper arms very tightly and shook her just a bit. "If something happened to you, I would not want to go on. I must keep you from danger, or else I fail myself. Do you understand?"

She didn't, of course. That brain of hers was already racing ahead to a confrontation with the enemy. "Of course you would go on," she said. "All men go on. How long would you grieve for me? Mayhap a month?"

He sighed. "I will likely see you in a couple of days." He turned on his heel, paused a moment at the door, and said over his shoulder, "You could wish me luck. You could kiss me, tell me you will pray for my safety. You could wish me Godspeed."

"Aye, I will wish you all of those things."

He realized then that he could not trust her. "Do you swear, Chandra, that you will remain at Camberley?"

He rocked back in surprise when she said, "Nay, I will not swear to that, Jerval, but I do

268

wish you Godspeed."

"Very well." He pulled the heavy key from the door and jerked it closed behind him. As he grated the key in the lock, he expected to hear her yelling at him, cursing him, but he heard nothing at all.

"Good-bye, Chandra."

He met his father in the hall and pressed the key into his hand. "Release her to-morrow, after we are well away. If you would give her supper, take care."

Lord Hugh looked at his son, finally nodded. "Has the girl no sense at all?" At his son's silence, he added, "Kill one of the jackals for me."

"Aye, Father, I will."

"Where is Chandra?" Mary asked, and Jerval saw her looking closely at each of the mounted men.

"I locked her in our bedchamber," he said. "Where she will stay." He strode away to mount his destrier.

"Poor Jerval," Julianna said as they watched the men ride from the keep, "wed to such an unnatural creature."

Mary wanted to slap her, but she didn't, just turned on her heel and walked back into the Great Hall. The truth burst upon her when she saw Lord Hugh with a huge key in his hand, speaking to an outraged Lady

Avicia. Mary stared upward, wondering what Chandra was doing, locked in her bedchamber.

Chandra was tying the ends of the sheets together, cursing her husband with every breath she drew. Satisfied finally with her knots, she carried the sheets to the window, only to discover that it would not open wide enough for her to squeeze through. She looked for a long time at the costly glass panes. She couldn't break them — they were too beautiful. But there was no hope for it.

She had to prove herself, once and for all. She had to prove to Jerval that she wouldn't shame him, that she could fight and fight well and that the men would grow accustomed to her going with them. She would always be at his side, and she would protect him. Aye, she would prove herself this time. She simply had to, or her life, as she had lived it at Croyland, as she wanted more than anything to continue living it, would end. His heel would be on her neck.

She shattered the glass with a wooden stool and felt pain at the sight of the shards of glass on the floor. She snaked the line of sheets out the windowframe and watched them tumble down the stone wall of the keep. She threw down her quiver and her bow and sword, squeezed through the narrow frame, and slithered slowly down. A group of small boys were looking up at her as she came down the sheets. She said not a word to them or to the servants she passed as she strode across the inner bailey to the stables. Hopefully they wouldn't even think to say anything, particularly to Malton, who was likely inside, speaking with Lord Hugh.

She looked toward Wicket, but knew that Jerval would spot him in an instant. She chose instead one of Jerval's other horses, an older roan stallion with a broad back, strong legs and a stout heart. When she led him from the stables, she looked about, wondering if anyone would try to stop her. She made for the cooking shed, where she found a loaf of bread and wrapped it in the none-too-clean blanket she had taken from the stable.

She rode the stallion through the outer courtyard, head up, as confident as a warrior on a quest, and waved to Beglie. The drawbridge was still down. She prayed he would let her pass. He waved back to her, his expression sour, and yelled something about bad weather on its way. He even pointed in the direction Jerval and his men had ridden. She realized then that he probably didn't recognize who she was. She was wearing a woolen cap over her hair. So much the better. Chandra laughed, dug her heels into the stallion's belly when he crossed the drawbridge, and let him lengthen his stride.

Chandra settled comfortably in her saddle. She kept a good half mile back from Jerval's men, planning to approach only when they made camp for the night. She was not foolish enough to believe herself invincible, and she would need the protection of their camp. She thought about Mary. She would speak to Jerval as soon as this fight with the Scots was over. He would know what to do.

Why did she assume that?

Why could she not solve the problem? Her mind went blank. What to do? What to do?

Well, what would Jerval do? He was a man, a man just like Graelam, who had raped Mary, made her pregnant. Oh, God, would Jerval say they had no choice? Would he say that since Mary was shamed she had to go to a convent? Chandra had to think; she had to save Mary.

She leaned forward in her saddle, her face on the roan's neck. She closed her eyes, smelling his sweat, feeling the steady rhythm of his hooves.

For the tenth time, she told herself that she had done nothing dishonorable. This time she would prove to Jerval that she was skilled and competent, that he needed her. This would end the strife between them. He would admire her, praise her, approve, finally, of what she was.

He simply had to.

She loved his mouth on her, loved him inside her, wanted those frantic wild feelings.

No, she wouldn't think about that.

Her exhilaration began to dim when the late afternoon air became damp and chill as the road snaked closer toward the sea. It was odd, she thought, pulling the wool cap tighter over her hair, how slowly the time passed when one was alone. Her stomach growled, and she thought of the single loaf of bread that would be her evening meal, indeed, all of her meals until — until what?

Fools acted in anger. Bigger fools acted in haste. And the very biggest fools acted out of vanity and arrogance. She had done all three. She should be riding in the midst of his men, not trailing after them, alone and at risk. She turned in her saddle to stare back in the direction of Camberley. She didn't see the keep, naturally; she saw Jerval's face, grim and set, and knew that even if she returned to Camberley now, he would know that she had disobeyed him, and his anger would be nearly as great. It was possible that she would be in more danger than she was in now were she to try to return to Camberley alone.

She was beyond a fool.

She could think of nothing to do except see this through. She slapped her arms against the cold and started singing to her horse. She didn't know his name.

Mark turned about to let the fire warm his back and tossed the pork rind over his shoulder. "You are quiet tonight, Jerval. What ails you?"

"Nothing."

"Do you brood on a new strategy for the Scots?"

Jerval raised his head, forced a smile. "If you would know the truth, I was wondering if my father will chance taking Chandra any supper."

"If he's wise, he'll send Mary. The girl handles Chandra better than you do. Even your mother treats Mary well, almost as if she were another daughter."

"But not another daughter-in-law."

Mark grinned. "I never forget the day poor Trempe wandered into the hall looking totally bewildered, Chandra's hauberk tucked under his arm, not having a single idea what he should do. Your mother just stood there beside him, the both of them staring at that damned hauberk."

"One of the links had come loose. Chandra had very nicely asked him to repair it for her."

"Which he did, I gather, once you gave him the order. I remember that at Croyland, her word was law, even with her father's armorer."

"You think I should have tied her up as well as locked her in her room?"

"Nay. As it is, she will likely starve herself, out of anger against you. It is difficult to balance the cocky, arrogant boy with the soft, beautiful woman."

"Aye," Jerval said only, but Mark knew him very well. They'd been raised together, after all. *He loves her*, Mark thought, hence his patience with her. Yet Chandra admired strength, and Mark wondered if Jerval would not more quickly gain her compliance if he simply buckled down and beat her. No, he couldn't, wouldn't do that. And if he did, Chandra would probably stick a knife between his ribs. Mark hated that there was nothing he could do.

"You know," Jerval said after a moment, to all of his men, "I have been thinking. I'm now firmly convinced that Sir John of Oldham is in league with the Scots. We have spoken of it before, but now my father agrees with me, even though he wishes he did not. It is odd that they appear so suddenly, as if they were in hiding near to us. My father remarked upon that first thing when we heard of this raid."

Ranulfe said, nodding, "Oldham's keep is but five miles to the east of Camberley, in the direction of the latest attack. I have never trusted Sir John, for he is a greedy man."

"Aye, and disloyal, I wager," Mark said. "I agree. He is involved with them."

"We will know for certain soon," Jerval said. He paused a moment, then smiled. "I have spoken to Chandra of Sir John and his dealings. She has plans of her own for him." He broke off, grinning into the fire.

Rolfe called out, "What does your lady wife say?"

"That we should visit Oldham, as well as the other keeps, and introduce her to our people. It is her idea to go sniffing about to see if Sir John is up to anything."

Mark said, "That is a good idea. A lady is more apt to be allowed to pry and ask questions. Sir John would likely fall all over himself to impress her."

"Aye. My wife can be quite reasonable. She has a good mind. But I will not let her go with us, for it could be dangerous. After we have dispatched the Scots to hell, we will ride to Oldham."

"And catch Sir John by surprise?"

"Aye. I look forward to the meeting."

They broke camp early the next morning and huddled close to their horses' necks for warmth as they rode, for a cold wind was blowing in from the sea. The demesne farm was naught save smoldering ashes when they reached it, and the peasants had just buried the three men slaughtered by the Scots. They did not tarry there. Jerval pushed them throughout the morning northward toward the border, over terrain that became ever more wretchedly stark and barren.

"Jerval — there is a man trailing us. Lambert spotted him but a few minutes ago."

Jerval reined in Pith and turned in his saddle at Arnolf's shout. "Is he alone?"

"For the moment he is. Lambert says he looks English."

Jerval was silent for a moment. "Still, there is a chance he may be tracking us for the Scots."

"One of Sir John's men?" Mark said, reining in his horse.

"Possibly. Have Lambert hang back and keep him in sight. I have no wish for the lot of us to be ambushed. Don't let the man catch sight of Lambert."

Their horses climbed a steep rise, and Jerval raised his hand for a halt behind some boulders that had scrubby oak trees growing in amongst them. Stretched before them was a wasteland of rocky, shallow hills dotted only with splashes of green moss. Jerval looked again behind them, tightening his grip on Pith's reins. The man trailing them had shortened the distance and was now riding but a mile behind them, his horse holding a steady pace.

"Let us wait for the fellow," he said to his men. "I wish to know what manner of fool he is."

They watched the man ride through a narrow stretch of road, bounded on each side by desolate heaps of rocks. They realized that he didn't see the four riders gallop from behind the rocks until they had formed a half circle around him. From where he sat, Jerval could hear their banshee cries as they swung their claymores in great arcs through the air.

"God's blood," Jerval shouted, "it's certain now that the fellow isn't one of them. It is four Scots against one. Don't they know that we are not that far ahead of them? Are they stupid?"

Mark said, "Evidently they don't know. Whoever he is, he's a fool, likely a dead one very soon. Can you imagine riding out here by yourself? At least he's brought them out into the open for us."

"We might as well try to save the fellow," Jerval said. He whipped Pith about, dug his heels fiercely into his destrier's sides and galloped back down the hill. He was yelling at the top of his lungs, as were his men, hopeful of turning the Scots' attention toward them and away from the single man.

Chapter 17

"Ye wish to taste death, do ye?"

Chandra nearly fell off her horse in shock to see the ferocious-looking Scot riding right at her, his huge claymore stretched above his head, a wide grin splitting his bearded face.

She felt equal amounts of fear and excitement pour through her. She yelled at him, "Come then, you ugly bastard. You will feel my sword cold in your guts!"

But she had no time to pull her sword from its scabbard, for the four men were closing swiftly about her.

"It's but a boy, lads," one of the Scots shouted. "Look at his pretty, smooth face! Just a little nipper, coming to find us."

"Aye, a wee English bastard."

"Let's slice him up and take his horse. He's old, but he's sound."

Four of them. Too many, too many. They were Scots, savages, without honor. They were the ones Jerval was hunting.

They had formed a loose circle around

her, coming no closer; even that huge, ugly one had drawn back. They were taunting her, waiting, she guessed, for her to lunge at one of them so that the others could slash at her back. No, it was simpler than that. They wanted her to drop her weapons and give up. They didn't want to take a chance of harming her horse.

She didn't move, just held the roan steady. The man she thought was their leader — he was a large man with a thick black beard and long black hair that flowed over his shoulders, eyes as black as a moonless night.

She whipped her horse to face him. "Are you so afraid of one man that you must hang back? I see now that you are naught but a worthless pack of scavengers. Cowards, the whole lot of you."

"Aiee, Alan," one of the men cried, "yer brave lad calls us cowards. What think ye o' that? Let me take him." He lashed his horse toward her, and Chandra turned to meet him. She slashed at him with her sword, and felt the blade tear into his arm. He lurched back, grabbing his arm, yelling, and she saw blood spurting out between his fingers. Chandra felt her wool cap suddenly jerked from her head, and her long, thick braid fell free down her back.

Jerval recognized the roan stallion in the next instant. It was Thunder, old now, but strong, steady, still valuable. He saw the man slash out at one of the Scots, draw blood, but then another of them closed behind him and jerked off his cap. A thick golden braid swung free.

By all the saints, it was Chandra.

No, no, it simply couldn't be his wife, that damned stubborn girl he'd locked in their bedchamber to keep her safe. Instant fear froze the blood in his veins.

But he wasn't surprised. He was many thing in that moment, but no, he wasn't surprised. He closed his eyes a moment against the fear of it.

He cursed even as he prayed that her hair would save her life. No man — even a Scot — would want to stick his sword through a woman. No, a man would want to rape a woman, not kill her.

"A girl," Alan Durwald shouted. "It's a bloody girl." He could not believe his eyes, and his men pulled their horses back, gaping at her in surprise. Alan slewed his head about to see the mounted Englishmen bearing down on them, their swords at the ready. They'd used this girl for bait? She was their tethered goat? He hated the English to his very soul, always had, but he had never imagined they could be so devious, so conniving.

He gazed for a moment at that beautiful dirty face, recognized the wild fury in her eyes for what it was. What was going on here? He reached out his hand and grabbed her long braid, pulling her off balance. With his other hand, he brought his knife down and severed part of the braid.

Chandra tried to pull away, but in the next instant, the man Alan had smashed his horse against hers, jerked her out of her saddle and thrown her facedown over his thighs. Her sword went spinning from her hand and clattered to the rocky ground. He ripped the quiver off her shoulder and flung it away.

"Let's be gone, lads, quickly, quickly." Alan Durwald knew they had but a few moments to escape the Englishmen galloping furiously toward them. "Aye, it's a marvelous prize we've won this trip!"

Chandra yelled at the top of her lungs and tried to rear up, but he smashed his hand down, pinning her.

"Hush, my little lad," Alan said, and stroked his fingers over her.

She cursed him, but her voice was muffled against his thigh. He laughed harder.

He was ahead of his men now. He shouted back over his shoulder, "I will meet ye at the border. Angus, ye go fetch the other men and the cattle. The rest of ye, fight off the English bastards. I will see that our prize is kept safe."

Jerval rode straight toward the first of the yelling Scots, his powerful arm raised. The man hacked at him, spittle spewing from his mouth as he shouted curses, but it was quickly over. Jerval's sword plunged into the man's chest and emerged a foot from his back. He yanked his sword back and saw the man's eyes widen in astonishment as he slid off his horse and sprawled on the rocky ground.

Jerval wheeled about in his saddle, looking frantically for Chandra. He saw her, in the distance, thrown facedown in front of one of the Scots. "Mark, kill the rest of them, and then follow me." He wheeled Pith about and dug in his heels.

"Faster, Sunnart," Chandra heard the man Alan yelling at his powerful stallion. He looked over his shoulder and saw that one of the Englishmen had turned from his men and was galloping after them. "Well, lass," Alan said, his hand hard against the small of her back to hold her still, "it appears that one of the English wants ye for himself."

She knew it had to be Jerval. He would save her. She managed to rear up just a bit and yelled, "It is my husband, and he will kill you. You must let me go."

"Yer husband? That lie will bring ye many a fair night in hell. If he were yer husband, ye stupid wench, ye wouldn't be here now. Ye'd be safe, far away from here. No husband would let his wife dress like a boy and ride into battle. No husband would be such a fool unless he wanted to rid himself o' ye.

"And ye were by yerself. Ye lie, for even a gutless Englishman wouldn't be that stupid. Now ye think that coward will kill me? I dinna think so, lass. I'm hard to catch, much less kill. He has a bit o' distance to cover to catch us. Already his beast is tiring. My Sunnart will get us to safety. Ye will bring me a fine ransom, my little lad. Mayhap that man is yer lover? Aye, but ye no longer please him in his bed? He wants to be rid of ye now? Aye, that's it, isn't it?" And he laughed.

Chandra could see nothing, for the dust the stallion kicked up was clogging her nostrils and burning her eyes. Her plan had gone wrong. Everything had gone wrong. She had broken the glass window in the bedchamber. She had, quite simply, ruined everything.

She had to get away from this man, else he might try to use her to kill Jerval. She would not let that happen. She closed her eyes against the dust, then gritted her teeth. He had to make a mistake soon — he had to. Patience, she had to have patience, and remain alert and ready.

"An insistent man, that Englishman," Alan said after a few more minutes of hard riding. "He doesn't know the eastern forest — that will slow him. Aye, we'll lose him in amongst the trees."

He raised his hand from her back. Instantly, Chandra tried to wrench herself free. She reared up, twisted even as she was readying to hurl herself to the ground. She nearly made it, knew that when she hit the ground, she had to roll fast. She felt the point of a dagger pressing through her clothes, its razor tip nipping the flesh of her side.

"Hold still, wench, else yer lover will find a dead mistress in a ditch. Does he dress ye like a boy because it pleases him to do so? The English are pederasts — all know that — but to dress a lass like a little warrior and send her out as bait — by a man's balls, that's a gutless thing to do. Are ye worth so little to him?"

He believed Jerval was so dishonorable that he'd used her as bait to draw out the Scots? What was a pederast? She lay like a sack of peat, afraid even to breathe. They gained the forest. She saw the blur of trees, heard the crunch of leaves and the tear of bushes beneath Sunnart's hooves. A branch slashed her face. She pressed her face downward against his thigh to protect herself.

He laughed — the madman actually laughed as he said, "There'll be time enough later for that, lass. Aye, I'll show ye what a man can be. A Scotsman is no pederast. It's pleased I am to see ye so interested. Yer tired of yer cold Englishman? Well, it matters not since he is obviously tired o' ye." He jabbed the tip of the knife into her flesh again, and she felt the brief sting, then the wet of her blood beneath her clothes.

Jerval pulled Pith to a halt to wait for his men. He knew he wouldn't find the Scotsman in the forest; he needed Thoms to track him. Christ, he thought, cold with fear for her, he should have tied her down, left two men to stand over her, guarding her every waking hour. Her pride, her damnable pride. He steeled himself against the sight of her flung facedown before the Scot.

Lambert shouted, "We killed the three bastards. But there's no sign of the cattle."

"They split up," Mark said. "We need to send our men after them."

Jerval motioned for six men, Rolfe at their head, to go after the cattle.

"Where is milady?" Thoms asked.

"Their leader has her," Jerval said, and the sound of his own words froze him all the way to his bones, but only for an instant. "He rode into the forest. Thoms, you must track him."

Then he paused, thinking. "Ranulfe, I don't believe he will hide in the forest for long. He needs to get to the border, needs to see to the cattle he stole, come together with his other men. We will skirt the forest northward, by the sea. With luck, he'll veer eventually our way and we'll have him. But Thoms, find his tracks and keep close to him. It's possible he may go to the east. We have enough men. Set up a relay so if he decides to come out to the west, we will have warning."

Jerval was right. Not an hour later, Rolfe shouted, "You were right, Jerval. The bastard is headed northwest, out of the forest. Thoms will stay well behind him, but he said it was obviously the man's direction.

Aye, the damned Scot wants to make better time and he cannot do it in the forest. It's nearly dark."

They rode hard, hoping to get well ahead of the Scot before he broke out of the trees. "We must catch them before dark," Jerval said once, then said it again, and all the men knew what he was thinking.

"Don't forget that he's carrying Chandra," Mark said. "It will slow him even more. You know too that she will fight him at every opportunity."

Jerval knew it well. He prayed the Scot wouldn't finally decide she wasn't worth risking his life for and slit her throat.

But night was falling. It wouldn't be long now. Jerval thought of the man alone with his wife and thought he'd choke on his rage, and his helplessness.

Alan Durwald reined in his exhausted stallion and slewed his head back. A gentle rise blocked his view, but he could see no clouds of dust from pursuing horses. They'd been out of the forest for only a few minutes now. There was no one about. He was safe. He'd lost the Englishman. He said, even as he pressed his fingers inward on her hips, "Well, my cheeky little lady, it appears that yer lover has at last given up, or I've outsmarted him or mayhap he just didn't care. Another half hour, and it will be dark. And then, wench, we can take our rest. I do hope yer lover will still want to pay yer ransom when I'm done with ye."

You will have to kill me first, Chandra thought. She tried to pull herself upward, but he grabbed her hair, wrapping it tight about his hand, making her scalp burn, and pressed her face down again. She saw the crimson of the sun setting over the sea. Please, she prayed silently, please be close by.

Alan Durwald clicked Sunnart forward toward the next rise, swiveling about in his saddle again to look back at the rutted path behind them. He was pleased until he turned forward again. Chandra felt him tense, and then he cursed, a torrent of Scottish oaths she did not understand, but she felt the fury of them to her bones. He whipped his horse about and rode back south, back toward the forest. He cursed again. He saw more of the English coming out of the forest. They'd been tracking him. Somehow the others had gotten ahead of him. What to do? He was pinned between the two groups.

Suddenly, Sunnart stumbled, and his great body heaved with effort, throwing

Chandra up against the man's chest. She gave a howl of fury and mashed her fist into his groin as the stallion reared. Alan grunted in pain, tried to control the panicked Sunnart. Chandra threw herself sideways, breaking free of his arm.

Her joy lasted only until she struck the rocky ground. The impact knocked the breath from her, and she rolled head over heels down a sharp incline. Jagged rocks tore through her clothes and flesh. She couldn't stop herself, her fingers grabbing at rocks, at bushes, but she couldn't keep a hold. Then her head struck a rock and she didn't know when she finally rolled to a stop.

"Wake up, Chandra. Damn you, don't you dare die on me."

She slowly opened her eyes at the sound of his furious voice. Jerval? Her head felt as though it would explode, the pain was so bad.

"Look at me, you damned woman!"

She blinked then and looked up into her husband's face. He looked angrier than she'd ever seen him. He looked ready to kill. She managed to wet her lips. "Did you catch him?"

"Good, you're awake." He paid her no

more attention. He was feeling each of her arms, her legs. "Is there pain?" He was pressing his hand against her belly.

"No."

"And here?"

His hands were splayed on her ribs. She winced.

"I don't think they're broken. By all the saints' white teeth, you're a mess." Jerval lifted her slowly to her feet. "Can you stand?"

"Please, Jerval, did you catch him? He is their leader."

"My men are chasing him, but he's veered into the forest again between our two forces. I decided to see if you were alive."

"You must ride after him, Jerval. You mustn't let him escape."

"Shut up," he said and released her. There was blood on his hands, her blood. "Your head will hurt from that rock you hit, but you deserve it."

He had believed he could forgive her anything if only he found her alive. He'd been wrong. He took a step back from her, knowing that if he touched her again, he would thrash her, mayhap even strangle her. He wiped her blood on his trousers.

She saw his fury, knew that fury of his was greater than it had been just the moment before, but it didn't matter. She said, "He saw you coming after him and whipped his horse about, but his horse stumbled and I hit him in the groin and managed to jump. His name is Alan. That's what his men called him. He is their leader. We must hurry, Jerval, before he gets too far ahead of us."

Jerval stared down at her, angry cords straining in his neck. He was nearly incoherent with rage. He drew a deep breath, still not approaching her. He said, his voice as low and soft as a gentle mist, "Do you have any idea what would have happened to you if we had not seen the Scots surround you?"

"Of course I know. My father trained me well, if you would just but recognize it. I would have killed two of them, but then I would have been hurt or killed myself."

It was true. He closed his eyes a moment, words beyond him.

"Thank you," she said low. She lightly touched her dirty fingers to his shoulder.

"Do not touch me."

He'd spaced each word apart. She dropped her hand. "Thank you for coming after me."

"I should have let you fend for yourself."

"I did fend for myself. I managed to get away from him."

"I saw what happened. When he realized that he was caught between my men, his horse panicked and you took your chance, as I would expect anyone to. Now, you know what he intended, don't you? He would have raped you, and then if he had not killed you, you would have been hauled across the border and held for ransom. By God, it might have been good riddance."

"Aye, I know what he intended. I would have died first before I let him rape me. He thought you had used me as bait, that I was your mistress, that since all Englishmen were pederasts, it pleased you to dress me up like a boy."

"Now I am a pederast," he said, and then he laughed. "The truth of it is that you did make excellent bait. We had ridden past him, as you know. I doubt we would have caught him if he hadn't come out to get you." And he laughed more.

"What is a pederast?"

"It is a man who prefers other men, not women."

"But that makes no sense at all."

"No, it doesn't."

"I don't feel well," she said then, and fell to her knees and vomited, shaking and heaving, wanting to die. She hurt all over.

He didn't touch her, just stood over her,

his arms crossed over his chest. When she was done heaving, he said, "He sliced off your braid, a good foot of it. You look more like a boy now than before. Oh, yes, his name is Alan Durwald. He is rather infamous for the ferocity of his raids."

She felt too wretched to touch her hair, but she felt it dangling to her shoulders, no further. "It is just hair," she managed to say at last. "It isn't important."

Thoms shouted, "He escaped us, Jerval. Damnation, but he knows every hiding place in the forest. That wouldn't matter so much, but now it is dark and we haven't a chance of tracking him."

"I know," Jerval called back. "It doesn't matter."

"Is Chandra all right?" Mark said as he swung off his horse's back.

"She is herself," Jerval said, his teeth clenched. He strode to his destrier and leapt into the saddle. "We will hope Ranulfe and his men find and secure the cattle. Now there is nothing more for us here. We will ride down the coast a bit until we find a sheltered inlet for the night. Tomorrow we return to Camberley."

Bayon was leading the roan stallion to her. He nickered as she walked to him. She stood there a moment, staring up. She hurt everywhere, felt the chill evening air and the blood drying against her flesh through her torn clothes. But it didn't matter. Alan Durwald was gone. She was safe. She gritted her teeth and pulled herself up into the saddle.

Jerval watched her from the corner of his eye, but did not turn to face her. When she rode up next to him, he said, "Just how did you get out of my bedchamber?"

"I knotted sheets and climbed out the window."

A muscle jumped in his jaw. "Did it not occur to you that everyone would be frantic when they found you gone?"

"I was sorry for that. Truly I was, but don't you see, I had to prove myself to you?"

"Aye, you did just that, didn't you? And look at the outcome. Not so very skilled, are you? You didn't stand a chance."

"I would have if I had been one of your men, if I had fought at your side, if I had not been alone. No one could have managed by himself. Perhaps you would have, but it would have been very difficult, even for you."

She was utterly serious. He said nothing for a very long time, then, "I have been wondering if I can haul you out to sea and drown you."

She wondered if he meant it. Then she felt too numb to care.

Chapter 18

They stopped to make camp twenty minutes later. It was dark, with thick clouds rolling across the sky and a half moon giving enough light to collect wood for a fire. Chandra found herself alone, for the men as well as her husband ignored her and kept their distance. It was cold. She pulled her blanket around her shoulders and moved closer to the fire. She was jerking the burned rabbit meat away from the bone when Mark came around the fire to sit cross-legged beside her.

He saw that she was covered with cuts and bruises. He said, however, "You are eating, so you must feel all right."

"Aye. My head hurts, that is all."

"Jerval said you took quite a blow, but that your head is so hard, it wouldn't hurt you very long." He paused a moment, then said very clearly and slowly, "I was forced to tell him that I am very grateful to God that you are neither my wife nor my responsibility."

His words struck her to the bone, adding to the pain that swamped her, but she said nothing for the moment, just sucked her fingers, for the meat was hot. Then, "It was not my choice to be any man's wife or responsibility."

Mark shook his head, and when he spoke again, his voice was as cold as the sea breeze chilling her flesh. "Jerval is my best friend. We were raised together. It is unfortunate what has happened to him. You say that you never wanted to be any man's wife or responsibility. By God, I'll wager that he now wishes he had known that."

She chewed on a bite of rabbit, knowing what he said was true. She just wished the knowing didn't hurt so much. But even that didn't matter now. Nothing, at the moment, appeared to matter. She said, "I wonder why Alan Durwald chopped part of my braid."

"A trophy. If he manages to survive this raid, and now I am certain that he will, I can see him wearing it about his arm for all the world to see. He took Jerval de Vernon's woman, be it only for a few hours. He will tell the world about that, about the golden hair he wears. He might even boast that he took you, that he returned you to your husband mayhap with his babe in your belly."

"Then he would lie. Who is he?"

"He is a very hard man, smarter than he should be, merciless to his enemies, a man who is also a very dangerous renegade."

"What do you mean?"

"Durwald was in line for a rich estate in Galloway, but King Alexander would not back his claim and gave it instead to his cousin. You see, Durwald would not swear fealty to his king. Unfortunately, the trouble is now ours. He's not stupid. He never wreaks enough damage to gain the attention of King Henry or King Alexander. He has been until recently content to raid farther to the east. But now he is here, and we must kill him or he will pick our bones."

"Thank you for telling me."

"There was no reason not to tell you. There is nothing harmful you can do with the information. Good night, Chandra."

"Do you hate me so much?"

Mark rose to his feet, looked down at her for another moment, then turned on his heel and left her without a backward glance.

A short time later, Jerval wrapped himself up in his blanket and lay down near his wife. He knew she had to be in some pain. That was too bad. He wondered why he'd bothered to give her a blanket. She had her conceit, her god-awful arrogance, to keep the chill night air at bay.

The fire was nearly out, but from the dim shadows cast by the orange embers, he could see clotted blood over a cut near her jaw. She deserved it.

They were a few miles north of Camberley late the next morning when Jerval turned in his saddle and waved his hand toward Chandra, who was riding by herself at the rear of the troop.

For a moment, he believed she would ignore him.

Then, just a moment later, she reined in beside him. "Aye?"

He never looked at her, just said, "I have thought about what to do with you. I gave you all the freedom you had at Croyland, until you broke trust with me. Even then, I allowed you your manly trappings. After your ridiculous performance with the Scots in the tiltyard, I ordered you to learn from my mother, hoping, praying, it would temper your actions. That did naught but make my mother howl in frustration.

"But now, I will make no more excuses for you. No, you will not interrupt me. Close your mouth and listen carefully, for I can assure you that all hell will break loose once we are home." He felt the pain rumbling through him even as he forced himself to say, "I have done all that I can to change your feelings for me. I give you a woman's pleasure every night. Then I feel your tears against my shoulder at what you believe to be your humiliation, your subjugation, by me, your husband. You see it as a battle and see yourself, after you have recovered from the pleasure I give you, as having somehow lost something and been bested by me, your enemy. I believe you are incapable of recognizing that there is caring between us, and your passion with me is a sign of your caring for me."

Her face was frozen.

He continued, his voice harsher now, because the pain cut him so deeply. "Every morning, you flee from me. Tell me why you must run away."

He did not believe she would answer him, but she did. "I have no choice. I cannot stay."

"Why?" She remained silent, and he said, "If you did stay, and I awoke with you, then I would bring you pleasure yet again and that is something you would never forgive yourself for. Is that it?"

She said nothing. The dried blood itched on her cheek.

"It would be in the light of day, and you would have to see me in that full light, not in the dim shadows of night, and you would know I was looking at you and you would see my mouth and my hands on you and you cannot bear that, can you?"

He didn't think she would answer that, but she did, saying slowly, "You're right. I cannot bear it."

"Why the hell not?"

And that she couldn't, or wouldn't, answer. Which, she didn't know. She stared down at her scraped and torn hands and remained silent.

He said at last, "This last example of your thoughtlessness, your childishness, your absolute selfishness, has shown me clearly that you have not a pittance of sense, or maturity, and no regard at all for my wishes." Indeed, he thought, as a husband, as her lord, as a man to whom she owed respect, he had failed spectacularly. She'd accused him of changing after they'd wed. Now, he knew that he must change.

"You will practice no more with the men, nor will you again wear your men's clothes. You will spend all of your time learning from my mother the things a lady should know. Never again will you set yourself against me, or I will deal with you as befits a disobedient, ill-tempered wife."

It was more than she could bear, more than she would let pass. "I am not ill tempered."

He nearly laughed at that one. "Mayhap that wasn't what I meant exactly. You are more heedless, mayhap more oblivious, than ill tempered. There, does that suit you?"

She said nothing at all.

"Just look at you. Some lady I bound myself to. You're filthy. Your hair is tangled around your face."

"The same applies to you, Jerval, save that you have a dirty, scratchy growth of beard on your face to hide the dirt."

She was right.

"It will take me an hour to bathe and soothe ointment into all the cuts and scratches on your body."

"I will do it myself."

"Aye, if I did it, then I would see your body in the full light of day. I would touch you, and you are afraid that you would like the feel of my hand on you and would want more."

"All right, then you will do it. I care not. You think I would want you to touch me more? That is a man's conceit. By all the saints, I hurt too badly."

Again, he nearly laughed. "If I wish it, then I will. Now, do you have any questions about what you will do?"

She said nothing, just dug her heels into the stallion's sides and rode away from him.

He wondered what she would do.

A half hour later, he saw her beside the rutted road. He would have grinned had he been able, for he realized that she did not have the courage to enter the keep without him.

He merely nodded to her, and she guided the roan beside him, not looking at him. There were shouts from the men lining the outer walls, and as he expected, his parents were awaiting them in the inner bailey. He could hear his father's sigh of relief upon seeing Chandra. There were two spots of angry color on his mother's cheeks.

Chandra slithered slowly off the roan's back. She heard her mother-in-law call her name, but kept her head down and walked quickly to where her husband stood.

"Jerval," said Lady Avicia, "thank the Virgin you have brought her back safely."

"By all the saints, we did not know what she would do," Lord Hugh said, limping toward them, for his gout was particularly noxious today.

"I know," Jerval said. "Let us go within and I will tell you everything."

Once in the hall, Lord Hugh said, "What of the Scots? Did you get our cattle back? Capture the bastards?"

Jerval pulled Chandra down beside him

on a trestle bench. He said, "We killed many of them, but their leader, Alan Durwald, escaped. I expect Ranulfe will catch up with the other Scots and will bring back the cattle."

"Oh, my God, your hair!" Lady Avicia was staring at Chandra, pointing.

Chandra hurt, both in body and in spirit, but it appeared that there was nothing she could do about either. She shrugged, but it cost her dearly. "Their leader, Alan Durwald, chopped off my braid. Mark believed he did it because he would have a trophy. It doesn't matter. It is just hair."

Lady Avicia's eyes bulged. "You were in the fighting? But, Jerval, you told me you would not allow it."

"She did it anyway," Jerval said, and nothing more.

"You smashed my glass window," Lord Hugh said. "By all the saints' blessed deeds, you should be beaten."

Lady Avicia rose to stand over her daughter-in-law. "This nonsense must stop, Jerval, before she is killed through her own foolishness."

Jerval rose and brought Chandra up beside him. When she would have pulled away, he just tightened his hold. He said very calmly, "Yes, it will stop. Now Chandra and

305

I will bathe off our dirt. Mother, please have some ointment sent to my bedchamber. As you see, my wife is covered with cuts and bruises that must be tended to." He paused a moment, then said over his shoulder, "When Alan Durwald saw that we had cut him off, Chandra managed to fling herself off his horse and save herself. Unfortunately, the ground was not smooth."

"Hold still."

She had no choice. Before he'd stripped off her torn, filthy clothing, he'd given her a potion to drink. "It will ease your pain. Now you will bathe; then I will see how badly you are hurt."

He hadn't left the bedchamber while she bathed. Indeed, he'd held a towel for her when she stepped out of the tub. "Lie down," he'd said, and she did, on her stomach on the bed.

"Hold still," he said again, only she hadn't moved. Her body hurt and her spirit wanted to die.

He said nothing more, but she felt his hands on her, gentle, his fingers covered with the ointment, touching her here and there, looking at her everywhere. "Turn onto your back now."

She turned onto her back. She hated it.

She lay there, naked, and he was sitting beside her, only there was no caring in his eyes as he looked down at her, only duty, perhaps also impatience, and anger still simmering in him at what she had done.

"I played my part well even though you hadn't given it to me. I was a fine tethered goat. I brought them out for you to fight and capture. You managed to kill most of them."

His fingers were on her belly. They stilled. "Tethered goat? Oh, yes, you were my bait." He didn't tell her that when he'd first seen her surrounded by the Scots, he'd nearly lost all control, he'd been so afraid for her. But she was all right. He looked down at his fingers still lightly touching her smooth belly. He wanted her, and it surprised him. He wanted her very badly.

She said, "I managed to get away from Alan Durwald by myself."

He moved quickly away from her belly. "Aye, you did. I even told my mother and father that."

He was rubbing the ointment into several cuts on her legs.

"I do not believe that I should be punished to such an extreme. It was just that I was unlucky. Surely —"

"Be quiet. I don't care a single damn what you believe. You have even cut your feet. No, don't say anything more. I am tired of your excuses, your justifications." When he was done, he rose and covered her with a light towel. "Do not move until I tell you to."

She closed her eyes, feeling the ointment leach the pain out of the worst of the cuts and bruises.

She heard him speaking, knew he was ordering clean hot water for himself. She said nothing, merely lay there, not understanding why she wasn't yelling at him to free her, to take part of the blame for what had happened. But the fact was, there was nothing inside her now — no anger, no fear, nothing at all. She felt both numb and battered. At that moment she truly didn't care if she lived or died. She closed her eyes.

He was dressed when he sat beside her again. "Has the pain lessened?"

She nodded, her eyes still closed.

"Sit up and let me comb your hair."

She did. It didn't take him long. "At least he didn't make you bald. I never liked you wearing a braid. Now your hair is too short to allow it. After you feel strong enough, you will dress in one of your gowns. I will speak to my mother and tell her what, when you are well enough, it is you will do from now on."

He looked over at the window. All the

broken shards of glass had been removed. "If you are industrious enough, I might consider it payment for breaking the glass, though I doubt that my father will. Did you ever bother to consider that Camberley is the only keep in the north of England that has glass?"

"A warrior's keep shouldn't have glass windows. But it was beautiful. I am sorry I had to break it."

Well that was something, particularly since Lord Richard had raised her in his very image, with all his beliefs, all his prejudices. "As I said, you will now learn all the responsibilities of a lady. If I am pleased with your progress, see clear evidence of your cooperation, if your moods and conversation are pleasant, then mayhap I will allow you to once again ride, practice your archery. Perhaps I will even allow you to hunt again. But you will do none of these things without my permission."

She heard herself say, as if from far away, "I want to go home to Croyland."

"It is a pity, but you cannot. Your father would not want you back. No, you don't believe that, do you? Actually, I would just as soon you returned as well, but it is not to be. We are wed, and that's an end to it. You believe you are trapped? Believe me, Chandra,

I am caught in the same snare with you."

She flinched. He wondered why, but he didn't ask.

He wondered if he should simply take all her boy's clothes, her armor, her weapons. But no, he wouldn't. He would gladly beat her if she dared to flout him again.

When he saw her two hours later in the Great Hall, Mary at her side, he smiled. If the smile didn't reach his eyes, everyone knew why it didn't. Her hair fell to her shoulders, a golden band holding it back from her face. Her gown he recognized as one she had worn at Croyland, soft pink silk, its long, loose sleeves lined with bands of miniver. The cut on her cheek ruined the effect.

He had spoken privately to his parents and told them the details of what had happened, preferring them to hear it from him rather than from the men. He had also told them what he now expected from his wife. "It is over," he'd said. "I believed I could ease her into being a wife. I was wrong. I have no choice now. Mother, I would ask that you try to go easily with her. As much as she knows about a warrior's weapons and skills, she knows nothing about a lady's duties. You wondered why her mother, Lady Dorothy, didn't teach her. I don't know the whole of it, but I do know that she dislikes her daughter intensely. I also know it wasn't Chandra's fault. Now, do not try to break her. Just instruct her. Will you try?"

"The girl should be thrashed every day," Lady Avicia said. "She is worse than a thorn — she is a blight. Oh, very well, I will treat her as well as I can."

"She could have been killed so easily," Lord Hugh said, shaking his head even as he stroked Hawk's massive head. "I do not understand how her brain is fashioned."

"I have wondered many times myself," Jerval said. "I will have the glass replaced, Father. Then it is her debt to me."

The evening meal, luckily, passed without any unpleasant incident. Chandra was as silent as the roasted pheasant on her trencher. She didn't eat much of the meat and kept her head down even when Julianna mentioned to all those within hearing how a woman's hair was her pride, and a woman who lost her hair, no matter the reason, wasn't a woman any longer, now was she? Not a word out of Chandra. Jerval wasn't used to this. He almost told Julianna that she was being cruel and to shut up, but he managed to keep his mouth shut.

He didn't touch her that night, though he wanted to very much. No, she was too sore;

there were still too many painful cuts on her body. Still, when he awoke at dawn the next morning, she was gone.

What had he expected?

That afternoon, Jerval and two dozen men set out from Camberley for Oldham. Jerval cast one last look over his shoulder at the huge towers, shrouded in early fog.

"She will come about, Jerval."

"It seems you are privy to all of it, Mark. You spoke to Mary?"

"Aye. She told me some of it. It is a strange and wonderful thing, but Mary would fight to the death for Chandra. She refuses to hear any criticism of her friend. All she told me really was that Chandra acquitted herself quite well, that she'd fought as well as any of us — I couldn't deny it — and that I was just being an oaf and blindly following your lead, which wasn't fair of me. She stuck her chin in the air as if to challenge me, and then said this was according to Bayon and he wouldn't lie to her."

"Bayon much admires her."

"I don't like that. Mary deserves better than he," Mark said.

"No, I meant that Bayon admires Chandra."

"He is young yet. Now, I saw Mary and Chandra speaking together last night and it seemed like a very serious conversation."

"Mary is probably advising her how to behave with your mother."

After a few moments, Jerval said, "Soon we will know if Sir John is in league with Alan Durwald. Even though I am certain that he is guilty, I still have difficulty believing the fool has the gall to betray us."

"I agree with you. Oldham is not well fortified. We could take it in a week, if he tried to break his oath of fealty. Do we stop at Penrith?"

Jerval shook his head. "Nay, I wish to see what Sir John is about, then return to Camberley."

Mark smiled. "Ah, back to the eye of the storm."

"She's held herself remarkably silent."

"Do you know, Jerval, I believe she was truly frightened. The tales I have heard about Alan Durwald make my blood run cold. He held her captive for several hours."

"If she was frightened, I was too angry to notice."

They reached Oldham early that evening. It was a small keep that sat on a flat stretch of ground on the northeast perimeter of the de Vernon lands, its thick stone outer walls its only noteworthy defense. Jerval searched the walls for signs of resistance, almost disappointed when he saw none. He was itching for a good fight, as much as were his men. He called a halt and rode forward to the edge of the moat. Men lined the walls, but none said anything.

The drawbridge was lowered slowly, its winches groaning, and Jerval wondered if they had ever been oiled. He gave Malton orders to scout all the outbuildings for signs of the Scots once they were within, and their troop filed into the bailey. Sir John stood awaiting them, surrounded by his ill-kempt men and even filthier servants.

Jerval had not seen Sir John in over a year, and time, he saw, hadn't improved him. Heavy-jowled, his face ravaged by too much ale, his belly fat from too much food and too little exercise, he was dressed richly in a long robe of red velvet. His fingers were beringed. He looked like royalty amongst beggars. Beside him stood a thin scrap of a woman, as ill kempt as the servants. It took Jerval a moment to recognize that she was Lady Faye, Sir John's wife.

"Welcome, welcome, Sir Jerval," Sir John said, rubbing his hands together as Jerval dismounted and strode toward him. "Come into the hall. Your esteemed father does well? Your mother?"

Jerval only nodded before turning to Lady

Faye and saying, "I give you fair greeting, my lady."

Sir John grunted, his eyes narrowing on his wife's face as she whispered greetings to Jerval. "Are you stupid, Faye? Have wine brought for our guests."

Lady Faye skittered away. Jerval said nothing, merely nodded to Malton, then turned to follow Sir John into the keep, Mark at his side.

He was used to Camberley, used to smells of food and wax and rosemary, and now Hawk, his father's boarhound. A healthy smell. But here he both saw and smelled filth. The reeds strewn over the stone floor of the hall hadn't been changed in a very long time. When his boots crunched over some bones, the remains of a long-ago supper, a rat scurried out, darting between his feet.

Sir John spread his hands in front of him, seeing the look of disgust on Jerval's face. "Last winter was hard, my lord, and many of the sheep died. As for the serfs, they are lazy louts, and the crops not what I expected. My wife has not the wit or will to keep the hall as clean as I would wish."

Jerval nodded toward Sir John, thinking that he did not appear to have suffered at all. "And the Scots? Have you lost stock to them?"

Sir John answered quickly, "Aye, my lord, the dirty mongrels. My men can never catch them, but they try, they always try."

Sir John's wife leaned over Jerval's shoulder to pour wine into a tarnished silver goblet. She slipped on some refuse in the rushes and some of the wine splashed onto his surcoat.

"Clumsy bitch!" Before Jerval could assure the poor woman that no harm was done, Sir John had struck her and sent her sprawling.

Chapter 19

Sir John was breathing hard, his fist raised to strike again. "Women. They are such useless, whining creatures. And this skinny sheep cannot even give me a son."

"Leave her be," Jerval said. He rose slowly and towered over Sir John. Sir John, no fool, backed up. Jerval leaned down to help Lady Faye to her feet. She was all right, just pale. At least she was all right this time. He imagined that Sir John hit her fairly often. "It was a simple accident, no cause to strike her."

Sir John looked at his cringing wife, then calmed himself. He would see to her later. He cleared his throat. "I hear you have taken a wife, my lord. I wager she is not a silly sheep like this one."

"Actually, Sir John, my wife would cut your throat for what you just did to your wife, were she here with me."

Sir John looked appalled, then stuttered a laugh. "Ah, that is a jest, isn't it, my lord?"

"No, it isn't." Then Jerval said abruptly, "I will see your accounts now, Sir John. Your payment to the de Vernons this year was not according to your pledge."

"As I said, Sir Jerval, the crops did not yield much." Jerval saw the lie in Sir John's eyes, but kept his expression bland. "As to the accounts, I did not expect you, my lord, and I fear that my steward, a rascally fellow I dismissed from Oldham just last week, was cheating me."

"I see," said Jerval. "I will see the accounts anyway."

"Certainly, my lord," Sir John said. He looked toward the unshuttered windows, smiled to himself, and said, as jovial as a man could be, "It grows dark. Perhaps you would like to wait until tomorrow? Tonight, after you have eaten, I will send you a lovely morsel to while away the long night."

To Mark's surprise, Jerval said in the voice of an eager young man, "An excellent suggestion, Sir John."

Sir John very nearly rubbed his hands together.

Mark waited until he and Jerval had been shown to the one private chamber above the hall by a furtive serving maid before he opened his mouth to protest. Jerval shook his head and placed his fingertip to his lips until the girl had slipped from the room. He remained silent as he gazed about at the oddly bare chamber. There was but one stool and an old chest against the end of the bed, and the bed itself, though large and comfortable, was covered with worn, tattered blankets.

Jerval said thoughtfully, "It is too bare and poor, as if someone had stripped the chamber of its trappings. Did you notice the rings on Sir John's fingers, Mark?"

Mark nodded slowly, and a smile spread over his face.

"I wonder," Jerval continued, thoughtful still, "where his lady wife sleeps."

Rough tables were pressed together to accommodate Jerval, Mark, Malton and three of their men at supper. Lady Faye was nowhere to be seen. The girl, Dora, was seated next to Jerval. She had been hastily bathed, but there was still dirt under her fingernails. She wasn't uncomely, and she was very young. There was a smug, assessing look in her dark eyes, and he grinned to himself. The meal was surprisingly well prepared, and Jerval, Mark and Malton were careful to eat and drink only what Sir John did, as were all their men.

Jerval smiled at Dora and deliberately cupped his hand over her full breast. "More wine, my lord?" she whispered against his ear, pressing her breasts against his arm.

"Aye," he said, though he had no intention of drinking it.

"I have another girl for you, Sir Mark," Sir John said as the meal progressed. "You need have no fear that you will spend the night alone."

Jerval sent his host a lustful grin and said in a slurred voice, "Send her to the chamber, Sir John. We will enjoy the both of them together."

Sir John could scarce keep his satisfaction to himself. Young men had mighty appetites, and it would serve him well tonight.

The other girl was neither as clean nor as comely as Dora, yet she appeared eager enough. She too, Jerval saw, had been hastily bathed. He bade Sir John a drunken good night and allowed Dora to take his hand and pull him with her up the stairs.

Jerval's expression did not change when they entered the bedchamber. "Take off your clothes, girls," he said, leaning his back against the closed door. "Mark, shall we draw lots to see who takes them first?"

"And you, my lord?" Dora said. "Will you not allow me to help you remove your tunic?"

"In a moment, Dora."

Jerval watched dispassionately as the girls quickly stripped off their clothes. When they both stood naked, their young bodies white in the light of the one torch, Jerval walked forward and stroked his chin, as if assessing them. Dora grabbed his hand and guided it to her breast.

"I will make you forget everything, my lord," Dora whispered, her hand stroking down his belly. Jerval lightly shoved her away before she could discover that he was as flaccid as a man who'd just jumped into a cold river.

"Hand me your shift, Dora." The girl cocked her head in question but did as she was told. Jerval ripped it into strips, paying no heed to Dora's squawk of anger.

"I suggest," Jerval said, "that both of you keep your mouths shut."

When both girls were bound and gagged, Jerval and Mark carried them to the bed and covered them with blankets.

"Did you tell Malton to alert the men?"

"Oh, aye," Mark said.

"Good. Now we wait."

Chandra jabbed a needle into Jerval's burgundy-velvet tunic.

"Nay, Chandra," Mary said. "You must be more careful, else you'll make a greater rent in the fabric."

"By all the saints' woes, I don't care,

Mary. One of those silly girls could do this."

Mary was relieved that Lady Avicia had left Chandra with her and had not chosen to oversee the mending herself.

"Perhaps, but that is not the point. It is your responsibility to care for your lord's clothing. Don't you see? When another sees Jerval, sees that he is richly clothed, that his tunics are finely made, then he knows he is well stationed, that his wife cares well for him."

To Mary's consternation, a tear slid down Chandra's cheek and dripped off her chin.

"Oh, dear, don't cry. I've only seen you cry once before and I hated it, mayhap even more than you did. Listen to me. To be a wife is no shame, Chandra. Just think, once you have learned all the housewifely skills, then you can easily supervise whilst the servants do it. And do you know what will be true then?"

"No, dammit."

"You'll know what both men and women alike know. You will be unique."

"I don't want to be unique. I want to go home."

Mary, for the first time in her life, wanted to slap her friend. "I do not understand you. Here you are, given all you could desire. You are safely wed and your husband is a very fine man. I begin to believe that you do not deserve him. The good Lord knows that he wants to please you, if only you will let go of your ridiculous pride and allow it. Aye, I am nearly ready to hit you and that must mean that you have pushed me very hard."

Chandra dropped the needle and swiped her palm over her cheek. "Please do not hit me," she said, and there was a smile through that deadening pain on her face. "And the other — I haven't forgotten, Mary. You will not live in dishonor, I swear. It is just that I must wait for Jerval to return."

"Jerval? Oh, please, I don't wish for him to know."

"There is no way for him not to know. You said yourself that he is a fine man. Does that mean you believe him fair? Honorable?"

"Well, yes."

"Fine, then stop worrying."

"So you believe your husband to be fair and honorable as well?"

"Yes, I suppose that I do."

"Then mend his tunic well, and count your blessings. Oh, I'm sorry, Chandra. I know that you will do your best, and mayhap even Jerval will think about it as well, but time is growing short. Just this morning I very nearly vomited on Lady Avicia's slippers."

"Trust me, Mary. Everything will be all right."

Mary watched her poke the needle through the fine fabric and shook her head. "Let me show you again how to take a stitch just there. Come, you can learn. It is not that difficult."

"I hate that old hag. She yelled at me this morning, actually yelled."

"You had overcooked the eggs. They weren't edible. But I was proud of you. You did not threaten to wring her neck, nor did you yell back. Pray accept what you must do. I am so tired of all the fighting."

"I haven't fought anyone in a full day now. I even ignore Julianna, and that, I will tell you, is more difficult than you can imagine."

"All right, then more often than not, you are now fighting with your damnable pride. You must know that Jerval will ease his hold once you prove to him that you can be reasonable. He has told you he will."

"If only he had taken me with him to fight the Scots. I would have done well, you know that I would have. But he put me in a terrible position. It isn't my pride here, Mary."

"It isn't? Listen to me. There was no way Jerval could have taken you. All would have believed him beyond foolish to take such a chance with your life."

"He was beyond foolish to leave me behind."

Mary sighed. "Yes, you smashed that beautiful glass window."

"I hated to do that but there was no choice."

"It is too late to be sorry. Now, Chandra, I wish you would forget Lord Richard. He is your father, Chandra. He could never be your husband."

"Speaking of husbands, I hope Jerval doesn't need me right now. I've heard talk that Sir John of Oldham is a mangy, paltry man. I hope the man doesn't try anything foolish. Jerval would gullet him."

Mary rolled her eyes.

Chandra pricked her finger on the needle.

Alan Durwald stroked the thick hank of hair that was braided about his wrist, and was satisfied. Jerval de Vernon, the man who had killed too many of his men, taken back the cattle he'd stolen, would die by his hand tonight, and his lady would be left without a husband to protect her. Sir John's man had told him that there were a dozen men. Alan would trust Sir John's men to take the Camberley men who were sleeping in the hall and in the barracks.

He would kill Jerval de Vernon. It was late

enough now, and the young knight was likely snoring after slaking his lust. He would also be drunk, if Alan knew Sir John, which indeed he did. He motioned his three men up the narrow stairs of the keep and paused to listen outside the oak door of the bedchamber. All was quiet, as it should be. He quietly pressed the latch and swung the door open, his fingers tight about the bone handle of his dagger. Through the darkness, he saw the outline of two figures in bed, and motioned for his men to enter. They stepped toward the bed, their swords and knives at ready.

Suddenly, the silence was rent by a blood-curdling yell, and he saw the glint of a sword slicing toward one of his men.

He couldn't believe it. "It's a trap!"

Jerval slashed his sword into the man's belly, then jerked it out. "Take that one, Mark," Jerval shouted, "I want this bastard." He leapt aside as Alan Durwald swung his claymore high above his head and brought it down in a vicious blow.

Jerval blocked the claymore, but he felt the force of it all the way to his shoulder. Now it was his turn. Excitement flowed through him.

He brought his own sword down, and he felt Durwald's arm weaken under the blow.

Jerval heard a low, gasping sound, felt a cold chill touch him. Even as Mark shouted, "Behind you, Jerval!" he wheeled about and saw another man run through the doorway, his sword raised. Jerval flung his knife. It sliced cleanly through the man's neck, and arcs of blood spurted toward him.

"You damned English bastard!" Alan Durwald saw Geordie fall, his hands clutching at the knife in his throat, saw him fall backward, driving the knife back out. He whirled on Jerval, nearly beside himself with rage. He fought with all his strength, but de Vernon did not falter or fall back. Durwald heard another man fall, and knew with certainty that he was now alone against two men.

"No, Mark, he is mine."

But de Vernon did not leap toward him as he'd hoped. He saw a blur of movement, nothing more.

Alan Durwald felt the blade slice deep into his shoulder, and he roared with the pain of it, stumbling back. Another knife, he thought blankly, pain numbing him now — he'd thrown another knife at him. His claymore fell from his fingers, and he sank to his knees. He felt de Vernon's boot strike his belly, and he fell to his back. He felt de Vernon's heel dig into his chest, and saw his enemy lean over to jerk the dagger from his shoulder. With a scream of pain and fury, Alan managed to clutch the dagger, and with all his strength, he jerked it out of his flesh. He plunged it toward de Vernon's stomach. Jerval jerked back, twisted away. There was an instant of silence, such cold silence it was. Then Alan Durwald, panting, his palms pressed against his own shoulder, felt a sudden blinding pain in his chest. He realized in that instant that de Vernon had plunged his sword downward this time. Then he felt no more.

"Light the torch, Mark."

Jerval stared down at Alan Durwald.

"He is dead?"

"Aye." Jerval rose to his feet. "As for Sir John, he will look quite well hanging from the gibbet at Camberley."

Jerval rode into the inner bailey at Camberley with Sir John and his wife, Lady Faye, beside him, and three Camberley men-at-arms at his back. He had left Mark, Malton, and the rest of Camberley's men at Oldham to restore some kind of order to the keep.

Sir John faced his overlord in the Great Hall, and knew by the implacable look on Lord Hugh's face that he was lost. He listened in silence while Sir Jerval recounted the events at Oldham.

"The Scot leader, Alan Durwald, is dead," Jerval said. "Our northern border should be peaceful for a time."

"The Scot threatened me, my lord," Sir John said, rushing forward to grab Lord Hugh's arm. "He stole my cattle and sheep and bribed my steward and some of my men. I told your son about my steward. He was in league with Durwald. I had no choice but to obey him. He said he would kill me and my poor wife if I did not hide him when he needed Oldham as a base."

He waved his beringed hand toward his hapless wife, who stood trembling with fear, her eyes upon her feet. Stupid bitch, he thought with impotent anger, could she not at least plead for him? "Aye, Faye was Durwald's mistress, the faithless bitch. She is the one who is guilty here, not I."

Chandra broke the silence. "You wear valuable rings on your fingers, Sir John, and very costly garments. Yet I look at your lady wife and see that she wears a tattered gown, and is thin and pale. And the bruise beside her mouth, Sir John, does not become her. It would appear to me that you have not protected her well from harm."

"Durwald struck her."

"Oh, no," Jerval said. "That is a lie."

Sir John had forgotten that he'd hit Faye in front of Jerval de Vernon. Damnation, such a mild blow it had been, it had barely marked her. "She was the one who must have warned him that you would be there."

Chandra said, "If your wife is behind all this wickedness, Sir John, then why do you wear the rings and the velvet?"

Sir John looked at the beautiful young woman who was undoubtedly Sir Jerval's new wife. Why did he allow her to speak so freely? To question him?

"I have offered to give her anything she wishes, but she refuses," said Sir John.

It was so ridiculous that Chandra couldn't help herself. She laughed. "You are a pathetic man, Sir John. Soon, at least, your lady wife will be free from your abuse."

Sir John stared at the girl. That she was even allowed in the men's presence still shocked him. But that she would speak of executing him — she was naught but a worthless woman — angered him beyond reason.

"She is a stupid cow," Sir John yelled. "She is barren. You have naught to say about any of this, girl. Shut your cursed mouth!"

"Enough!" Lord Hugh bellowed.

Jerval said, "Chandra is right, Father. There is no doubt at all that Sir John has been in league with the Scots for a long time now. He is responsible for the loss of our stock. I think the money from the sale of all his rings will provide Lady Faye enough to live comfortably. She bears no blame in this, I am certain."

He looked toward Lady Faye, and was surprised to see the haunted look gone from her eyes and her thin shoulders drawn back. Jerval said to his wife, "Chandra, would you please see that Lady Faye is made comfortable?"

"Aye, my lord, it would be my pleasure." She smiled at Lady Faye and took her hand to lead her away.

"You should not be swayed by foolish women, Lord Hugh."

Sir John saw only a blur of movement. Jerval's fist smashed against his jaw, and he dropped where he stood. "I have wanted to do that since the moment I saw him." Jerval rubbed his knuckles. "To see his fat body swinging from a gibbet will please me even more."

And so it was done.

Lady Faye, Chandra discovered, was the eldest of four daughters of an impoverished knight from the south of England, near Rye.

She was shocked to learn that Lady Faye was only twenty-seven years old, for she was so bowed and thin, her hair as scraggly as Alma's. There was a look of hopeless suffering etched into her pale face. "But why did you wed Sir John?" she asked as she herself helped bathe Lady Faye.

Lady Faye winced slightly as the washcloth touched her bruised ribs. "Not everyone is as lucky as you, Lady Chandra," she said, without rancor. "Sir Jerval is not only an extremely handsome young man — he is also kind, an uncommon quality in a husband."

Chandra said absolutely nothing, though she was thinking about his body over hers, his mouth touching her, caressing her. Lady Faye didn't know the half of it.

"Sir John is — was — a mean, greedy man," Lady Faye said, no emotion in her voice. "My father, poor man, had four girls to contend with. Ten years ago, I suppose that Sir John looked at my meager dowry as sufficient, but of course it did not last long."

Mary helped alter one of Chandra's gowns to fit Lady Faye, who was some inches shorter, and much thinner. Chandra presented her proudly at supper the evening after Sir John's hanging, an event to which Lady Faye appeared oblivious, and placed her in her own chair.

"You are such a kind child," Lady Faye said to her, "but is it wise to bring me to sup with the family?"

"No one has ever called me kind, Lady Faye. Nor am I a child. You are but a few years older than I, and soon, after you have added some pounds, you will look even younger. I doubt not that I will be telling folk that you are my younger sister."

Lady Faye smiled. "You are as kind as your husband, and I will never let you forget it. I thank you, Chandra."

Jerval greeted Lady Faye, smiling because he'd heard her words. He was surprised at the change in her, though he had no idea what they were going to do with Sir John's widow.

Lady Avicia inclined her head politely and offered Faye a huge helping of roast lamb. "A man will not want you again unless you fill out my daughter-in-law's gown."

"Mayhap," Chandra said, her chin up, "Lady Faye does not want another husband. Her first was a monster."

Lord Hugh said, "Sir John's jewels will bring sufficient funds for another dowry if Lady Faye wishes it." For the first time Hugh saw the potential of the young woman.

Julianna said, "Chandra's gown is not a

becoming color for you, Lady Faye. I have a pink wool that you may have."

Chandra stared at Julianna, so surprised that she did not at first see that Faye was silently weeping.

"You are all so very good," she said, hiccupping.

"You cannot eat if you are crying," Lady Avicia said matter-of-factly, and the newly created widow meekly swallowed her tears, and a goodly portion of lamb.

After supper, Chandra fidgeted about in her bedchamber, waiting for her husband. She had finally left Lady Faye in Mary's capable hands.

"You will wear out Mother's new carpets," Jerval said as he came into the room.

"Oh, good, you are here. Jerval, I must speak to you. It is very important. Now."

"I must needs speak to you as well. I believe this is yours, Chandra." He pulled a foot-long plaited rope of golden hair from his tunic and tossed it to her. She caught it and stared at the dusty hair.

"He was wearing it braided around his wrist — like a gallant knight with his lady's favor."

"It is my hair," she said. "My hair — he was wearing it? That is ridiculous. It is no favor."

Jerval walked slowly to her, stopping only inches away. "Listen to me. Durwald was a vicious animal. Had he escaped with you, there would have been no ransom. He would have kept you and raped you until you were dead or wounded deeply, like Lady Faye. He would have broken you, Chandra, doubt it not."

"Just like poor Faye? Aye, you're right. God, what you men do to women. You didn't see all the bruises. She is only twenty-seven years old, Jerval." She was trembling, so angry that she blurted out, "And like Mary? Mary is pregnant, raped by another one of you animals! And none of it her fault either!"

Jerval stared at her silently for a long moment. He said finally, "By the virgin, the child is Graelam de Moreton's?"

"I didn't mean to tell you like that. I meant to speak slowly, in a very reasoned manner. Oh, damn. There is no hope for it now. Yes, Graelam raped her, you know that. Now she is pregnant, and she doesn't know what to do. It wasn't her fault, but now she will be damned. Please, we must do something. I just don't know what."

She was over three months gone with child. He cursed softly. "I can see that you are greatly disturbed by this. So am I. Don't worry. I will take care of the matter."

"Just like that?" She snapped her fingers. "I know that you are very kind, that your mind works wondrously well, but what is it you will do? Come, tell me."

But he was gone.

Chapter 20

Lord Hugh bellowed to the nearly eighty people in the Great Hall of Camberley, "Oldham needs a master who will not cheat its people, and who will rebuild its defenses. Sir Mark of Oldham. Ah, I like the sound of it. Come forward, Mark."

Malton laughed at the stunned look on Mark's face. "Go ahead," he said, poking Mark in his ribs, "leap for joy."

Mark just couldn't believe it, but it was true — it really was true. He was now a landed knight. Lord Hugh wouldn't lie about that. Absolute euphoria filled him.

"Will you, Sir Mark of Oldham, swear fealty to your overlord?"

A cheer went up from the men-at-arms. Mark, who didn't think there were any words in his head that could make their way out of his mouth, did not have to answer until the noise died down. He walked slowly to Lord Hugh, who sat in his grand chair, his left hand on his boarhound's head, Jerval standing beside him. Jerval was grinning at him from ear to ear.

Then Mark threw back his head and said, loud and strong, "I swear upon my honor and my life to be your loyal vassal, Lord Hugh." He could have well understood if he had been appointed castellan of Oldham, but now he was the master of Oldham, and no longer a landless knight in the service of another. When Jerval asked to speak to him privately later that evening, Mark was still both bewildered and elated at his good fortune.

"I have a favor to ask of you, Mark."

"I would hesitate to cut off my arm," Mark said, that foolish, happy smile of his widening even more, "but anything else I will seriously consider —"

"Oldham will need a mistress, and if you have no strong objection to the lady, I would offer you Mary."

Now this was a blow to the belly. Mark said slowly, "That makes a man serious very quickly. I suppose you have seen that I believe her comely and gentle, that I know she is honest and open, and she smiles at my jests. Perhaps I would have come to this myself, but I doubt it, being a landless knight with nothing at all to offer a wife. No, I would have had no right to ask her to wed me. But now — well, it is all different now, isn't it?"

"Yes, things are different now. I know that her father, Sir Stephen, will provide her a sufficient dowry. As I said, Oldham will need a mistress."

"She is a woman grown," Mark said even more slowly now, looking past his friend's right shoulder. Then he shrugged and smiled. "It is just that you have taken me by surprise. I had not thought of marriage. And now it is staring me in the face. Ah, Jerval, Mary is also an innocent babe."

"Have you wondered why she accompanied Chandra to Camberley?"

"Not really. She and Chandra grew up together. They have been friends since they were children. Also, I've been told that her father doesn't care for her very much, simply views her as a pawn, as barter."

"All that is true, and there is more. There is no easy way to say this, Mark. Mary was raped by Graelam de Moreton when he took Croyland. He raped her in front of Chandra to bring Chandra into line. Mary is pregnant, over three months gone."

For a moment Mark could find no words. Rage filled him. But then he realized fully that what was done was done. "I am to be the father to Graelam's child? I wonder if God will grant that the child not be a boy and I have another man's son as my heir."

"It is something you must consider closely, Mark. I will not try to coerce you, even though Chandra is very nearly distraught over it."

"Yes, she would be. Naturally, that would add to her dislike of men."

"Aye, it has."

"I will do it, Jerval. I like Mary very much. She soothes me, she makes me smile, she is generous. Please ask Lord Hugh to send a messenger to Mary's father to gain his permission."

Jerval nodded. "He will do it tomorrow. At the very least, her portion should enable you to buy what you need to provision the keep properly, make repairs to the walls, and provide feed and seed for the farmers."

Mark smiled. "I suppose that I am to have dallied with Mary, and am doing the honorable thing by her."

"Aye, you will doubtless be cast as the lecher, particularly by my mother, when Mary's belly becomes nicely rounded in the next couple of months." The two men rose, and Jerval placed his hands on Mark's shoulders. "I thank you, Mark, as will Chandra. She has been frantic with worry."

"Have you told Mary?"

Jerval looked at him, surprised. "Nay, of

course not. I trust she will be overcome by her good fortune. No, of course I could not tell her. Do not worry that her father will turn you down. He won't. My father thinks he will hear soon enough from Sir Stephen and you can wed by early next week."

"This moves very quickly. It makes a man roll his eyes, Jerval."

"Aye, that and a good deal more. Are you certain you wish to wed her?"

"Aye, but I wish I knew whether she wanted me."

"But I couldn't tell her, could I? What if you had not wished to become master of Oldham? I could not foist a landless lout on her, now could I?"

"Your wit fells me."

"I know, but I am trying. Now, you must marry the girl quickly. Do you feel that you can safely leave Oldham in Malton's hands until you return with your bride?"

"My bride," Mark said, and swallowed. "Aye, I can leave Malton with a half-dozen men under his command. Lord Hugh said that I could recruit more men from Penrith and Carlisle. I must do that quickly. I hope the Scots will not attack until I have the additional men I need at Oldham."

An hour later, Jerval found his father with

a roll of parchment on his lap, his gouty foot propped up on a stool. He was smiling.

"Sir, what is it?" Chandra said to Lord Hugh, drawing closer, Lady Faye at her side.

Hugh drew himself up, and that smile stretched his mouth even wider. "It is a letter from King Henry. Prince Edward and Princess Eleanor are touring the lake region on their way to Scotland, and will be our guests. So what do you think of that?"

"When, Father?"

"In a week, no more."

"Only seven days from now?" Lady Avicia whirled about to yell at her husband, "By the Virgin, Hugh, I must have a new gown. Oh, and all the preparations. I haven't the time to get it all done. Oh, my."

"How exciting it is," Mary said to Mark, who had walked to stand beside her.

"Aye, it is an honor," he said. "It will also drain Camberley of some of her winter stores."

"I had not thought of that."

"It is still wonderful," Mark said, smiling down at her, seeing her with new eyes, the eyes of her future husband. Please, God, he prayed as he looked at her still slender waist, do not let it be a male child.

Jerval said, "It will be good to see Edward

again. You will like Edward's ready wit, Chandra, and Eleanor's gentle grace." He frowned suddenly at the old gown his wife was wearing. "I trust you have something more fitting to wear?"

"I am learning how to weave," she said, her voice as flat as the tapestry against the stone wall behind Lord Hugh. "It is dirty work."

Jerval grinned at her. "I trust you are growing as skilled with the loom as you are with a bow."

"No," she said. "I am not." She shook her head and couldn't help herself — she smiled from ear to ear. "I cannot believe it! Prince Edward will be coming here?"

He smiled at her excitement.

"The king writes that my poor Matilda's husband, Eustace, will be accompanying them," Lord Hugh said. "It appears he has been hanging about Windsor since his return from France."

"I wonder what Eustace was up to in France," Jerval said thoughtfully. "Louis, after all, has already left for the Holy Land."

"Whatever it is, it won't be good," Lord Hugh said. "Eustace is a rotten whoreson, and I doubt that he's improved with the years. Now, I also think the prince has more reason for visiting the lake region than just to tour his lands and to kick any Scots warriors who happen to get in his way."

"I think you are right, Father," Jerval said, then smiled at Mark. "I have more good news for all of you," he called out. "It would seem that my mother has more to do in the way of preparations than just for the prince and princess's visit."

Lady Avicia, who had just begun to make lists in her mind, bent a sharp eye to her son at his words. "Whatever do you mean, Jerval?"

Jerval studied Mary's lovely face for a moment, then winked at Mark. "I believe I will savor the telling until this evening."

"He did naught but *inform* you?" Chandra said.

Mary's happy smile did not dim. "Not exactly," Mary said. "Jerval is always kind to me, and I know he means me well."

"I should have insisted that he tell me what he was planning."

"But, Chandra," Mary said, "what does it matter that he did not tell you? After all, he had first to gain Sir Mark's agreement. Mark will be a fine husband, and he is too kind ever to reproach me about the child. I am more pleased than I can tell you."

"But you were given no choice, Mary.

How can you be pleased that Jerval simply decided that you would wed Mark, without even asking what you thought of him?"

"It would have been my father's duty to find me a husband," Mary said reasonably, "and I cannot tell you how thankful I am that my father will never know about the child. Because Jerval took it upon himself, I am now to marry an honorable man who likes me and will treat both me and the child well. What more could I ask? I will have a gentle lord, be mistress of his keep, and bear his children. Mark knows that I will try to make him a good wife. It is more than I ever could have wished for."

At Chandra's sigh, Mary said with a rare show of temper, "Would you prefer that I bear a bastard in shame?"

"Nay, of course not. It's just that I would have liked to know what he was thinking, what he was planning. After all, it is I who am your friend first."

Mary couldn't help herself. She laughed aloud, laughed even louder, holding her stomach. "Oh, my, Chandra, it is just that Jerval did not even consider asking you that makes you snipe about all of it. But surely you cannot disagree with the outcome. After all, what meaning would life have if one did not marry and have babes, and live together, and share joy and sorrow? Such a sad life it would be." She laid a light hand on Chandra's arm.

Sharing, Chandra thought, sharing. With a man, with a husband, with Jerval. It was a very difficult thing. It meant giving over — it meant no longer holding what you were, deep inside, close.

It meant being less than yourself, giving part of yourself over to the other. Over to Jerval. No, he would demand that she give him everything she was. It was a terrifying thought.

Chandra said, suddenly brisk, "You are right, of course. Now, we have little time to prepare your bridal clothes. And the prince is coming as well. I hear he is terribly tall, isn't he?"

"Aye, he is called Edward Longshanks. And Lady Avicia is already bustling about. She must wonder why we are to wed so quickly, but she said nothing of it to me. She is so very kind to me, and I fear I have done little to deserve it."

"Nonsense, you are an angel, and Mark the luckiest man alive. I hope my mother-in-law doesn't clout Mark in the head when she hears of this."

Five days later, Chandra, her husband beside her, waved one last time to Mary from atop the outer wall.

"Mother packed the baggage mules so high, I was beginning to wonder if we would have anything left at Camberley," Jerval said. He looked down at his wife's clear profile, so elegant, so pure. Her hair was pulled back from her face, and she was gowned beautifully in soft yellow, with yellow ribbons threaded through her hair. He wanted her, right that moment. But he didn't move.

He said, "You will miss her. We will visit them. Do not fret." He paused a moment, then said slowly, "Mother tells me that you are learning. Not as quickly as she would like, but nonetheless, it appears you are trying a bit. She tells me that most of the time you even manage to keep your mouth shut — a miracle, she believes — but there is still the cursing under your breath."

"Does that mean I may go hunting with you and the men on the morrow?"

"No, but perhaps by next month you will have the skill that will change my mind. You will tell me when you are ready to demonstrate what you have learned." He added, "I will miss Mary. She mended my tunics. I will be favorably impressed if you can show me that sort of skill with a needle."

"I mended the last one — the blue wool

you had ripped under the arm. See, you did not even think that it might not have been Mary's work."

"I simply wondered if perhaps Mary had decided to sew with larger stitches."

He was laughing at her. She wanted to clout him and she wanted to throw herself against him and beg him to make love to her. He hadn't touched her for well over a week. She wanted him — she admitted it. She wanted him to touch her, to kiss her in that special way he had; she wanted him inside her, deep, a part of her. She didn't say anything, but the tears gathered and fell.

"Chandra."

"Nay," she said and held up her hand to ward him off, then turned to walk away.

He stared after her, praying that his teasing hadn't led to her tears — no, impossible. He'd realized some time before that keeping the upper hand was the only way to save himself from being ground beneath her heel. Why had she cried? Surely not because he'd laughed. He wished she'd hit him instead. He wanted her, always wanted her; it was a low ache in his groin. But he saw his avoiding her as punishment for what she'd done. Punishment for him as well. He was a fool, he knew, but he didn't know what he could do about it.

★ ★ ★

The next morning everyone at Camberley was caught up in the preparations for the coming of the prince and princess. Under Lady Avicia's sharp eye, the tapestries were taken down and beaten free of dust, the feather-down mattresses were hauled from the keep and aired for two days, leaving everyone to sleep wrapped in blankets on the floor. Even the jakes did not suffer from lack of Lady Avicia's attention. She saw to it that even with a south wind, there was no odor to offend the nose. Weaving and sewing went on far into the night, and the serving wenches were fitted with new kirtles of green wool. The lavers were polished until they sparkled enough to show the prince and princess their reflections while they washed their hands. The accumulated ashes were swept away from the huge hearth and the cavernous fireplace scrubbed.

It was only when Lord Hugh saw several boys dangling from tall ladders trying to clean the crossbeams in the hall ceiling that he threw up his hands, crying enough. Hawk, with Lord Hugh's agreement, was kept out of the keep, and Chandra — who spent most of her waking hours directing servants and weeding the garden herself, for Lady Avicia was certain that Princess Eleanor would wish to inspect the tiered vegetable plots — was too tired from all the work to complain much.

"I wonder which of us will have to wash the castle walls," was all she said.

It was Jerval, in fact, who directed the cleaning of the barracks and stables, for in Lady Avicia's mind, the prince's men would surely tell him if they found filth. Although the men grumbled, they too were infected with the growing excitement, for royalty had not visited Camberley in over twenty years, when King Henry had once deigned to pass the night there. The rotted hay — of which there was very little — was swept from the stables and burned in the bailey.

Meals were meager the several days before the prince's arrival, and the smells from the cooking sheds made everyone's mouth water. Lady Avicia had even sent for a baker from Carlisle, and the little man, his scrawny frame wrapped in a huge white linen apron, had quickly spread terror among the rest of the cooks, until, under his snapping orders, piles of pastries and breads filled the larders.

Everyone but Lady Avicia was delighted when Anselm, high in the north tower, sounded three loud blasts on his hunting horn. She still wasn't ready — oh, by all the saints, what would the princess see that would offend her? At the sound of the horn, even the smallest child in the keep lined up beside his mother, his hands reverently clasped in front of him, awaiting the royal review.

Chandra wished she were in the tower with Anselm to witness the prince's vast retinue, but her silk gown was new, as were her soft leather shoes, and she was left to wait at Jerval's side in the inner bailey. He was dressed, she was certain, as finely as the prince must be. His fair hair fell shining and thick in loose waves at his neck. His surcoat of vivid dark blue velvet fell to his ankles, its full, fur-lined sleeves wide and loose over his large hands. His mother had made his surcoat.

"I do hope," Jerval said to her, "that the prince has bathed in the last week, else my mother will likely have him bathed before he's allowed to eat at the trestle tables."

Chandra smiled at that, but didn't reply, for the inner bailey was suddenly a blaze of deep purple and crimson. Edward and Eleanor, dressed in rich velvet shot with gold thread, rode at the fore of their retinue, astride two matched, glossy-white stallions.

"She is beautiful," Chandra whispered, her eyes on the exquisite woman who rode beside the prince, her black hair held in a net of gold, her gloved hands, covered with sparkling pearls, lightly holding her reins. "Never have I seen a more beautiful lady."

"Aye," Jerval agreed, and could but shake his head. Chandra was the most beautiful creature he had ever seen. Had she no idea what she looked like? That a man wanted to fall to his knees just looking at her? "If you think me tall, Chandra, wait until your neck creaks looking up at the prince."

"Aye, I know he is called Longshanks."

Prince Edward leapt gracefully from his destrier and tossed the reins to one of the gape-mouthed stable boys. He was as magnificent as his princess, Chandra thought, taller even than she'd imagined, broad shouldered, and slim hipped. He was not, she thought objectively, as handsome as Jerval, but his features were strong, and his light-blue Plantagenet eyes seemed to take in everything and everyone about him. His hair was pale yellow and hung to his shoulders.

There was a babble of voices until Lord Hugh stepped proudly forward. "God's grace on you, sire." Lord Hugh bowed deeply to the prince, and then to Princess Eleanor. "And to you, my lady."

Chandra saw Prince Edward meet Jerval's eyes, his lips parted in a grin, but it was to

Lord Hugh and Lady Avicia that he said, "Thank you for your excellent friendship. Eleanor and I are pleased to be here."

"Aye," Eleanor said, her voice sweet and full, "we thank you for your hospitality."

It was then that the prince turned to Jerval and clasped his hand, then hugged him. "Aye, it's even more handsome a rogue you've become," Edward said.

"And even more a giant you've become."

"It is good to see you again, Jerval." Edward wrapped his arms about Jerval's shoulders. "Eleanor, I beg you not to fall in love with this very short man just because you feel sorry for him. It's true too that he's but a boy, a good five years less of ripening than I have."

"After seeing only your face for so many years, and watching you grow old, I vow I will look my fill," Eleanor said and gave Jerval her white hand. "It has been too long, Jerval. I trust all goes well with you."

No, he thought, things weren't going all that well for him, but those thoughts didn't show on his face. "Aye, it has been far too long, my lady," he said, then added, "Sire, my lady, this is my wife."

"What? You have finally tied yourself to one woman? Show me this amazing creature who has brought you low." The laughter left

Edward's blue eyes when he looked down at Chandra. The girl curtsying before him would take away a man's breath. She was glorious. Golden hair hung loose to just below her shoulders, held back from her face with plaited yellow ribbons. He wanted to touch that hair. Actually, he wanted to touch all of her. And then she looked up at him, and he wondered what one said to such an exquisite creature. There was no shyness in her as she straightened to look at him full-face.

"Who are you, my lady? Surely such a lovely girl would not pass unheard of to me, even at Windsor."

"I am Chandra de Avenell. My father, Lord Richard, is one of your marcher barons. His castle is known as Croyland."

"Sir Jerval is a lucky man," Eleanor said, smiling. "Come, my lord, have we not heard tell of Chandra de Avenell?"

"My daughter-in-law," Lady Avicia said to everyone's astonishment, "has long been known for her beauty."

"I can certainly see why," Eleanor said. "Do you not remember, my lord? Your father approved their marriage not long ago."

"Aye," Edward said slowly. "I remember you well now, my lady. Lord Graelam de Moreton, as I recall, approached my uncle about wedding you." He turned to Jerval, a wicked gleam in his eyes. "You beat out a fine warrior, Jerval, and stole yourself a prize."

It was on the tip of Chandra's tongue to inform the prince that it was Graelam who had nearly done the stealing, but Eleanor said suddenly, "A French minstrel, Henri, visited the court last year. He sang about you, Chandra, your beauty and your warrior deeds."

"This lovely girl a warrior?" Edward gave a great belly laugh.

Chapter 21

"She is now more a wife," Jerval said smoothly, taking Chandra's hand in his. "As for Graelam de Moreton — that, sire, is a long story. Perhaps late one night when we are deep into my father's fine wine from Aquitaine, I will tell you of it."

After the prince and princess were swept into the hall by Lord Hugh, Jerval turned to give orders for the prince's vast retinue.

"Well, cousin, you must be relieved that the prince is happily wed and doesn't have the habit of consorting with his nobles' ladies."

Jerval drew up at Eustace's deep voice. "You keep high company, Eustace." His eyes turned to his wife. "Chandra, this is Eustace de Leybrun. He was my sister Matilda's husband."

Chandra nodded politely at the dark man, hearing the barely veiled dislike in Jerval's voice. He was dressed nearly as richly as the prince, his thick velvet cloak covering a surcoat of burgundy, its wide sleeves lined with miniver. He was not of Jerval's height, but he was built like a bull, his neck thick and corded, and she could see that beneath his noble clothes, his body was hard with muscle. She guessed him to be about thirty, or perhaps older, for there were lines etched about his dark eyes and his wide mouth.

"Welcome to Camberley, sir. I understand you have been in France."

"Aye, my lady," Eustace said. "Had I known that my little cousin was wedding himself to such as you, I would have returned and relieved him of his bride." His glance swept toward Jerval. "I saw de Moreton, you know, cousin. He was surly, his manner more abrupt than usual. None wanted to cross him. I had no idea that it was you who was the cause of his black humor. He said nothing to me, of course, but his squire's tongue became loose with drink, and he spoke of his master's defeat at Croyland, and of his shoulder wound at the hands of a gently bred lady."

Eustace turned to Chandra and said in a soft voice that made her skin crawl, "So the victor won the prize, my lady. It is seldom that an heiress has claim to such beauty, as well as skill with a dagger. You are a prize to be treasured. Were you mine, I would hold you above all my possessions."

Chandra had listened to him in silence. She wanted to strike him on both his ears. He hated Jerval — that was easy enough to see. It was jealousy, but no matter. Soon he would be gone again. She said, "Your compliments, Sir Eustace, ring hollow as the chapel bell. Mayhap you'd best strive for more sincerity."

"Well met, my lady," Eustace said. "What is this about your gentle wife being a warrior, Jerval, and hurling daggers at the greatest fighters of our land?"

"Go assist my mother," Jerval said, and gave Chandra a light shove. She wanted to remain, to challenge Eustace, but she saw the anger in her husband, anger that was deep and abiding.

"My wife, Eustace," he said, watching Chandra gracefully mount the staircase to the hall, "is many things. But most important, she is now a de Vernon."

"Do not, I beg you, Jerval, challenge me for admiring your wife's beauty. I see that you are surrounded by beauty. The fair Julianna has grown quite comely. I trust that she is still a virgin? Or did you already relieve her of that commodity?"

Jerval wanted to strike him, to break both his legs, but he couldn't, at least not at this moment, so he ignored his words and said,

"You have a new neighbor at Oldham. Sir Mark is now master there." He saw the tightening in Eustace's jaw and smiled.

"How generous you are toward a landless knight." Eustace said it with a sneer, which marred his face, had he but known it.

"The de Vernon lands need proper protection from the Scots," Jerval said smoothly, "and Sir Mark's loyalty to the de Vernons, as well as his honor, cannot be questioned."

Eustace shrugged. "From what I heard, Sir John kept a tight hold on Oldham. Did he have the misfortune to look lustfully at your wife?"

"Nay, he lacked the wit to see me for what I am, and he now rots in a shallow grave just beyond the keep. He betrayed us, dealt with Alan Durwald, who is also dead now. You will see Lady Faye, his widow. She has much changed since we freed her of that bastard. Let us go within. Doubtless you would like to refresh yourself."

"What lovely rugs," Jerval heard Princess Eleanor say to his mother as they entered the hall.

Lady Avicia beamed. "This one is from Castile, my lady, your homeland."

"How long do you stay at Camberley, sire?" Lord Hugh asked.

Edward tossed down the rest of his wine before saying with a disarming grin, "Actually, Lord Hugh, our trip north is for two purposes, the first being to travel to Scotland to celebrate my aunt's birthday. If it pleases you, we would be your guests for two days. My wife much enjoys the lake region, and it is always a pleasure to see my father's faithful barons."

"And your other reason?" Jerval asked, having a good idea what was in Edward's mind.

"Do not press me, Jerval," Edward said. "I plan to get you drunk, then gain your agreement."

"That will be a sight worth seeing," Jerval said, and laughed. "I could always outdrink you. You'll be snoring and sodden in your chair and likely forget what it is you're after."

"Very true, my lord," Eleanor said. "But at least you are always sweet and regretful the next morning."

Edward said to Chandra, just shaking his head at his wife, "My lady, Lord Richard, your father, is one of the king's favorite men, and he has done well against the Welsh. But even castles like Croyland are not enough to contain them."

"You are right, sire," Chandra said.

"There is more need of protection. However, I must say that because of the Welsh, life at Croyland was never dull."

Edward sat forward in his chair, needing no more encouragement, and rubbed his large hands together. "Aye, someday I will build castles along the border, mighty fortresses that will hold even Llewelyn. Englishmen will need have no fear that they will awake with their throats cut." Edward said to Chandra, "You find life at Camberley dull then, my lady?"

What to say? That she was forced to mend sheets? To pull endless weeds next to the rosemary in the wretched gardens? Well, no, they weren't exactly wretched, those magnificent gardens, but to spend three hours on her knees, pulling up weeds, patting those plants as if they were children to be encouraged. Aye, life had to be dull if she wasn't allowed to hunt until she proved to her husband that she could sew him a wretched tunic. There were needle marks on the pads of her fingers. She hated sewing. She said finally, aware that Jerval was looking at her, his head cocked to one side, "It has not been so since we heard of your coming, sire."

"She misses her armor," Julianna said. "Did you not know, sire? Chandra boasts

361

that she can rout any man on the battle-field."

Edward's brow shot up. "What is this, Jerval? You have another warrior at Camberley, yet you do not use her skills?"

"My wife is currently enlarging her skills, sire. My mother is teaching her the duties of a chatelaine. Now, sire, you have need to re-fill your goblet."

What Chandra wanted more than any-thing at that moment was to fetch her sword and go toe to toe with the damn prince.

She looked at her husband and knew he saw exactly what was in her mind. He smiled at her even as he shook his head. That smile of his, she knew, was dead serious.

She sighed and escorted Princess Eleanor to her chamber.

The trestle tables groaned under the weight of the food Lady Avicia provided that evening. Silver plates held the trenchers of bread, set amid pastries filled with chicken, venison, salmon, and eel. The mixed aroma of onions, garlic, carrots, arti-chokes, peas, and potatoes wafted through the hall, filled with over a hundred people, many of them eating seated on the stone floors, Avicia having wisely rolled up the carpets to prevent them from being soiled.

"Indeed a royal feast," Edward said as servants carried in huge platters of roasted stag, cut into quarters, crisped, and larded. He watched, rubbing his hands in anticipation, as one of the cooks poured a hot, steaming pepper sauce over the stag.

"And such a wealth of vegetables, Lady Avicia," Eleanor said.

"The vegetables are from Camberley's own gardens," Lady Avicia said. "Chandra has nearly made the garden her own."

"Not the garden," Chandra said, "merely the weeds."

"It is one and the same thing," Avicia said.

As if on cue, Lady Avicia's specially hired cook ushered in three servants who were carrying an enormous platter. Lord Hugh, grinning widely, stepped forward, eyed the huge pastry, and slashed it open with his dagger. A score of small swallows fluttered out and flew wildly about the hall, amid the men's shouts and the ladies' cries. Eventually, they winged to the crossbeams and to safety.

When he was sated with food and wine, Edward sat back in his chair with a satisfied groan.

"Do you wish more wine, sire?" Lord Hugh asked.

"Perhaps," Jerval said, "Prince Edward will finally tell us his real reason for his visit to Camberley."

Edward grinned at him. "You know, Jerval, why I am here. I want you to come with me to Tunis, to join King Louis and fight the heathen in Outremer."

"The Holy Land," Jerval said to Chandra.

"A crusade?"

"Aye, my lady," Edward said. "I have taken my vow before God, as have many others. It is a holy cause and we will not fail. But we must leave soon, before winter sets in and makes travel impossible. Join me, Jerval, and bring as many men as Camberley can spare."

"How many men does Louis command?" Lord Hugh asked.

"Well over ten thousand. Although our numbers will not be so impressive, together we can crush the Saracens."

"I have heard it told," Jerval said, "that the Saracen sultan, Baibars, commands an army in the hundreds of thousands."

"Aye, it is true. But I am convinced, as is King Louis, that our cause will bring the other kings of Christendom to our aid."

"King Louis failed miserably in his first effort," Lord Hugh said sharply. "He was captured, ransomed, and released back to

France, weak and old before his time."

Eleanor said quietly, "But, my lord, his spirit inspires the most profound loyalty and admiration in Christendom, and fear in its enemies. The Saracens fear us, and our God."

"It will be a costly venture," Jerval said.

"Aye," Edward agreed, "but think of the glory and honor we will gain in serving God by ridding the Holy Land of its heathen."

"It is a request that I must not answer quickly," Jerval said quietly, closing his hand over Edward's arm.

The talk continued, but Chandra wasn't listening. She had never been out of England; indeed, the Scottish border was the farthest she had ever traveled from Camberley, and that journey was not a pleasant memory. She remembered her father telling her of the mighty Templars, a fierce military order as skilled in the art of finance as in that of fighting, and of the Saracens, who were threatening the very existence of the Kingdom of Jerusalem. If only she were a man, a knight, to be free to join Prince Edward. To go to the Holy Land — ah, it was a dream, a magnificent dream.

Lord Hugh said suddenly, "My daughter-in-law is talented, sire. Would you care to hear her perform?"

The talk of the crusade was over. Chandra looked briefly at Jerval and saw his brow furrowed in thought.

Edward called out, "Aye, let Chandra play and sing, and then I can retire to my bed to dream about her."

"You have eaten so much, my lord," Eleanor said, "I wager it is nightmares you'll have."

Chandra's lyre was fetched and she settled it on her lap, running her fingers lightly over the strings. She sang of King Richard and his final battle with the great Saladin, a song she herself had written. Her eyes sparkled as the notes rose to a crescendo at Richard's victory, then fell muted and sad at the treachery that imprisoned him, far away from England, in the dark dungeons of Leopold of Austria.

There was silence for a brief moment when she had finished; then Edward leaned forward in his chair and said, his voice low and serious, "My great-uncle taught the heathen that the Christian God would not be denied, that our Lord makes us strong and brave in battle. I thank you for your tribute."

Eustace called out, "Ah, sire, she is a warrior, do you not remember?"

Edward's Plantagenet-blue eyes lightened. "Tell me, then, my lady, what other talents do you possess?"

"I joust, though I do not have a man's strength. I hunt. I am good with a knife. And, sire, I should not be surprised if I could best you on the archery range."

Edward looked taken aback; then he threw back his head and gave way to booming laughter.

"A soft, delicate girl best me?" Edward wiped his eyes on his sleeve. "I admire your wit, my lady."

"I was not jesting, sire."

"Chandra."

She twisted about to see her husband's face, his eyes narrowed on her face. She saw the anger in his eyes even though his voice, saying her name, had been soft, gentle almost. She looked down at her slippers. She had not meant to flout him. She hated herself at that moment — worried that she had unwittingly flouted a man, flouted her husband, who was a man and her master. Oh, God, she was becoming nothing at all.

Jerval rose abruptly to his feet, his hand closing tightly about Chandra's arm. "My wife is tired, my lord."

"And you, my lord," Eleanor said to her husband, "have drunk too much wine."

"Nay," Edward said, his eyes resting with

laughter on Chandra's face. He rose and slowly pulled a heavy emerald ring from his finger. "If you, my lady, can indeed beat me, the ring is yours. And will you, Jerval, give your colors to your wife so she may wear them on her sleeve?"

Chandra heard a gasp from Lady Avicia.

"You have to accept me in my wife's stead, sire," Jerval said. His fingers tightened over her wrist. "Tell him that it is so, Chandra."

She wanted to howl, to curse every foul word she'd heard since she was a little girl, to tell her husband and the world that she wasn't a useless bit of nothing. But he knew that. He didn't care. He didn't want that girl as his wife. She said, "Indeed, sire, it is so."

She watched Edward slide the ring back onto his finger, saw Eleanor tug on his sleeve. He leaned down to hear her softly spoken words. When he straightened, he said, "Perhaps, then, my lady, we can speak again on the morrow."

Not two hours later, a messenger arrived from Oldham, from Mark. The Scots had attacked the demesne farms and killed many of Sir Mark's people. Retribution for Alan Durwald's murder, it was said. And Oldham itself would be next. There was anger and fear in the woods, both in equal measure.

Chandra rode at the rear of the thirty men who left Camberley within the next hour. There was a full moon. It was late, very late. She thought of Mary, and what the messenger had told her. She'd known there was no choice at all, despite what her husband would probably say, despite what he would do to her. He would never forgive her, she knew, but she had no choice. Mary, the messenger had said, was begging her to come. She needed her.

She waited until they were a mere mile from Oldham before she rode up beside her husband.

At first he did not pay her any attention, his eyes straight ahead, his brow furrowed in thought.

"I will be very careful," she said. "You need not worry about me. Mary is afraid, perhaps even in danger. I need to help her."

Jerval slewed around in his saddle, not wanting to believe what he was seeing with his own eyes.

"I can weave, I can mend your tunics, I can weed the vegetable gardens. It is time to let me do what I was trained to do. I can help you. Truly, I had no choice but to come."

"I don't believe this," Jerval said, slapping

his gauntleted hand to his thigh. "I just don't." He wanted to strangle her in that moment.

"I'm here only because of Mary. She needs me. The messenger told me she is very afraid, and she asked me to come to Oldham. She is the only reason I am here. She is very afraid, both for Oldham and Mark."

"You will not fight."

"I know. I came to be with Mary."

When they arrived at Oldham, Mark was preparing to ride out with his men. He was leaving six men to guard Oldham keep. "You have made excellent time. I thank you, Jerval. We hear that the Scots have ridden north. We are going after them. I cannot allow this to remain unpunished."

"We will ride with you." Jerval turned to his wife. "You will remain here, with Mary." He paused a moment, then smiled an evil smile. "Aye, you will protect the lady of Oldham. Didn't you say that was the only real reason you came?"

"Aye." He'd believed she'd lied to him. She hadn't. They rode into the inner bailey. Chandra leapt off her horse and ran to Mary, who was standing on the wide steps to the Great Hall, pale, her hands clasped over her belly.

Chandra didn't hesitate. She pulled Mary to her, stroking her hands over her back. "It will be all right. There are enough men. Jerval and Mark will catch them, and it will be over. I will not leave you. Come inside now; you must rest."

"You look like a warrior again."

"Aye, I am *your* warrior, here to guard you."

"Thank you, Chandra, for coming. Was Jerval angry?"

"Only for the last mile."

"Well, that is an improvement."

"I didn't show myself until then."

"Ah."

Chandra shrugged. "It matters not. Now, we have six men to guard the keep?"

"And you, Chandra, and you."

It was nearly dawn when Chandra, who had finally fallen into a light sleep, awoke to a strange gurgling sound. It was deep and low and it sounded like — She jerked fully awake, her knife in her hand, realizing that what she'd heard was the sound of a man choking to death on his own blood. A man usually didn't choke to death by accident.

It took her but an instant to realize the truth. The Scots weren't headed north with Mark and Jerval on their heels. They'd circled back. They were right here, and somehow they'd gotten into the keep.

Jerval said, looking up at the bright moon, "We have come too far. There is no sign of them. It isn't right."

Mark sniffed the air. "It's cold, too cold," he said, "and I don't like this either. It doesn't smell right. You're right. The Scots aren't ahead of us. I know it."

"Then where are they?"

"I don't know, but they're not in that copse of trees yon."

"They wanted retribution for Durwald's death — that is what you told me."

"Aye, one of our own men-at-arms told me that, said a bandit had told him to tell me that. That this was their first onslaught, that soon, not long from now, perhaps in the dead of winter, they would return and they would drive us from Oldham and torch the keep."

"What was an Oldham man-at-arms doing at a demesne farm? Wasn't that where the Scots were?"

"Aye. He fancies the daughter. He was there wooing her when the Scots attacked."

"Why didn't they steal any cattle?"

"If it was revenge they wanted this time, as my own man told me, why would they bother with cattle? Herding cattle would slow them down, give us a better chance to catch up with them. No, they just wanted to strike us hard, quickly, then retreat. Vengeance, that's what it is."

Jerval said slowly, "I wonder why they had this man-at-arms tell you of their plans."

"To boast of their prowess, I suppose. After they stabbed my man in the shoulder, they must have realized it would make an excellent jest to send him to me and tell me what had happened and what they planned for the future."

Jerval was shaking his head as he said, "It doesn't make sense, Mark. Why would they give you warning of their intent? No, it simply doesn't ring true to me. Wasn't there another demesne farmer who managed to get to Oldham to tell you what was happening?"

Mark nodded. "Both my man-at-arms and the farmer managed to make it to the keep, my man first."

"Where is your man-at-arms? I would speak to him."

"As I said, he — Alaric — was covered in blood, unable to fight. He just told us we must hurry, that the Scots hadn't gotten too far, that they'd believed him very badly wounded, and thus he couldn't get to me quickly. He was too ill to come and so he remained behind."

And there was the answer, staring him in the face. He was an idiot. He'd moved too quickly, hadn't really thought about the attack, about the man-at-arms' words, hadn't weighed the possibilities, hadn't really assessed the Scots' intent, and he'd been brought low.

Dear God, Chandra was at Oldham. He'd left her there himself to guard Mary, to sit with her and give her milk and pat her hand. Aye, he'd thought she would be safe, and there would be no danger for her. By the saints, he should be hanged for his stupidity.

She was there with naught but six men.

Jerval jerked back on Pith's reins, the destrier rearing on his hind legs. "We're fools, Mark. Alaric, the man who stayed behind with his wound — he stayed in the keep?"

"Aye, he did. Why wouldn't he?"

"I think he's a traitor."

"Oh, God, you don't really think that it was all a ruse, do you?"

"He's a traitor," Jerval said again. "It was a plan to get you away from Oldham, and me as well since you sent a messenger to me. We are bloody fools." Jerval turned in his saddle and yelled to the men, "We've been betrayed! Back to Oldham!" And all he could think about was his wife, so brave it frightened him, unyielding in the face of overwhelming odds, ready to face down the devil himself, willing to die for Mary. She was there with a traitor, and the Scots.

Chapter 22

Chandra quickly pulled on her woolen cap, stuffing her hair beneath. She stood slowly, her knife in one hand, her sword in the other, looking around. There was no one in the Great Hall save her and Mary. The servants were up in the solar, the six guards in the bailey or on the ramparts. She walked quietly toward the front doors, out of habit looking right and left, ready, her muscles bunched, her heart pounding, but her mind was cold and sharp. There was only silence now, and the first soft gray light of dawn pearling in the quiet air through the open front doors to the Great Hall. Chill morning air also seeped through the open front doors, shifting the silent air within. Oh, God, she thought, the front doors were open.

The doors should be closed, the heavy wooden and steel bars firmly in place, but they weren't.

Someone had opened them and she hadn't heard a thing. Mary was seated in a chair at the back of the hall near the huge fireplace, her cheek pillowed on her palms, finally asleep. No, Chandra didn't want to awaken her yet. Maybe there was nothing wrong, maybe —

The six men-at-arms were all outside in the bailey — they had to be, aye, on the walls, watching, searching all around the keep for any sign of the enemy. Surely they weren't asleep. There was too much at stake here. Their lives for one thing. There'd been no attack. If there had been, there would have been shouts, cries of warning, sounds of battle, but there'd been only that one death sound deep in the man's throat. Where was he? As for the servants, she didn't know where they were, but none were here in the Great Hall. She'd believed the hall stingy in its size, but now, in the utter stillness, with that death sound still echoing in her ears, she believed it huge, filled with echoes and evil and danger, and she was alone, no one to help her.

When she couldn't bear it any longer, she walked to where the front doors to the Great Hall were cracked open and gently shoved them outward. The man whose death sound she'd heard was lying there in his own blood, his eyes wide and staring. He'd been stabbed, then somehow managed to crawl this far. He'd wanted to warn them, but he hadn't made it. He'd just died, and that meant the enemy was here, waiting, probably watching her, wondering how many men were within the keep.

No, she wasn't alone, not any longer. The Scots had managed to get into the keep. Were all the six guards dead? She had to assume they were. What to do?

She held perfectly still, listening. She heard the sound of boots, not many, perhaps three men, coming toward the keep, over the uneven cobbles in the inner bailey. Soon they would see the dead man on the steps; they would see the front doors open.

She didn't have time to get the doors closed, and it wouldn't have mattered in any case because she wasn't strong enough by herself to place the huge bars into their thick wooden slots on the doors.

She ran back to Mary and shook her, saying quickly, "Don't be afraid, Mary, but there is trouble. I need you to get beneath this trestle table. The cloth on it is long and will hide you. Quickly, quickly."

"But, Chandra, our men —"

"They're dead. Hurry, Mary, you must hurry. You must protect your babe."

Once Mary was beneath the trestle table, Chandra crept back toward the front doors of the Great Hall. More footsteps, at least six men, moving quickly now, with purpose. They must have discovered that there was no one in the Great Hall except two women. There was no more reason for them to hang back. How long had they been inside the walls?

She stood there, knife and sword raised, waiting, waiting.

Their leader came first through the front doors, and she saw him clearly in the dawn light, harsh now, steel gray, framing the wild-haired man dressed in his animal skins, his face pocked, his eyes flat and hard.

Even though she'd never seen him before, she knew immediately that he was Alan Durwald's brother. Their features were so similar, even the way they carried themselves. It was like meeting the devil for a second time.

The devil had come for revenge. Someone had betrayed them.

He stopped when he saw her standing there, a boy facing him with a single sword and a single knife, both raised and ready to do battle, tall and slim, this boy, pride in those shoulders, pride bred into his very bones. What was he doing here?

"What," Robbie Durwald said, coming to a stop, his voice filling the dead silence of the Great Hall, "a single little lad left to defend Oldham? What think ye of this, men?"

The men behind him laughed. Some didn't because they were looking around, searching every corner of the hall, ready, nervous.

"A little lad," Robbie Durwald said again, and he walked to the lad, pulling up a good six feet distant because he wasn't stupid and the lad could be good with a sword. "Who are ye? Why are ye here? Sir Mark leaves ye here unguarded?"

Chandra said nothing at all.

"Come now, answer me. What do ye here, lad? Where is the lady of the keep? I was told only she and her friend were here."

"She and her friend left hours ago for Camberley, for safety."

"And why are ye the only one here?"

"I wanted to remain. I commanded the guards. You've killed them, haven't you?"

"Aye, they're all dead, the miserable English bastards. Aye, everything came to pass as I believed it would. Ye English have cocks for brains, so easy it was. And now there is only ye."

Then she realized what had happened, how they'd been betrayed. The man-at-arms who'd told Mark that the Scots had fled back northward had not been wounded at all. He was the traitor. He'd opened the gates; he'd taken off the bars from the front doors.

"Well, lad, how wish ye to die?"

"If I die, it will be after I've ripped out your guts, you filthy bastard. You won't feel it because you'll be in hell with the devil, just watching and weeping at your failure."

The man paused then, staring at the boy, and something sounded in his memory, something Alan had told him, and then he'd shown him that beautiful rope of hair he'd sliced away from her. No, it wasn't possible. That girl couldn't be here. She was a lady and at Camberley. But Alaric had said it was only two women.

"What be yer name, lad? Afore I kill an enemy, I like to say his name aloud and curse him to his death."

"I am Alaric. Unlike the other Alaric, I am not a traitor."

"Ah, the boy knows ye for what ye are, Alaric," Robbie Durwald yelled behind him. "Come forward and tell me who this lad is?"

"No wound, I see," Chandra said, watching the man stride toward them. She wished she could run the man through his belly.

"No," Alaric said, "there is no wound. Wait, Robbie. I did not intend for Lady Mary to be harmed. Where is she?"

"She is gone, to Camberley."

Alaric was shaking his head. "No, she did not leave Oldham. I was watching." Then he stopped cold and stared. "You're Sir Jerval's lady. You're that girl warrior."

She didn't move, just smiled at him.

"Aye, I believe ye're right, Alaric," Robbie Durwald said. "I believe I would like to have a lady serve me ale. What think ye, men?"

"Robbie," Alaric said, coming forward to lightly touch his hand to the man's forearm. "We don't want to remain at Oldham any longer than we have to. Sir Mark and Sir Jerval aren't stupid. We got them out of here, but they will realize what happened, that we doubled back, and they will come back. We must take Lady Mary's dowry gold and leave, now."

"They're English, Alaric, just like you. They're stupid and thoughtless. Just ye look — they left two ladies here unprotected at Oldham. What man would leave his lady unprotected?"

"She's not a lady. I have heard the men talk of her. They say that she fights as well as they do, that she shows no mercy, that she will run a sword through your belly, smiling all the time. We must leave, Robbie, we must."

"Ye bore me, Alaric. As I said, ye English are stupid filthy louts." He turned slowly about to face Alaric, slipped a thin-bladed knife from his belt and, fast as a snake, slid it into his chest. "Go to hell," Robbie said, watching Alaric's eyes go wide and unseeing as he fell silently to the stone floor.

"Now, lady, for that is what ye are, despite yer boy's clothes, I wish ye to fetch me some ale. Aye, and ye will serve me, and then maybe ye'll sit on my knee and I'll let ye beg me for yer little life and that of Lady Mary. Aye, and I'll see that hair of yers. Alan had a foot of it wrapped around his wrist. Yer husband took it from him when he killed him. Where is Lady Mary?"

"Alaric was wrong. Sir Mark sent her through the postern gate, to Camberley, to safety."

"If I find her, and I will look very soon now, then I will kill her right in front of ye. Believe me, for I do not lie."

"Mary," Chandra said very quietly. "Come out."

Slowly, Mary came from beneath the trestle table. Slowly, she stood.

"Ah, she carries a babe, does she? Sir Mark seduced ye, little one? Planted a babe in yer belly? But he married ye — a good man, all say, but I don't care about that."

Mary stood straight and tall, her chin up. She said, her voice loud and clear, "My husband will kill you."

Robbie Durwald threw his head back and laughed. "He's not here, if ye'll notice, my lady. He's probably near the border by now, chasing shadows and clouds."

"It's nearly daylight now," Chandra said.

"Aye, and he'll ride and ride because that's what he's supposed to do, thinking he will see us fleeing like cowards just over the next rise. An Englishman's brain can't work as quickly as a Scot's."

"As well as your brother's worked?" It was out of her mouth before she could curse herself. She held herself very still. She had to keep him there, talking, bragging, because she knew to her bones that Jerval would come. And this wasn't the way to do it.

Robbie Durwald jerked about to face her. "Ye don't sully my brother's name, hear ye? Ye don't insult him."

She couldn't help herself, just couldn't. "He was the cowardly one. He came at Sir John's appeal to kill my husband, but my husband wasn't stupid. He was waiting for him because he knew Sir John had betrayed us, and he trapped him in his own web and he killed him, just as he'll kill you."

"Ye think so? Go get me ale, wench, now."

Mary said quickly, "I can call the servants

to fetch you ale. I am very thirsty myself."

"Nay," said Robbie Durwald, "I want the lad to fetch it. Go, lad, or my knife slides into Lady Mary's sweet belly." He saw her determination, that steel that came from deep within her, and he remembered what his brother had said — "I wanted to break her, but I don't know if I ever could have." He pressed the tip of his knife against Mary's stomach. "Now, drop that little knife and sword on the floor."

Chandra didn't want to give up her weapons, but there was no choice. Slowly, she bent down and laid the knife and sword side by side on the floor.

"Hurry, little lad, hurry."

It gave them more time, Chandra thought, as she ran out of the Great Hall into the silent inner bailey. Durwald's men shouted at her, but she ignored them. There were three servants in the kitchens, hiding behind flour bins. She told them to stay where they were and keep quiet. She picked up two pitchers of ale and all the goblets she could carry and brought them back to the Great Hall. If only she had some poison to pour into the ale, if only — but there was no time to search about. He would hurt Mary if she didn't hurry — she had no doubt about that at all.

When she came running into the Great Hall, it was to see Robbie Durwald standing even closer to Mary, his knife extended, its point resting just above her left breast. She saw him reach out his hand to touch her and something inside her broke. Once she had let Mary be raped, but not this time.

She ran as fast as she could, the men parting as she came. She raced to Robbie Durwald, and yelled, "Don't you touch her, you bastard! Here!" And she threw a pitcher of ale in his face. His arm jerked up, and she kicked him square in his groin as hard as she could, grabbed the knife as it loosened in his fingers, and went down with him as he clutched himself and fell onto his knees. She jerked him up against her as he moaned and whimpered in agony, her arm tight around his neck.

"Now," she said to his men over his moans, for she'd kicked him harder than she'd ever kicked a man in her life. He was nearly insensible with the pain, and for the moment he was helpless. She tightened her hold around his neck and lightly sliced his own knife across his throat. A thin line of blood welled up. His men stopped dead in their tracks.

"Robbie, what should we do?"

"He'll not answer you just yet," Chandra

said, and jerked him back to keep him off balance. "All of you will drop your swords and knives, now!"

"Nay," Robbie Durwald managed to say, and he brought up his hands to claw at her arm. She stuck the knife tip into his throat. Blood welled out. He froze.

"If you move, you will be dead," she said against his temple. "Now, stay on your knees and don't move." Slowly, she eased her hold and stood over him, leaning only slightly, her knife point firm against his neck.

She said now, "All of you, take three steps back. That's right, do it now. Three steps."

Slowly, the men moved backward.

"Mary, fetch their knives and swords and put them behind me. Hurry, but take care."

"I'll kill ye, ye bitch, and it'll be slow and I'll laugh whilst I —"

She eased the knife further into his neck. He gulped and shut up.

What to do now?

She'd won. She couldn't really believe it, but she'd managed because of her red-eyed rage about Mary, and she'd won.

Where were the bloody servants?

It was dead silent in the Great Hall save for the still, harsh breathing of Robbie Durwald. The pain was leaving him, she realized, and she knew he would try to get away from her.

"Mary, hand me my own knife and sword."

She held her own knife in her hand, eased up the other and slipped hers into place. She said to Robbie Durwald, "Feel my knife. It's sharper than yours, and it'll go through that coarse neck of yours in but an instant. Don't move or you'll be dead before you keel over."

"How long do ye think ye can hold us here all by yerself?"

"As long as I —"

It happened so fast that she didn't even see it. One of Durwald's men pulled a knife out of his tunic belt and hurled it at her. It struck her shoulder and Chandra felt a blaze of fire slam into her. Her knife wavered and Robbie Durwald moved quickly, twisted her wrist until she dropped the knife, and then jumped back from her.

He was laughing.

At her.

Chandra had thrown her knife at Graelam and struck him in the shoulder. The irony of it ate deep. She didn't appreciate it. The pain was so strong, so overwhelming, that it took every bit of her strength, pulled from the deepest part of her, to keep a hold.

"Mary," she said. "Mary, stay behind me."

"Aye, Lady Mary, do whatever ye wish, but first, ye will very nicely return my weapons to my men."

"Chandra —"

"I'm all right, Mary. Do as he says. I'm all right."

Mary looked at her friend, her face deathly pale, the knife stuck in her shoulder, blood pouring over her hand.

"Do as he says, Mary."

"Aye, Lady Mary, do as the little lad here asks."

Robbie Durwald came to stand over her. He took her chin in his palm and forced her face upward. He sank his knife point into her woolen cap and jerked it off. Her hair fell about her face.

"Ah, now I see ye as ye really are. The knife hurts? Aye, I can see that it does." He reached down and jerked it out.

Chandra felt as if someone had pulled her heart from her chest. She had time only to suck in her breath at the pain; then she fell over onto her side.

Durwald knelt beside her, ripped off strips of her tunic, wadded the cloth and pressed it against her wound. He called to his men, "Once you have yer weapons, we're off." He stared down at her, willing her to open her eyes.

But she didn't.

"We'll torch the keep," he said and rose. Mary raced to Chandra and pressed the blood-soaked cloth to the wound.

"Nay, don't," she said, looking up at Robbie Durwald. "Don't fire the keep."

"I'll do whatever I wish to do," Durwald said, and turned toward his men.

Chandra felt his movement away from her. She felt the pain deep in her shoulder, but she also felt more determined than she ever had in her life. She felt for her sword, clutched her fingers around the grip, and lurched to her feet. She was on him in an instant, her sword going through his side. He yelled and whirled about, his men staring, not believing that the girl was even alive.

It was what Jerval saw when he and Mark burst into the Great Hall. Chandra was jerking her sword out of a man's back even as he was turning, his knife raised.

He saw blood covering her.

He meted out death even as his howls of rage filled the Great Hall of Oldham.

It was Mark who gave Robbie Durwald his death-blow.

Chandra stood there, panting, her sword in one hand, its tip bloody, her other hand pressed against her shoulder, blood everywhere, so red against her white face, and he couldn't believe it. She was smiling.

"I knew you would come," she said. "Thank you, Jerval. It was close, very close."

He was striding toward her when she collapsed where she stood.

"I'm going to strangle you," he said, his mouth against her cheek. "Aye, the instant you're well again, I'm going to strangle you."

She tried to smile, but it was difficult. She'd lost a lot of blood, she knew, and she knew that most men wounded as she'd been easily bled their lives away. But he wouldn't let her die. She knew that as well.

"Thank you," she said.

"You were supposed to be safe, holding Mary's hand, reassuring her." He was speaking more to himself than to her, and she realized it even though the pain was building now and it was hard to hold on, to keep the pain at bay so she could see him clearly and hear his words.

"Thirsty," she whispered.

He held her head up and put the goblet to her lips. She drank slowly, so slowly. He wiped water from her chin.

"There is a healer here at Oldham. Her name is Agnes. She has sworn to me that you will live. You've been very sick for three days now."

"Is Mary all right?"

"Aye, she is fine. When I am not with you, she is. You have but to lie still and mend. I have sent Prince Edward and Princess Eleanor on their way. They are sorry that you were wounded."

"Will you go to the Holy Land with them?"

He was silent a moment. "I don't know," he said at last. "First you must get well again. Then we will see."

"I want to go too," she said. Then her eyes closed and she slept.

He thought of her fighting Robbie Durwald, her life bleeding away, and — and what? he wondered. It was his fault that he'd left her unprotected at Oldham. Yet it was her fault that she'd even come with him, sneaking in with his men. And he knew to his bones that she would never waver, she would never back down, she would always fight.

He sighed. He had no idea what he would do.

"Aye, it is a good sleep," Agnes said, coming up to stand beside the bed. "The lass is strong, stronger than most men I've tended. She'll live to give ye gray hair."

"I think she already has," Jerval said.

It was three nights later, in the deepest part of the night, when Jerval awoke to her moan.

He quickly lit a candle and came down beside her. "What is wrong, Chandra? Does your shoulder pain you?"

"My stomach, Jerval," and she cried out, clasping her arms around herself, drawing up, and then she moaned deeply, jerking, finally lying back, panting hard.

"What's wrong? My stomach feels like it's ripping apart."

"I don't know," he said and was gone in the next moment to fetch Agnes.

He heard her screaming even before they returned to the bedchamber. Agnes pushed him aside and came down over his wife. He saw her pull back the covers, saw her jerk up Chandra's bedgown. Then he saw the blood, so much blood, and it was coming from her body. And he knew then, knew that she had lost a babe.

She was moaning quietly now, her eyes closed, her palms up at her sides as Agnes bathed her.

He turned and left the bedchamber.

It had happened so quickly. The child had existed for such a short time and now it was gone.

Simply gone.

Chandra lay quietly, bathed, wrapped in a clean bedrobe, and she felt empty.

She heard him come into the bedchamber. She said nothing until he was standing beside her and his palm was flat on her forehead.

"I've no fever," she said.

"No."

"I want to go home."

"I told you. You cannot return to Croyland."

"No, I meant Camberley."

His eyes narrowed on her pale face. So much pain she'd endured, so much blood she'd lost. He opened his mouth, then closed it. Then he said, unable to keep the words back, "You lost my babe."

She said nothing, just stared ahead toward the narrow window cut into the far wall. Both of them were staying in Mark and Mary's bedchamber. It had been nearly seven days now.

He waited, and finally she said, "I did not even know that I carried a babe."

"Why should you? You won't accept that you're even a woman. A woman conceives a child, a man doesn't."

"When Mary told me she was pregnant with Graelam's child, I thought about it for the first time. You came to me always, every night, but then I just forgot about it, and then you no longer came to me."

He paced to the far wall, then back again. He said, his voice flat and hard, "You will never change. I have to accept that. I failed. I will go to the Holy Land. As for you, when you're well, I will take you back to Camberley. You may go fight the Scots, you may weed the gardens. I care not. You are free now, Chandra. Do what you will."

She turned her head to look up at him. It brought her pain to look at him. He had given up on her, but why should that lance her with pain? She had lost the babe. She'd been so unthinking, so unwomanly, that it just hadn't occurred to her. She still didn't know how she felt about it — the pain was too recent.

She closed her eyes and turned her head away from him.

But he wasn't through. There was just too much, all of it festering inside him. "You challenged the damned prince! You wanted to challenge him to archery. Do you have any idea what a fool you made me look?"

She said quietly, not looking at him, "I did not mean to make you look foolish, nor did I mean to make you angry, or to flout you."

"Then why did you do it?"

"Are you afraid that I could best the prince?"

He stared at her. "By all the saints' name days, do you think it pleases me to have my wife bragging like a bloody man? Do you never think? Nay, don't answer that. You don't. You do only what you want to do. You don't care about anyone else, just yourself."

"I wasn't bragging. What is wrong with my pitting my skills against the prince, or anyone else for that matter?"

Jerval turned abruptly away from her, his fists clenched at his sides. "I have said everything I wished to. As I said, there is little reason for me to remain at Camberley. When you are well, I am going to the Holy Land with Edward."

As it turned out, Jerval de Vernon didn't go alone. He took two knights and their squires, six soldiers, three archers, and his wife.

Chapter 23

Tunis
Four Months Later

There was a growing swell of noise from the soldiers, and shouts suddenly rang out, not only from their ship, but from the man-of-war that sailed off their bow. Chandra strained her eyes through the haze in the distance, but it was several minutes before she could be sure she saw the sprawling mass of buildings that was the city.

Tunis! After week upon dreary week aboard their small vessel, they'd finally arrived.

Chandra felt excitement bubble up like fresh water from a spring. "Look, Jerval, at those tall towers with the oddly shaped domes. Whatever are they?"

"They are called minarets. The Moslem religious men climb to their tops to call the people to prayer. Payn told me about them."

Their ship sailed close in to the rest of the fleet as they neared the point of land.

Chandra saw one of the soldiers hurl a bag of spoiled flour overboard and shout, "Food at last!"

"You'll kill the fish," someone shouted back.

"I must join the men soon, Chandra. You find Joanna and stay with her."

Ah Joanna, Sir Payn de Chaworth's wife, had become her friend during the long voyage. Joanna, plump, dark-haired, filled with laughter, always optimistic. She nodded.

"By God," Lambert said when they were finally in sight of the harbor, "behold all the ships. With King Louis, we will make a fearsome sight when we sail to Acre."

Their ship eased behind a huge man-of-war, and the rowers held to a narrow channel between the French ships. Chandra could make out scores of men waving wildly toward them from the rough wooden docks. Their ship scraped an anchor line as they neared the docks, and the sailors' fierce shouts rang out over the soldiers' cheering.

It took several hours for their ship to take its turn at the dock. Chandra fidgeted impatiently as she waited with Joanna on the forecastle. They could see clustered buildings, low stone huts separated by narrow alleyways, rising behind the dock. From their vantage point, it seemed that all of Tunis was French soldiers, loitering about on the docks, waving and shouting toward the English ships.

"Everything looks so very strange," Joanna de Chaworth whispered to Chandra when they finally stepped onto the rolling dock. "So very foreign."

"Aye," Chandra said, "it does, but that doesn't matter. Finally, we're here. I wondered if we would ever arrive."

It was difficult to walk after being aboard the ship for so many long weeks. They were flanked by a dozen soldiers, Rolfe and Lambert at their head, balance difficult for all of them. After weeks at sea, the noise made her ears ring. Outside their line of soldiers, she saw a knot of Moslem men ogling them, most of them short and wiry, all with dark faces. They were dressed in baggy white trousers and loose shirts, their heads wrapped in thick white turbans. They looked insolent and angry, and Chandra felt a quiver of fear. Skinny-legged children, many of them naked, darted between their legs, yelling and pointing wildly toward her and Joanna.

"They hate us," Joanna said. "Look, Chandra, at the women."

Chandra looked toward a small knot of

women who stood hunched like a flock of black crows in an open doorway. Unlike the men, they were covered from head to toe in black, even their faces shrouded with thin black veils.

"I feel naked compared to them," Joanna said, touching her fingers to her face.

"I wonder why they are all covered up. Surely that black must be terribly hot."

"My lady," Rolfe shouted, shoving the men aside to reach her. "The king is dead!"

"Which king?"

"King Louis — he died over a month ago of the stomach flux. All these soldiers and ships belong to King Charles of Sicily."

Poor Edward, she thought. He had dreamed of joining with the sainted Louis on the crusade. "Who is King Charles?"

"King Louis's youngest brother. Sir Jerval has asked me to escort you to King Charles's encampment outside the city. He said he would join you as soon as he could."

Joanna clasped her hands over her bosom. Usually one to see the good in every situation, she closed her eyes and moaned this time. "What will happen to us now?"

Bathed and gowned, Chandra paced the narrow width of the tent, awaiting Jerval's return. She had sent away the Moslem slave

400

woman after her blessed bath, a gift, Rolfe told her, from the bey. She opened up the tent flap and stepped outside, hoping for a breeze from the sea, but she soon retreated within, for the sun was beating down mercilessly upon the treeless camp. As far as she could see, small, stiff-topped tents were being raised over the rocky terrain. English soldiers were still arriving, their belongings slung over their shoulders. Chandra could make out Edward's pavilion, larger by far than the other tents, set atop a small rise. His personal guard, some dozen soldiers dressed in his blue-and-white livery, were clearing a defensive perimeter about his pavilion.

Chandra stared at Jerval in surprise when he strode into the tent. His beard was gone, and he was dressed in a long robe of white linen, hemmed with purple.

"What happened to you?"

"Like you, the bey provided all of us baths and clothing. I begin to feel human again."

"Rolfe said that King Louis is dead."

Jerval ran a hand through his thick hair. "Aye, and Edward is bowed with grief. I left him with King Charles of Sicily — he is — was — King Louis's brother."

"Yes, I know. What will happen?" She was asking Joanna's question, to which there had been no answer.

He smiled, as if seeing her for the first time. "I had forgotten how you look with your hair loose. Were you also allotted a slave?"

She nodded and shook her head, feeling soft hair against her cheeks. "It will be a long time before I wear another braid. It was so dirty after all those long weeks at sea, I feared my hair would fall out when I unplaited it."

He wanted to touch her hair, but he knew if he did, they wouldn't leave the tent, and he'd been commanded to attend the prince. And so he merely smiled at her as he said, "This evening we will go to a banquet at the bey's palace, in Edward's honor. The bey is anxious to be rid of us all, both English and French. We will likely leave Tunis very soon."

"Where will we go?"

"To Sicily for the winter. Edward will try to persuade King Charles to take up his brother's holy cause, though I doubt he will succeed. Charles has not admitted it, but there are rumors that he has signed a treaty with Sultan Baibars." Jerval watched her frown as she considered what he had said. He found himself staring at her for a long moment, uncertain if he should allow her to accompany him through the city to the bey's palace. He had seen few Moslem women, and those he had passed had been heavily veiled and eerily silent, their eyes downcast.

He found himself wondering what it would be like if she had not accompanied him. He hadn't wanted it, but Eleanor had pleaded with Edward, and in the end, Jerval had practically been ordered to bring his wife. To date, he hadn't regretted it, but of course aboard ship, there'd been nothing outrageous for her to attempt. And, he thought, the wonder of it still in his mind, they had become friends. He remembered the times she had cut his hair, the one time she had shaved him. He remembered the nights when the moon was full overhead, the air warm, the stars filling the sky, and they'd lain together, side by side, on the deck of their vessel, just speaking of this or that. And she'd told him she wanted him, but he' hadn't wanted to take the chance that someone would see or hear them, which was a very likely thing, and so he'd just kissed her and held her hand. He'd said, "There is no privacy. There are three people standing just yon. No, we must be strong about this. You will suffer as will I. This isn't the place, more's the pity."

"I heard Payn and Joanna," she said.

"We will wait," Jerval said, and it nearly killed him to say it.

And now he wanted her, very badly. He looked at her, thought her beautiful, and wanted to take her this very moment. He said abruptly, "Are you ready?"

"To leave Tunis?"

"Nay, ready for a banquet with real food."

"Aye, I am. Have you seen Eleanor?"

"Aye, I walked through the encampment with Edward to his pavilion. Eleanor is with child. His ship had some privacy, I gather."

"A child? Is she very ill? Aboard ship and with child?"

"She is quite well and very happy, as is Edward." If Chandra hadn't lost their babe, her belly would be rounded by now. He wondered if he would have left if she hadn't — No, he refused to think about it. He said only, "Eleanor is fine, as I said. Come, it is time to leave."

Rolfe, Lambert, and Arnulfe escorted them to the camp perimeter, where they were met by a turbaned man, short and black-bearded, who was to guide them through the city to the palace. He looked curiously at Chandra, but said nothing. The streets were a labyrinth of narrow, rutted paths, with low stone houses on either side, piles of garbage climbing their dusty walls.

Chandra felt her belly knot at the overpowering stench.

"The peasants do not bury their dead animals," their Moslem guide said calmly. "The ground is too hard."

They passed a group of Moslem men smoking pipes that gave off a sickeningly sweet smell. Chandra felt their dislike, their contempt. One of the men stepped toward her, smiled at her insolently, and spat. His spittle landed inches from the hem of her gown.

Jerval's hand clapped his sword scabbard, and he cursed.

"Do not, my lord," the Moslem said. "You are strangers here. A woman, a Moslem woman, is not allowed to flaunt herself unveiled in the streets." He turned and said something in harsh, guttural sounds to the man who had spat at her. The man backed away, but Chandra saw his hatred and scorn. She found that she was trembling, and she drew closer to Jerval. He closed his hand over her arm. She carried a knife strapped to her thigh, but she didn't even consider once moving away from her husband.

The banquet held by the Bey of Oran was opulent, the food plentiful and strange to the English contingent, the torches and candles bright and hot.

Chandra wondered what would come of all this outward deference, all this ceremony, if Prince Edward would gain more supporters. Then she looked across the huge chamber and saw Graelam de Moreton staring at her. A slave girl was at his elbow, but he was paying her no heed. He just kept staring. His expression was calm and very cold. She nodded to him, then turned away and spoke to Joanna, who was at her side, laughing at something another lady had said.

She'd known Graelam had come to crusade, but he'd voyaged here on another ship and this was the first time she'd seen him.

She hoped she wouldn't see him again after this night. On the walk back to Prince Edward's encampment some three hours later, Chandra walked very close to her husband.

"Just as we all expected, it was nonsense," he said. "A show, a sham. No one wishes to fight the Saracens, but they will provide us food and drink and as many slaves girls as we can service. I hate this, Chandra. And now we're off to Sicily."

Sicily, she thought, a foreign name that sounded smooth and flowing on her tongue.

"Place your hand here, Chandra," Eleanor said. "That's right. Do you feel the babe?"

A small foot kicked against Chandra's palm. She raised surprised eyes to Eleanor. "Does that not hurt you?"

"Nay." Eleanor laughed. "But sometimes it is difficult to sleep, with the little one so active. Edward delights in pressing his ear to my belly and telling me he can hear the babe's heartbeat. I am very sorry that you lost your child, Chandra, but these things happen, far too often. I feared you would be cast down about it and thus I wished you to come with your husband to the Holy Land. But there will be other children. Aye, and you will see, Chandra, what a wonder it is when you carry Jerval's child and you feel him moving inside you."

Chandra turned abruptly away and stared out over the palace grounds toward the beautiful city of Palermo below. She breathed in the sweet scent of the flowers that splashed their bright colors over the hillside.

"Even the market stalls are sweet smelling," she said after a moment.

Eleanor leaned back against the soft, gold-embroidered cushions and regarded Chandra quietly for a moment. She knew that Chandra was bored and restless — just like the men, she thought, smiling to herself. Although King Charles was gracious and surrounded them with every luxury, Edward and the men itched to be gone from Sicily, for it was becoming clear that Charles was unwilling to accompany them to Palestine. She sighed as Chandra rose and began to pace the balcony.

"You are thin, Chandra," she said, resting her hands on her rounded belly. "And pale. I hear that Jerval and Edward just returned from their weeklong hunt in the hills. He will be concerned when he sees you."

"Jerval should not be surprised that I am pale, Eleanor. I have been allowed to ride out only once into the hills, and then only in the company of two dozen soldiers. I would have liked to go on their hunt. I am tired of being useless."

"There is no question of that. You remain here for your own safety. I'm told the peasants grow more discontented by the year with their French masters. Even the men ride out armed. Why don't you speak to Jerval? He would arrange for you to be out of doors more often, if it is your wish."

"He is always busy with Payn, Henry, Roger, John — so many men — and, of course, Edward."

"Men," Eleanor said, smiling, "they cannot seem to be happy unless they are busy with something, and now they are fighting, or at least preparing to fight. I feel sorry for them in a way, for when they are wounded, or old, and can no longer fight, they grow bored and think themselves useless. There are few men I have known who have found the serenity that women seem to possess naturally. Most women, that is. Now, my dear father-in-law is an exception. He much prefers directing the architects in Westminster Abbey or playing with his grandchildren."

Chandra remembered her father cursing King Henry for bleeding his subjects to the point of rebellion to fund his building, but let it pass.

"Do you know," Eleanor continued, "that I was married to my lord when I was but ten years old, and he but a young, long-legged lad? How the years have flown by. I can still remember my father, Ferdinand, soothing me, telling me about my new home and my future family, all in a language that no longer comes easily to me." She drew a bloodred hibiscus to her nose and sniffed the sweet fragrance. "I came to England as a child, and was fortunate enough to love my husband the moment I saw him. It is odd to be a wife when one is barely a girl, but thus it was."

Chandra cocked her head to one side. "I had not thought of it before," she said, "but even you had no choices. You were bartered for political gain. What if you had not loved Edward?"

"Then my life would be a series of events with no particular sorrows and no particular joys. But of course, even if a lady does not care for her husband, she still has her children. What if Edward had taken me into grave dislike? What would he have had to fill his heart?"

"Mayhap a quiver of women would have filled it."

Eleanor only laughed at that. "That is very possible. However, the truth is that he had no more choice than I did, you know."

"But it is fathers, Eleanor," Chandra said sharply, "who choose their daughters' husbands, and then the husbands who rule their wives just as their fathers did. And what of all the widows in England whose husbands are scarce laid under the earth before another man comes to claim them, despite their wishes? Why should they at least not have the right of choice?"

Eleanor arched a sleek black brow. "Choice? It is only when I see a black-veiled Moslem woman, drawn back with her head bent in the shadow of her husband, that I see a woman with no choices, no freedom. She is the slave, not you or I."

"Even our own husbands can beat their wives, if they wish."

"Has Jerval ever beaten you?"

"Nay, but still he thinks himself my lord, and he is angry if I disobey him." Which she hadn't done since they'd begun their voyage to the Holy Land. There'd been naught but peace between them, and a friendship that was still growing by the day, and she feared that her liking for him would grow so great that when he did become angry with her, that liking wouldn't disappear. But his liking for her might, and she didn't know if she could bear that.

"When you discover a perfect world, dear child," Eleanor said, "I beg you to invite me to visit you. Edward is stronger than I, just as Jerval is stronger than you, and it is to them that we must trust our safety, and the safety of our children. We — not our husbands — are the givers of life. It is through us that life continues."

"But why must we be less than men? Why

must we always live in the shadow of their wishes?"

"I have never believed myself less than my lord, nor do I perceive that Jerval yearns for the cowering, veiled Moslem women. I have my responsibilities, my duties, just as does Edward. Together, we make a whole and a meaningful life. Our marriage vows bind us, but it is our love and our respect for each other that give us joy. Are you so unhappy, child?"

Chandra shook her head. "Nay, I have not been so really since we left England. I thank you, Eleanor, for convincing Jerval to allow me to come with him."

You were so miserable at Camberley, Eleanor wanted to say, *so unknowing of yourself and your husband, I only wanted to help you,* but she said only, "I believe I hear Edward. Ah, Jerval is with him."

Chapter 24

"My lord," Eleanor said, rising to greet Edward. He took her hand and pressed her back gently onto the cushions. "Nay, my love, do not disturb our babe." He sank down on a cushion next to his wife and rested his hand on Eleanor's stomach, grinning with pleasure. "Jerval, it is time you filled Chandra's belly. I vow she'll look nearly as beautiful as Eleanor when she is with child."

"Such things take time, my lord," Jerval said. And he thought of the long weeks he hadn't touched her, then of the endless nights in Tunis and here on Sicily that he'd spent loving her. He nearly shuddered thinking about how it felt to be deep inside her, touching her womb. And then he realized that she hadn't wept, not once since he'd made love to her after they'd left England. Nor had she left their bed before he'd awakened the next morning.

"You, my lord," Eleanor said, "seem to take all the credit."

"I would kill any other man who dared

to," Edward said.

Chandra jumped to her feet and said to Jerval, "Cannot we walk for a while? Along the palace walls?"

Jerval rose gracefully and looked toward Edward.

"Aye, get you gone, Jerval. I have no need of you until tonight; then it's yet another meeting with Charles. The man is more stubborn than a goat with an old boot. Aye, go bring roses back into your wife's cheeks."

As they strolled away along the marble balcony, Chandra heard Eleanor giggle. "They are so happy," she said. "They are what they are and they are happy."

He said, not looking at her, "That is because they accept each other for what they are."

"And you do not accept me for what I am."

He looked at her then. "Do you know that I was furious when I knew you were coming with me?"

"Aye, I know it."

"But my anger fell away quickly enough. You change daily, Chandra." He shrugged. "I know that I would give anything to carry you into the gardens below and have my way with you."

She realized she wanted him as well, right

this moment. She looked away from him. They stopped along the balcony wall, and Jerval leaned his elbows on the smooth mosaic tiles to look out over the blue Mediterranean.

"It's beautiful here," she said. "Not at all like the winters at home. I have yet to spend a winter at Camberley. Is there much snow?"

"Aye. Three years ago the lake froze. We rubbed wooden planks with duck lard and held races." He grinned. "You should have seen Bayon. Rolfe gave him a mighty shove and he went flying over the ice, flailing his arms, screaming for God to save him. He smashed into bushes, but he didn't get hurt because there was so much snow." He turned to face her. "When we are home, the lake will freeze again. Mayhap I will allow you to race against me."

"I am grown so soft, I would likely break my neck." She thrust her arm toward him and pushed up her loose sleeve. "Feel, Jerval, I have scarce any muscle left."

He closed his fingers about her upper arm and squeezed gently. "Aye, you are soft, but it is not at all displeasing, at least to me."

"You'd best be careful that I become too weak to ply my needle on your tunics."

He couldn't believe it. She hadn't taken

offense. Maybe she really was changing, growing more content to be a woman, to be his wife and not some proud and vainglorious warrior. He lightly touched his fingertips to her cheek. "How are you passing your days? I scarce see you."

"You know I spend most of my time with the women. Sometimes I grow so tired of their chatter. And the waiting. How went your hunt?"

"Well. We brought down three deer and one boar. I also grow tired of all the men's talk. Waiting is the same for all of us."

"Hunting would not be boring. I would surely love to go hunting the next time."

"I'm sorry, Chandra, but it is only men. I wouldn't want you to be the only lady on the hunt."

"I was always the only lady at home."

"Not here. It simply isn't done. I'm sorry, but we must both be patient."

She said nothing, and he realized indeed how much she'd changed. She was willing to accept his word. "You really have changed since we left England."

"There has been little chance for me to commit the sin of angering you."

"All you need is opportunity, and we would be at each other's throats again? Is that what you mean?"

Jerval lightly touched his fingertips to the tendrils of hair on her forehead and brushed them back. "Do you know that you would look beautiful with your belly rounded with child?"

She turned away from him, looking out over the gardens. "I lost a child. It hurt, Jerval, both my body and my spirit."

"I know. I remember, too well. All the blood, your screams. It was very bad, Chandra. I am also sorry for blaming you. I was wrong. I hope you can forgive me. You know, of course, that Camberley must have an heir."

"Aye, I know. Since you are with me each night now, I will probably conceive your heir a long way from Camberley."

"I will keep you safe if you do conceive. I do not want you to be afraid."

"I am, but it doesn't matter. What we do each night — I don't wish you to stop and thus I will have no choice in whether or not I conceive."

"I know."

She thought of his mouth on hers, the feel of him deep inside her, pushing and pushing until she was screaming with the pleasure of it, holding him tightly.

"You haven't cried."

She knew exactly what he was talking

about. She said only, not looking at him, "I do not understand it."

"Change," he said. "You are changing."

"And so are you, Jerval. You are changing back to the man I married."

Was he? he wondered.

A silent Sicilian woman had brought Chandra buckets of steaming, lavender-scented water for her bath, and at Chandra's distracted wave, had left her. Chandra sat on an ornately carved stool in her bed-chamber, her legs resting over the side of the wooden tub, soaping herself as was her custom before rinsing herself in the clear water. She was thinking of Croyland, of the days before her marriage, when she had competed with Jerval in every sport she could devise. She could practically hear his laughter mingling with hers, hear his voice teasing her. She had felt a sense of freedom, and of belonging with him then. Her washcloth slowed its path over her breasts as she remembered watching him riding tall and ramrod-straight in his saddle, his lance held firmly in his strong hand, his eyes bright with concentration as he galloped Pith toward Rolfe on the tiltyard. She re-membered the sunlight illuminating the darker golden streaks in his hair the day he had galloped toward her on the promontory. She sighed, and felt her body still pulsing from the early morning when he'd awakened her, his mouth on her breast, his hand on her belly, kneading her, then going lower until she was panting.

She did not know herself. She was not what she'd been, she realized, and Jerval knew it as well. It pleased him. She wondered what was happening to her.

Jerval opened the door of their chamber, grumbling silently at himself for his stupidity. He had forgotten a sheaf of notes Edward needed for discussions with King Charles. He drew to a halt, all thoughts of the notes wiped immediately from his mind. Chandra sat naked on a stool beside a wooden tub, her profile toward him, her back arched as she trailed a soapy cloth downward over her shoulders. He watched her touch the cloth as would a gentle lover over her breasts. She threw her head back, showing him the graceful line of her throat. She looked exquisite, her firm breasts thrusting outward, almost too heavy now for her slender torso. His eyes dropped downward to her waist, so slight that he could encircle her with his hands. He had, just that morning.

She began to hum softly to herself as she

rubbed the soapy cloth downward over her belly. When she at last parted her thighs and touched herself, slowly caressing the cloth over herself, he was hard, painfully so. It had happened so very quickly. At last he recognized the song she was humming, a song of love she herself had written and sung to him, in all innocence, he knew, long ago at Croyland.

She rose slowly and leaned over to rinse the cloth in the water and wring it lazily over her body. His eyes swept down her long legs, sleek and smooth, endlessly beautiful legs. In that instant, she saw him. For a long, still moment, she simply stared at him, her eyes locked on his, the cloth quiet in her hand.

Jerval could think of nothing but her, being inside her, kissing her, every bit of her. He strode to her and closed his hands about her waist, lifting her to him. At the touch of her, he moaned deep in his throat and swept her upward, pressing her against the length of him. He tugged at the thick knot of hair at the back of her neck, spilling her hair over her shoulders and down her back. He pulled her toward him until he had her mouth beneath his. He buried his face against her throat and breathed in the lavender scent of her.

"Dear God," he whispered against her

temple. "It has been but three hours since I had you beneath me, and now I would willingly hurl myself in front of a Saracen army to have you again, right now." He took her mouth again and moaned her name against her lips.

She didn't hesitate. She welcomed the leap of pressure deep in her belly, the fierce hardness of him, his fingers curving over her hips to find her. She'd felt an immediate awakening when he'd appeared so suddenly, so unexpectedly. And then, when he'd nearly run to her, she saw herself as he must have seen her — languid, her every movement inviting. Actually, she'd been thinking of him, weaving him into the soft, incoherent thoughts and memories that had held her as she bathed herself.

She felt him bend her gently against his arm, felt his fingers trembling as they caressed her breast, then swept lower to her belly. "Surely it must be against the commandments of the Church to feel this way," she said, and her hands were on him now, trying to pull off his clothes. He was laughing, slapping away her hands, and soon they were together, naked, on their bed, and he was kissing her and laughing between the kisses, telling her what he was going to do to her, and then she managed to get him onto his back and she was over him, telling him what she was going to do to him. Before he could do anything other than suck in his breath, her mouth was on his belly, and he tensed tighter than a bowstring. When she took him in her mouth, he yelled, nearly beside himself.

Just before he lost control, he heard her laugh, felt her warm breath all the way to his soul.

He was so felled by pleasure that it was many moments before he could speak, much less think. She was on her knees beside him, her palms on her thighs, and she was grinning down at him.

"I have brought you down," she said.

"Aye, you have. Now it is my turn to show you that I'm your master in all things." And he did. When she cried out, her body arching madly, he tried to laugh, but couldn't.

And he said against her mouth when her breath was still fast and jerking, "I love you, Chandra."

Her eyes flew open and she stared up at him, helplessly, so shaken with the power of his words that she couldn't think, much less speak. At last, she whispered, "I don't know. I just don't know." She wrapped her arms tightly around his back and pulled him to her. She held him tightly. "I'm so afraid."

"Of what?"

"Of what it will all mean. Of what will happen to me." And then she opened her legs and brought him into her again. They both forgot her fear then.

Later, he wondered if it were indeed fear in her mind, or it if wasn't more likely her damnable pride. He wondered if she would always suffer him as her husband — enjoy his body, but never give herself fully to him.

They left Sicily in early March and sailed to Acre on a storm-tossed sea. Chandra lay moaning on her pallet, so seasick from the storm that she prayed for oblivion. She felt a damp cloth on her forehead and forced her eyes to open. "I want to die," she said.

"Nay, little one," Jerval said, kissing her nose. "Here, drink some wine."

She did as she was told, but after only a moment, she knew it wouldn't work. "Oh, God. Please leave me alone, Jerval."

"No, I won't leave you."

"Damn you, don't you feel anything?"

"I cannot be ill. Who would take care of you if I were puking up my innards there beside you?"

She vomited into the pan he held for her. He gave her just a taste of water to wash out her mouth, then settled her back onto some blankets and stroked her shoulders. "You were also sick during that storm off the coast of Spain. I'm sorry, Chandra. It cannot be pleasant. The first thing we must do when we reach Acre — other than fight the Saracens — is to fatten you up."

"You must hate me to speak of food." She clutched her belly, drew her knees to her chest and moaned.

He rose and looked down at her clammy face. He was worried. "I must leave you with Joanna now, sweeting, and don my armor."

"Why? What has happened?"

"The watch has sighted Acre, and it is under attack by the Saracens. Our timing could not be better. King Hugh of Cyprus and Jerusalem is within the city walls, and thus the attack."

She tried to rise, but he gently pushed her down. "Joanna," he called, "see that she rests."

"Please take care."

"You may be certain that I shall," he said, kissed the tip of her nose, patted her cheek and left.

Chandra had been so excited when they had finally set sail for Acre with the thousand men in Prince Edward's army. Now that it was in sight, she could not even rise to see it. She closed her eyes, remembering how Edward had slowly risen to his feet in King Charles's magnificent banquet hall and kicked the soft pillows on which he had been seated away from him.

"Hear me, all of you," he had said in a voice filled with passion. "King Charles has told us why we should not journey to the Holy Land. Now I will tell you that I made an oath before God. If my life is to be forfeit for keeping my holy vow, so be it." He had thrown out his arms, embracing the entire company. "Do what your consciences dictate. I pledge before God that I will go to Acre to fight the Saracens if naught but my groom be with me!"

Payn de Chaworth had jumped to his feet and shouted, "You, sire, your groom, and I!"

Soon all were shouting, and Edward, flushed with pleasure, had clasped each of his nobles in his arms, tears in his eyes.

"You will feel better soon," Joanna said, lightly patting her face as though she were a child. "We are in the calmer waters of the harbor."

"I want to see Acre," Chandra said and pulled herself to her feet.

"Chandra, I promised Jerval to keep you quiet."

"How can you look so healthy? I know, you have made a pact with the devil. Come, Joanna, I will not fall overboard, though I am tempted to end my own misery. Are you coming with me?"

"Aye, I would see that Payn is all right."

From a ladder on the forecastle, Chandra looked toward the walled city of Acre. It was the largest city she had ever seen, its long white seaward wall towering over the water, seemingly impenetrable. There was smoke rising above the white stone walls that hugged the dock, and the acrid smell of fire. She saw Jerval in his glistening silver armor, the de Vernon lion emblazoned across the breast of his blue surcoat, standing at the fore of his men, poised to jump ashore when they reached land. Their ship scraped against the wooden dock, and Jerval leapt ashore, soldiers swarming after him. A huge seaward gate opened to them, and he was soon lost to her sight.

She called after him, but of course he did not hear her. The seaward gate opened several more times as groups of soldiers ran to it from the docking ships, and then there was an almost eerie quiet. She could hear only muted shouting, and the sound of the waves slapping against the ships that lolled near the dock. Chandra watched until the storm clouds over the city turned a deep crimson as the sun fell into the sea. She turned to see Joanna on her knees, praying, she thought, for Payn's safety. There was no messenger to tell them what was happening. Her stomach cramped viciously, and she doubled over, moaning.

She awoke that evening to see her husband staring down at her, his blue surcoat splattered with blood. She lurched up, terrified. "Oh, God, you're hurt, you're —"

"No, I'm not hurt. I'm much better than you are, by the looks of you. What in God's name are you doing up here on the forecastle?" He shook his head, expecting no sensible answer, and turned to the knight beside him. "Sir Elvan, this is my wife, Chandra. Chandra, this is Sir Elvan, a Templar, and a physician. He is here to help you." A tall, leather-faced man in full armor stood beside him, a huge red cross stitched on his white surcoat.

"I am sorry." She moaned, clutching her belly. "The boat isn't moving. The seasickness is supposed to stop. Please, don't waste your time with me. I will be well in but a moment. Or maybe two."

He smiled at her as he laid his hand upon her forehead. "Your belly will continue to cramp until I stop it, which I will. Just hold still whilst I mix you one of my magic potions."

She nodded, clearly disbelieving him, as she said, "Jerval, what of the wounded? What has happened?"

"The Saracens fled," Jerval said, "and Acre is once again safe. King Hugh wasn't harmed. We lost only a few men. Now, shut your mouth and let Sir Elvan take care of you."

"How did you know I would still be sick? How dare you worry about me and not about yourself?"

Sir Elvan laughed as he mixed a white powder in a wooden mug of wine.

"Drink this," he said as he held the mug to her lips. "When you awaken, the cramps will be gone and you can hear all about what happened. You don't believe me, but you will see."

"Jerval, I don't know about this. You swear you are not harmed?"

"I am quite fit. Now, be quiet and close your eyes."

She said, her voice slurred, "Now I shall have to mend that wretched surcoat. It is badly ripped."

And he laughed.

Chapter 25

Eustace followed a silent, olive-skinned slave into the cool interior of Ali ad-Din's private chamber. He drew up at the sight of the merchant — black-eyed, heavily bearded, his huge belly held in place by a wide, gold-threaded sash, and felt a tug of envy. His long robe was of cool light yellow silk, richly embroidered and studded with gems. He wore stiff brocade slippers with the same oddly pointed toes the other local men of wealth wore. Only these were crusted with gems. Ali ad-Din was rich, a member of the High Court of Acre, and as Eustace's eyes swept across the opulent chamber and the dark-skinned slaves, he wished he owned but a portion of his wealth.

Ali ad-Din sighed to himself, softly cursing the early arrival of Sir Eustace de Leybrun. He had hoped to see Princess Eleanor's milk-white skin stretched over her belly as she stepped into his bathing pool, but she had not removed the silk robe his women had provided her. Though the golden-haired girl with her was beautiful, her breasts full and white, she was a bit too thin for his taste. He had given only a cursory glance at the plump, dark-haired girl, pretty enough, but of little interest compared to the full-bellied princess.

Although Ali ad-Din was nominally Christian, he proffered Eustace the Moslem greeting, touching his forehead with his beringed fingers. "Ah, Sir Eustace," he said, not the smallest shadow in his voice to show that his guest wasn't welcome. He walked away from the veil-covered wall where he had been standing when Eustace entered the room. "You have come to remove your beautiful English princess and her ladies from my humble house?"

Eustace nodded, and at Ali ad-Din's graceful wave of his hand, sank down on a pile of soft pillows that surrounded a low sandalwood table inlaid with ivory.

A slave girl poured him a goblet of sweet red Cypriot wine and held a huge, fruit-filled bowl toward him. He selected several sticky soft dates, a delicacy that seemed to be everyday fare in Palestine.

"I hope your noble Prince Edward and his mighty lords are in good health?"

Eustace had grown used to the round-about questioning, a disconcerting trait of all the heathen in the Holy Land, be they Christian or Moselm. "Aye," he said only, his teeth tingling at the flavor of the tartly sweet dates.

Ali thought Sir Eustace as boorish an oaf as most of the arrogant nobles who had traveled with the English prince, but the smile never left his mouth. He continued in his soft voice. "I fear that you must rest awhile in my company, Sir Eustace, for the beautiful ladies have not yet finished their bath."

"I will wait," Eustace said, chewing on another date. "The prince has commanded that the ladies be escorted at all times, as you know." He added the words Edward had bade him speak. "The prince does, of course, treasure your kindness in offering your house for the ladies' comfort."

"It is an honor," Ali said, his black eyes hooded. He prided himself on his judgment of a man's character, and Sir Eustace's envious glances had not been lost on him. He suspected that Sir Eustace was not a religious fool like the English prince, nor, he thought, did he seem capable of the almost blind loyalty of Lord Payn de Chaworth and Sir Jerval de Vernon, the two English nobles whose wives were at this very moment enjoying his bathing room with the child-swelled Princess Eleanor. The man would make himself sick if he continued to eat the sweet dates. Ali silently clicked his fingers together toward the boy slave. The bowl of fruit was removed and Eustace's goblet was filled with more wine.

"It is a pity that the saintly King Louis did not succeed," Ali said. "But he was a sick old man, and Tunis such an infested rat hole. The Saracens believed, of course, that Acre would be an easy plum to pick now that the new French king, Philip, and King Charles of Sicily have made peace with the Sultan Baibars. All of Acre, my lord, is grateful to you English nobles for your bravery."

Eustace's belly felt warmed by the sweet wine. They had indeed saved a beautiful city, one of the few Christian fortresses left in Palestine. The Venetians and Genoese had garnered great wealth here, and the Sultan Baibars's lust for the city was under-standable. But Christ, to pit one thousand men against Baibars's vast armies — even Edward had not understood why the Saracens had fled the besieged city, for the sultan commanded ten times their numbers. It was still a mystery.

"You seem to have weathered the siege well."

Ali shrugged. "A merchant, even such a

humble one as myself, must arrange his affairs so that he will survive, no matter the outcome." He added on a smile, "Since I am neither Genoese nor Venetian, I have not had to concern myself with their bickering, and have been able to trade with both of them."

"You have many slaves," Eustace said, as a lithe young girl clothed only in a filmy silk robe stepped toward them.

Ali's mouth split into a wide smile over his white teeth. "And many beautiful women, my friend," he said. "Several of my slave girls are with your English ladies now, attending them at their bath."

"The prince," Eustace said, "is grateful for your offer of a banquet tonight. He has grown tired of the rations."

"It is not unexpected. My humble house is his to command. I understand that he thinks to leave Acre soon."

Eustace looked up quickly, surprised that the merchant knew of the prince's plans. He had cursed Edward under his breath when he had learned they were to leave even the nominal comforts of Acre to scout the blistering inland.

"I am not certain," Eustace said.

"No matter," Ali said agreeably, waving his beringed hand toward the slave girl. She silently stood next to Eustace, her olive features expressionless. When Eustace raised his face, his eyes fell upon the supple flesh of her bare belly. "Her name is Loka," Ali said smoothly. "She is only thirteen years old, but skilled in the art of men's pleasure. Perhaps tonight, after the banquet, you would wish to enjoy her gifts."

"Aye, perhaps," Eustace said. What he wanted to do was to see Chandra, naked, in her bath, and he wondered what she was doing.

Just behind the wall, in the bathing room, Beri, their translator, said of one of the slaves, "She has never before seen anyone like you, madam. She says that you are golden everywhere, even between your thighs."

Joanna de Chaworth held her sides with laughter, but Chandra blinked and turned red, looking down at the slave girl who was on her knees before her, a soapy sponge in her hand.

"I wish that you would be quiet," Chandra said, frowning toward Joanna and wishing the girl would stand up again. She still hadn't shaken the sense of embarrassment she felt at being naked around the women, and the slave girls seemed to delight in looking at her and touching her. "I think I am clean now, Beri. I would like to swim in the pool."

Beri said a few swift phrases to the girl. She rinsed the sponge free of soap and poured warm, perfumed water from a pottery jug gently over Chandra's head. Chandra stretched and pushed her heavy wet hair out of her face.

"There can be nothing more wonderful than this. If only we had this in England. You really must try it, Joanna." She then smiled at Beri and slipped beneath the surface of the cool water of the pool, enjoying the absolute stillness. When she couldn't hold her breath any longer, she flipped onto her back and floated, her hair fanning out about her head. She cocked an eye open and raised her head from the water at Joanna's shriek of laughter as the soft sponge glided over her body.

Chandra wondered, looking at Joanna, how she remained so plump. She would swear that Joanna ate less than she did, and yet Chandra was still thin — at least that was what Jerval kept telling her just before he stuck food in her mouth. At least she was fit again. She had seen the Templar physician, Sir Elvan, but once since they had settled in their sprawling tent encampment just beyond St. Anthony's Gate, outside the walls of Acre. He had treated her kindly, gently kneading her belly and nodding his approval to Jerval. "As I told you, when the stomach cramps so much it becomes a reflex, and medicine is necessary to stop the cramping. Now you are well, and I want you to stay that way."

Chandra stood up in the water. It came to her waist. Joanna said, "If only Payn would take a few moments from his infernal plotting and join me in this pool, I vow he would soon have the son he so desperately wants."

"I think you should have a daughter, Joanna. She would laugh and make everyone happy."

"A son first, then I may bring my glorious daughter to this world. Aye, it is only fair — Payn has worked so very hard, he deserves a son first. Do you not think Sir Jerval would enjoy himself with you in this pool, floating and whatever else in the water?"

"Aye, he would." Chandra remembered so clearly that day she'd been bathing in their chamber in Sicily. She had felt so languid, lazily dreaming, enjoying the touch of the soapy cloth and the warm water. And Jerval had watched her and wanted her, had held her so tightly that she felt the pounding of his heart against her breast. Ah, that afternoon, he had told her he loved her, and it had been the first time in so very long. And she'd said nothing because she was afraid. She was a fool.

As one of the slave girls toweled her dry, Chandra raised her eyes to see Beri looking at her, a thoughtful expression on her lovely face. Chandra smiled, cocking her head in question. Beri motioned Chandra to lie on her stomach atop a cushioned table. "The girls will rub a soothing oil into your skin. It will protect you from the fierceness of the sun."

Chandra felt a warm liquid run down to the small of her back before gentle hands rubbed over her, smoothing the oil into her skin. She felt light-headed, and so relaxed that she could not keep her eyes open.

"You are very beautiful," Beri said, "and golden everywhere." A slight smile indented the corners of her mouth. "I had thought you would be ugly, perhaps lumpy and fat."

"Why did you believe I would be ugly, Beri?"

Beri paused a moment, then smiled sadly. "You are lucky in many ways, my lady. You are wellborn, a great lord's wife, and have the choice to do whatever you wish. I am a slave, and but do my master's bidding. My mother was also a slave. An Armenian merchant sold me to Ali ad-Din when I was thirteen years old."

Beri turned away and calmly directed a slave girl to fetch another jar of perfumed oil.

"My master," Beri continued after a moment, "has taken a great liking to your husband, Sir Jerval. He took my master's side before the High Court against a Genoese merchant who wanted to strip him of his trade route to the Mongols. The Genoese are dirty and so greedy that they would give Acre itself to the Sultan Baibars if they could fatten their purses by it."

"Aye," Chandra said. "My husband told me of it, though he said that Ali ad-Din would have won his case anyway."

"Your husband is a very handsome man," Beri said matter-of-factly. "There is another, an English noble whose name I cannot pronounce. He has such intense eyes, dark as a velvet midnight, and they burn deep when he looks at me."

Chandra searched her mind. "Do you mean Sir Eustace de Leybrun?"

"Never that one. He is outside with my master, waiting for you to finish with your bath. I dislike him. He frightened me. It is how he looks at a woman. It isn't healthy."

Intense eyes, Chandra thought, reviewing the nobles in Prince Edward's retinue. She said quietly, not looking up, "You mean Lord Graelam de Moreton."

Beri nodded. "Am I right about him? Is he intense? Do his passions burn strong? Do you know him well?"

"I know him. I suppose you could say that his passions burn strong, perhaps even out of control. He is ruthless, Beri, take care."

"Men should be ruthless," Beri said with great seriousness. "It makes them more desirable."

Now that was something to think about.

"Come, Chandra," Joanna called, lowering her towel. "It is my turn to be oiled down."

Chandra obligingly rolled off the table and rose. She pulled the towel from about her hair and shook it out free. "It will take an hour to dry," she said. She turned to see Beri looking after her, her expression puzzled.

The banquet was held in the tent-covered inner courtyard of Ali ad-Din's palace. The air was redolent with fragrant incense, and the oil lamps burned softly, casting blurred shadows on the rich silk and brocade furnishings. Chandra was gowned in a pale blue silk robe, and her hair hung over her shoulders, held back from her forehead with a band of twisted gold. There was no breeze blowing off the Mediterranean this night, and Chandra felt her gown sticking to her back. The aging archbishop of Liege, Tedaldo Visconti, looked at her approvingly, and she found herself wondering if it was her soul or her person that pleased him.

Chandra greeted Sir Elvan warmly. "I have never seen a sword scabbard studded with precious stones," she told him.

"A physician receives many gifts in payment for his services," he said.

"Don't believe him, Chandra," Jerval said. "He is more than a physician. He is a Templar, and he shows equal skill in commerce."

"I have heard it said that you do not always agree with another military order, the Hospitalers."

"And you find that strange, Lady Chandra? It is true, and the reasons for our disagreements precede my birth. If we take one side of an issue, you can be certain that the Hospitalers will take the other."

"As Christians," Chandra said, "I believe we should all fight on the same side."

Sir Elvan merely smiled. "Nothing, my lady, is ever so simple, I fear."

"No," she said after a moment, nodding, "I think you are right."

Chandra took her place beside her husband on the soft, down-filled pillows. Small sandalwood dining tables were set close together across the courtyard, a red-robed slave standing beside each of them. Along a long table at the far end of the courtyard, Prince Edward and Princess Eleanor sat with Ali ad-Din and King Hugh of Cyprus and Jerusalem. Although Edward wore a pleasant smile, he had a distracted air about him that seemed to Chandra to be shared by all of his nobles present tonight.

She heard Roger de Clifford say to Jerval, "It seems that King Hugh has arranged a farewell banquet for himself tonight, Jerval. He is returning to Cyprus."

"He should remain. He should show support for Prince Edward," Jerval said.

"He cannot afford to remain here much longer, else he might lose Cyprus to his greedy barons."

Chandra took a bite of the roasted lamb, then turned toward Jerval when he said, "I suppose you're right, Roger. Now that his barons have sent word that they will only serve in the defense of Cyprus, there is little reason for him to stay. Edward, at least, took it well. Though King Hugh had promised us men to defeat the Saracens, in truth, their numbers would not have added much."

Chandra said, "I can scarce believe that a

king has so little control over his kingdom. Methinks King Hugh should muzzle his barons."

Roger de Clifford blinked in surprise. "I did not think you ladies had any interest in or knowledge of the matter."

Chandra cocked an eyebrow. "Why would you think that, Sir Roger?"

Jerval said, after a moment, "Where did you hear of our problems with the Cypriot barons, Chandra?"

"From Ali ad-Din. I asked him why King Hugh of Cyprus was here with so few men."

"He fears treachery, that's why," Eustace said. "What chance have a thousand men against the damned Sultan Baibars and his hordes of Saracen soldiers?"

"Do not forget," Graelam de Moreton called out, "that the Venetians — our Christian brothers — are busily supplying Baibars with all the timber and metal he needs for his armaments. And the equally Christian Genoese supply them the slaves to build their weapons."

"Do you know that when Edward reproved the merchants," Payn de Chaworth said, his brow knit in an angry frown, "they simply showed him their licenses from the High Court at Acre? By God, I would drive them all into the sea."

Joanna de Chaworth, smiling at her husband with a lustful eye, interrupted the grim conversation. "I cannot get used to these white grains called sugar." She held up a sweetmeat made of dates and lemons, sticky with the sweet substance, for her husband's inspection. "I still cannot believe, my lord, that it will replace honey, as you keep telling me."

Payn smiled, leaning toward his wife. "It is one of Palestine's main trade goods to the West, Joanna."

The rich meal and heavy wine did not lighten the men's mood, and when Ali ad-Din called for the dancers, Jerval, Payn, and Roger de Clifford left the table to join the prince.

Graelam de Moreton eased himself down beside Chandra. She did not move away from him because that would show fear. She had seen little of him since they had left England. In Sicily, if rumor was correct, he had amused himself by indulging freely in the women offered to the English nobles by King Charles. She eyed him, wanting to send her fist into his smiling face.

"I don't like it when you smile," she said. "It means you are up to no good."

"Ah, we will have to see about that, won't we? Do you enjoy the music, Chandra?"

"I suppose it is music," Chandra said, the clacking cymbals and the tinkling bells still sounding strange, even after weeks of hearing them every waking hour. "Do you not wish to join the prince and my husband?"

"Aye, perhaps in a moment. Is not the girl in the red veils Beri, Ali ad-Din's slave?"

She nodded, frowning as she said, "It is a pity that such a lovely, soft-spoken girl must be a slave."

He looked for a moment into his silver goblet, into the deep-red Cyprian wine, then said, "Doubtless even Beri has some amusement in her life."

"I have seen what amusements you promise for women, Lord Graelam. But of course you look upon women — slaves or free — as naught but instruments for your pleasure, do you not?"

He watched her for a long moment, before saying easily, "You still fear me."

"I'm not afraid of you, my lord. I was merely thinking of Mary, the young girl you raped at Croyland."

Graelam raised a black brow. "I did not wish to do it. I could think of nothing else to make you tell me where your brother was hidden."

"She was innocent." Of course, it was too late now. She added, "The slave girl yon,

444

Beri — I told her you were ruthless."

"Fair enough. Your dagger, Chandra — my shoulder was raw for weeks, and each time I flexed my shoulder, I thought of you. Then, of course, when my men returned with your noble father's message, I found myself a bit angered." He shrugged his broad shoulders, adding, his voice deeper now, "Let me give you warning. We are in a treacherous land where men trade their souls to gain an advantage. You must take care."

"Is that a threat, Lord Graelam?"

"A threat? It is an interesting question, but one that is much too simple."

"I have wondered why you are here."

"The truth is that we are a pitiful lot. If you would know another truth, Chandra, my motive for being here is not quite as noble as it could be."

"You wish for glory."

"Glory?" His voice was incredulous. "By God, your father did you a great disservice. Take our lauded conquest of Acre. Be thankful your husband did not allow you in the fighting for this wretched city. In that, at least, I must admire him. You imagined the glory of our victory from a distance. I felt flies crawling over my face. The heat was so intense that I felt baked beneath my armor, and I was blinded by my own sweat. There is no glory in this hellhole, Chandra. Edward's noble cause is doomed; you have but to listen to know that. There is nothing in this miserable land save disease and death and treachery. Look yon at Ali ad-Din, our fawning host. He is as treacherous and ruthless as any of Baibars's emirs, as dishonorable as the damned Venetians and Genoese, and he licks Edward's boots only to ensure his own safety. Do not blind yourself with the myth of glory, Chandra."

"I do not blind myself, Lord Graelam, particularly to your treachery."

He laughed. "Your memory pleases me, Chandra." He shrugged, but his voice once again became serious. "Think on what I have said, though I imagine that your proud husband has told you much the same things."

"Nay, Jerval said nothing of the fighting when we arrived at Acre."

"But you saw his surcoat — it was covered with blood."

"Aye, but it wasn't his blood. A man fights as he must — a woman as well. There is honor in fighting, Lord Graelam, if the man or woman fighting knows honor to his soul." She rose quickly. "Princess Eleanor is waving to me, my lord. I must attend her now."

Graelam watched her walk gracefully toward the princess, his eyes narrowed thoughtfully on her back. It seemed that she hadn't yet heard that her husband had taken Beri to his bed. He had been told by Eustace de Leybrun, a kinsman of Jerval de Vernon's. Was it true?

Edward looked about the faces of the nobles inside his pavilion and loosened the tie of his tunic. It was near to midnight, for Ali ad-Din's banquet had lingered long.

"King Hugh is leaving shortly to return to Cyprus," he said.

"Not that it much matters," Jerval said.

"Christ, it is so infernally hot," Payn de Chaworth said.

Edward felt as though he was drowning in his own sweat, but he said, "I understand that the Sultan Baibars considers us a sufficient threat to hold in his steel claws, at least for the moment." He suddenly slammed his fisted hand against his open palm. "What chance have we against Baibars?"

Payn de Chaworth gave Edward a tired smile. "We must be patient."

"Nay," Edward said, rising. "I will not sit idly here in Acre watching the bloody Genoese and Venetians trade all the wealth of Palestine to the damned Saracens."

"My lord," Jerval said. "We came to Palestine to reconquer the cities and castles captured by Baibars. I suggest that we do just that, beginning with Nazareth. By God, it is our Christ's city and it is in heathen hands."

Edward's eyes gleamed with sudden decision, and his fine chiseled features hardened with purpose. He walked to stand beside Jerval, towering even taller than he, his head brushing against the top of the pavilion. His mouth widened into a pleased smile. "Sir Jerval is in the right. With God's aid, we will succeed in this venture. Gather the men and provision them for the march to Nazareth. We leave in the morning."

Jerval did not return until very late. Chandra felt his cool hand upon her cheek, and she smiled at him, still half asleep. "Is something wrong?"

"Nay. We leave for Nazareth in the morning."

"I go with you?"

"I'm sorry, but we must take Nazareth first; then you will come when all is secured. Sleep now. I will wake you at first light."

Chapter 26

The dust kicked up from the rutted road by the horses' hooves was a hazy white under the sweltering morning sun. Chandra craned her neck westward for a glimpse of the Mediterranean, but they were too far inland to make it out. Nothing grew here save an occasional yellowish shrub. Even the hearty olive trees, gnarled and bent, lay a mile or so to the west, still within sight of the sea, across a barrier of dunes and craggy rocks.

Although Chandra's head and most of her face were covered with thin white gauze, she felt gritty sand in her mouth each time she breathed. She, Eleanor, and several of her ladies were on their way to Nazareth to join Edward and his army. They were well protected, surrounded by a hundred soldiers, Payn de Chaworth at their head. Eleanor rode in a covered litter, her only concession to her pregnancy. She had been as excited as Chandra to leave the confines of Acre, thanking God for their victory in Nazareth.

Chandra clicked her nimble-footed bay

mare to the fore of the troop, to search out Arnolf. Instead, it was Payn who reined in beside her. He wore a white linen surcoat over his armor, his only defense against the baking sun, and his head and face, like hers, were covered with swaths of white cloth.

"I was trying to find Arnolf," she said, smiling at him. "You look tired, Payn."

"Nary a bit," he said, looking back briefly toward Joanna, who rode next to Eleanor's litter. "I wager you want to hear all about the battle."

She heard amusement in his voice and turned in her saddle to see his eyes crinkled above the line of cloth. "Certainly more than that we won, and God be praised."

Before he spoke, Payn once again twisted in his saddle to check the troops behind them. Their party formed a wide phalanx, the ladies in the middle, surrounded on all sides by Edward's men.

"My Joanna would likely prefer spending this day in the cool bathing room at Ali ad-Din's residence."

"It is dreadfully hot," Chandra said, wiping sand from her forehead as she spoke. "Come, Payn, please tell me how you took Nazareth."

Payn raised a sandy brow at her excitement. She leaned toward him as he said,

"All right. Edward's spies told us the Saracen garrison at Nazareth had grown lax, especially at night. We were able to form in a semicircle, twenty men deep, about the walls before dawn. You are probably picturing the thick walls of Acre, but Nazareth was besieged by the Saracens several years ago, and they had not bothered to rebuild. Our Lord's city is a filthy, devastated place, its wealth long ago looted, and truth be told, the Saracens had little heart to defend it. We lost few men breaching the walls. But the Saracens did not want to leave us any gain. Instead of fighting us, they butchered Nazarenes as they fled through the streets. I did not see much, for Edward sent me back to fetch the ladies, but what I did see was not a pretty sight."

"War is never pretty," Chandra said.

Payn looked at her, his head cocked to one side, knowing that she was mouthing words without really comprehending their meaning. There had been no devastation in Acre, and she still had no concept of what armies could do to a people caught in their midst. "Perhaps your father raised you to picture war as the battles of gallant knights, riding in honor," he said. "It is not the heroic Roland, my lady, dying with dignity, a prayer to God on his lips. War in the Holy Land

451

against the Saracens is a hell most men would give their souls to forget."

She said nothing to that, but Payn saw that she was looking very thoughtful.

Chandra's first impression of Nazareth from a distance was a peaceful one. The city was set upon a rise, and to Chandra's surprise, there were lush date and palm trees surrounding it.

"Nazareth was built," Payn said, "as a trading center. There is water, and once the city was as beautiful as Acre, so I'm told. It isn't beautiful now."

As they drew nearer, she saw that the city was like a giant ravaged carcass, its dirty brown stone walls in ruin. There was a pungent odor in the air, a nauseating smell that made her stomach roil. She looked a question toward Payn.

"It is the stench of the dead and dying," he said. "It was here before we arrived. As I told you, the Saracens killed and maimed as many people as they could, believing, I suppose, that we would take whomever they left unharmed as slaves."

Their horses picked their way through the rubble in the narrow streets. Children in pitiful rags stood huddled in doorways, staring at them with dull eyes. They were too weak for the Saracens to bother with, Payn told her matter-of-factly.

"But they are only children," she said blankly, fury and helplessness filling her.

"That is why they still live. The Saracens knew they would die before they could be sold as slaves."

She saw bedraggled women, their stomachs bloated with hunger, tending to men whose cries of pain rent the air. Her mare snorted and sidestepped a pool of blood. A man's body, covered with a rag, lay alone at its center, blackened by the ferocious hot sun. She gagged, unable to help herself.

"How can this be our victory, Payn?"

He shrugged, weary and saddened. "It is worse than I thought. You, Joanna, and the other ladies will stay with Eleanor," he said, pointing to a small stone house that lay ahead of them beneath the collapsed northern wall of the city. "That is Edward's headquarters."

Chandra followed Eleanor into the bare, derelict interior of the house. Wounded English soldiers lay on blankets along its walls. "Where is Jerval?" she asked Lambert, who was kneeling over a wounded soldier.

He raised his once-happy boyish face to her, and she drew back at the haunted look in his eyes. "He will return," Lambert said, his voice dead.

She saw Graelam holding a gourd of water to the pinched lips of one of his squires, the look on his face one of fury mingled with despair. His eyes met hers briefly, and for the first time, it was Graelam who looked away.

Chandra stayed close to the women, praying for the sun to set on the misery. She heard Edward say to Eleanor, "If I had known that it would be so wretched, I would not have sent for you. We lost few men. But the people, by God, the people."

Eleanor's face was pale, her dark eyes dimmed with the suffering she had seen. "It is beyond anything I could have imagined," she said, her hands against her swelled belly.

"You will stay within. I do not want you outside."

Chandra helped Eleanor and her ladies prepare a small chamber in the back of the house for them, but she could not remain with them, hidden away. She stood in the doorway of Edward's headquarters, awaiting Jerval. When he finally strode toward her, his surcoat drenched with sweat, she saw that he was carrying a small girl in his arms, one of her legs wrapped in the bloody hem of his surcoat. He nodded at her, and she felt suddenly like an outcast, her body clean and whole, her belly filled with food. He looked unutterably weary. She felt tears start to her eyes when the child looked at her, for she did not utter a sound or a groan, and her dark eyes were glazed with shock.

"I saw a Saracen hack at her leg," Jerval said blankly, the first words he spoke. "He simply leaned low off his horse's back and slashed his scimitar. I killed him, of course, but it was too late for the child."

She remembered her glib words to Graelam the night of Ali ad-Din's banquet, idiocy about glory and honor, and her meaningless words to Payn just hours before that war wasn't pretty. She'd had no idea, none at all. They were just words she'd spoken, just silly words spoken by an ignorant fool. "I'm sorry," she said. "Oh God, I'm sorry." But her words meant nothing in the face of the horror that surrounded them, and she knew it.

She watched him lay the child tenderly down upon a blanket and force some water between her pinched lips. Her small head lolled to one side. He rose and looked about the wall at the English soldiers.

"You are all right?" she asked him.

"Nay," he said, "I am not all right, but I am alive and healthy, which is more than I can say for these poor wretches." He shook his head, as if to block out the chaos outside the house. "I wish that you had not come."

"Is there nothing we can do?"

He ran his fingers through his matted hair. "Aye, many of the people are starving. I am taking some men to give them what food we can."

"I would go with you, Jerval."

She saw that he would refuse, and quickly added, "If I must be here, do not deny me a useful task."

He seemed to struggle with himself for a moment, then shrugged. "Very well, but you will stay close beside me. I do not know if there is still danger. You can help us gather the food."

It was late afternoon when they left the English quarters, and the sun still blazed overhead, making the stench almost un-bearable. She would have given away all the bread she carried to the men and women huddled close by Edward's headquarters had Jerval not stopped her, his voice grim. "Nay, there is much need. You must dole it out, else you'll have nothing for the rest of the people."

She just shook her head, but she heeded him and followed him through the labyrinth of rubble in the narrow streets. They saw women crouched down in the piles of waste, burrowing for food or clothing.

"The Saracens took pride, I think, in beggaring the Nazarenes," Jerval said wearily. He turned to see Chandra leaning over a ragged woman in the doorway of a small house. She was shaking her, begging her to take a hunk of bread. Her voice rose, almost angrily, when the woman did not raise her head.

He felt a stab of impotent pain and touched his hand to Chandra's shoulder. "She is dead, sweeting. Come, there is nothing you can do for her."

Chandra raised angry eyes to his face. "No, you are wrong, Jerval. No, she isn't dead, she isn't. She's merely sleeping. It is so very hot, you see, and there was such violence. Sleeping, aye, she's just sleeping."

He saw that she could not accept it and forcibly drew her to her feet. He said to one of the soldiers, "Tell the men that there is another for the funeral pyre.

"Come," he said, forcing her away. "There are living who need our food."

She said not another word throughout the rest of the afternoon, even when they passed one of the burning funeral pyres. When they had no more food, she raised glazed eyes to Jerval's face. "What are we to do?"

"Nothing. I'm sorry, Chandra." He drew her against him for a moment to block out the squalor around them.

He led her back to Edward's headquarters as evening fell. Chandra passed by the wounded English soldiers and fell to her knees by the small girl whose leg the Saracen had hacked off. There was a film of white over her staring dark eyes. She was dead.

Geoffrey Parker, one of Edward's surgeons, knelt down beside her. "The child had no chance," he said.

Chandra heard Jerval give a low growl in his throat behind her. She watched him lift the small child in his arms and carry her from the house. She rose to accompany him, wishing there were something she could say to him, but he strode away from her as if she were not there.

"She is beyond pain," Geoffrey Parker said, touching his hand to her arm.

"He is taking her to be burned," Chandra whispered, and felt the pain so deep, she knew it would never leave her.

"Aye. Come, my lady. If you wish it, I could use your help with our wounded."

She looked up some time later to see Jerval strapping on his helmet. She jerked to her feet, filled with sudden fear. "What are you doing? Where are you going?"

"There are reports of Saracens outside the walls. Stay here and do not worry. I will be back soon." He left her without another word, Lambert at his side.

Joanna de Chaworth handed her a piece of bread. "Here, Chandra, you must eat something. Eleanor sent me to fetch you. She wants you to rest now."

Chandra looked at the bread, held out to her as the dead woman should have seen it. "Nay," she whispered. "I have no wish for food. Oh, God, Joanna, the waste of it, all the suffering, it is too much to bear."

When the wounded men were tended, Chandra walked to the doorway and sank down, waiting again for Jerval to return. The night air was cool upon her face. Over the housetops beyond, she could see black smoke billowing upward from the funeral pyres.

"Lady Chandra!"

She looked up to see Lambert running toward her.

"It's my lord," he said, clutching at her arm. "He has been wounded. The Saracens came upon us from the rocks."

Geoffrey Parker, Edward's physician, jumped to his feet and hurried to the door. For an instant, Chandra could not move.

She could bear no more suffering, no more death. Oh, God, please, not Jerval.

"My lady!" Geoffrey shouted to her. "Prepare a place for him, quickly."

"God's teeth!" she heard Jerval bellow, pain deep in his throat. "Do not tear my flesh from my damned bones!" He was carried through the door by Payn, Rolfe, and two men-at-arms.

"Do not worry," Payn de Chaworth said, casting her a quick glance over his shoulder. "The wound is not deep, but the blood has congealed and stuck to his shirt."

Chandra could only nod. She smoothed down a bed of blankets, and Jerval was lowered, cursing, onto his back.

"By all the saints' misery, Payn," he said, gritting his teeth, "would that you were not such a clumsy oaf."

"Aye, and you not such a noble lout."

Chandra fell to her knees beside him, pushed back the sweaty hair from his forehead and held his face between her hands. "You told me you would be all right, damn you. You promised me you would take care, but you didn't. You lied to me. I am very angry at you about this, Jerval."

He smiled up at her through the gnawing pain in his side. "I did promise you, and I meant it. I swear that I did not mean to get hurt. Now, the wound isn't deep. Stop your worrying."

"My lady," Geoffrey Parker said, and pushed her away. She watched as Lambert and Payn unstrapped his armor and stripped off his bloody clothes. Geoffrey probed at his torn flesh. "I am relieved, Sir Jerval," he said. "It is but a needle and thread I'll need for you." He yelled for more water.

Edward leaned over Jerval, shaking his head in grim humor. "What have you to say, sir? I send you forth to dispatch the heathen, and it is you who are on your back."

"I will survive, sire," Jerval said.

"The blood is clotted," Chandra said. "I will bathe him. He will be all right, sire. If he isn't, I will kill him."

Geoffrey saw shock in her eyes, and nodded. It was better to let her care for her husband. "Aye, you bathe the wound, then call me."

Jerval looked up at her and smiled. "I am not going to die, Chandra, even though you were not at my side to protect me."

"I should have been with you. I can fight, as you well know. I don't know how you can laugh about it, damn you." She stared down at his naked body, at the dried blood clotted over his right side and streaking down his leg. "Damn you, you could have been killed."

He winced from the pain in his side, and it got worse. Jerval felt it deep, and knew he had to control it, else his wife would howl, steal his sword, and go after the Saracens by herself. He closed his eyes. He could still see the wild-eyed Saracen, hear his blood-curdling yell as he swooped down from his horse's back, his curved blade but inches from Payn's neck. Jerval's sword had slashed deep into the man's leg, so deep that its tip had wounded the horse beneath him. The beast had snorted in pain and fallen on the man, crushing him beneath its massive body. Jerval had pulled off his helmet to rub the burning sweat from his eyes, and it was then that two Saracens had come at him. He had thrown his helmet at one of them, but the other had reached his side with the tip of his scimitar. He had been unlucky, for their force had far outnumbered the Saracen band. He felt Chandra's hand lightly touch his shoulder, and he opened his eyes.

"Drink this, Jerval. It will ease the pain."

Lambert helped him to rise from the blankets enough to drink from the goblet. The liquid was sweet and cool, and almost immediately, Jerval felt a soothing warmth pervade his mind. When the pain lessened, he opened his eyes to see Chandra, a bowl of water and a cloth in her hand.

"Thank God," he said, grinning up at her, "that Geoffrey will stitch me up. I don't want to look like the surcoat that you mended for me."

"Please don't jest about this," she said in a whisper. He stared up at her, but he said nothing as she dropped to her knees beside him. "I will bathe the wound now. I will try not to hurt you more than I must."

She found that she had to scrub at the jagged flesh to cleanse away the clotted blood. She felt his muscles tense beneath her hand, and stilled.

"I'm sorry, Jerval, but it must be done."

"Aye, love, I know. Just get it over with." He closed his eyes again and clenched his teeth. "Forgive my foul odor. I smell like stinking death."

"I will bathe all of you when I am through." Her words sounded strangely distant to him.

When Geoffrey had finished stitching his flesh, he rose and said gently, "You did well, my lady. Sir Jerval is young and strong. He will be fit within the week. You may bathe him now, if you wish."

She sponged him with warm, soapy water. He cracked open his eyes and smiled hazily up at her. "Ah, that feels good," he said. Her hand stroked down his chest to his belly, and he felt her hesitate, but just for a moment.

"I'm sorry that I cannot show you my appreciation, Chandra, but even that part of me is beyond tired."

"I see that it is," she said.

He smiled, simply couldn't help it. Of course, she didn't leave his side. She talked and talked, of nothing really, or she just sat in silence, staring at him.

"Chandra," he said finally, "you need to walk about and get some fresh air."

She just shook her head. "There is no fresh air, not anywhere in this place."

"I have to relieve myself, and I would prefer Lambert to help me."

She left him for but a minute, but upon her return, he was surrounded by Edward, Payn, and Eustace de Leybrun. She sank down in a corner, listening to them speak quietly of their losses and what was to be done for the Nazarenes.

When she awoke the next morning, Jerval was sitting up, eating a hunk of bread and drinking ale. "You look better," she said. "It is a good thing that you do. I am still not happy with you."

He leaned back a moment, looking at her

from beneath half-closed eyelids. "I have never seen you so frightened," he said after a moment, "save after you were taken by Alan Durwald. I did not realize it then, for you were full of cocky bravado, but you were terrified."

"You believe me a fool? Of course I was scared, but it wasn't like this. Nothing has ever been like this. That was just me, but this is you."

She held him more dear than she held herself? He would have to think about this. He handed her a piece of bread. "I dreamed last night of Camberley, the lakes and the Cumbrian Mountains. I think I would gladly give a year of my life to be back there now, with you, even to hear my mother complaining about your throwing the distaff at her."

She stared at him, not smiling as he had intended. She said, "Why, Jerval?"

"Why what, Chandra?"

She waved her arm about her. "Did you know that it would be like this? The horror? The hopelessness?"

"I suppose so, for I have fought before, Chandra. But this bad? This is beyond what I have seen before. Here there is such poverty, such wretchedness, and this damnable heat that eats into your very soul. No, I

465

haven't seen anything like this."

"But you knew it would be bad. Why did you agree to come with Edward, if you knew that war was ever thus, and that you could be killed?"

He looked away from her a moment, weighing his words. "One wonders why God, in His infinite mercy, wishes His followers to win battles in His name, if this is the outcome. We have spoken many times, Chandra, about a woman's responsibilities, and a man's. It is my duty to keep all that I hold dear safe against my enemies. It does not mean that I am less enraged than you by the waste of it. But my duty forbids me to turn away and leave other men to fight, and possibly die, in my stead."

"But this was different. It was me you wished to escape, wasn't it? That was why you agreed to come with Edward. You no longer wanted me."

"A part of that is true. I believed you would never come to me. That you would never realize that together we could be more than we are separately. I still wonder, despite all we have been through together."

She was silent.

Chapter 27

They rode out of the city three days later, the wounded English either tied to their horses or drawn by them on litters at the center of the phalanx of troops. Chandra rode next to Jerval, cursing his pride. He should not have refused a litter. She knew that he felt pain, but he was in his armor again, and in his saddle. Edward had done what he could for the Christians of Nazareth, but beyond providing all the food he could spare and leaving two of his physicians behind with a hundred soldiers, there was little he could do.

Chandra looked up to see Eleanor ease her palfrey next to the prince's destrier. She had given up her litter to a wounded soldier. She extended her hand and laid it gently upon her husband's mailed arm. It was an offer of comfort, a sign of love and trust. Chandra saw Edward close his hand over hers. They rode, touching, for some minutes, speaking quietly to each other.

"I hope that Eleanor and her babe will not suffer from this," she said.

Jerval did not answer her. She turned to him and saw his mighty shoulders slumped forward, his head bowed in sleep.

Acre now seemed like the most comfortable haven in the world. At least there Jerval could rest on a cot, protected from the scorching sun. The thought that he could easily have been killed still haunted her. Tentatively, as she had seen Eleanor do, she stretched out her hand and lightly touched his mailed arm.

"My lord," she said quietly.

"I shall survive, Chandra. The wound is naught. Stop your fretting."

"Is it so unmanly to admit that you feel pain? I am still angry with you about this wound."

He grinned at her. "Nay, Chandra, I will admit it, I feel pain. However, you did pull me from a pleasant dream."

The column narrowed as they rode through the Neva Pass, a barren grotto with jagged boulders jutting from its walls around them like armless sentinels. Beyond the pass, she knew, the dusty road veered toward the coast.

Suddenly the air was rent by yells that seemed to come from everywhere as they echoed off the surrounding rocks. Chandra scarce had time to pull in her frightened mare before the screaming Saracens jumped from their crevices, their scimitars whirling over their heads.

"Go to the women!" Jerval shouted at her, and slapped his mailed hand on her palfrey's rump. Her palfrey jumped forward toward a small clearing, where Edward's personal guard were forming a circle three men deep around Eleanor and the other women. The English horses were careening into each other, snorting in trapped fear. Dimly, she heard Edward shouting orders even as a screaming Saracen broke through the raging throng toward him. Edward's sword dipped gracefully downward.

She looked toward Jerval, fear for him clotted in her throat. He was cut off from the men, hacking his sword methodically at three bearded Saracens around him, but he wasn't up to his full strength. Payn de Chaworth yelled at her to keep close to the women. But she saw her husband's face, grim with determination. She knew the strength of his arm, and saw that he was weakening. Damn him, he'd been wounded less than four days before, and he was fighting. He could so easily be killed. No, she would not allow it. She yelled at him, but he didn't hear her. She remembered her promise to him, and knew that she could not keep it. She would not let him die.

She gritted her teeth, reached beneath her robe, and pulled her hunting knife from its leather sheath. She dug her heels into her palfrey's side and sent him galloping toward her husband. A wild-eyed Saracen lunged toward her, his curved sword arched high above his head. She hurled her knife, and it pierced the man's chest. He stared at her even as he choked on his cry. She kicked her horse forward and jumped from her saddle to wrench the sword from the man's hand as he lay on the rocks.

In an instant, she was on her palfrey's back again, riding frantically toward Jerval, the screams of wounded men filling her ears. She was frightened, so frightened that she could scarce breathe, but it didn't matter. She couldn't let him be killed. She flung the heavy scimitar from her left to her right hand, and slashed out with it as she had been taught on the tiltyard. She saw a surprised look on a beardless face, a boy's face. Dear God, he was young, so very young, and he was staring up at her blankly until his blood spurted from his mouth. She screamed his agony for him, feeling his death as if it were her own. She felt a sharp pain in her right arm, and saw her own blood oozing from her flesh. She looked at her arm stupidly, knowing that his blade could just as easily have entered her breast, but somehow the knowledge of it didn't really touch her. She felt beads of sweat sting her eyes, and dashed her hand across her face. She had to get to Jerval.

"Chandra!"

She heard Jerval's shout, and whipped her horse forward. He was at her side in the next instant, hugging his destrier close to her horse's head. He was trying to protect her, she thought wildly, pushing her behind him toward the rocks. She saw blood at his side and knew that his wound had opened. She would not allow him to die for her.

"À Vernon," she yelled, and broke away from him, bringing her horse's rump around to protect his flank. She heard an unearthly shriek and whipped her horse about to see a Saracen leap from an outcropping of rock toward Graelam de Moreton's back.

Graelam jerked about to see Chandra's sword slicing into the screaming man's belly. For an instant, he was frozen into stunned silence. Then a faint smile touched his lips, and his eyes met Jerval's.

Jerval turned away to meet two Saracens who were bearing down on him. He jerked back on his destrier's reins, and the mighty horse reared back, striking the neck of one of the Saracens' mounts. The Saracen went flying, and the other had little chance against Jerval's sword.

Jerval looked through a blur of sweat to see Chandra, still astride her horse, next to Payn de Chaworth, who had fallen to the ground. She was protecting de Chaworth, who was trying to struggle to his feet, only to fall back as his wounded leg collapsed beneath him. He watched her sword go through a man's chest, a man who would have killed de Chaworth had she not been there.

Suddenly, it was over. A shout of victory went up. The Saracens were fleeing over the jagged rocks, or riding on horseback like the devil himself back toward the boiling desert. The time had seemed endless, but only ten minutes had passed from the beginning of the assault to its end. The English troops were yelling obscenities and curses at the fleeing Saracens, and bloodcurdling cries of victory.

Jerval dismounted painfully from his destrier. Chandra was leaning over Payn de Chaworth, pressing her palm down as hard as she could over the gaping tear in his leg. Payn de Chaworth was looking up at her with a surprised, crooked smile before he fell on his back, senseless. Chandra ripped off the turban that now hung loose down her back and wrapped it tightly about his thigh to stanch the flow of blood. She pressed down even harder. "It's working. The blood is slowing."

Jerval knelt beside her, not speaking until he was certain that the wound had stopped bleeding. He raised his face and found that she was staring at him, relief, and something else he could not fathom, in her eyes.

"Your side," she whispered. "I saw the blood and knew the wound had opened. Oh, God, are you all right? Let me look at your wound, Jerval."

"I am fine." Then he saw the blood streaking down her arm, and felt himself go cold. "You're hurt," he said, his voice sounding so harsh that Chandra jumped.

"It's nothing at all. It all happened so quickly. From one instant to the next, they were on us. By God, we beat them off."

The memories of the battle rose in her mind. She saw the boy's face, so clearly, right there, staring at her. She rose shakily to her feet and stumbled away from Jerval toward a narrow crevice in one of the jagged rocks. Nauseating bile rose in her throat, and she fell to her knees. She wretched until her belly was empty, then wretched more, doubling over. She felt his hands on her shoulders, steadying her.

"Here, Chandra, drink this."

She accepted the water skin from Jerval

473

and forced herself to swallow the cool water, then rinse out her mouth. "What is wrong with me? I cannot even stand." And then she tried to stand again, but her legs wouldn't hold her. She felt his arms about her, and she leaned against him.

She said, her voice deep with pain and horror, "We are so fragile, our lives so easily snuffed out in an instant with the twist of a hand. It is just too much." She turned about on her knees to face him. "To know that you are about to die, to become nothing in but a moment. And to kill, to rob another of life. Dear God, he was only a boy, and I killed him. I didn't hesitate, just killed him, and I saw the surprise on his face."

Jerval fell to his knees and gathered her shaking body into his arms. "He did what he had to, just as you did. Fighting the Saracens isn't like fighting the bandits at home. These are not bandits, men ruled only by their greed — nay, these are men who believe as strongly as you and I that what they think is right. We are heathen to them. We are the evil ones.

"I think for the first time you were truly aware that the specter of death was on your shoulder." As he spoke the words, she felt him stiffen. "You could have been killed playing the hero for me."

She looked up at him wildly. "I could not bear it if you had fallen and I had done nothing."

"But I would not have borne the cost had you been killed. You saved de Moreton's life and probably de Chaworth's. I must thank you, yet it pains me to my soul."

Jerval looked over at Graelam de Moreton, who was seeing to another one of their wounded men. She'd saved him. Not so long ago, she would have gladly killed him, as would Jerval for that matter.

He tightened his hold about Chandra's shoulders. He could hear Payn cursing at the top of his lungs at one of the physicians, who was probing at his leg.

He looked down at Chandra. She was tugging at his arms. "Please, your side. I must change your bandage."

"Your arm first, Chandra." He ripped away the sleeve of her gown, and drew a relieved breath. He bandaged the shallow gash as best he could. "Is Eleanor safe?"

"Aye. She was well protected, surrounded by at least twenty men." She looked up at him, wanting to speak, wanting to beg him never again to place himself in danger, but she knew she could not. It was his duty to fight. She said simply, "I don't want to lose you, ever. Do you hear me?"

His eyes flew to her face at the raw passion in her voice, but she had turned away from him, pressing her cheek against his shoulder.

"Aye," he said, "I hear you. You will stay safe with me until we are once again back in Acre."

She sat on the ground beside the unconscious Payn de Chaworth while the English buried their dead. The hovering birds were but waiting, she thought, for them to be on their way, leaving the bodies of the Saracens.

She saw a large shadow from the corner of her eye and gazed up to see Graelam de Moreton towering over her.

She said nothing when he dropped to his haunches beside her. He simply gazed at her for a long moment, his hands fisted against his thighs.

"You hate me. You would have killed me at Croyland if you could have. Why did you save my life?"

She looked at him full face. "You were simply an English knight who would die if I did nothing. No matter what has happened, no matter what you have done, I could not let them kill you."

"Your arm," he said, his tone almost as harsh as Jerval's had been.

"It's nothing."

Payn groaned and twisted sharply. Graelam helped her ease him onto his back and straighten his wounded leg.

She felt Graelam's hand touch hers, and her eyes flew to his face.

"You will hear no more veiled threats from me, Chandra," he said quietly. He patted her hand and looked off into the distance. "You have no more reason to fear me. It's true that I thought still about taking you, even here in the Holy Land, and I know that I wouldn't have treated you well. I hated you almost as much as your father after the humiliation I suffered through Jerval and the king's order — and of course from that knife wound in my shoulder." He sighed deeply and looked back at her, a grim smile on his lips. "You have robbed me of my revenge, Chandra."

He rose suddenly, his shadow still blocking out the sun. "Your husband is returning. I thank you for saving me and I wish you and Jerval well. I owe you a debt now, Chandra." He turned and strode away from her to his destrier.

Chandra stared after him until she heard Payn de Chaworth moan. She laid her hand gently on his chest, and he opened his eyes to stare up at her. He said, pain rumbling in his throat, "I thank you, Chandra, for protecting my wretched skin. I had heard you could fight, of course, but I did not believe that it could be true. Sir Jerval must admire you greatly."

She raised her head, a bitter smile on her lips. Mayhap he did, she thought, despite his anger at her for fighting, but she found little pleasure in the notion. She felt free of herself for the first time in her life, free from the bonds of a meaningless pride. She heard wild cursing. It was Eustace, howling, as a physician stitched up a gash in his cheek.

"He is carrying on like a damned woman," Payn said, then realized what he'd said. "Nay, that isn't true, is it? Not any damned woman, in any case. However, I cannot imagine — damnation, forget that."

Chandra lightly punched his shoulder and laughed.

"You look as if you swallowed a prune," Joanna said to Chandra.

"Nay, I was just wishing we had word from Haifa. It has been nearly a week without news."

Eleanor, arranged comfortably on thick, soft cushions in Ali ad-Din's bathing room, said easily, "They will send word soon, Chandra. There is little to fear. My lord told me before they left that the Saracens had only a loose hold on the city and would likely flee at the sight of our army."

The slave girl who had been soaping Chandra rose at a word from Beri and poured a jug of warm, perfumed water over her. Chandra sighed with pleasure and slithered into the cool bathing pool. As was her habit, she floated in the water, listening to the giggling Joanna and the chattering slave girls. When she opened her eyes, she saw Beri staring down at her, an odd, assessing look in her dark eyes. She stood up, pulled her hair over her shoulder, and twisted out the water.

Beri handed her a towel. "Come, this time I have a very special perfumed oil for you."

"Will it remove this ugly scar?" Chandra asked, looking at the jagged ridge of flesh on her arm.

"Nay, but it will make men wild to be near you."

Chandra gave her a twisted smile. "It is not something I wish."

"Perhaps you should," Beri said.

Chandra stretched out on her stomach and felt the warm oil trickle down her back until a slave girl began to rub it lightly into her flesh. She turned her face toward Beri. "Why did you say that?"

Beri shrugged. "I told you once that I did

not understand. You are beautiful, your body glows with health, and you are not at all ill tempered."

"You have never seen me angry, Beri."

"You are proud. That is different, and perhaps that is what I do not understand. You must take care. There is a man who wishes you ill — Sir Eustace de Leybrun is his name. I heard that he was spreading rumors that my master had given me to Sir Jerval as payment for his help against the Genoese. He wishes to hurt both you and your husband."

Rumors that Jerval had bedded Beri? She wanted to know more, but there was no time because Eleanor called out, "Chandra? There is a message just delivered. We have taken Haifa, and our husbands are all safe."

Chandra gazed blankly toward Eleanor, who was waving a letter a slave girl had given her. "Thank God," she said. "Thank you, Beri, for giving me warning." She paused a moment, and smiled. "Actually, I believe I lost my pride when I saw my husband wounded. I won't let Eustace or anyone harm him again." She rose from the table and allowed a slave girl to help her dress.

She was aware of Beri watching her until she passed out of the bathing room with Eleanor.

"I am returned, hale and hearty, Chandra. Stop your pacing. I am not hurt — indeed, everything went easily."

She whirled about to see Jerval stride into the tent. She only stared at him.

"Are you surprised that I am clean? And out of my armor?"

She was at his side in a moment, feeling his arms, his shoulders. She fell to her knees, her hands on his legs. "You are all right? Your side did not pain you?"

"Aye, I am fit again." He stopped abruptly, staring at her. "You look pale. What is the matter?"

"I want you. Right now. I want you to kiss me."

He believed his eyes would cross. He was instantly hard, harder than he'd ever been in his life. He was on her in just a moment more. He lifted her against him, pressing her tightly to him.

She clutched at his shoulders and felt the power of him, felt the urgency of his need for her. His mouth was gentle, his hands lightly stroking, yet she knew he was holding himself back, that he was in control. She didn't want him to be in control. She wanted him to be as wild as she was. She rubbed herself against him.

Even as he said, "Our clothes, Chandra," she was tearing at the fastenings on her gown. He laughed, slapping her hands away, and stripped her within moments. Then it was her turn. She gave him a siren's smile, and once again he believed he would lose control. It was very close.

"Lie beside me," he said, and she believed him to be in pain. When she would have spoken, he lightly placed his fingertips against her lips. They lay facing each other, and for a moment, he feared to touch her, for if he did, he would be on her and deep inside her. He stared into her eyes, smoky and vague. Beautiful eyes, a deep blue, shimmering like the sea at dawn.

"Why do you stare at me?"

"I never want to forget what you look like at this moment." Then he clasped her hand and gently guided it down his belly. When her fingers closed over him, he smiled. "I want you, badly — you know that."

She still held him, her fingers clutching at him now, and it was almost pain, but not enough for him to stop her. Finally he pulled her hand away. "No more, or I will spill my seed and you will want to take your sword to me."

"No," she said into his mouth, "no." She felt his fingers pressed against her, feeling her, stroking, and she quite simply wanted to die from the frenzy of it, the immense wildness.

"Move against my fingers," he said, nuzzling her throat.

When her eyes went blank and wild, he reared over her and came inside her. He thought he would die at the feel of her, of them together.

She yelled, holding him tightly against her, feeling him inside her, so deep, part of her, and she wanted him, wanted, and when his fingers found her, she yelled again.

She was whispering love words to him and clutching his back, holding him down on top of her. For many moments, his mind was a vague blur, raw sensation warring with thought. He could feel her pounding heart against his chest, the giving softness of her breasts and belly. He shook his head, clearing away his passion, and balanced himself over her on his elbows to stare down into her face.

"Did I hurt you?" he asked.

She smiled, replete and satisfied. "Nay, but I am filled with you," she said in wonder. "Filled, and it is very good."

"Aye," he said, "but not quite so much now." He lowered his head and rubbed his chin against her neck.

She said against his temple, "So many things have happened, things I never expected. I thought I would die when you were wounded at Nazareth."

"And I must always try to protect you. There will be some things I cannot change, Chandra, some things that you will have to accept."

"Because you are a man."

"Aye, because I am a man, and because life, even at Camberley, is so damned uncertain."

"But I was not useless during the Saracen attack. I did save Graelam and help Payn."

"That is true. I suppose I sound like a fool, and if Payn heard me, he'd likely call me an ungrateful dog, but perhaps the next time it would be your life to be forfeit. Never could I bear that cost, never."

"So it must always be I who waits in fear?"

He rolled to his side and laid the flat of his hand in the hollow of her smooth belly. "When you carry my child, it is his safety that must be your only concern."

"I am to be the giver of life, and you its protector."

"Those sound like some philosopher's words."

"It is what you want."

"Mayhap, some of it. We are back to obedience, are we? We will have great fights, Chandra, and we will tug apart and then pull back together. The servants will cower in fright, and my parents will believe us mad. But there will be love between us, and respect. If you will agree to that, then all else will work itself out."

She snuggled her face into the hollow of his throat and smiled. "You won't ever leave me?" she asked him, her arms tightening about his back.

"I doubt if I could leave you even if the damned Saracens besieged Acre."

"I love you, Jerval." He was silent. For an instant, she tasted the fear of vulnerability.

"It took you long enough to realize it. You will not now forget, will you? Ever?"

"Nay, never."

"I have loved you since I saw you standing in the Great Hall of Croyland." He paused a moment as his fingers lightly probed the raised scar on her arm. "There has been too much between us — and not enough."

"I don't want us to be what we were in England, ever again."

"No, we have both changed."

There were no more words between them, and they slept within minutes, Chandra sprawled beside him, her hand curled upon his chest.

Chapter 28

The next afternoon, after little fuss, Eleanor birthed a girl child, named Joan of Acre — a fitting name, Jerval said to Chandra.

But two days after the birth of his daughter, Prince Edward sat alone in his tent, wearing only his tunic, having rid himself of his hellishly hot armor, wondering what the devil was keeping al-Hamil, an emissary from a local chieftain who had made a truce with the Christian knights. He was impatient to join Eleanor and their babe, Joan. The fly that kept hovering about his forehead did not improve his temper.

He heard conversation outside his tent, but did not rise. He looked up as the flap was raised and nodded welcome to al-Hamil, an unusually large man for a Saracen, nearly as tall as Edward, with black, bushy eyebrows that almost met across his forehead. Al-Hamil stepped inside the tent and bowed low to Edward.

"Sire," he said, and walked slowly forward.

"What have you to say to me today, al-Hamil?" Edward waved him toward a stool. Turning slightly to reach for a goblet of wine, he saw a shadow of swift movement from the corner of his eye. He flung the goblet of wine toward the Saracen and threw himself sideways even before he saw the gleaming dagger coming down fast. He felt a prick of pain in his upper arm, and with a growl of rage, he lunged at the Saracen, his fingers gripping the wrist that still held tight to the dagger.

"Christian dog!" al-Hamil yelled, spitting into Edward's face. "It is too late for you, for the dagger has pierced your flesh."

Edward felt the Saracen's arm weakening beneath his fingers and, slowly, he turned the dagger toward al-Hamil. Before the Saracen could wrench away from him, Edward brought up his knee and thrust it brutally into the other man's groin. Al-Hamil bellowed in pain, staggered, and fell to his knees. He saw the dagger's vicious point aimed at his throat.

"Allah!" he screamed.

Edward locked his arm behind the Saracen's neck and, with a final surge of strength, drove the dagger into al-Hamil's chest. The Saracen gazed up at the prince and smiled, even as his blood trickled from his mouth. He slumped backward, his eyes, now sightless, locked on Edward's face.

Edward jumped back, his chest heaving. He saw his guards flooding into the tent, staring at him in shocked silence. He wanted to speak to them, but he felt a wave of nausea close over him. *It is but a prick in the arm*, he thought as he crumpled to the floor.

Jerval, Chandra on his heels, burst into the crowded tent to see Edward's two physicians leaning over him, probing at the swelling flesh of his upper arm. Eleanor stood at the foot of his cot, utterly still, utterly silent, her face frozen.

Jerval, angry at the babbling disorder, shoved the bewildered soldiers from the tent. "For God's sake," he shouted at them, "keep everyone out."

"The dagger was poisoned," Payn said, "and the damned physicians are but wringing their hands."

Edward slowly opened his eyes. He felt a numbing chill radiate from the wound in his arm. He looked up at Geoffrey Parker. "Is there nothing you can do?"

"Sire, it is a heathen poison, a poison that we do not understand. We have cleaned the wound." He turned his eyes away from Edward's gray face. "We can do naught save sew the flesh together, and pray to God."

Jerval turned to Roger de Clifford. "Send a man to fetch the Templar physician, Sir Elvan. If it is a heathen poison, he may know what to do. Quickly, quickly!"

Eleanor raised her eyes at Geoffrey's words. For an instant, she looked about her blankly, at the hovering nobles standing impotently about, at the drawn faces of the two physicians.

"Poison," she whispered. There was a bluish tinge about her husband's lips, and he was trembling now, uncontrollably. Her eyes fell to the still-swelling gash in his arm. Edward gave a low moan, and his head fell back against the cushions.

"No!" Eleanor shouted. "You will not die." She rushed from the foot of the cot and shoved Geoffrey roughly out of the way.

"My lady, please," Geoffrey said. "You must leave. There is nothing you can do."

But Eleanor knew what she was going to do and no one was going to stop her. "Listen to me. I will not let him die. Get out of my way, all of you." She fell to her knees beside Edward and lowered her mouth to the gaping wound. She sucked hard, then spat the blood and the venom from her mouth, and sucked again at the wound until she could draw no more blood or poison from it. Slowly, she fell back on her knees, and bowed her head.

There was stunned silence until Chandra slipped away from Jerval and eased down to her knees beside Eleanor. "My lady," she said gently, lightly touching Eleanor's white sleeve, "I think you are the bravest person I have ever seen. You have done all you can for your husband. Come away with me now." She looked up, angry because the damned physicians had begun to argue with each other in hushed whispers.

"She likely killed our lord," she heard one of them say.

"To bring in a Templar physician, surely the prince would not approve."

Jerval, wanting to strangle the lot of them, shouted, "Why not? Do you think the prince would prefer to die?"

"That is not the point," said another of the men, but Jerval just turned away from them.

But Chandra didn't ignore him. "Then what is the point?"

"It is better to die a Christian than let a heathen save you."

"I have never heard greater nonsense," Eleanor said, raising her head to look at the man. "If the devil himself would save someone I loved, I would do it." Wisely, Geoffrey Parker held his tongue.

As for Eleanor, she was now oblivious of them and all their muttering. "Nay, Chandra," she said at last, raising her head, "I cannot leave my lord." She shuddered, wiping her hand across her mouth. "I tasted the poison. It was awful, like decaying flesh."

Chandra quickly poured her another goblet of wine. "Here, Eleanor, you must wash out your mouth again. I don't like it that you can even remember the taste of that horrible poison."

Jerval and Payn shoved aside the bickering physicians. Chandra helped Eleanor to her feet, and they watched silently as the two men vigorously rubbed Edward's arms and legs.

"By all the saints," Payn said, "he should not remain unconscious so long."

Eleanor sat beside her husband and lightly slapped his face. "My lord," she whispered. "Please, my lord, open your eyes. Come back to me. I refuse to tell our little daughter about you. You must see her for yourself. Open your eyes else I will be very distressed."

Edward's fair lashes fluttered. He heard Eleanor's voice from afar, vague and distant, and he was suddenly frightened that she needed him. He heard her voice again, closer now, and with a great effort, he forced his eyes to open. He felt light-headed, and the wound in his arm was a raging pain, so great that he clamped his lower lip between his teeth to keep from crying out. When he focused his gaze, it was not Eleanor he saw above him, but the dark-seamed face of Sir Elvan, the Templar physician.

"Hold still, sire."

Sir Elvan nodded to Jerval and Payn. They sat on either side of Edward and held him firmly.

Edward scarce felt the knife plunging into his flesh. He heard Eleanor telling the physician to go more easily. He wanted to soothe her, to tell her he didn't feel much of anything, but no words came to mind. A fiery liquid followed the path of the knife, and Edward lunged upward with a cry of agony.

"Payn, hold him!" Jerval shouted. It required all their strength to keep Edward down as Sir Elvan opened the wound still wider and poured more of the dark liquid into it.

Sir Elvan slowly straightened. "The poison should have bubbled up from the wound. It may have worked so rapidly that my remedy will have no effect."

Jerval smiled toward Eleanor. "I believe, Sir Elvan, that there is no poison because the princess sucked it from the wound."

Sir Elvan's expression did not change. He looked at Eleanor, still speaking to her husband, stroking her palm over his forehead, her black hair straggling about her pale face.

"My lady," he said very gently, "I believe you have saved your husband's life. Well done. You are very brave."

Edward heard his words, and gazed up vaguely into his wife's face. She was smiling.

"I am so blasted weak. Damn, but this is ridiculous."

"And ill tempered, and impatient to be well again," Jerval said, standing over Edward. "At least you are no longer worried about making out your will."

"You make my neck sore, Jerval. Sit down."

Jerval sat. "Eleanor is suckling her babe and will return to you soon." Jerval smiled suddenly, his white teeth gleaming. "Now, sire, both you and I owe our miserable lives to our wives."

"Aye," Edward said slowly, "it is a strange and daunting thought." His brows lowered. "Why did you not stop her? The poison could have killed her."

"It did not occur to me to stop her. Indeed, I believe if anyone had tried, she would have killed him."

"That is likely true," Edward said, and smiled. "She has been like a clucking mother hen, just as Chandra was when you were wounded at Nazareth." He shook his head. "Geoffrey Parker now meets with Sir Elvan daily, to learn from him. At least he will return to England with something."

Jerval looked at Edward steadily, saddened at his bitterness.

Edward laid his head back against the pillow and closed his eyes. "I wonder what would have happened had King Louis not died. He would have added another ten thousand men to our cause."

"As pious and well meaning as Louis was," Jerval said quietly, "he still fancied himself a leader of men —"

"Which he was."

"Not in battle. It would have been up to you to lead our armies in battle, sire, not Louis. I wonder, after seeing all the bickering among Christians here, if all would have gone as we hoped."

"I remember so clearly feeling that God himself laid the cross of his holy cause upon me," Edward said slowly, "that I was to be the instrument of his hand, to free his land of the Saracens. Even after hearing of Louis's death, I still believed that I was chosen to take Palestine."

"It was the thought and belief in all our minds."

What was he to do? Edward wondered silently, the pain of his spirit making his wound as nothing. "God knows we have tried," he said aloud, "but with a thousand men, we have achieved so little. Sometimes I feel the hideous desire to pray to God to rain destruction upon all the sanctimonious Christians who have refused to leave their comforts and come to our aid."

"The Holy Land is thousands of miles from most of Christendom, sire. It no longer holds the promise of great wealth, or even the promise of freedom for God's people."

"Aye, that's true, but still, when I think of King Hugh, him and his miserable barons, snug and safe in Cyprus, I want to kill the lot of them. And our sainted King Louis's brother, King Charles of Sicily — a ruthless, ambitious man, our Charles. I think he schemed only for control of the trade routes in the Mediterranean. I begin to believe that God has forsaken His land. We came with such hopes, like children who look only to God for succor."

"Acre would have fallen had we not come."

Edward said quietly, "Acre will fall, Jerval. It is but a matter of time. And when Acre does fall, the damned Venetians and Genoese will be slaughtered. I wonder if they will realize that it was their own greed over the control of Palestine that brought them to their end?"

"No, probably not," Jerval said and fell silent. He knew well that even Edward's near death had brought only mendacious letters of concern from Christians in the Holy Land. There was nothing more, never anything more. Duty to God and to Edward was a grave cross to carry.

"I have given it a lot of thought," Edward continued quietly. "What I sought to accomplish was a child's dream. I see clearly now that all we can hope for is a temporary halt to Sultan Baibars's mad desire for the rest of Palestine. I have heard it said that Baibars fears me." He laughed, bitterly. "Why, I cannot imagine. He probably believes that confronting me would bring the rest of Christendom to my aid. He seeks a treaty, Jerval."

"A treaty? I did not know, sire."

"You are the first I have told. I think he

grew restive at my delay and took a chance that the rulers of Christendom would simply mourn my death with pious prayers, as they did King Louis's. Had I been gracious enough to succumb to the assassin's dagger, Baibars would have gained what he wanted with no effort at all. Do you know that the bastard had the gall to send me his profound regrets that an assassin had nearly killed me, an assassin he, naturally, knew nothing about?"

"By God, I would like to stick my sword through his miserable belly."

"Save your anger, my friend. If I guess aright, he is even now taking advantage of my weakness to gather an army to attack us. It is sound strategy, I must admit. I need you to lead our troops, Jerval. I have no wish to be forced to negotiate a treaty with Baibars without an army."

"We have men scouting to the north. We will know soon enough if and where the Saracens are gathering." Jerval turned questioning eyes toward Edward. "You have decided upon the treaty with Baibars, then?"

"Aye, I have decided. Our failure will be a grave disappointment to my father."

"You have accomplished more than your great-uncle, Richard," Jerval said.

"My great-uncle — the Lionheart — what a fantastical man he was. I believe he was driven by the lust for adventure and battle." Edward added, his voice infinitely weary, "I was driven by God." He raised his eyes to look at Jerval. "It seems that neither is enough."

Amaric watched the Lady Chandra as she paced outside her tent, awaiting news of the battle. He had not liked being assigned as her personal guard so that Lambert and Bayon could join the battle. He wished she would at least go back into her tent, so he could find some shade and return to his dice without the sun beating down on his head.

They both looked up at the pounding of a horse's hooves. Amaric moved closer to his lady, saw that it was Sir Eustace de Leybrun, and eased away again.

"Eustace," Chandra said, her voice cold, for she wouldn't ever forget what Beri had told her about him.

"Chandra, thank God I have found you so quickly. I must speak to you."

She automatically took a step toward him, her heart pounding. "What is it, Eustace? Come, tell me, quickly, what has happened?"

Before he answered her, Eustace's gaze

flickered toward Amaric.

"Oh, God, something has happened to Jerval? He is wounded, isn't he?"

He nodded his head, not meeting her frantic eyes. "He has been wounded, Chandra, badly, and sent me to fetch you. I have already sent the physicians ahead, for the fighting is over. Quickly, get something to cover your head. The ride will be hard. We must hurry."

When Chandra came out of the tent but moments later, she saw Amaric standing by her horse. He tossed her into the saddle and jumped astride his own destrier.

"Amaric will help me protect you," Eustace said. He brought his mailed hand down upon her palfrey's rump, and the mare broke into a gallop

"He will be all right," she said, looking straight ahead. "He will." She refused to think anything else. She dug her heels into her palfrey's sides and lowered her head close to the mare's neck.

They rode north toward Caesarea, keeping the inland sea but a mile to their west. They had ridden but half an hour when she heard Amaric call out behind them, "Sir Eustace! The fighting was to the north. We are headed east." Chandra looked to her left, for she had not noticed they had lost sight of the sea.

Eustace drew in his destrier and waited for Amaric to rein in beside him. Chandra turned her mare, frowning. She saw Amaric slide to the ground from his horse's back. Eustace, smiling now, was rubbing his blood off a dagger. She stared at him in shock, and then at Amaric, sprawled dead upon his back.

She realized so much in that moment. She'd been a fool. He'd tricked her, using Jerval.

He grabbed her palfrey's reins and pulled her in.

"What is going on, Eustace? By God, what have you done?"

"So you have finally come out of your daze, Chandra. Well, no matter now — we will soon be far from Acre." He sent a quick gaze toward Amaric. "There will be no one to say what happened to you, save me."

"You bastard. Jerval isn't wounded at all, is he?"

Eustace laughed. "Your precious husband is well."

She weaved in her saddle with relief. Then she heard Beri's words again. He'd taken her, and with little effort. She'd been a fool. She said slowly, thinking frantically, "But what is it you mean, Eustace?

What are you saying?"

He laughed again and sat back in his saddle. "I will have to tell Jerval that his stubborn wife insisted upon joining him, and that Amaric and I, fearing for your safety, rode with you to protect you. How sad that we were attacked by Saracens, and only I will be alive to tell of it."

She hadn't strapped her dagger to her thigh, something she always did, except this time, because she was so frightened that she could scarce think at all. Here she was with a man who had betrayed her, and she had no weapon, nothing at all. This was madness. He was an English knight. He was Jerval's kinsman. "But why? What have I ever done to you? Or Jerval? Neither of us has ever harmed you."

"You think not? Well, it doesn't really matter, for I will be rich."

"What do you mean?"

Chapter 29

"My dear Chandra, you and I are going to the camp of al-Afdal, one of the primary chieftains of the Sultan Baibars. He heard of you from one of the Saracen soldiers who escaped from the Neva Pass. The man described a beautiful creature who fought like a man, all white-skinned, with golden hair. Al-Afdal gained a fortune from the looting of Antioch, and he is quite willing to share it with me, once I give you to him. Truly, this isn't due to hatred of you or Jerval. I want all the wealth he will provide me for delivering you to him."

"You are a fool, Eustace. The Saracens have no honor. He won't give you anything except a knife through your heart. Call a halt to this madness whilst you have a chance of coming out of it with a whole hide."

Eustace raised his hand to strike her, but drew it back. "Nay, I don't want to bruise your lovely face. Your new master would not like that."

Chandra dug her heels into her palfrey's sides, but Eustace held fast to the reins. "That was your one try, Chandra, and your last. I know all your tricks, so you needn't waste your time trying them on me. You have no weapons. You stand no chance against me. If you try to hit me, I'll break your damned arm."

She spat at him, full in the face. He stared at her for a moment, wiping her spittle from his cheek, before he smashed his mailed fist into her ribs. She doubled over in pain, and heard him say, "I told you only that I would not mark your face, Chandra."

"You will not succeed, Eustace." She was panting, trying to get back her breath. Her ribs pulled and ached. "Jerval will not believe you. He will find out what you did, and he will kill you."

"Did you not listen, my lady? The direction in which your captors lie will, unfortunately, be miles from where I lead your husband. Ah, the riches I will gain. And the joy of knowing that you will part your white legs for your heathen master the rest of your life — or until you lose your beauty and he tosses you away."

"You cannot do this. Even you. Beri told me to be careful around you. By God, she was right."

"Beri. I will see that she pays for that. Now, enough talk, Chandra. I wish to be farther away from Acre. You will ride with me, else you will feel my dagger in your breast." He brought his hand down again on her palfrey's rump and forced her to a gallop beside him.

They rode due east, and the ground turned hilly and brittle beneath the horses' hooves. It seemed like hours to Chandra before Eustace jerked on her palfrey's reins and pulled his destrier to a halt. "We will take our rest here." His eyes scanned the surrounding countryside, then turned back to her.

He saw it in her eyes. She was readying herself to leap on him. He drew his dagger. "You try it and I will slit your throat and bedamned to the wealth."

She believed him. Later, she thought, later she would catch him off guard.

Graelam de Moreton rode toward Acre to give Edward word of his victory in the company of one of his men-at-arms and his squire. Edward would be quite pleased with the outcome of the battle. They had attacked the ill-prepared Saracens as they gathered themselves for a final blow after the attempted assassination of Edward, and had scattered them easily.

Graelam stretched his tired bones in his saddle, and looked inland, away from the sun-reddened sea. He saw a riderless horse cantering toward them and frowned, recognizing Amaric's horse. For a long moment, he held his destrier still, his dark brows lowered. He knew that Jerval had ordered Chandra never to leave the camp without a guard. Without another thought, he ran the horse down and reined him in. He saw a drop of blood on the saddle.

What in God's name had happened? He turned to his men. "We ride east until we find Amaric."

It was Albert, Graelam's squire, who spotted Amaric's body on a flat stretch of ground, his legs covered with sand by the desert wind. There was a clean stab wound in his chest, and his sword was sheathed. Graelam raised his lifeless arm. It was not yet stiff in death.

"Albert, ride back to Sir Jerval. Tell him that we found Lady Chandra's guard murdered." Graelam studied the ground for several moments. "There are two horses riding to the east. Tell Sir Jerval that we will follow and will leave a trail for him. Quickly, man."

Graelam swung onto his destrier's back, wondering why in God's name Chandra could not be like the other ladies and remain safe in the camp until her husband's return. Had she been so reckless as to demand that Amaric accompany her to the battle site? No, wait. They were traveling east, not north. Perhaps Jerval's proud lady had not been at fault. He smiled faintly at this thought as he dug his heels into his horse's belly. There was but one other person with her. Had she been taken against her will? Damnation, he owed her his life, and it displeased him to owe his life to a woman, even the fierce maiden warrior of Croyland. It was time to repay his debt.

"Off your horse, my lady," Eustace said. "We wait here."

Chandra didn't move. "This is madness, Eustace. We still have time. Take me back."

He laughed, and picked a fingernail with the sharp tip of the dagger. "Not mad, my lady, never mad." He paused a moment then, and looked at her. "Besides the riches I will have, I will also have the memory of your lovely body, a very lovely body that you once denied me. Since you are not a virgin, it makes little difference how many men plow you before you become al-Afdal's sole property."

"I don't think so," she said, even smiling at him. He frowned, but she moved very

506

quickly, one eye on that dagger of his. She leaned over in the saddle and drove her fist into his jaw. More from surprise than from pain, Eustace reared back and dropped her palfrey's reins. Chandra scooped them up, and with a wild cry she sent her horse into a frenzied gallop.

Eustace's powerful destrier quickly overtook her, his shadow huge and black against the moonlit rocks. She gave a cry of fury when his thick arm closed about her waist and lifted her off her palfrey's back. She fought him with all her strength, but he simply held her against him, squeezing her ribs, squeezing, squeezing until she couldn't breathe.

Eustace pulled his destrier up and flung her to the rocky ground, and she felt the pain from the sharp rocks dig into her back. She looked up to see him jerking up his surcoat, ripping at the ties on his chausses. He was going to rape her. She had to stop him, but how? He was much stronger, and she was hurting, badly.

Eustace was grunting as he tugged at a knot in the ties. He looked down at her, sprawled before him, her gown torn and riding up her legs. "I begin to see why Jerval does not want to leave your bed." He tossed her his mantle. "Spread yourself on it. Else I'll gut you with my dagger."

Chandra rolled to her side away from him and jumped to her feet. She grabbed the mantle and flung it at his head. She heard him curse as she rushed toward her palfrey. Stones cut into her slippers, but she didn't slow. She heard him still cursing, close behind her now, too close, and she gave a cry of anger and whirled about to face him, knowing that she could not outrun him. She controlled the pain in her ribs. She had only one more chance before he raped her. She saw him raise the dagger just as she kicked him in his groin with all her strength, but her gown held firm above her knee, and her foot landed against his armored thigh. Eustace grunted in pain, but he managed to close his arms around her and fling her backward.

"No, I'm not going to kill you, but I am going to hurt you. Aye, I'm really going to hurt you." His voice was a mixture of pain and lust.

Chandra fought him, tried to throw him off balance, using every trick her father and his men had taught her, but he was like a bull, crushing her into the cold stones. She felt his hand ripping her gown, and she yelled curses at him. His hand was upon her bare leg, squeezing her flesh.

She could feel the cold night air against her skin. She managed to rear up in one final surge of strength and strike his face.

Suddenly, she heard low, angry voices — men's voices — and they were close by. She raised her head, painfully. She saw about a dozen desert-garbed Saracens, some still on their horses and several standing near her. Eustace's fist was raised to strike her. One of the men said something. She heard Eustace yell back, "You have no right to interfere. I was told I could enjoy her before she became al-Afdal's whore."

The Saracen who appeared to be their leader was speaking quietly. "The bargain was made, Sir Eustace, but you will not take the English girl here, on the rocky ground, and then turn her over cut and bleeding to my master."

"I won't use my dagger on her, though she deserves it. Listen, I want her now. She fought me. I want her."

"No, not here." Munza breathed a sigh of relief that he'd gotten here in time. If his master's physician found seed in the girl's body, his life would be worth less than an old slave's, of which there were very few. He turned and looked down at the woman. He knew all she could see was a dark face, framed in a white turban. "Ah, good, she is conscious."

He dropped to his knees beside her. She

did not move when he touched his fingers to her jaw. She thought she saw a glint of pity in his black eyes. "Are you in pain?"

She shook her head.

The Saracen said over his shoulder to Eustace, "You will pray to your Christian god that you have not harmed her."

"She fought me, Munza," Eustace said. "She is a bitch, and wants taming."

"Cover yourself," the Saracen said coldly, his eyes dropping to Eustace's open chausses. "It will be for my master to say what is to be done with her." His black eyes flickered over her, thoroughly assessing. "She is more beautiful than I believed possible. Al-Afdal will be pleased. It is a pity she is not a virgin."

Chandra raised her hand to clutch at his sleeve. "Do not do this. Of course I'm not a virgin. I'm a wife. My husband is Sir Jerval de Vernon. You must return me to Acre and my husband. You will be greatly rewarded, I promise you."

He shook off her hand and rose. "Can you stand?"

She nodded, knowing there was no hope with him. Slowly, she forced her knees to lock and hold her weight. "Here," the Saracen said, and threw her a mantle to cover her ragged gown.

She wrapped it about her. At least she was covered now. She wanted to kill Eustace. If only she could have gotten his dagger away from him. She also wanted to kill herself for being so stupid as to believe him. He'd killed poor Amaric. It was too much.

"When can I have her?" It was Eustace, so frustrated he sounded as though he was ready to fight all the Saracens to get to her.

Munza shrugged. "When my master accepts her, your bargain will be sealed. Come, al-Afdal awaits."

Chandra was helped to her feet and set upon her horse. There was no more talk among them, only the sound of the horses' hooves pounding over the rocky ground. They were riding to higher ground, and the night air became colder. She thought of Jerval, wondering if he yet knew that she was gone, wondering what he would do. She felt tears sting her eyes, tears of grief for what could have been, tears for what she had found so briefly, and lost. She knew Eustace would still rape her. The Saracen had agreed it was part of the bargain. Then he would take his money and return to Acre, full of righteous anger and grief at her capture. And she would be left, like Ali's slave girl, Beri, for the rest of her years as a man's whore.

She swallowed her tears. They couldn't help. She calmed. She would kill herself — aye, she would kill herself, before she would let Eustace or any of the Saracens touch her. She'd kill Eustace first, then herself. But the thought of suicide curdled like sour milk in her belly. She did not want to die, at least not by her own hand. It was a coward's way, and by Christ, she would not be a coward.

But what to do?

She would wait and see. She must be ready. Her father always said, "While there is life, there is hope." She'd never really thought about it before, but now it meant everything to her. Jerval would come. He must.

Graelam and his man-at-arms drew up in the shadow of a huge rock at the sight of a ghostly, white-garbed band of Saracens. Chandra was riding in their midst, Eustace with their leader at their fore. Graelam gripped his man's arm. "We can do naught against a dozen Saracens. Ride back and bring Sir Jerval and his men. You will have no difficulty tracking me. I will follow to see where they take her."

As he rode through the night, keeping well out of sight of the Saracens, Graelam smiled grimly, picturing his hands choking the life out of Eustace.

★ ★ ★

The mountainous terrain gave way to a barren plain of low sand hills pressed among scattered rocks and boulders. Chandra looked up as she shifted wearily in the saddle and saw lights in the distance. As they grew nearer, she could make out a cluster of palm and date trees, and the outline of tents set among them. They formed a small village at the edge of the plain, its back pressed against the mountains. Horses whinnied and groups of armed men shouted in welcome. They rode past a pool of clear water with women kneeling beside it, filling goatskin jugs. Thoughts of escape dimmed at the sight of so many people.

The Saracens drew to a halt before a huge, many-domed tent, and their leader jumped down from his horse and threw the reins to a boy standing beside its entrance.

"Come inside, Sir Eustace," Munza said in his lilting accent. "My master will want to see you."

Eustace dismounted and swaggered toward the huge tent. He turned as Munza helped Chandra off her palfrey and said, "It is just as well. I will enjoy her more once she is bathed and readied. I warn you, though. She is not a woman to be cowed and made fearful. Watch out for her. She is as ferocious as a warrior."

Munza said nothing, though for a moment he wanted to laugh. The Englishman sounded afraid of the girl, which was beyond ridiculous. He grasped her arm and forced her to walk beside him to the tent. He stopped her a moment in the light, and studied her face. "There is a slight bruise, that is all. My master will be pleased."

Chandra gazed at him coldly. "Your master will be pleased for only a short time. Then he will be dead."

Munza drew back and frowned at her. He was not a tall man, and the English girl's eyes were as cold as the northern winters he'd heard about. He knew that Christian women were not like Moslem women. But still it shocked him that she could speak so brazenly, and stare at him with such contempt. "You will learn how to behave, my lady," he said. "Else my master will flay the white skin from your beautiful body." That should silence her. He waited to hear her plead, perhaps even beg him to go gently with her.

She said, "Ah, another brave man. Take me to this courageous master who must steal a wife from her husband. Aye, I wish to look upon his noble face."

Munza didn't want to, but now he found himself worried. She was not behaving as she

514

should. He said slowly, "A slave does not look into her master's eyes unless he wishes it. I don't want you slain. Remember my words, my lady, else you will not live to say more."

Chandra shrugged and it angered him — she saw it, and it was something. She pulled the mantle about her torn robe and walked, stiff-backed, beside Munza into the tent.

She blinked her eyes, adjusting to the blazing resin torches that lit the interior of the tent. It was an immense structure, its floor covered with thick carpets, slashed with vivid reds and golds. Fat, brightly embroidered pillows were piled beside small circular tables, delicately carved in sandalwood. Flowing, translucent veils of cloth separated the tent into chambers, and it was toward a large central chamber that Munza led Chandra. She was aware of silent, dark-skinned women, their faces covered with thin veils, who briefly raised their downcast eyes at her. They were dressed as slaves, with flowing tops of light material fitted snug beneath their breasts, leaving their skin bare to the waist, and long, full skirts, fastened at their waists by a thin band of colored leather. She could see the line of their legs through the shimmering cloth. Dark, bearded men stared at her openly, and it was lust she saw on their faces. She would be strong; she wouldn't give up.

She began to feel as if she were walking through a gauntlet designed to humiliate her. At last, Munza drew apart a golden veil that hung from the roof of the tent to its floor, and shoved her forward. She stood silent for a long moment, drew in her breath. She could not believe that such riches could be gathered in a tent, set in a barren desert. There was gold everywhere: goblets glistened upon the low tables, chests bound with intricately carved gold bands, and thick pillows embroidered with gold thread. The light was not so bright here, and its softness added to the opulence of the room. Munza grasped her arm and pulled her forward.

"Bow to our master — al-Afdal," he said close to her ear.

She laughed; she actually managed to laugh. "I will see this jackal in hell first." She'd spoken loudly enough to reach the man sprawled at his ease on the far side of the chamber. She threw her head back and stared at him, not moving. His dress was different from that of the desert-garbed Saracens. He wore a short jacket, without sleeves, fastened across his wide chest by golden chains. His trousers, like his jacket, were of pristine white wool, full at the thighs, and bound by a wide golden belt at his waist. When her eyes traveled to his face, she was surprised to see a young man, with a beard curving to a sharp point at his chin. He was not ill-looking. His black eyes were cold, deep as an ancient well. She saw thick black hair on his chest curling about the golden chains. She forced herself not to move.

"This is Lady Chandra de Vernon," Eustace said in a loud voice, stepping forward. "She gave me a bit of trouble, but I barely marred her beauty. As I told you, she is known for her warrior skills. She did not come easily."

"Come here," al-Afdal said. He raised a heavily jeweled hand toward her. He did not answer Eustace or even acknowledge his presence.

Chandra jerked her arm free of Munza and strode forward. She drew to a halt some three feet before the man, al-Afdal, and crossed her arms over her breasts. "So, you are the jackal who bribed this weak fool" — she paused a moment, and cocked her head contemptuously toward Eustace — "to bring me here?"

"You damned bitch," Eustace yelled, and took an angry step toward her.

Chapter 30

"Quiet, my friend," al-Afdal said softly. He rose gracefully to his feet, and Chandra was taken aback at his size. In her experience, Saracens were small men, wiry and slight of stature. He wasn't. "I believe I told you to come here, Chan-dra." She started at the still-gentle tone of his voice. He spoke her name as two distinct words.

She shrugged and stepped forward, aware of a sigh of relief from Munza. "What is wrong with you? Are you so desperate that you must steal women? So ugly and ill formed that you cannot persuade women to come to you without force?"

He moved so quickly and gracefully that Chandra scarce had time to draw back. He unfastened her mantle and dropped it onto the carpet at her feet.

"I see that you did fight Sir Eustace," he said in that same soft voice. He turned his dark eyes to Munza. "Did the English knight rape her?"

Munza shook his head quickly. "Nay,

518

master, but he would have had I not stopped him."

"She is no virgin," Eustace said. "What does it matter how many men take her?" Al-Afdal did not reply, and Eustace continued, emboldened. "I would prefer to have her once she is bathed. Then I will take my leave of you, with the gold you promised me."

Al-Afdal nodded slowly. "As you wish, Sir Eustace." He raised his hand toward a group of women who had entered silently. One of them, a girl with skin and flowing hair as black as ebony, stepped forward, her eyes upon al-Afdal's pointed slippers. Even they, Chandra noticed, were braided with gold and studded with gems.

"Calla," he said to the girl, "take Chandra to the baths, then call for me. I wish to be present when the physician examines her." He said to Chandra, "Do as you are bid, else I will have my men hold you down. I do not make idle threats, particularly to women. Do you understand?"

Chandra nodded slowly.

"Calla," he continued, "speaks your tongue. She will give your instructions to the other slaves."

Again Chandra nodded. She knew that she must learn the extent of her confines before she could act. She quickly lowered her eyes, afraid that al-Afdal would guess her thoughts, so keenly was he looking at her.

Al-Afdal watched her as she followed Calla from the chamber. She was proud, he thought, proud and untamed and exquisite, like a white-petaled rose. He remembered that his father had once purchased a young girl from Persia, a fiercely proud girl, and he had crushed her spirit, and the beauty of her pride. He turned back to the English knight, his dark eyes hooded. Perhaps he would not give the English girl to Eustace as he had planned. She wore her pride like a maiden-head, and he wanted that prize for himself when he took her, when he made her realize that her life was different now, that she had to please him to live.

Chandra followed Calla into a smaller room at the far end of the tent, with several of al-Afdal's men close behind them. It was not unlike Ali ad-Din's bathing room, save there was no sunken pool and no mosaic tile covering the floor. A large brass tub, shaped like a hollowed-out lemon, was set in its center, and women were filling it with steaming, perfumed water. She did not know the scent, but it was heady.

"Please to undress now," Calla said.

Chandra looked quickly about her, but there were only women. As she shrugged out of her torn clothes, she gazed more carefully about the chamber. It was an inner room that did not touch the perimeter of the tent. The roof dipped down in scallops between slender wooden supports. She wondered what would happen if she managed to pull down one of the wooden poles. A bit of a commotion, perhaps, she thought, but that was all. She laid her clothing on a low, linen-covered table that she guessed was used to oil the bathers after their bath.

"Calla," she said suddenly, turning to the girl. "I am here against my will. I do not belong here. Please, you must help me."

Calla looked into the English girl's pale face. She said, "I know who you are. I have heard the men speak of you. There is naught I can do about it. My master seems to think you some kind of goddess."

"Goddess? That is ridiculous. I am but a woman, like you, Calla, and I have a husband, an English noble, who will miss me."

"You are prideful," Calla said as she slowly shook her head, "but you must take care. He believes he admires the pride in you, but he is wrong. He is like his father. No, al-Afdal is not a patient man. No one dares to gainsay his will, and especially not a slave or a woman."

Chandra said nothing more, and stepped

into the tub, unaware that Calla was studying her body, her eyes hooded.

She allowed herself to be bathed by the silent women. Like Ali's slaves, some of the girls were scarce into womanhood. She lay back and closed her eyes, trying to think what she was to do. *I will not let him touch me, him or Eustace, no matter what happens.* There, she'd finally made her decision. She felt strangely calm now. Much to Calla's surprise, she fell asleep in the swirling hot water.

Chandra started awake, feeling refreshed, and she smiled up into Calla's astonished face. At least her fatigue was gone from her. She felt strong and alert. Her ribs didn't hurt much anymore.

Calla motioned her to lie on the linen-covered table. Chandra lay on her back, staring up at the tent top, and did not bother to look up at Calla until she heard her say in her soft voice, "Do not move. I do not wish to cut you."

Chandra started up, balancing herself on her elbows. She saw that Calla held a thin razor in her hand.

"What are you doing?" She was scooting back, as far away from that razor as she could.

Calla's eyes traveled down Chandra's

belly to the damp golden hair covering her woman's mound. "My master does not like woman's hair," she said.

"He doesn't what? You can tell that miserable jackal to shave all that black hair from his chest then." Chandra swung her legs over the table and grabbed Calla's arm at the elbow. "Get that thing away from me."

There was no fear in the girl's eyes. Calla shrugged, and Chandra released her. "You are not like the rest of us. Perhaps the master will not notice."

Chandra watched her place the razor on a pile of linen towels and take some colorful gossamer cloth from the arms of another slave girl. "Let me dress you now. The master, as I said, is not a patient man."

Chandra did not resist. She had no intention of being naked in front of any of these heathen. The veils that covered her breasts were a pale lavender, as soft as a moth's wings. Calla fastened the material together beneath her breasts with a golden clip. She stepped into a floor-length skirt much like the one Calla wore, and let Calla tighten it in folds at her waist with a leather belt. She noticed that Calla was barefoot. She sat docilely while several slave girls, under Calla's direction, combed out her wet hair.

"What is this? Don't you want to shave my head?"

"You show no fear. I do not know what the master will think."

"Perhaps he will be intelligent enough to release me." She heard Calla sigh softly.

They fastened her damp hair back from her forehead with a gem-covered strip of stiff golden cloth.

"You are very beautiful," Calla said finally. "I will fetch the physician and my master now."

"Why a physician? I am not ill. My ribs aren't broken. I have no need of a physician."

Calla did not reply, and Chandra was left to stand among the whispering girls. She walked about the small enclosure, as if with great indifference. The girls watched her for a while, then resumed their duties. She stood next to the pile of linen towels, inching her hand toward the razor. Her fingers were hovering above the ivory handle when the veiled curtains parted suddenly and al-Afdal entered. She whipped her hand away and turned to face him.

She felt his eyes upon her, studying her, she thought, as if she were a prized bit of horseflesh. He lowered his head a moment and listened to Calla's softly spoken words,

words that Chandra could not hear.

She saw his dark eyes flash and one of his hands clench into a fist, the huge ruby ring he wore on his middle finger gleaming in the soft light. She noticed a man standing behind him, tall and painfully thin, dressed in a white turban and a full white robe that covered him from his throat to his toes. His eyes were small, black and never calm. Like his master, he wore a full beard that was trimmed to a sharp point at his chin.

Al-Afdal's anger grew as he watched Chandra. Even from where he stood, he could see purple bruises on the English girl's bare ribs. A man did not need to harm a soft-fleshed woman, unless he wanted to, of course. And Calla had said that there were other bruises on her body, and cuts on her arms and legs. He began to doubt Munza's assurances that he had saved the girl from being raped by the English knight.

He strode over to where she stood, staring at him, her head thrown back, her eyes hard. He couldn't look away from her eyes for a very long time. He'd heard about blue eyes, but he'd never seen them before. And her hair, like the fine gold thread on his slippers.

He waved his hand back toward the physician. "You will remove your clothes, Chandra. I wish my physician to examine you."

He could practically see the words of refusal forming in her mind. He continued patiently. "If you do not, I will have the clothes ripped from your body, and there will be no more for you. A woman without clothes is a more malleable creature. My men would appreciate it, I know."

"If you meant me to be naked, then why did you give me clothes in the first place? If you would call these ridiculous veils clothes."

A smile twisted his mouth. "My little Calla dressed you because I did not tell her not to. She tells me that you refused to have your woman's mound shaved."

Oh, God, it was nearly too much. She took a step back and saw him smile. No, she had to hold steady. She couldn't let him see that she was so afraid, she was ready to die from it.

"It matters not. I will decide if I wish you shaved after I have seen you."

"No, you will not. It is your hair that is disgusting — why do you not shave that black hair off your chest? You have the look of a matted animal."

She heard Calla gasp and saw the slave girl recoil, as if from a blow, but al-Afdal did not move. She saw his black eyes narrow in rage, and she readied herself. If she was to

526

die, she could not die cowering like a slave.

"Help her do my bidding," he said finally to the slave girls, his voice as cold as the air of the desert night. In an instant they had surrounded her, and were unclasping the fasteners and unwinding the soft material that covered her. Chandra tried to keep the killing fear from showing in her eyes when she at last stood naked before al-Afdal.

"Lie down," he said, his eyes on her face.

She did, holding herself stiff. She tried to cover herself with her hands, and turned her head away, her eyes closed.

She jumped when she felt fingers, light and probing against her bruised ribs. She turned her face and stared up at the physician's impassive countenance. He was speaking quietly to al-Afdal as his fingers roved over her. Her arm was raised and examined, then lowered back to her side. They spoke quietly again, words she didn't understand.

The physician left her side, and al-Afdal strode forward to stand beside her. "The physician finds you fit, Chan-dra." His eyes roved down her body, and he gave a crack of laughter. "I will not demand that you be shaved — indeed, the golden hair against the white flesh is pleasing." She jerked away at the touch of his hand.

"Fear me, Chan-dra — that is a good thing, but know that you have but to please me and your life will be contented."

"No," she said, "I will not fear you. You are nothing to me."

"I cannot allow you to continue insulting me. You will keep your mouth shut, else I will have your tongue removed."

"Then my eyes will tell you what you are to me. What will you do then — blind me?"

His jaw worked, and she held herself steady, in control now, forgetting for the moment that she was naked, and waited for him to strike her.

Al-Afdal turned away from her a moment and said abruptly to the physician, "You will examine her belly, to see if there is a man's seed within her."

Chandra grabbed at the embroidered linen cloth that covered the table and pulled it around her. "No more," she said, "no more. I am not a slave, nor am I your possession. I will not allow this."

Before al-Afdal could raise his arm to strike her, his patience at an end, Chandra lunged toward the pile of towels and grabbed the ivory-handled razor. "Now let us see what a brave man you are, al-Afdal."

Al-Afdal took a step toward her, for a moment so angered that he forgot the reports

528

of the Saracen soldiers that the English girl was a fighter, swift and deadly. He was drawn up suddenly by an unearthly shriek of pain from outside the chamber. He whirled about, his dagger unsheathed, to see a huge English knight lunge into the chamber, his sword flailing over his head, three of al-Afdal's men swarming behind him.

"Graelam!"

Graelam took in the white cloth that was wrapped about her, and the razor clutched in her hand. "Get behind me, Chandra," he shouted. "Cut through the tent — there is a women's chamber beyond. Hurry."

For an instant, she believed that the entire English army would follow him. But there was no one, only more of al-Afdal's men. She whirled about and slashed out at one of the Saracens as he passed her.

Al-Afdal heard the man yell out, and whipped about to see him fall to his knees, grabbing his shoulder, and Chandra's razor red with his blood. One of his men tossed him a scimitar, and he caught it handily, only to see that Chandra had grabbed the sword of the man she had wounded. The small chamber was fast filling with his men, rushing toward them. If the fighting continued, she would be killed, and likely a half-dozen of his men with her.

He came to a quick decision. "Surround him," he shouted, raising his scimitar toward Graelam. "And keep away from the girl. I will kill the man who draws her blood."

Graelam knew that he would die, and he cursed himself for being a noble ass and a fool to believe that he alone could save her. Only his heavy broadsword was holding back the men who surged toward him, and their number grew with every moment. He felt the flat side of a scimitar strike the back of his legs, and he went hurtling to the floor onto his back. He saw a black-eyed Saracen above him, his scimitar raised in an awful arc, and a prayer came to his lips as he prepared himself to die.

"Do not kill him!" Al-Afdal's voice cut through the din. The man above Graelam stiffened, his scimitar poised to strike. Even as Graelam tried to push himself up, another pointed blade touched the flesh of his throat.

"Chan-dra!" Al-Afdal shouted. "Throw down the scimitar, else the English knight will die."

Her scimitar was poised to strike down at a Saracen's blade when she heard al-Afdal's words. She saw Graelam upon his back, some five men pinioning him. She gave a cry of fury and defeat, and drew back, panting.

"Drop the scimitar."

Slowly, she let the scimitar slip from her hand. One of the men, dazed with a blow she had given him, lunged toward her before al-Afdal could stop him. He looked on in horror and then in utter surprise.

Chandra jumped to the side, the cloth that covered her pulling from her body, and tripped the man as he lunged past her. She grabbed his wrist and brought her foot down on his elbow. In the next instant the man lay on his back, clutching his broken arm, shrieking. Her foot was poised to crash into the man's ribs when she heard al-Afdal shout at her again to back away.

She looked toward Graelam, and knew she could do no more.

Al-Afdal grabbed the fallen cloth and threw it over her. She clutched the material to her and took a stumbling step away from him.

"Do not kill him," she whispered, still panting so that she could barely speak.

"Is he your husband?"

"No, he is a friend."

"A brave man," al-Afdal said, "but stupid to believe that he alone could save you." He saw the bleakness in her eyes, and pivoted about. "Well, Englishman," he continued, "it appears that Sir Eustace was not so careful as he thought." He motioned to his men, and they pulled Graelam to his feet.

"Chandra," Graelam said, his voice heavy, "I am sorry."

"Don't be," she said, "don't be." She turned toward al-Afdal. "You will not kill him."

"No," al-Afdal said thoughtfully, staring at her. "I have other plans for your brave knight."

He saw Munza standing in the entrance. "Was the Englishman alone?"

Munza nodded. "He must have seen Sir Eustace and the English girl and followed them, master."

"Post more guards. I think we would be wise to leave for Montfort soon."

Montfort. The once-Frankish castle captured by the Saracens. It would be impenetrable. Once inside the fortress, all of Edward's army could not rescue her.

Graelam's arms were bound and he was dragged from the chamber. Al-Afdal looked a moment toward the slave girls still cowering against the walls, the physician beside them, then back to Chandra, a slight smile curving his wide mouth.

"Calla, dress her and bring her to me." He

touched his hand to Chandra's bare arm. She did not flinch. "You will, of course, do as you are told now, Chan-dra."

He nodded toward the physician, and in the next moment, Chandra was once again alone with the slave girls. The women seemed afraid to come near her. She shrugged out of the cloth and said sharply, "Bring me clothing."

Chandra followed Calla through the tented corridors to the chamber where al-Afdal waited. She looked about for Grae-lam, but he was not there. Eustace stood next to al-Afdal, who lay sprawled on soft cushions, in much the same pose she had first seen him, a golden wine goblet in his hand. She felt numb. Was Graelam dead? And if not, what was al-Afdal up to, that Graelam would not be here?

"Come here, Chan-dra."

She walked toward him, the shimmering fabric of her skirt clinging to her legs.

"Is she not exquisite, Sir Eustace?"

Eustace took in the gem-studded clasp at her waist and followed the movement of her legs through the translucent veils. Her hair, now dry, fell down her back. He felt lust swirling in his belly. "Aye," he said only.

"I suppose you would like to take her now, as we agreed."

"Aye," he said again, his voice thick, "and then I will take my leave of you."

"Would you care to take her here, in front of my men? They have never seen an Englishman rut a woman."

"She will fight me," Eustace said. "I have no wish to hurt her. That is for you to do if she is disobedient. You must tie her down to spare her bruises."

To Eustace's surprise, al-Afdal threw back his turbaned head and laughed. "Yes, she would fight you. She would also likely unman you before you thrust yourself into her. But, my friend, you are right. I don't want her bruised. See what you already did?" Al-Afdal rose gracefully to his feet and walked to Chandra's side. He did not touch her, only pointed to the dark purplish bruises over her ribs.

"She fought me."

"Perhaps," he said thoughtfully, turning back to Eustace, "Chan-dra needs a man to fight for her." He watched, a half-formed smile on his lips, as Eustace glanced contemptuously about at his men.

"Give me a sword," Chandra said. "I will fight him."

Al-Afdal glanced at her face and saw that she was serious. "I cannot risk that you would be harmed, Chan-dra."

Eustace started forward, uncertain what was going on here. "Just give me my gold, and I will leave. I have decided she is not worth the trouble. I do not want her."

Al-Afdal stroked the point of his beard. Eustace did not like it. He tasted fear. He wanted to leave this place.

"Is it not a practice among you English," al-Afdal said, "to provide a champion for the weaker?"

Chandra felt the blood rush to her temples. Al-Afdal had Graelam, and it would be he who fought Eustace. Did Eustace not know anything of Graelam?

Eustace's hand clapped about his sword, and he slowly backed away.

"Do not be so anxious to leave, my friend," al-Afdal said. "I have another English knight for you to meet, someone worth your mettle." He nodded toward Munza, and Graelam was shoved into the chamber, flanked by four of al-Afdal's men, his arms bound behind his back.

"De Moreton!" Eustace exclaimed.

Chapter 31

"Aye, you filthy bastard!" Graelam said.

Al-Afdal returned to his seat of cushions. "I will make you a bargain, Sir Eustace," he said. "If you can defeat Lord Graelam, you will leave here with your gold."

Eustace had seen Graelam fight. The man was strong, and he showed no mercy. Eustace was afraid, very afraid now.

"If Lord Graelam defeats him, will we be allowed to leave?"

Al-Afdal smiled toward Chandra. "Not you, Chan-dra, but your noble Graelam will be free."

"Release me," Graelam said hoarsely. "I will carve his guts from his belly." He did not trust al-Afdal to free him if he killed Eustace, but at the moment, he didn't care. He turned his dark eyes toward Chandra, and saw that she was looking at him with great sorrow. He wanted to tell her that it didn't matter, but of course it did. He didn't want to die, but for now, there seemed to be nothing he could do. Except kill Eustace, and that he wanted to do very much. He smiled at her, nodding almost imperceptibly.

"Clear the chamber," al-Afdal said. "I do not wish my possessions hacked to bits. Come stand beside me, Chan-dra." He held out his beringed hand toward her, and she had no choice but to obey him.

"May God be with you, Graelam," she said as she passed him. "I thank you. You owed me no debt. No matter what happens here, it is I who owe you."

For the first time, Eustace saw the bloody gash in Graelam's arm. It was his sword arm, and Eustace knew that he must be weakened. He drew his sword, ran the tip of his thumb along its sharp edge, and smiled at Graelam. "Aye," he said, "you have lusted after her, have you not? You lost her to Jerval, but you still wanted her. You will die, Graelam, and the little bitch will spend the rest of her days serving the heathen paynim."

Graelam did not answer him. As the Saracens unbound his hands, he concentrated on his memories of Eustace in battle. He knew that Eustace thought that his wounded right arm would do him in. His sword was placed in his right hand, and he left it there. Nay, he thought, let the fool believe he will have an easy time of it. He flexed his arm, and grimaced. Eustace slashed his sword before him, his mouth set, his eyes alight with the victory he knew would be his.

"Well, Chan-dra," al-Afdal said, closing his hand about her wrist. "I do not need to ask you whom you favor, do I?"

"I favor the only brave man here," she said. She heard him suck in his breath, but didn't look at him. She kept her eyes on Graelam. Her heart pounded with fear for him. Like Eustace, she saw the blood on his arm.

Al-Afdal raised his arm, and brought it down. And then he laughed.

With a loud roar, Eustace lunged toward Graelam, his sword high above his head. In the instant Eustace's sword arced downward in a blur of silver, Graelam tossed his sword to his left hand. The clash of ringing steel jarred the silence of the tent.

Al-Afdal watched calmly as Graelam and Eustace joined swords, hacking at each other. They moved slowly, their armor restricting their freedom, and he saw that it was a test of strength between them. His men would have dashed in and out, whirling about to avoid the crunching blows, relying on their quickness rather than a grueling contest of sheer strength. Both men were soon panting heavily, their brows beaded with sweat.

Eustace suddenly disengaged and took several jerking steps backward. He saw Graelam holding his sword easily in his left hand, and cursed aloud.

"Come back to me, Eustace. Come, you puking coward." But Graelam didn't wait. He strode toward Eustace, his sword flailing before him, cutting a wide path of control.

As he neared, Eustace kicked his leg out and smashed it against Graelam's thigh. Chandra cried out as Graelam fought to keep his balance, but his foot caught on a fringed edge of the carpet, and he hurtled onto his back. Eustace lunged toward him, his sword raised high. He gripped it in both hands to send it downward to Graelam's chest.

Graelam saw Eustace's face above him. He did not have time to twist out of the sword's path, for his armor was like a coffin of dead weight, making him slow and clumsy. He saw the blur of steel, and heard Chandra cry out. Dear Christ, he thought, his mind strangely detached, to die because of a kick in the leg and a clumsy fall on a carpet.

The instant was like an eternity of time.

Eustace opened his mouth to shout his victory, but the words never emerged. He heard an odd hissing sound, and a soft thud. Eustace raised his eyes in astonishment, his sword slipping from his grasp. Graelam awkwardly jerked himself onto his side, just as Eustace, a thin-bladed knife in his throat, fell heavily to the floor.

Graelam heaved himself up. He looked toward al-Afdal, then at Eustace, who lay dead, his blood welling from his pinioned throat.

"You killed him," he said, staggering to his feet.

"Yes, my friend," al-Afdal said easily. He nodded to Munza. "Bring me my knife. Wipe the infidel's blood from it."

Chandra felt al-Afdal's hand, the one that had hurled the dagger, close about her wrist. She looked up at him. "Why did you save him?"

He did not immediately answer her. "Take Lord Graelam to your tent, Munza, and guard him well. Give him food and drink, and a girl, if it pleases him."

Graelam shook his head, still disbelieving that he was alive, and the heathen Saracen had saved his life. He gazed at Chandra, but he had no chance to speak to her before he was prodded from the chamber.

"Sit down, Chan-dra. You do not look well."

"Why did you spare Graelam?"

He gave her a long, considering look, his fingers lightly stroking his bearded jaw. "It is really quite simple. You hated Eustace and are grateful to the other man, Graelam, for trying to save you. It would do me no good were Graelam to die. While I have him, I have his life to give you, and you will obey me because you will not want me to kill him as you watch."

Al-Afdal smiled, adding, "Come with me now, for I would enjoy your body and the touch of your mouth upon mine." He saw her shake her head and said, his voice softer still, "You will never deny me or fight me now, Chan-dra, for if you do, my dagger will pierce Graelam's throat, and your brave knight will die because of your pride."

She forced herself to look up into his face. So calm he was, so certain of himself, of his power, of his strength. She said, "I hate you. I will always hate you."

She finally realized that she'd lost. He said nothing, merely shrugged. But he was angry, very angry; he would punish her for that. He sent for the physician to accompany them. He would humiliate her, make her realize that he could do with her what he wished. He took her arm and led her through a curtained doorway.

Chandra drew up, staring about her. She had believed the larger chamber was his own, but it was not. Here was luxury she would not have imagined. Vivid colors of gold and crimson, and the smell of incense, strangely sweet, filled the chamber. Slender tapers were set in golden-branched holders about the chamber, filling it with soft, shadowy light. There were no furnishings save for a small sandalwood table that stood on delicately carved legs beside a wide bed of flat cushions covered with animal furs. A brass brazier was set beside it, filled with glowing coals for warmth.

Al-Afdal stood watching her. "You are unused to such beauty," he said. "I do not relish returning to Montfort. The Frankish castles are drafty, and all my wealth cannot disguise their ugliness." He smiled thinly. "But until I know that Prince Edward and all his men, including your husband, have been pushed into the sea, it is there we shall stay." He looked about him with negligent pride. "Tonight, at least, we will enjoy these comforts."

He looked beyond her and raised a beckoning hand. Chandra turned about to see the gaunt-faced, silent physician behind them. She wanted to beg him not to make her endure this, but she knew that al-Afdal would only be even more pleased, even more certain of his victory."

"Take off your clothes and lie upon your back."

There was no choice, none at all. She unfastened the golden clasp beneath her breasts. It was the strangest thing, but she felt a tear fall down her cheek. Crying, a silly, stupid thing for her to do. No more, no more, else he would see and know he'd beaten her, shamed her. The clasp came loose, and slowly, she loosed the soft cloth that covered her breasts.

Al-Afdal felt immense lust. He wanted to touch her now, take her.

Chandra's hands hovered about the gemmed clasp at her waist. She didn't want to die. But perhaps death would be her only escape from al-Afdal. The clasp fell open. She knew he was looking at her. She stood very still as the material fell from her hips to the thick carpet at her feet. She turned away, unaware that the sight of her white back and hips gave al-Afdal as much pleasure as her breasts and belly, and walked with a hesitant step to the cushioned bed.

She closed her eyes tightly for a long moment, praying that she wouldn't break. She lay down upon her back, her legs locked together.

She heard al-Afdal say to the physician, "Quickly, examine her, and be gone." There was an urgency in his voice, and she knew that he wanted to take her, and quickly. She felt a hand touch her thigh, and she tensed. Because she could not bear to hear his humiliating order, she parted her legs.

The physician's hands were delicate and curiously gentle as he probed at her. When his thin finger, slippery with some kind of ointment, slipped inside her, she felt such shame that she wanted to choke on it. She stiffened, drawing upward, when she felt him deep within her, and al-Afdal pressed his hands on her shoulders to hold her still. When the physician's hand was gone from her, she forced her eyes to open. He was standing over her, but his eyes were upon al-Afdal. He said quietly, "She has been with no man in the past day. The Englishman, Eustace, did not take her."

"She is healthy, without blemish?"

"She is healthy."

"I want many sons from her."

The physician bowed. "She is narrow, but will bear as many sons as you wish."

Al-Afdal waved his hand in dismissal, and the physician bowed again, and backed out of the chamber.

"Are you hungry, Chan-dra?"

She shook her head, and reached for the fur cover. He stilled her hand. "No. I wish to look at you. You are mine now. Do not forget it. I am not hungry either."

He stood over her then, his eyes on her as he stripped off his clothes.

"Look at me, Chan-dra," he said. "I want you to look at me and see me, know me, and recognize me as your new master. I want you to imagine the magnificent sons you will bear me."

"I want you to think only of my hatred for you." She looked at him, contempt hard in her eyes, looked down the hard length of him. He was lean and wiry, hard with muscle. She looked at his groin. "My hatred," she said, "and my pity, for you are scarce a man, I see."

Her words, ridiculous in truth, made him want to kill her. She saw his anger, and smiled. "Must I also lie to you, as I am certain your other women do, and tell you how very magnificent you are?"

No woman had ever in his life scorned him. His first impulse was to beat her until she cried for mercy and swore to him that she had lied. He saw the hard coldness in her eyes, and knew that beating her would not have the result he wished. No, he would thrust himself into her until she was raw, until he saw the pain fill her eyes.

"Open your legs. Now."

She struggled against him as he clutched at her thighs and jerked them apart. With a growl of fury, he reared over her and smashed the flat of his palm against her cheek.

The dizzying pain snapped her eyes open, and for an instant, she stared at his angry face. She forgot his threat to kill Graelam, indeed forgot everything except her rage. "Filthy savage!" She kicked at him with all her strength, and landed her foot squarely in his naked belly. He was thrown off balance and fell heavily onto his back on the carpet. She picked up the small table, and before he could fling up his hands to protect himself, she crashed it blindly against the side of his head. She was raising the table to strike him again when her mind suddenly cleared, and she stared down at him. He was moaning, his eyes closed. There was a gash at his temple, and blood was streaking down the side of his face. Suddenly, he lunged upward and struck her jaw with his fist, flinging her backward. As she weaved, dizzy from the blow, she saw him clutching his head, then falling again, sprawling naked upon his back.

She grabbed at the empty air to save herself, but she fell, striking the coal-filled brazier. She heard a soft hiss as the flame-red
coals rolled over the silken cushions.

Chandra struggled to her knees, shaking
her head to clear her mind, and rubbed her
burning eyes. Murky gray smoke swirled
about her, and licking flames were curling
up behind the cushioned bed, climbing the
thin veils to the roof of the tent. She staggered to her feet and looked down at the
Saracen chieftain. Suddenly one of the
wooden supports gave way, bringing a
flaming cloud of azure material with it. She
watched in horror as it crashed down over
him.

The heat and smoke were choking her,
and she whipped about. She grabbed the
thick embroidered cloth that had fallen
from the small table, clutched it about her,
and lunged toward the veiled entrance of
the chamber.

The roaring flames blazed over her head,
spreading across the roof with amazing
speed. She crouched over in the dense
smoke, pressing the edge of the cloth against
her face, and struggled forward. She heard
women screaming, saw shadows of men
running toward the entrance. She dashed

past two of al-Afdal's soldiers, but they paid her no heed. They were rushing back to his chamber, intent upon saving their master.

She fell forward onto her knees in the cool night. For a moment, she could not move as she gulped in the clean night air. Even outside the crumbling tent, she could feel the raging heat gushing outward. She struggled to her feet and looked wildly about her. Frenzied horses were screaming at the towering flames, and Saracen men and women ran past her, intent upon saving themselves and their belongings.

She had to find Graelam. She looked back at the blazing tent, but remembered that al-Afdal had ordered him taken to Munza's tent. The flames were leaping from the tent roof, orange embers and burning swatches of cloth falling onto the smaller tents around it.

"Graelam!" She yelled out his name as she rushed from one tent to another until her voice was a hoarse whisper. Saracen men slammed into her, but paid her no attention. She pulled back the flap of an outer tent and rushed inside, Graelam's name on her lips. She found him there, struggling frantically against the ropes.

He saw her, a white apparition, and a strange laugh broke from his throat. "By

Christ's blood, Chandra, I should have known that it would be you to bring the heathen to their knees."

She dropped down beside him and quickly unfastened the knots on the rope that bound him. When his arms were free, he worked at the knots at his ankles.

He jumped to his feet, then stood a moment, staring down at her. "Thank you," he said. "Now, I do not wish to join the devil in a heathen camp."

"The horses — they are behind this tent. Hurry, hurry."

They both whirled about at a cry of rage. Munza stood in the entrance, his eyes burning red from the flames, his scimitar raised. "You," he yelled at her. "You have killed my master." He lunged forward, readying his scimitar to strike her.

Graelam flung Chandra out of the way. She lurched to her feet, grabbing a clay pot that lay on the earthen floor.

"No!" she screamed, bringing Munza's eyes toward her. She flung the pot at his chest. As Munza stumbled backward, Graelam lunged at him, his fist smashing the side of his head. The scimitar went flying and Munza fell to the ground.

"Graelam!" she yelled, pulling at his arm. For a moment, his mind was locked against her, and he smashed his fist again against the Saracen's face.

"The tent is on fire!"

Graelam smelled the bitter smoke and tore himself away from the Saracen. He grabbed the scimitar, and together he and Chandra rushed from the flaming tent.

The horses had broken free and were galloping from the camp through the masses of men and women. Chandra saw a man with his clothes aflame running in blind frenzy and pain. Graelam jerked her back as a maddened stallion galloped in front of them, flinging clots of dirt in their faces. He tried to clear his mind of the raging spectacle about them, and plan their escape. He grabbed Chandra's hand and pulled her with him toward the cliffs, away from the people and the trampling horses.

Jerval felt a numbing band of pain in his chest. His eyes followed Payn's shout and pointing finger.

The dark sky was cast in orange. "By God, it is the Saracen camp."

"We are too late!"

Jerval did not hear Roger de Clifford's voice. He kicked his spurs into his destrier's side and pushed him across the plain toward the eerie orange glow in the sky. He heard

Payn's shouts behind him, a battle cry to the fifty men that followed.

They thundered into the camp, their swords ready to strike, but the Saracens fled away from them, leaving whatever they could not carry.

Jerval pulled his destrier to a halt in the center of the camp, his eyes burning from the acrid smoke, straining to find Chandra. He saw the huge tent, collapsed on itself. He spurred his horse toward it.

Jerval yelled over his shoulder as he pointed toward Chandra and Graelam, "Stay close to me, and then fan out!"

Graelam saw a crazed horse veering toward them. He slammed Chandra against the cliff, covering her body with his. He splayed his hands on either side of her, flattening her against the rocks to protect her. He felt her heart pounding against his breast.

"If we are to die, Chandra," he said, pressing his cheek against her temple, "I would say that we have given life a fine ride."

"We won't die," she said. And he knew she believed it.

Graelam laughed. "It has come to me, my lady, that had I succeeded in claiming you, we would have likely killed each other. You are not a restful woman, Chandra."

Graelam pressed her tightly against him, closing out the din about them. Chandra struggled to look beyond him. He heard her say in a strangely calm voice, "I knew he would come. I knew we wouldn't die. Jerval is here. We will be all right now."

He jerked about to see Jerval and a dozen men forming a barrier around them. "Aye, Chandra," he said, shaking his head in disbelief. "You were quite right."

He stepped back, allowing Chandra to see what was happening. She did not move, even now that the danger was past, merely stared toward her husband as he shouted orders and rode toward them.

"Chandra?"

She ran to him. As he caught her in his arms, he looked over her head at Graelam, who stood silently, watching.

To his surprise, Graelam smiled. "Your wife and I," he said, "are very pleased to see you."

Jerval looked down into her beloved face, blackened with soot, and couldn't believe his eyes. She was crying. He said nothing, just tightened his arms about her back and felt the cloth that covered her begin to slip.

"I cannot have you naked, love." He forced himself to release her for a moment, pulled off his mantle and wrapped it about her. She hiccuped as she tried to swallow her tears, and he laughed, deep and rich, a laugh filled with relief.

"Come, Chandra, there will be no fighting here tonight. Let us go home." He lifted her into his arms and set her upon his destrier. He turned back to Graelam. "You have saved what I hold dearest on this earth. I thank you, my lord. I am forever in your debt."

Graelam grinned, just shaking his head. "Even though you see her crying now, like a weak woman, my hide would be naught but fodder for desert vermin if not for her. It galls me, but it is she who has saved me twice. I will never raise my sword against you."

Chandra said, "It is all the smoke that is making my eyes water."

"Aye," Jerval said. "The smoke. I feel my eyes beginning to water as well. Come, let us all get out of this place. I wish to come no closer to hell."

Graelam said, "The devil of this hell died in his own flames this night."

Epilogue

Chandra stood beside Jerval at the harbor mole, a thick breakwater of sandstone, watching their provisions being hauled aboard the ships. The sun was a bright white ball overhead, and the day, as always, was unmercifully hot.

"You do not look very happy," he said.

"I am afraid I will be ill again."

He reached inside his tunic and drew out a small parchment square. "Sir Elvan gave me some medicine for you, just in case."

"Ah, I think he is the one I will miss. He is a kind man."

"He accompanied Edward, with his own physicians in tow, to Caesarea for the signing of the treaty."

"I saw Edward this morning. He seems to have thrown off his depression and looks stronger."

"Edward has realized that the treaty is not so meaningless an accomplishment." He suddenly pulled her to him and gave her a great hug. "Do not," he whispered fiercely, "ever again get yourself abducted. I found a gray hair in my head this morning, doubtless there from worry."

"I swear," she said, nuzzling her cheek against his shoulder, "I know of no other Alan Durwalds to take me by force from Camberley."

He held her silently, then gave a tug on her hair to make her look up at him. "If Mary's letter is to be believed, you, my love, will not even have anyone to fight with. Mother, it seems, has grown positively benign under Lady Faye's influence."

"Give her one day with me," Chandra said, laughing.

"Perhaps by the time we reach Camberley, your belly will not be so flat. Your carrying my heir would make her more than pleasant toward you."

"But there will be no privacy aboard our ship."

"We will have sufficient privacy so you should not forget the pleasures of lying with your husband."

"I like the sound of that." Suddenly, she frowned and said, "Oh, dear."

"What bothers you?"

"What will happen to me when we are home again?"

"I will bully you and love you. Can you

ever doubt that?"

"No, but our life has been so different here."

"When you are not heavy with child, we will doubtless argue about what is proper for you and what is not." He saw that she was still frowning and added quietly, "I believe that at least you and I have learned that we can disagree, and not rant at each other. You may be certain, Chandra, that our children will know that my wife saved my worthless hide in the Holy Land."

"I never wish to look upon blood and death again. I shall never forget the horror of it, and my fear for you."

It was on the tip of his tongue to tell her how pleased he was that she had finally come to her senses, but he was wiser with her now. Nor did he tell her that he loved to fight, if his opponents were soldiers, and not innocent women and children. Aloud, he said only, "Always fear for me, Chandra. It will make me all the more careful."

"Have you decided what we will say about Eustace?"

"That he died honorably. There is no reason to let his treachery be known."

"But it is Graelam who is now our friend. Life is very strange."

"Aye, it is. I thank God that Mary birthed

a daughter. Did you hear? Graelam will be the only noble to leave Palestine with great wealth. Al-Afdal's treasure trove, what remained from the fire, was an unbelievable find."

"You accepted the jewels he offered you?"

"Aye, and the rubies will adorn your white neck."

"Look yon, Jerval," Chandra said, pointing toward the open seaward gates of Acre.

"The Christians of the city are gathering to bid us farewell."

It was probably the only time, Chandra thought, that Templars had stood next to Hospitalers in temporary truce, and Genoese next to Venetians. Now, thanks to Edward, they would have ten years to bicker and fight among themselves, without threat from the Saracens.

She saw Payn de Chaworth limp aboard his ship, Roger de Clifford at his side. Jerval laced his fingers through hers. "Lambert is waving to us, Chandra. It is time to leave."

She looked one last time toward Acre and saw a veiled woman atop the wall, her hand raised. Beri? She could not be certain. Aye, she thought, smiling sadly to herself, I am the lucky one. I am free.

Chandra turned to see Eleanor smiling at her, the babe, Joan, in her arms.

"You will take care, Chandra," Eleanor said. "It will be some time before I see you again. As you know, my lord has no wish to return to England immediately. We are to see more of the world."

"I will write to you, Eleanor."

"I pray that you will. My lord's heart is heavy, and I will need happy news to cheer him."

"I trust that I will have only happy news to tell you," Chandra said, smiling toward her husband. She hugged Eleanor, touched her fingertip lightly beneath the baby's dimpled chin, and straightened.

"Chandra."

"Good-bye," she said to the future queen of England, laughed, and ran to Jerval. When she reached him, she threw her arms around him, hugging him fiercely.

She stepped back, took his hand, and tugged him forward. "Let us go home, Jerval, to England and to Camberley."

"Aye," he said, kissing her ear, the tip of her nose. "Just think of all the warm evenings we'll spend together on deck."

She ran her fingers lightly over his chest. "You will hold my hand and tell me how beautiful you believe me to be?"

"Well, not exactly. I learned more about the stars from Sir Waymer, a Templar who